GHOST SUMMER:
STORIES

GHOST SUMMER: STORIES

Tananarive Due

PRIME BOOKS

GHOST SUMMER: STORIES

Prime Books
Germantown, MD
www.prime-books.com

For more information, contact Prime Books:
prime@prime-books.com

Print ISBN: 978-1-60701-453-9
Ebook ISBN: 978-1-60701-461-4

Contents

To my true-life
Forever Man,
Steven Emory Barnes.
I love you.

Introduction

Nalo Hopkinson

SEE, I KNOW TANANARIVE DUE. Have known her for years. Have read her fiction, even published some of it. She's a sweet, upright woman. Journalist, fiction writer, strong black woman. Strong woman, period. Loving wife and daughter. Fierce mama, as mamas must be. Strong roots in the civil rights struggle. A good woman.

But maybe I forgot something along the way, because from the first line of the first story in this collection, my arms were prickling with unease. At the end of the story, I found myself gaping at the page and sitting up in bed so I could snug my back right up against the wall for its safe solidity. The second story contained an image which, like the mother in the story, I will never be able to unsee. Eerily, a part of me doesn't want to. And the twist . . . how can a good child be such an unsettling thing? By the third story, I was reading between my fingers, captivated by Tananarive's gentle characters and the lush sensoria of her landscapes, completely caught by stories of the most mundane situations tumbling end over end into a darkness all the more eerie because it all feels so normal.

The best horror is simultaneously unflinching and humorous. It gazes calmly at the fragility of life, at how easily good intentions can fray if the face of the Void opens its crazy eyes and looks back at you. Good horror examines all this, and then it giggles. I know Tananarive well enough to see that she's writing about the possibilities that terrify her, that would terrify anyone. Of the inevitability of pain and death. Of having thoughts you know you shouldn't. Of losing what you love the most. Of hurting the ones you love. Of the ones you love hurting you. What I hadn't realized before is how playful her writing is, like juggling with butchers' knives.

So yes, a good woman. A good woman who dares look at scary things. And a bloody good writer.

Nalo Hopkinson

9

GRACETOWN

No one warned her
about summers in Gracetown . . .

The Lake

The new English instructor at Gracetown Prep was chosen with the greatest care, highly recommended by the Board of Directors at Blake Academy in Boston, where she had an exemplary career for twelve years. No history of irregular behavior presaged the summer's unthinkable events.

—Excerpt from an internal memo,
Gracetown Preparatory School
Gracetown, Florida

ABBIE LAFLEUR was an outsider, a third-generation Bostonian, so no one warned her about summers in Gracetown. She noticed a few significant glances, a hitched eyebrow or two, when she first mentioned to locals that she planned to relocate in June to work a summer term before the start of the school year, but she'd assumed it was because they thought no one in her right mind would move to Florida, even northern Florida, in the wet heat of summer.

In fairness, Abbie LaFleur would have scoffed at their stories as hysteria. Delusion. This was Gracetown's typical experience with newcomers and outsiders, so Gracetown had learned to keep its stories to itself.

Abbie thought she had found her dream job in Gracetown. A fresh start. Her glasses had fogged up with steam from the rain-drenched tarmac as soon as she stepped off the plane at Tallahassee Airport; her confirmation that she'd embarked on a true adventure, an exploration worthy of Ponce de León's storied landing at St. Augustine.

Her parents and her best friend, Mary Kay, had warned her not to jump into a real estate purchase until she'd worked in Gracetown for at least a year—*The whole thing's so hasty, what if the school's not a good fit? Who wants to be stuck with a house in the sticks in a depressed market?*—but Abbie fell in love with the white lakeside colonial she found listed at one-fifty, for sale by owner. She bought it after a hasty tour—too hasty, it turned out—but at nearly three-thousand square feet, this was the biggest house she had ever lived in, with more room than she had furniture for. A place with potential, despite its myriad flaws.

A place, she thought, very much like her.

The built-in bookshelves in the Florida room sagged. (She'd never known that a den could be called a Florida room, but so it was, and so she did.) The floorboards creaked and trembled on the back porch, sodden from summer rainfall. And she would need to lay down new tiles in the kitchen right away, because the brooding mud-brown flooring put her in a bad mood from the time she first fixed her morning coffee.

But there would be boys at the school, strong and tireless boys, who could help her mend whatever needed fixing. In her experience, there were always willing boys.

And then there was the lake! The house was her excuse to buy her piece of the lake and the thin strip of red-brown sand that was a beach in her mind, although it was nearly too narrow for the beach lounger she'd planted like a flag. The water looked murky where it met her little beach, the color of the soil, but in the distance she could see that its heart of rich green-blue, like the ocean. The surface bobbed with rings and bubbles from the hidden catfish and brim that occasionally leaped above the surface, damn near daring her to cast a line.

If not for the hordes of mosquitoes that feasted on her legs and whined with urgent grievances, Abbie could have stood with her bare feet in the warm lake water for hours, the house forgotten behind her. The water's gentle lapping was the meditation her parents and Mary Kay were always prescribing for her, a soothing song.

And the isolation! A gift to be treasured. Her property was bracketed by woods of thin pine, with no other homes within shouting distance. Any spies on her would need binoculars and a reason to spy, since the nearest homes were far across the lake, harmless little dollhouses in the anonymous subdivision where some of her students no doubt lived. Her lake might as well be as wide as the Nile, protection from any envious whispers.

As if to prove her newfound freedom, Abbie suddenly climbed out of the tattered jeans she'd been wearing as she unpacked her boxes, whipped off her T-shirt and draped her clothing neatly across the lounger's arm rails. Imagine! She was naked in her own backyard. If her neighbors could see her, they would be scandalized already, and she had yet to commence teaching at Gracetown Prep.

Abbie wasn't much of a swimmer—she preferred solid ground beneath her feet even when she was in the water—but with her flip-flops to protect her from unseen rocks, Abbie felt brave enough to wade into the water, inviting its embrace above her knees, her thighs. She felt the water's gentle kiss between her legs, the massage across her belly, and, finally, a liquid cloak upon her shoulders. The grade was gradual, with no sudden drop-offs to startle her, and for the first time in years Abbie felt truly safe and happy.

That was all Gracetown was supposed to be for Abbie LeFleur: new job, new house, new lake, new beginning. For the week before summer school began, Abbie took to swimming behind her house daily, at dusk, safe from the mosquitoes, sinking into her sanctuary.

No one had told her—not the realtor, not the elderly widow she'd only met once when they signed the paperwork at the lawyer's office downtown, not Gracetown Prep's cheerful headmistress. Even a random first-grader at the grocery store could have told her that one must never, ever go swimming in Gracetown's lakes during the summer. The man-made lakes were fine, but the natural lakes that had once been swampland were to be avoided by children in particular. And women of childbearing age—which Abbie LaFleur still was at thirty-six, albeit barely. And men who were prone to quick tempers or alcohol binges.

Further, one must never, *ever* swim in Gracetown's lakes in summer without clothing, when crevices and weaknesses were most exposed.

In retrospect, she was foolish. But in all fairness, how could she have known?

• • •

ABBIE'S EX-HUSBAND had accused her of irreparable timidity, criticizing her for refusing to go snorkeling or even swimming with dolphins, never mind the scuba diving he'd loved since he was sixteen. The world was populated by water people and land people, and Abbie was firmly attached to terra firma. Until Gracetown. And the lake.

Soon after she began her nightly wading, which gradually turned to dog-paddling and then awkward strokes across the dark surface, she began to dream about the water. Her dreams were far removed from her nightly dipping—which actually *was* somewhat timid, if she was honest. In sleep, she glided effortlessly far beneath the murky surface, untroubled by the nuisance of lungs and breathing. The water was a muddy green-brown, nearly black, but spears of light from above gave her tents of vision to see floating plankton, algae, tadpoles and squirming tiny creatures she could not name . . . and yet knew. Her underwater dreams were a wonderland of tangled mangrove roots coated with algae, and forests of gently waving lily-pads and swamp grass. Once, she saw an alligator's checkered, pale belly above her, until the reptile hurried away, its powerful tail lashing to give it speed. In her dream, she wasn't afraid of the alligator; she'd sensed instead (smelled instead?) that the alligator was afraid of *her*.

Abbie's dreams never had been so vivid. She woke one morning drenched from head to toe, and her heart hammered her breathless until she realized that her mattress was damp with perspiration, not swamp water. At least . . . she *thought* it must be perspiration. Her fear felt silly, and she was blanketed by sadness as deep as she'd felt the first months after her divorce.

Abbie was so struck by her dreams that she called Mary Kay, who kept dream diaries and took such matters far too seriously.

"You sure that water's safe?" Mary Kay said. "No chemicals being dumped out there?"

"The water's fine," Abbie said, defensive. "I'm not worried about the water. It's just the dreams. They're so . . . " Abbie rarely ran out of words, which Mary Kay knew full well.

"What's scaring you about the dreams?"

"The dreams don't scare me," Abbie said. "It's the opposite. I'm sad to wake up. As if I belong there, in the water, and my bedroom is the dream."

Mary Kay had nothing to offer except a warning to have the local Health Department come out and check for chemicals in any water she was swimming in, and Abbie felt the weight of her distance from her friend. There had been a time when she and Mary Kay understood each other better than anyone, when they could see past each other's silences straight to their thoughts, and now Mary Kay had no idea of the shape and texture of Abbie's life. No one did.

All liberation is loneliness, she thought sadly.

Abbie dressed sensibly, conservatively, for her first day at her new school.

She had driven the two miles to the school, a red-brick converted bank building in the center of downtown Gracetown, before she noticed the itching between her toes.

"LaFleur," the headmistress said, keeping pace with Abbie as they walked toward her assigned classroom for the course she'd named *Creativity & Literature*. The woman's easy, Southern-bred tang seemed to add a syllable to every word. "Where is that name from?"

Abbie wasn't fooled by the veiled attempt to guess at her ethnicity, since it didn't take an etymologist to guess at her name's French derivation. What Loretta Millhouse really wanted to know was whether Abbie had ancestry in Haiti or Martinique to explain her sun-kissed complexion and the curly brown hair Abbie kept locked tight in a bun.

Abbie's itching feet had grown so unbearable that she wished she could pull off her pumps. The itching pushed irritation into her voice. "My grandmother married a Frenchman in Paris after World War II," she explained. "LaFleur was his family name."

The rest was none of her business. Most of her life was none of anyone's business.

"Oh, I see," Millhouse said, voice filled with delight, but Abbie saw her disappointment that her prying had yielded nothing. "Well, as I said, we're so tickled to have you with us. Only one letter in your file wasn't completely glowing . . . "

Abbie's heart went cold, and she forgot her feet. She'd assumed that her detractors had remained silent, or she never would have been offered the job.

Millhouse patted her arm. "But don't you worry: Swimming upstream is an asset here." The word *swimming* made Abbie flinch, feeling exposed. "We welcome independent thinking at Gracetown Prep. That's the main reason I wanted to hire you. Between you and me, how can anyone criticize a . . . creative mind?"

She said the last words conspiratorially, leaning close to Abbie's ear as if a creative mind were a disease. Abbie's mind raced: The criticism must have come from Johanssen, the vice-principal at Blake who had labeled her argumentative—*a bitch*, Mary Kay had overheard him call her privately, but he wouldn't have put that in writing. What did Millhouse's disclosure mean? Was Millhouse someone who pretended to compliment you while subtly putting you down, or was a shared secret hidden beneath the twinkle in her aqua-green eyes?

"Don't go easy on this group," Millhouse said as when they reached Room 113. "Every jock trying to make up a credit to stay on the roster is in your class. Let them work for it."

Sure enough, when Abbie walked into the room, she faced desks filled with athletic young men. Gracetown was a co-ed school, but only five of her twenty students were female.

Abbie smiled.

Her house would be fixed up sooner than she'd expected.

ABBIE LIKED to begin with Thomas Hardy. *Jude the Obscure.* That one always blew their young minds, with its frankness and unconventionality. Their other instructors would cram conformity down their throats, and she would teach rebellion.

No rows of desks would mar her classroom, she informed them. They would sit in a circle. She would not lecture; they would have conversations. They would discuss the readings, read pages from their journals, and share poems. Some days, she told them, she would surprise them by playing music and they would write whatever came to mind.

Half the class looked relieved, the other half petrified.

During her orientation, Abbie studied her students' faces and tried to guess which ones would be most useful over the summer. She dismissed the girls, as she usually did; most were too wispy and pampered, or far too large to be accustomed to physical labor.

But the boys. The boys were a different matter.

Of the fifteen boys, only three were unsuitable at a glance—bird-chested and reedy, or faces riddled with acne. She could barely stand to look at them.

That left twelve to ponder. She listened carefully as they raised their hands and described their hopes and dreams, watching their eyes for the spark of maturity she needed. Five or six couldn't hold her gaze, casting their eyes shyly at their desks. No good at all.

Down to six, then. Several were basketball players, one a quarterback. Millhouse hadn't been kidding when she'd said that her class was a haven for desperate athletes. The quarterback, Derek, was dark-haired with a crater-sized dimple in his chin; he sat at his desk with his body angled, leg crossed at the knee, as if the desk were already too small. He didn't say "uhm" or pause between his sentences. His future was at the tip of his tongue.

"I'm sorry," she said, interrupting him. "How old did you say you are, Derek?"

He didn't blink. His dark eyes were at home on hers. "Sixteen, ma'am."

Sixteen was a good age. A mature age.

A female teacher could not be too careful about which students she invited to her home. Locker-room exaggerations held grave consequences that could literally steal years from a young woman's life. Abbie had seen it before; entire careers up in flames. But this Derek . . .

Derek was full of possibilities. Abbie suddenly found herself playing Millhouse's game, noting his olive complexion and dark features, trying to guess if his jet-black hair whispered Native American or Latino heritage. Throughout the ninety-minute class, her eyes came to Derek again and again.

The young man wasn't flustered. He was used to being stared at.

Abbie had made up her mind before the final bell, but she didn't say a word to Derek. Not yet. She had plenty of time. The summer had just begun.

As she was climbing out of the shower, Abbie realized her feet had stopped their terrible itching. For three days, she'd slathered the spaces between her toes with creams from Walgreens, none helping, some only stinging her in punishment.

But the pain was gone.

Naked, Abbie raised her foot to her mattress, pulling her toes apart to examine them . . . and realized right away why she'd been itching so badly. Thin webs of pale skin had grown between each of her toes. Her toes, in fact, had changed shape entirely, pulling away from each other to make room for webbing. And weren't her toes longer than she remembered?

No *wonder* her shoes felt so tight! She wore a size eight, but her feet looked like they'd grown two sizes. She was startled to see her feet so altered, but not alarmed, as she might have been when she was still in Boston, tied to her old life. New job, new house, new feet. There was a logical symmetry to her new feet that superseded questions or worries.

Abbie almost picked up her phone to call Mary Kay, but she thought better of it. What else would Mary Kay say, except that she should have had her water tested?

Instead, still naked, Abbie went to her kitchen, her feet slapping against her ugly kitchen flooring with unusual traction. When she brushed her upper arm carelessly across her ribs, new pain made her hiss. The itching had migrated, she realized.

She paused in the bright fluorescent lighting to peer down at her ribcage, and found her skin bright red, besieged by some kind of rash. *Great*, she thought. *Life is an endless series of challenges.* She inhaled a deep breath, and the air felt hot and thin. The skin across her ribs pulled more tautly, constricting. She longed for the lake.

Abbie slipped out of her rear kitchen door and scurried across her back yard toward the black shimmer of the water. She'd forgotten her flip-flops, but the soles of her feet were less tender, like leather slippers.

She did not hesitate. She did not wade. She dove like an eel, swimming with an eel's ease. *Am I truly awake, or is this a dream?*

Her eyes adjusted to the lack of light, bringing instant focus. She had never seen the true murky depths of her lake, so much like the swamp of her dreams. Were they one and the same? Her ribs' itching turned to a welcome massage, and she felt long slits yawn open across her skin, beneath each rib.

Warm water flooded her, nursing her; her nose, throat and mouth were a useless, distant memory. Why hadn't it ever occurred to her to breathe the water before?

An alligator's curiosity brought the beast close enough to study her, but it recognized its mistake and tried to thrash away. But too late. Too late. Nourished by the water, Abbie's instincts gave her enough speed and strength to glide behind the beast, its shadow. One hand grasped the slick ridges of its tail, and the other hugged its wriggling girth the way she might a lover. She didn't remember biting or clawing the alligator, but she must have done one or the other, because the water flowed red with blood.

The blood startled Abbie awake in her bed, her sheets heavy with dampness. Her lungs heaved and gasped, shocked by the reality of breathing, and at first she seemed to take in no air. She examined her fingers, nails and naked skin for blood, but found none. The absence of blood helped her breathe more easily, her lungs freed from their confusion.

Another dream. Of course. How could she mistake it for anything else?

She was annoyed to realize that her ribs still bore their painful rash and long lines like raw, infected incisions.

But her feet, thank goodness, were unchanged. She still had the delightful webbing and impressive new size, longer than in her dream. Abbie knew she would have to dress in a hurry. Before school, she would swing by Payless and pick up a few new pairs of shoes.

DEREK LINGERED after class. He'd written a poem based on a news story that had made a deep impression on him; a boy in Naples had died on the football practice field. *Before he could be tested by life,* Derek had written in his eloquent final line. One of the girls, Riley Bowen, had wiped a tear from her eye. Riley Bowen always gazed at Derek like the answer to her life's prayers, but he never looked at her.

And now here was Derek standing over Abbie's desk, on his way to six feet tall, his face bowed with shyness for the first time all week.

"I lied before," he said, when she waited for him so to speak. "About my age."

Abbie already knew. She'd checked his records and found out for herself, but she decided to torture him. "Then how old are you?"

"Fifteen." His face soured. "'Til March."

"Why would you lie about that?"

He shrugged, an adolescent gesture that annoyed Abbie no end.

"Of course you know," she said. "I heard your poem. I've seen your thoughtfulness. You wouldn't lie on the first day of school without a reason."

He found his confidence again, raising his eyes. "Fine. I skipped second grade, so I'm a year younger than everyone in my class. I always say I'm sixteen. It wasn't special for you."

The fight in Derek intrigued her. He wouldn't be the type of man who would be pushed around. "But you're here now, bearing your soul. Who's that for?"

His face softened to half a grin. "Like you said, when we're in this room, we tell the truth. So here I am. Telling the truth."

There he was. She decided to tell him the truth too.

"I bought a big house out by the lake," she said. "Against my better judgment, maybe."

"That old one on McCormack Road?"

"You know it?"

He shrugged, that loathsome gesture again. "Everybody knows the McCormacks. She taught Sunday school at Christ the Redeemer. Guess she moved out, huh?"

"To her sister's in . . . Quincy?" The town shared a name with the city south of Boston, the only reason she remembered it. Her mind was filled with distraction to mask strange flurries of her heart. Was she so cowed that she would leave her house in a mess?

"Yeah, Quincy's about an hour, hour and a half, down the 10 . . . " Derek was saying in a flat voice that bored even him.

They were talking about nothing. Waiting. They both knew it.

Abbie clapped her hands once, snapping their conversation from its trance. "Well, an old house brings lots of problems. The porch needs fixing. New kitchen tiles. I don't have the budget to hire a real handyman, so I'm looking for people with skills . . . "

Derek's cheeks brightened, pink. "My dad and I built a cabin last summer. I'm pretty good with wood. New planks and stuff. For the porch."

"Really?" She chided herself for the girlish rise in her pitch, as if he'd announced he had scaled Mount Everest during his two weeks off from school.

"I could help you out, if . . . you know, if you buy the supplies."

"I can't pay much. Come take a look after school, see if you think you can help." She made a show of glancing toward the open doorway, watching the stream of students passing by. "But you know, Derek, it's easy for people to get the wrong idea if you say you're going to a teacher's house . . . "

His face was bright red now. "Oh, I wouldn't say nothing. I mean . . . anything. Besides, we go fishing with Coach Reed all the time. It's no big deal around here. Not like in Boston, maybe." The longer he spoke, the more he regained his poise. His last sentence had come with an implied wink of his eye.

"No, you're right about that," she said, and she smiled, remembering her new feet. "Nothing here is like it was in Boston."

That was how Derek Voorhoven came to spend several days a week after class helping Abbie fix her ailing house, whenever he could spare time after football practice in the last daylight. Abbie made it clear that he couldn't expect any special treatment in class, so he would need to work hard on his atrocious spelling, but Derek was thorough and uncomplaining. No task seemed too big or small, and he was happy to scrub sand and tile in exchange for a few dollars, conversation about the assigned reading, and fishing rights to the lake, since he said the catfish favored the north side, where it was quiet.

As he'd promised, he told no one at Gracetown Prep, but one day he asked if his cousin Jack could help from time to time, and after he'd brought the stocky, freckled youth by to introduce him, she agreed. Jack was only fourteen, but he was strong and didn't argue. He also attended the public school, which made him far less a risk. Although the boys joked together, Jack's presence never slowed Derek's progress much, so Derek and Jack became fixtures in her home well into July. Abbie looked forward to fixing them lemonade and white chocolate macadamia nut cookies from ready-made dough, and with each passing day she knew she'd been right to leave Boston behind.

Still, Abbie never told Mary Kay about her visits with the boys and the work she asked them to do. Her friend wouldn't judge her, but Abbie wanted to hold her new life close, a secret she would share only when she was ready, when she could say: *You'll never guess the clever way I got my improvements done,* an experience long behind her. Mary Kay would be envious, wishing she'd thought of it first, rather than spending a fortune on a gardener and a pool boy.

But there were other reasons Abbie began erecting a wall between herself and the people who knew her best. Derek and Jack, bright as they were, weren't prone to notice the small changes, or even the large ones, that would have leaped out to her mother and Mary Kay—and even her distracted father.

Her mother would have spotted the new size of her feet right away, of course. And the odd new pallor of her face, fishbelly pale. And the growing strength in her arms and legs that made it so easy to hand the boys boxes, heavy tools or stacks of wooden planks. Mary Kay would have asked about the flaky skin on the back of her neck and her sudden appetite for all things rare, or raw. Abbie had given up most red meat two years ago in an effort to remake herself after the divorce tore her self-esteem to pieces, but that summer she stocked up on thin-cut steaks, salmon and fish she could practically eat straight from the packaging. Her hunger was also *voracious,* her mouth watering from the moment she woke, her growling stomach keeping her awake at night.

She was hungriest when Derek and Jack were there, but she hid that from herself.

Her dusk swims had grown to evening swims, and some nights she lost track of time so completely that the sky was blooming pink by the time she waded from the healing waters to begin another day of waiting to swim. She resisted inviting the boys to swim with her.

The last Friday in July, with only a week left in the summer term, Abbie lost her patience.

She was especially hungry that day, dissatisfied with her kitchen stockpile. Gracetown was suffering a record heat wave with temperatures hovering near 110 degrees, so she was sweaty and irritable by the time the boys arrived at five-thirty. And itching terribly. Unlike her feet, the gills hiding beneath the ridges of her ribs never stopped bothering her until she was in her lake. She was so miserable, she almost asked the boys to forget about painting the refurbished back porch and come back another day.

If she'd only done that, she would have avoided the scandal.

Abbie strode behind the porch to watch the strokes of the boys' rollers and paintbrushes as they transformed her porch from an eyesore to a snapshot of the quaint Old South. Because of the heat, both boys had taken their shirts off, their shoulders ruddy as the muscles in their sun-broiled backs flexed in the Magic Hour's furious, gasping light. They put Norman Rockwell to shame; Derek with his disciplined football player's physique, and Jack with his awkward baby fat, sprayed with endless freckles.

"Why do you come here?" she asked them.

They both stopped working, startled by her voice.

"Huh?" Jack said. His scowl was deep, comical. "You're paying us, right?"

Ten dollars a day each was hardly pay. Derek generously shared half of his twenty dollars with his cousin for a couple hours' work, although Jack talked more than he worked, running his mouth about summer superhero blockbusters and dancers in music videos. Abbie regretted that she'd encouraged Derek to invite his cousin along, and that day she wished she had a reason to send Jack home. Her mind raced to come up with an excuse, but she couldn't think of one. A sudden surge of frustration pricked her eyes with tears.

"I'm not paying much," she said.

"Got *that* right," Derek said. Had his voice deepened in only a few weeks? Was Derek undergoing changes too? "I'm here for the catfish. Can we quit in twenty minutes? I've got my rod in the truck. And some chicken livers I've been saving."

"Quit now if you want," she said. She pretended to study their work, but she couldn't focus her eyes on the whorls of painted wood. "Go on and fish, but I'm going swimming. Good way to wash off a hot day."

She turned and walked away, following the familiar trail her feet had beaten across her back yard's scraggly patch of grass to the strip of sand. She'd planned to lay sod with the boys closer to fall, but that might not happen now.

Abbie pulled off her T-shirt, draping it nonchalantly across her beach lounger, taking her time. She didn't turn, but she could feel the boys' eyes on her bare back. She didn't wear a bra most days; her breasts were modest, so what was the point? One more thing Johanssen had tried to hold against her. Her feet curled into the sand, searching for dampness.

"It's all right if you don't have trunks," she said. "My back yard is private, and there's no harm in friends taking a swim."

She thought she heard them breathing, or maybe the harsh breaths were hers as her lungs prepared to give up their reign. The sun was unbearable on Abbie's bare skin. Her sides burned like fire as the flaps beneath her ribs opened, swollen rose petals.

The boys didn't answer; probably hadn't moved. She hadn't expected them to, not at first.

One after the other, she pulled her long legs out of her jeans, standing at a discreet angle to hide most of her nakedness, like the Venus de Medici. She didn't want them to see her gills, or the rougher patches on her scaly skin. She didn't want to answer questions. She and the boys had spent too much time talking all summer. She wondered why she'd never invited them swimming before.

She dove, knowing just where the lake was deep enough not to scrape her at the rocky floor. The water parted as startled catfish dashed out of her way. Fresh fish was best. That was another thing Abbie had learned that summer.

When her head popped back up above the surface, the boys were looking at each other, weighing the matter. Derek left the porch first, tugging on his tattered denim shorts, hopping on one leg in his hurry. Jack followed, but left his clothes on, arms folded across his chest.

Derek splashed into the water, one polite hand concealing his privates until he was submerged. He did not swim near her, leaving a good ten yards between them. After a tentative silence, he whooped so loudly that his voice might have carried across the lake.

"Whooo-HOOOOO!" Derek's face and eyes were bright, as if he'd never glimpsed the world in color before. "Awesome!"

Abbie's stomach growled. She might have to go after those catfish. She couldn't remember being so hungry. She felt faint.

Jack only made it as far as the shoreline, still wearing his Bermuda shorts. "Not supposed to swim in the lake in summer," he said sullenly, his voice barely loud enough to hear. He slapped at his neck. He stood in a cloud of mosquitoes.

Derek spat, treading water. "That's little *kids*, dumb-ass."

"Nobody's supposed to," Jack said.

"How old are you, six? You don't want to swim—fine. Don't stand staring. It's rude."

Abbie felt invisible during their exchange. She almost told Jack he should follow his best judgment without pressure, but she dove into the silent brown water instead. Young adults had to make decisions for themselves, especially boys, or how would they learn to be men? That was what she and Mary Kay had always believed. Anyone who thought differently was just being politically correct. In ancient times, or in other cultures, a boy Jack's age would already have a wife, a child of his own.

Just look at Mary Kay. Everyone had said her marriage would never work, that he'd been too young when they met. She'd been vilified and punished, and still they survived. The memory of her friend's trial broke Abbie's heart.

As the water massaged her gills, Abbie released her thoughts and concerns about the frivolous world beyond the water. She needed to feed, that was all. She planned to leave the boys to their bickering and swim farther out, where the fish were hiding.

But something large and pale caught her eye above her.

Jack, she realized dimly. Jack had changed his mind, swimming near the surface, his ample belly like a full moon, jiggling with his breaststroke.

That was the first moment Abbie felt a surge of fear, because she finally understood what she'd been up to—what her new body had been preparing her for. Her feet betrayed her, their webs giving her speed as she propelled toward her giant meal. Water slid across her scales.

The beautiful fireball of light above the swimmer gave her pause, a reminder of a different time, another way. The tears that had stung her in her back yard tried to burn her eyes blind, because she saw how it would happen, exactly like a dream: She would claw the boy's belly open, and his scream would sound muffled and far away to her ears. Derek would come to investigate, to try to rescue him from what he would be sure was a gator, but she would overpower Derek next. Her new body would even if she could not.

As Abbie swam directly beneath the swimmer, bathed in the magical light fighting to shield him, she tried to resist the overpowering scent of a meal and remember that he was a boy. Someone's dear son. As Derek (was that the other one's name?) had put it so memorably some time ago— perhaps while he was painting the porch, perhaps in one of her dreams— neither of them yet had been tested by life.

But it was summertime. In Gracetown.

In the lake.

I wrote this story for Christopher Golden after he invited me to submit to the anthology Monster's Corner: Stories Through Inhuman Eyes. *The theme: stories from the monster's point-of-view. Some of my favorite stories have been written to themes, from places I would not have explored otherwise. The first monster that came to mind: a sexual predator. If only real monsters grew webbed feet and gills.*

Summer

DURING THE BABY'S naptime, a housefly buzzed past the new screen somehow and landed on Danielle's wrist while she was reading *Us Weekly* on the back porch. With the Okeepechee swamp so close, mosquitoes and flies take over Gracetown in summer.

"Well, I'll be damned," she said.

Most flies zipped off at the first movement. Not this one. The fly sat still when Danielle shook her wrist. Repulsion came over her as she noticed the fly's spindly legs and shiny coppery green helmet staring back at her, so she rolled up the magazine and gave it a swat. The fly never seemed to notice Angelina Jolie's face coming. Unusual for a fly, with all those eyes seeing in so many directions. But there it was, dead on the porch floorboards.

Anyone who says they wouldn't hurt a fly is lying, Danielle thought.

She didn't suspect the fly was a sign until a week later, when it happened again—this time she was in the bathroom clipping her toenails on top of the closed toilet seat, not in her bedroom, where she might disturb Lola during her nap. A fly landed on Danielle's big toe and stayed put.

Danielle conjured Grandmother's voice in her memory—as she often did when she noticed the quiet things Grandmother used to tell her about. Grandmother had passed three summers ago after a stroke in her garden, and now that she was gone, Danielle had a thousand and one questions for her. The lost questions hurt the most.

Anything can happen once, Grandmother used to say. *When it happens twice—listen. The third time may be too late.*

It was true about men, and Danielle suspected it was true about the flies, too.

Once the second fly was dead—again, almost as if it had made peace with leaving this world on the sole of her slipper—Danielle wondered what the flies meant. Was someone trying to send her a message? A warning? Whatever it was, she was sure it was something bad.

Being in the U.S. Army Reserves, her husband, Karl, didn't like to look for omens. He only laughed when she talked about Grandmother's beliefs, not that Karl was around in the summer to talk to about anything. His training was in summers so it wouldn't interfere with his job as county school bus supervisor. Last year, he'd been gone only a couple of weeks, but this time he was spending two long months at Fort Irwin in California. He was in training exercises, so the only way to reach him was in a real emergency, through the Red Cross. She hadn't spoken to him in three weeks.

Karl had been in training so long, the war had almost come and gone. But he still might get deployed. He'd reminded her of that right before he left, as if she'd made a promise she and Lola could do fine without him. What would she do if she became one of those Iraq wives? Life was hard enough in summer already, without death hanging over her head, too.

With Grandmother gone from this earth and Karl in California, Danielle had never been so lonely. She felt loneliest in the bathroom.

Maybe the small space was too much like a prison cell. But she didn't fight the feeling. Her loneliness felt comfortable, familiar. She wouldn't have minded sitting with the sting awhile, feeling sorry for herself, staring at the dead fly on the black and white tile. Wondering what its message had been.

But there wasn't enough time for that. Lola was awake, already angry and howling.

LONG BEFORE the bodies were found, Grandmother always said the Okeepechee swampland was touched by wrong. Old Man McCormack sold his family's land to developers last fall, and Caterpillar trucks were digging a man-made lake in the soggy ground when they uncovered the bones. And not just a few bones, either. The government people and researchers were still digging, but Danielle had heard there were three bodies, at last count. And not a quarter mile from her front door!

Grandmother had told her the swampland had secrets. Lately, Danielle tried to recall more clearly what Grandmother's other prophecies had been, but all she remembered was Grandmother's earthy laughter. Danielle barely had time to fix herself a bowl of cereal in the mornings, so she didn't have the luxury of Grandmother's habits: mixing powders, lighting candles, and sitting still to wait. But Danielle believed in the swampland's secrets.

All her life, she'd known Gracetown was a hard place to live, and it was worse on the swamp side. Everyone knew that. People died of cancer and lovers drove each other to misery all over Gracetown, but the biggest tragedies were clustered on the swamp side—not downtown, and not in the development called The Farms where no one did any farming. When she was in elementary school, her classmate LaToya's father went crazy. He came home from work one day and shot up everyone in the house; first LaToya, then her little brothers (even the baby), and her mother. When they were all dead, he put the gun in his mouth and pulled the trigger—which Danielle wished he'd done at the start. That made the national news.

Sad stories had always watered Gracetown's backyard vegetable gardens. Danielle's parents used to tell her stories about how awful poverty was, back when sharecropping was the only job for those who weren't bound to be teachers, and most of their generation's tragedies had money at their core. That wasn't so true these days, no matter what her parents said. Even people on the swamp side of Gracetown had better jobs and bigger houses than they used to. They just didn't seem to build their lives any better.

Danielle had never expected to raise a baby in Gracetown, or to live in her late grandmother's house with an Atlanta-born husband who should know better. The thought of Atlanta only six hours north nearly drove her crazy some days. But Karl Darren Richardson was practical enough for the both of them. Coolheaded. That was probably why the military liked him enough to invest so much training. *Do you know how much houses cost in Atlanta? We'll save for a few more years, and then we'll go. Once my training is done, we'll never be hurting for money, and we'll live on a base in Germany somewhere. Then you can kiss Gracetown good-bye.*

In summer, with Karl gone, she was almost sure she was just another fool who never had the sense to get out of Gracetown. Ever since high school, she'd seen her classmates with babies slung to their hips, or married to the first boy who told them they were pretty, and she'd sworn, *Not me.* All of those old friends—each and every one—had their plans, too. Once upon a time.

Danielle wasn't sure if she was patient and wise, or if she was a tragedy unfolding slowly, one hot summer day at a time.

LOLA CRIED harder when she saw her in the doorway. Lola's angry brown-red jowls were smudged with dried flour and old mucus. Sometimes Lola was not pretty at all.

Danielle leaned over the crib. "Go back to sleep, Lola. What's the matter now?"

As Danielle lifted Lola beneath her armpits, the baby grabbed big fistfuls of Danielle's cheeks and squeezed with all her might. Then Lola shrieked and dug in her nails. Hard. Her eyes screwed tight, her face burning with a mighty mission.

Danielle cried out, almost dropping all twenty pounds of Lola straight to the floor. Danielle wrapped her arm more tightly around Lola's waist while the baby writhed, just before Lola would have slipped. The baby's legs banged against the crib's railings, but Danielle knew her wailing was only for show. Lola was thirteen months old and a liar already.

"No." Danielle said, keeping silent the *you little shit bag.* "Very bad, Lola."

Lola shot out a pudgy hand, hoping for another chance at her mother's face, and Danielle bucked back, almost fast enough to make her miss. But Lola's finger caught the small hoop of the gold earring in Danielle's right earlobe and pulled, hard. The earring's catch held at first, and Danielle cried out as pain tore through. Danielle expected to see droplets of blood on the floor, but she only saw the flash of gold as the earring fell.

Lola's crying stopped short, replaced by laughter and a triumphant grin. Anyone who says they wouldn't hurt a fly is lying.

If Lola were a grown person who had just done the same thing, Danielle would have knocked her through a window. Rubbing her ear, she understood the term seeing red, because her eyes flushed with crimson anger. Danielle almost didn't trust herself to lay a hand on the child in her current state, but if she didn't Lola's behavior would never improve. She grabbed Lola's fat arm firmly, the way her mother had said she should, and fixed her gaze.

"No," Danielle said. "Trying to hurt Mommy is not funny."

Lola laughed so hard, it brought tears to her eyes. Lola enjoyed hurting her. Not all the time, but sometimes. Danielle was sure of it.

Danielle's mother said she was welcome to bring Lola over for a few hours whenever she needed time to herself, but Mom's joints were so bad that she could hardly pull herself out of her chair. Mom had never been the same since she broke her hip. She couldn't keep up with Lola, the way the child darted and dashed everywhere, pulling over and knocking down everything her hands could reach. Besides, Danielle didn't like what she saw in her mother's eyes when she brought Lola over for more than a few minutes: *Jesus, help, she can't even control her own child.*

Danielle glanced at the Winnie the Pooh clock on the dresser. Only two o'clock. The whole day stretched to fill with just her and the baby. Danielle wanted to cry, too.

Karl told her maybe she had postpartum depression like the celebrity women she read about. But her family had picked cotton and tobacco until two generations ago, and if they could tolerate that heat and work and deprivation without pills and therapy, Danielle doubted her constitution was as fragile as people who pretended to be someone else for a living.

Lola could be hateful, that was all. That was the truth nobody wanted to hear.

Danielle had tried to conceive for two years, and she would always love her daughter—but she didn't like Lola much in summer. Lola had always been a fussy baby, but she was worse when Karl was gone. Karl's baritone voice could snap Lola back to her sweeter nature. Nothing Danielle did could.

"SHE STILL a handful, huh, Danny?"

"That's one word."

Odetta Mayfield was the only cousin Danielle got along with. She was ten years older, so they hadn't started talking until Grandmother's funeral, and they'd become friends the past two years. The funeral had been a reunion, helping Danielle sew together pieces of her family. Odetta's husband had been in the army during the first Iraq war and come back with a girlfriend. They had divorced long ago and her son was a freshman at Florida State, so

Odetta came by the house three or four times a week. Odetta had no one else to talk to, and neither did she. If not for her cousin and her mother, Danielle might be a hermit in summer.

Odetta bounced Lola on her knee while the baby drank placidly from a bottle filled with apple juice. Seeing them together in the white wicker rocker, their features so similar, Danielle wanted to beg her cousin to take the baby home with her. Just for a night or two.

"Did she leave a mark on my face?"

"Can't see nothing from here," Odetta said. But Danielle could feel two small welts rising alongside her right cheekbone. She dabbed her face with the damp kitchen towel beside the pitcher of sugar-free lemonade they had decided to try for a while. The drink tasted like chemicals.

"People talk about boys, but sometimes girls are just as bad, or worse," Odetta said. "We went through the same mess with Rashan. It passes."

Danielle only grunted. She didn't want to talk about Lola anymore. "Anything new from McCormack's place?" she asked, a sure way to change the subject. Odetta worked as a clerk at City Hall, so she had a reason to be in everybody's business.

"Girl, it's seven bodies. Seven."

Seven bodies left unaccounted for, rotting in swampland? The idea made Danielle's skin feel cold. Mass graves always reminded her of the Holocaust, a lesson that had shocked her in seventh grade. She'd never looked at the world the same way after that, just like when Grandmother first told her about slavery.

Danielle said, "My mother still talks about the civil rights days, the summer those college kids tried to register sharecroppers on McCormack's land. He set those dogs loose on them."

"Unnnnnhhhhh-hnnnnhhhhh . . . " Odetta said, drawing out the indictment. "Sure did. That's the first thing everybody thought. But the experts from Tallahassee say the bones are older than forty-odd years. More like a hundred."

"Even so, how are seven people gonna be buried out on that family's land? There weren't any Indians living there. Shoot, that land's been McCormack Farm since slavery. I bet those bones are from slave times and they just

34

don't wanna say. Or something like Rosewood, with a bunch of folks killed and people kept it quiet."

"Unnnhhhh-hhnnnnnhhh," Odetta said. She had thought of that, too. "We may never know what happened to those people, but one thing we do know—keep off that land."

"That's what Grandmother said, from way back. When I was a kid."

"I know. Mama, too. Only a fool would buy one of those plots."

The McCormack Farm was less than a mile from Danielle's grandmother's house, along the unpaved red clay road the city called State Route 191, but which everyone else called Tobacco Road. Tobacco had been the McCormacks' business until the 1970s. Another curse to boot, Danielle thought. She drove past the McCormacks' faded wooden gate every time she went into town, and the gaudy billboard advertising LOTS FOR SALE—AS LOW AS $150,000. The mammoth, ramshackle tobacco barn stood beside the roadway for no other reason than to remind everyone of where the McCormack money had come from. Danielle's grandfather had sharecropped for the McCormacks, and family lore said her relatives had once been their slaves.

"How old's this baby?" Odetta said suddenly. "A year?"

"Thirteen months."

Lola had only been a month old last summer, when Karl went off to training. But Danielle didn't want to talk about Lola now. She had enjoyed forgetting all about her.

"Your grandmama never told you nothing about summer and babies?"

Danielle stared at her cousin, whose eyes were slightly small for her face. "You lost me."

"Just be careful, is all. Especially in July. Summer solstice. Lola may seem strong to you, but you gotta pay special attention to any baby under two. It's always the young ones. And now that those bones have been unburied, you need to keep an eye out."

"What are you talking about, girl?"

"I'm surprised your grandmama would let you raise a baby in her house. When your mama was young, she moved in with her cousin Geraldine. She never told you that? Lived in their basement until your mama was two."

35

The story sounded vaguely familiar, but Grandmother had died soon after Danielle married Karl, when Danielle had still been convinced she'd be moving to Atlanta within six months. She hadn't even been pregnant then. Not yet. She and Karl hadn't planned on a baby until they had more money put together. If not for Lola, they might be living in Atlanta right now.

"What do you mean? Is the water bad?" Now Danielle felt alarmed.

Odetta shook her head. "Leeches."

Danielle remembered the flies. Now she could expect leeches, too? "You mean those nasty things people put on their skin to suck out poison?" A whole army of leeches could crawl under the back door, with that half-inch gap that always let the breezes through. "Those worms?"

"Not that kind," Odetta said. "Swamp leeches are different. It's just a name Mama used to call them by. You could call them lots of things. Mostly people call them demons, I guess."

Danielle would have thought she'd heard wrong, except that Odetta had a sense of humor. She had Danielle cracking up at Grandmother's funeral, of all places, when Odetta whispered to point out how everyone who gave remembrances called Grandmother by a different surname. Grandmother had been married four times. *When I knew Mrs. Jenkins . . . When I knew Mrs. Roberts . . .* And on down the line. Once Odetta pointed it out, Danielle had to pretend to be sobbing to stifle her giggles. That laughter was the only light that day.

"What did you put in that lemonade after I fixed it? I know you're not sitting there talkin' 'bout demons in the swamp like some old voodoo lady," Danielle said.

Odetta looked embarrassed, rubbing the back of her neck. "I don't know nothin' 'bout no voodoo, but just ask folks. Nobody has young children near the swamp in summer, or there's trouble to follow. Cece's baby got crib death. But usually it just lasts the summer. The babies change, but by fall they change back."

"Change into what?" Danielle said, still trying to decide if Odetta was playing.

Odetta shrugged. "I don't know. Something else. Somebody else. You watch this baby real close, hear? Anything happens, ask me to take her by

Uncle June's. He's my granddaddy's brother, and he knows what to do. He says it's like those spirits flock to the swamp in summer, the way fish spawn. And they leech on to the young ones. That's why Mama calls them leeches."

Danielle almost asked about the flies she had seen, but she caught herself. What was she thinking about? Grandmother might have kept her candles lit, but this was plain crazy talk. The minute you start letting family close to you, turns out they're bent on recruiting you for the funny farm, too. No wonder Karl was so happy living so far from Atlanta and his relatives. He might never want to go back home.

"Don't look at me like that," Odetta said, grunting. She handed Lola back, almost as if to punish her. Danielle watched the sweetness seep from Lola's face, replaced by the mocking glare she saved only for her mother. If Odetta hadn't been sitting here watching, Danielle would have glared right back.

"I got to get home and see my stories. Just remember what I said. Watch over this girl."

The swamp leeches can have her, Danielle thought. God as her witness, that was the exact thought in her mind.

JUST TO BE on the safe side—and because she knew Grandmother would hound her in her dreams otherwise—Danielle brought Lola's crib into her bedroom so the baby wouldn't be alone at night. Danielle hadn't let the baby sleep in the master bedroom since she was four months old, and Lola never had liked the nursery. Now Lola fussed less at bedtime, and Danielle rediscovered how much she enjoyed the sound of another person breathing near her at night.

The strange thing didn't happen until nearly a week after Odetta's visit, when Danielle had all but forgotten the flies and Odetta's story about leeches. A loud noise overhead woke her one night. It sounded like a boot clomping on the rooftop.

Danielle opened her eyes, staring at the shadow of the telephone pole on her ceiling. Her bedroom always captured the light from the single streetlamp on this end of Tobacco Road. Sometimes her eyes played tricks on her and made her think she could see shadows moving. But shadows don't make noise, Danielle thought.

Karl would have sprung from bed to get his rifle out of the closet. But Karl wasn't here, and Danielle didn't know the first thing about the rifle, so she lay there and stared above her. That hadn't sounded like breathing wood or any of the old house's other aches and pains. Someone was on the roof. That was plain.

Not a rat. Not a raccoon. Not an owl. The only thing big enough to make that noise was a deer, and she'd stopped believing in creatures with hooves flying to the roof when she was eight. The clomping sound came again, and this time it was directly above her.

Danielle imagined she saw a large shadow on the ceiling above her, as if something was bleeding through. Imagined, because she couldn't be sure. But it seemed to be more than just the darkness. It was a long, large black space, perfectly still. Waiting. Danielle's heart galloped, and she couldn't quite catch her breath.

The thing on the rooftop made up its mind about what to do next. The shadow glided, and Danielle heard three purposeful strides on the rooftop above the mass. The sound was moving away from her bed—toward the baby's crib. The baby was still asleep, breathing in slow, heavy bursts. Danielle could hear Lola over the noise.

Too late, Danielle realized what she should have done: she should have jumped up, grabbed the baby, and run out of the room as fast as she could. It wouldn't have hurt to grab her Bible from inside her nightstand drawer while she was at it. But Danielle had done none of that, so she only lay there in helpless horror while a shadow-thing marched toward her baby girl.

As soon as the last clambering step sounded above—*CLOMP*—the baby let out a loud gasp.

The rooftop went silent, and the baby's breathing was normal again. Well, almost. Lola's breathing was shallower than it had been before, more hurried, but it was the steady breath of sleep.

After listening in the dark for five more minutes, feeling muscle cramps from lying so still beneath her blanket, Danielle began to wonder if the horrific sound on the rooftop had been in her imagination. After all, Lola woke up if she sneezed too close to her door—so wouldn't the baby have heard that racket and started wailing right away? Suddenly, it seemed all too plausible that the sound had been from a raccoon or an owl. Just magnified in the darkness, that was all. Served her right for letting family too close to her. Just crazy talk and nightmares.

But although she didn't hear another peep from the rooftop—and Lola's breathing was as steady as clockwork running only slightly fast—Danielle couldn't get back to sleep that night. She lay awake, listening to her baby breathe.

THE NEXT THING Danielle knew, sunlight was bright in her bedroom.

Lola woke up at six o'clock every morning no matter how late she went to bed, so Danielle hadn't lingered in bed long enough for the sun to get this bright all summer. Danielle looked at her alarm clock: It was ten o'clock! Midmorning. All at once, Danielle remembered the racket on the rooftop and her baby's little gasp. She fully expected to find Lola dead.

But Lola was sitting up in a corner of the crib, legs folded under her tailor-fashion patiently waiting. She wasn't whining, cooing, babbling, or whimpering. The baby was just staring and waiting for her to wake up.

Danielle felt a surge of warmth and relief, a calm feeling she wished she could have every morning. "Well, look at Mommy's big girl!" Danielle said, propping herself up on her elbows.

The baby sat straighter, and her mouth peeled back into a wide grin as she leaned forward, toward Danielle. Her eyes hung on Danielle, not missing a single movement or detail. She looked like a model baby on the diaper package, too good to be true.

And Danielle knew, just that fast. Something was wrong with the baby.

This isn't Lola, she thought. She would swear on her grave that she knew right away.

There were a hundred and one reasons. First, Lola started her days in a bad mood, crying until she got her baa-baa. The new sleeping arrangement hadn't changed that. And Lola never sat that way, cross-legged like a Girl Scout by a campfire. The pose didn't look right on her.

Danielle went through the usual motions—seeing if Lola's eyes would follow her index finger (they did, like a cat's), testing her appetite (Lola drank a full bottle and ate a banana), and checking Lola's temperature (exactly 98.6). Apparently, Lola was fine.

Danielle's heart slowed down from its gallop and she laughed at herself, laying Lola down flat on the wicker changing-table. The baby didn't fuss or wriggle, her eyes still following Danielle's every movement with a contented smile.

But when Danielle opened the flaps of the Pampers Cruisers and the soiled diaper fell away between Lola's chunky thighs, something dark and slick lay there in its folds. Danielle's first glance told her that Lola had gotten her bowel movement out of the way early—until the mess in her diaper *shuddered*.

It was five inches long, and thin, the color of the shadow that had been on her ceiling. The unnamable thing came toward Danielle, slumping over the diaper's elastic border to the table surface. Then, moving more quickly with its body hunched like a caterpillar, the thing flung itself to the floor. A swamp leech. A smell wafted up from its wake like soggy, rotting flesh.

For the next hour, while Lola lay in silence on the changing table, Danielle could hardly stop screaming, standing high on top of her bed.

DANIELLE DIDN'T remember calling Odetta from the portable phone on her nightstand, but the phone was in her hand. The next thing she knew, Odetta was standing in her bedroom doorway, waving a bath towel like a matador, trying to coax her off the bed. Danielle tried to warn Odetta not to touch the baby, but Odetta didn't listen. Odetta finished changing Lola's diaper and took her out of the room. The next time Danielle saw Lola, she was dressed up in her purple overalls, sitting in the car seat like they were on their way to lunch at Cracker Barrel.

"We're going to Uncle June's," Odetta said, guiding Danielle into the car.

Danielle didn't remember the drive, except that she could feel Lola watching her in the rearview mirror the whole way. Danielle was sure she would faint if she tried to look back.

Uncle June lived at the corner of Live Oak and Glory Road, near the woods. He was waiting outside his front door with a mug, wearing his pajama pants and nothing else. A smallish, overfed white dog sat beside him. Odetta kept saying Uncle June could help her, he would know just what to do, but the man standing outside the house at the end of the block looked like Fred Sanford in his junkyard. His overgrown grass was covered with dead cars.

Odetta opened the car door, unbuckled Lola from her car seat, and hoisted the baby into her arms. As if it were an everyday thing. Then she opened Danielle's car door and took her hand, helping her remember how to come to her feet.

"Just like with Ruby's boy in ninety-seven," Odetta told Uncle June, slightly breathless.

Uncle June just waved them in, opening his door. The dog glared back at Lola, but turned around and trotted into the house, where it made itself scarce.

"Let's put her in the bathtub, in case another one comes out of her," Odetta said.

"Won't be, but do what you want." Uncle June sounded sleepy.

Lola sat placidly in the center of the bathtub while the warm water came up to her waist. Her legs were crossed the way they had been in her crib. Danielle couldn't stare at her too long before she was sure a madwoman's wail would begin sliding from her throat.

She looked away.

Danielle gasped when she saw a long blue bathrobe hanging on a hook on back of the bathroom door. It looked like a man floating behind her. And the mirror on the medicine cabinet was askew, swinging to and fro, making her reflection tremble the way her mind was trembling. Danielle wondered how she hadn't fainted already.

"I told you," Uncle June said, and Danielle realized some time must have gone by. Uncle June had been standing before, but now he was sitting on top of the closed toilet lid, reading a well-worn copy of *The Man Who Said I Am*. "Won't never be but one o' them things." When the water splashed in the tub, they all looked down at Lola.

Danielle didn't look away this time; she just felt her body coil, ready for whatever was next. Lola's face was moony, upturned toward Danielle with the same intense gaze she had followed her with all morning. But the water around her still looked clear. No more leeches. Lola had only changed position slightly, one of the rare times she had moved at all.

"That thing I saw ..." Danielle whispered. Her fingers were shaking, but not as much as they had been up until then. "Was it a demon?"

Uncle June shook his head. "What you saw . . . the leech . . . that ain't it. Just a sign it's visiting. Evidence. They crawl for dark as fast as they can. Slide through cracks. No one's been able to find one, the way they scoot. Probably 'cause most folks head in the other direction."

"It's under my bed," Danielle said.

"Not anymore, it's not. It's halfway back to the swamp by now."

Danielle shivered for what seemed like a full minute. Her body was rejecting the memory of the thing she had found in her baby's diaper. She waited for her shivering to pass, until she realized it wouldn't pass any time soon. She would have to get used to it.

Lola, in the tub, wrapped her arms around herself with a studious expression as she stared up at Danielle. Lola was still smiling softly, as if she was going out of her way not to alarm her, but her creased eyebrows looked like a grown woman's. On any other day, Lola would be splashing water out of the tub, or else sliding against the slick porcelain with shrieks of glee. This creature with Lola's face might be a child, but it wasn't hers. Water wasn't novel anymore.

"If that isn't Lola . . . then where is she?" Danielle said, against the ball of mud in her throat.

"Lola's still in there, I expect," Uncle June said. "Dottie Stephens's baby was touched by it for a month . . . but come fall, it was like nothing happened. And Dottie's baby is a doctor now."

"Unnnnh-hnnnh . . ." Odetta said with an encouraging smile.

Danielle's heart cracked. A month!

"Course, you don't have to wait that long," Uncle June said. He stood up, lifted the toilet lid, and spat into the bowl. "I've got a remedy. They'll eat anything you put in front of them, so it won't be hard. Put about six drops on a peanut butter cracker, or whatever you have, but no more than six. Give it to her at midnight. That's when they come and go."

"And it won't hurt Lola?" Danielle said.

"Might give her the runs." Uncle June sat again.

"Lola's gonna be fine, Danny," Odetta said, squeezing her hand.

Karl's nickname for her was Danny, too. She should call Karl to tell him, she realized. But how could she explain this emergency to the Red Cross?

"What if . . . I don't give her the remedy? What would happen?" God only knew what was in that so-called remedy. What if she accidentally killed Lola trying to chase away the demon?

Uncle June shrugged. "Anybody's guess. It might stay in there a week. Maybe two. Maybe a month. But it'll be gone by the end of summer. I know that."

"Summer's the only time," Odetta said.

Danielle stared at Lola's face again. The baby's eyes danced with delight when Danielle looked at her, and the joy startled Danielle. The baby seemed like Lola again, except that she was looking at her with the love she saved for Karl.

"So how many is it now, Odetta? At McCormack's place?" Uncle June said. He had moved on, making conversation. Unlike Danielle, he was not suffering the worst day of his life.

"Six. Turns out they'd counted one too many. Still . . . "

Uncle June sighed, grieved. He wiped his brow with a washcloth.

"That's a goddamn shame." The way he said it caught Danielle's ear, as if he'd lost a good friend a hundred years ago who had just been brought out to light.

"Nobody has to wait on C.S.I. experts to tell us it's black folks," Odetta said.

Uncle June nodded, sighing. "That whole family ought to be run out of town."

Six dead bodies on McCormack Farm. Six of Gracetown's secrets finally unburied.

The other one, in the bathtub, had just been born.

"TEL-E-VI-SION."

Lola repeated the word with perfect diction. "Tel-e-vision."

All morning, while Danielle had sat wrapped up in Uncle June's blue bathrobe on the sofa with a mug of peppermint tea she had yet to sip from, Odetta had passed the time by propping Lola up in a dining room chair and identifying items in the room.

Lola pointed at the bookcase, which Uncle June had crammed top to bottom.

"Bookcase," Odetta said.

"Bookcase," the Lola-thing said. She pointed up at the chandelier, which was only a skeleton, missing all of its bulbs. "Chan-de-lier," Odetta said.

"Chandelier."

Danielle shivered with each new word. Before today, Lola's few words were gummy and indistinct, never more than two syllables. But Lola was different now.

Odetta laughed, shaking her head. "You hear that, Danny? Ruby's baby did this, too. Like damn parrots. But they won't say anything unless you say it first."

The baby pointed at a maroon-colored book on the arm of Uncle June's couch.

"Ho-ly Bi-ble," Odetta said.

"Ho-ly Bi-ble."

At that, honest to God, Danielle almost laughed. Then she shrank further into a ball, trying to sink into the couch's worn fabric and make herself go away.

Lola gazed over at Danielle, the steady smile gone. The baby looked concerned. *Mommy?* That's what the baby's face seemed to say.

"Your mama's tired," Odetta said.

Tears sprang to the baby's eyes. Suddenly, Lola was a portrait of misery.

"Don't worry, she'll be all right after tomorrow," Odetta said.

All misery vanished. The baby smiled again, shining her big brown eyes on Danielle. Just like Odetta's joke on the day of Grandmother's funeral, that smile was Danielle's only light.

"Ain't that something else?" Odetta whispered. "Maybe this ain't Lola, but they seem to come here knowing they're supposed to love their mamas."

No, it sure isn't Lola, Danielle thought ruefully.

A deep voice behind Danielle startled her. "Gotta go to work," Uncle

June said, and the door slammed shut behind him. Danielle had forgotten Uncle June was in the house.

"He never gave me the remedy," Danielle said, remembering.

"Later on, we'll carry Lola with us over to his gas station. It's just up the street. Besides, I'm hungry. Uncle June's got the best burgers under his warmer."

Some people could eat their way through any situation, Danielle thought.

After a time, Odetta turned on the television set, and the room became still. The only noise was from the guests on Oprah and a quick snarl from Uncle June's dog as he slunk past Lola's high chair. Lola didn't even notice the dog. Her eyes were still on Danielle, even when Danielle dozed for minutes at a time. Whenever Danielle woke up, Lola was still staring.

"What do they do?" Danielle asked finally. "Why are they here?"

"Damned if I know," Odetta said. "They don't do much of anything, except smile and try to learn things. Ruby said after she got over her fright, she was sorry to see it go."

"Then how do you know they're demons?"

"Demon ain't my word. I just call them leeches. What scares people is, they're unnatural. You don't ask 'em to come, and they take your babies away for a while. Now, it's true about that crib death, but Cece can't say for sure what caused it. Might've happened anyway." Odetta shrugged, her eyes still on the television screen. "They don't cry. They eat whatever you give 'em. And after that first nasty diaper, Uncle June says they hardly make any mess, maybe a trickle now and then. I bet there's some folks who see it as a blessing in disguise, even if they'd never say so. Lola, can you say *blessing*?"

"Bles-sing," Lola said, and grinned.

Danielle had never been more exhausted. "I need a nap," she said.

"Go on, girl. Lie down, and I'll get you a blanket. You could sleep all day if you want. This thing won't make no noise."

And it was true. Once their conversation stopped, the Lola-thing sat in the high chair looking just like Lola, except that she never once whined or cried, or even opened her mouth. She just gazed at Danielle as if she thought Danielle was the most magnificent creature on Earth. That smile from Lola was the last thing Danielle saw before she tumbled into sleep.

Uncle June had owned the Handi Gas at the corner of Live Oak and Highway 9 for at least twenty-five years, and it smelled like it hadn't had a good cleaning in that long, filled with the stink of old fruit and motor oil. But business was good. All the pumps outside were taken, and five or six customers were crammed inside, browsing for snacks or waiting in line for the register. The light was so dim Danielle could barely make out the shelves of products that took up a half dozen rows, hardly leaving room to walk.

Uncle June was busy, and he didn't acknowledge them when they walked in. Odetta went straight for the hamburgers wrapped in shiny foil inside the glass display case by the cash register.

"You want one, girl?" Odetta called.

Danielle shook her head. The thought of food made her feel sick. She had ended up with the stroller, even though Odetta had promised her she wouldn't have to get too close to Lola. But Danielle found she didn't mind too much. Being at Handi Mart with the truckers and locals buying their lunch and conducting their business almost made Danielle forget her situation. As she pushed the stroller aimlessly down aisle after aisle, hypnotized by the brightly colored labels, she kept expecting to feel Lola kicking her feet, squirming in the stroller or screaming at the top of her lungs. Her usual antics.

Instead, Lola sat primly with her hands folded in her lap, her head turning right and left as she took in everything around her. Odetta had spent the rest of the morning braiding Lola's hair, entwining the plaits with pretty lilac-colored bows alongside the well-oiled grooves of her brown scalp. Despite her best efforts, Danielle had never learned how to do much with Lola's hair. Mom hadn't known much about hair, either. This was the best Lola had looked in ages.

"I'll get to you in a minute," Uncle June called to Danielle as the stroller ambled past the register line. "I know what you're here for."

"Take your time," someone said, and she realized she had said it. Calm as could be.

Although Odetta was kin to Uncle June, she had to stand in line like any other customer. She'd helped herself to two burgers, a large bag of

Doritos, and a Diet Coke from the fountain in back. It's no wonder she was still carrying her baby weight eighteen years later, Danielle thought. With nothing left to do, Danielle stood beside her cousin to wait.

"Well, ain't you cute as a button?" a white woman said ahead of them, gazing back at Lola in the stroller. The woman was wearing an ostrich feather hat and looked like she was dressed for church. Was it Sunday? Danielle couldn't remember.

"But-ton," Lola said, the first sound she'd made in two hours.

The woman smiled down at Lola. Danielle almost warned her not to get too close.

"Thank you," Danielle said. Lola didn't get many compliments, not with her behavior.

"How old is she?" the woman asked.

"Thirteen months," Danielle said, although it was a lie. As far as she knew, the thing in Lola's stroller was as old as the swamp itself.

"Lovely," the woman said. She turned away when Uncle June asked her pump number.

And Lola was lovely today, thanks to Odetta. There was no denying it. Maybe that was why Danielle could touch her stroller without feeling queasy, or getting goose bumps. The nasty thing that had crawled out of Lola's diaper that morning was beginning to seem like a bad dream.

"One minute," Uncle June said when it was their turn in line. He vanished through a swinging door to the back room. As the door swung to and fro, Danielle saw a mess of boxes in the dank space, and she caught a whiff of mildew and ammonia. Danielle felt her heart speed up. Her fingers tightened around the stroller handles.

"You sure you don't want your own burger? These are mine," Odetta said.

Danielle only shook her head. A fly landed on one of the ribbons on Lola's head.

Uncle June came back with a brown iodine bottle with a black dropper. He set the bottle on the counter next to Odetta's hamburgers. "Remedy's free. Odetta, you owe me five-fifty."

While Odetta rifled through her overstuffed pocketbook, Uncle June leaned over, folded his hands, and stared Danielle straight in the eye. His eyes looked slightly bloodshot, and she wondered if he had been drinking that morning.

"Remember what I said," Uncle June told her in a low voice, so the man in the Harley Davidson T-shirt behind them wouldn't hear. "Six drops. No more, no less. At midnight. Then you'll have your baby back."

Danielle nodded, clasping the bottle tightly in her hand. She had questions about what was in the remedy, or how he'd come to concoct it, but she couldn't make her mouth work. She couldn't even bring herself to thank him.

Another fly circled, landing on the counter, and Uncle June killed it with his red flyswatter without blinking. He wiped it off the counter with a grimy handkerchief, his eyes already looking beyond Danielle toward the next customer.

"Won't be long now, Danny," Odetta said.

Danielle nodded again.

Odetta opened the gas station's glass door for her, and Danielle followed with the stroller. She was looking forward to another nap. Hell, she might sleep all day today, while she had the chance. She hadn't had a good night's sleep since Karl had been gone.

Danielle almost ran down an old white man in a rumpled black Sunday suit who was trying to come in as they walked out. "Sorry—" Danielle began, but she stopped when she saw his face.

Danielle and her neighbor had never exchanged a word in all these years, but there had been no escaping his face when he ran for Town Council in ninety-nine and plastered his campaign posters all over the supermarkets. He was Old Man McCormack, even though his face was so furrowed with lines that he looked like he could be his own father. He was also very small, walking with a stoop. The top of his head barely came up to Danielle's shoulder.

Odetta froze, staring at him with a stupefied expression, but McCormack didn't notice Odetta. His eyes were fixed on the stroller, down at the baby.

He smiled a mouthful of bright dentures at Lola.

"Just like a little angel," McCormack said. Some of his wrinkles smoothed over when he smiled, as if a great burden had been lifted from his face. He gently swatted away a fly that had been resting on the tip of Lola's nose. Danielle didn't know how long the fly had been there.

"Lit-tle an-gel," Lola said.

McCormack's smile faded as he raised his head to look at Danielle, as if he expected to find himself staring into a harsh light. His face became tight, like hardening concrete.

"Afternoon, ma'am," he said. His voice was rough, scraped from deep in his throat. And his eyes flitted away from hers in an instant, afraid to rest on hers too long.

But Danielle had glimpsed his runny eyes long enough to see what he was carrying. She could see it in his stooping shoulders, in his shuffling walk. She felt sorry for him.

"Afternoon, Mr. McCormack," she said.

He paused, as if he was shocked she had been so civil. His face seemed to melt.

"You and your pretty little girl have a good summer, hear?" he said with a grateful smile.

"Yessir, I think we will," Danielle said. "You have a good summer, too."

Despite the way Odetta gaped at her, Danielle wasn't in the mood to pass judgment today. Everyone had something hidden in their past, or in their hearts, they wouldn't want dug out. Maybe the McCormack family would have to answer to God for those bodies buried on their land, or maybe they wouldn't. Maybe Danielle would give Lola six drops of Uncle June's remedy at midnight tonight, or maybe she wouldn't.

She and this old man deserved a little peace, that was all.

Just for the summer.

Danielle rubbed the top of Lola's head, gently massaging her neatly braided scalp. Her tiny visitor in the stroller turned to grin up at her with shining, adoring eyes.

~~

"Summer" was written for Brandon Massey's Whispers in the Night, *the third anthology he edited in the Dark Dreams series featuring black writers. As the mother of a young son, I wanted to explore difficulties in parenting—and how any parent might make an unconscionable choice. Just for the summer.*

Ghost Summer

DAVIE STEPHENS was sure he must be dreaming when he heard his mother singing softly in his ear. It was an old call-and-response song she used to sing to him when he was young: *"Kye Kye Kule . . . Kye Kye Kofisa . . . Kofisa Langa . . . Kaka Shilanga . . . Kum Adem Nde . . . "*

The sound nearly made him clap his hands in rhythm to the song, reminding him of the game they had played. His first name was Kofi, just like in the song, from his mother's family in Ghana. But he had used his middle name since first grade because other kids called him Coffee and tried to pick fights. It was like a stranger's name. He preferred to be All-American David, like his father.

"Kye Kye Kule . . . "

When Davie felt a cold fingertip against his ear, he jumped up with a gasp.

He wasn't sleeping! A shadow sat beside him on the bed, washed in darkness. Davie's heart thumped. He opened his mouth to yell, but the shadow planted a firm palm across his lips.

"Don't be loud. You'll wake your sister," his mother said.

Only Mommy! He smelled the smoky scent of her shea butter as she flicked on his light. She was wearing her "home clothes," as she called them; green and gold and red and blue woven into her dress from Ghana. Davie looked at his Transformers clock radio, confused. Four a.m.

"I thought you left," he said.

"I'm leaving now. One last goodbye," she said, and kissed his forehead. Davie thought he saw tears shimmering, but Mommy was always emotional about trips and airplanes. She thought it was every airplane's destiny to crash from the sky, and the pilots had to fight for their lives the whole way. For months, she had talked about nothing but her visit to Accra to see her family, and now she seemed sad to be leaving. "I'll pack you in my bag, I think."

"You'll be back soon, Mommy," I said.

Mommy didn't answer, except to sigh. Suddenly, Davie was *sure* he saw tears.

"Saida?" Dad called from the hallway, his voice hushed in the dark. "Van's here."

Davie was glad Mommy had lost the argument, but he felt sorry for her. She wanted to take them all to Ghana with her, but this was time to go to Grandma and Grandpa Walter's in Gracetown, Florida. The summer trip had been planned since Christmas, but Mommy wanted them to go to with her instead. Mommy had said they should take a vote, and Davie had felt guilty raising his hand to choose Dad's parents over hers. Of course, Neema raised her hand to side with him too, because she mimicked his every movement.

Gracetown won, even though their older sister, Imani, had refused to vote because she was going away to Northwestern for the summer anyway. The relief Davie felt only had a little bit to do with the farmer in Gracetown who let them ride his tractor and horses whenever they wanted to, or Grandma's fried chicken and sweet potato pie. Mommy and Dad knew exactly why he and Neema wanted to go to Gracetown instead.

It was never the same at Christmas. The best time to go was in summer.

"Hope you see your ghosts," Mommy said, and kissed his forehead. She was smiling; a sad, empty smile, but still a smile. Mommy's smile made Davie's heart leap. Maybe she wasn't mad about his vote against her, or how he had led Neema to his side. The injured look on her face when he'd raised his hand had pierced him in a strange new way, as if she was his child—and he a parent who had made a terrible, unthinkable choice.

"I'll get video this time," Davie said. "Proof. You'll see."

Mommy made a *tssk* sound. "You think I never saw ghosts? On my street, they lived in the acacia trees. They sang us to sleep! We never saw it as a special thing. Not like you. Take care of your sister. I'll miss you, Kofi."

"I'll miss you too, Mommy."

Her hug lasted so long that Dad called for her twice more. The last time, he came to the doorway and stood there as if to block her way. "You'll be late. Come on." His voice was clipped, like he was mad. But he was only tired. That was what Davie told himself then.

It would be a month and two days before he would see Mommy again. He had never been away from her so long, so he didn't move from her arms even after Dad huffed out an annoyed sigh. More than annoyed, actually. Later, Davie would wonder why he hadn't realized right then that something was very, very wrong.

He'd known, maybe, but he hadn't wanted to.

That summer wasn't going to be like the rest. Not one tiny little bit.

Davie heard the shuttle drive off beneath his window, taking his mother far away from them. But as he tried to go back to sleep, twisting and turning beneath his sheets until they bound his legs, ghosts were the only thing on Davie's mind.

THE WEEKS in summer usually fly by, but the two days before they would leave for Florida passed as slowly as the last two days of school. The day of the trip passed even more slowly. First, the flight itself was endless. One plane to Atlanta to took forever, landing at the airport that was more like a city, with a transit system and far-flung terminals. The next plane was so teeny that they climbed up metal stairs from the hot tarmac in the rain, and Dad had to stow his computer case because the attendants said there wouldn't be room.

Neema, of course, complained the whole way. She always complained more when Mommy wasn't around, because Dad would cluck and tug her braids gently and try to make her smile as if she were still a baby instead of eight already. She really played it up when Mom was gone, carrying around her brown-skinned Raggedy Ann doll and batting her eyelashes. Pathetic.

Maybe Mommy is right about planes, Davie thought when the second plane landed with a terrible shaking and squealing. But then they were on the ground and everyone clapped with relief, and Mommy's fears seemed silly again.

Not *Mommy*, he reminded himself. He was twelve years old now. He was going to middle school in the fall, and he'd heard enough nightmarish stories about middle school to know that if any of the other kids heard him call his mother Mommy, he'd come home with a bloody nose every day. He'd already seen evidence of it: A hard glare from a teenager watching him play with Neema on the playground equipment at the McDonald's Playland had been Davie's first hint that the Punk Police were watching him now. He wasn't a kid anymore; he was a target. His mother was *Mom* now. Nothing so hard about that. Like Dad told him, she would keep him a baby forever if it were up to her. He had to be stronger than that.

As if in confirmation, when the plane rocked to a halt Dad patted Davie's knee the way he patted his business partner's knee when he came over for dinner. (His father was a movie producer, except not the rich kind.) That pat made Davie feel grown, even important.

"Well . . . we're here now," Dad said. He didn't look happy the way he usually did when he visited his parents. He said it as if flying to Tallahassee to drive to Gracetown were like being flown to the moon against their will, held prisoner for ransom by space pirates camping on moon rocks. Dad sounded like he wished he could go anywhere else.

There was no rain during the long drive past acres of thin, scraggly pine trees on I-10 east of Tallahassee, and Davie was disappointed to realize how much daylight was left even after such a long trip. Maybe two whole hours. He was ready to go to bed right now, even if it was only two o'clock in Los Angeles, not even time for SpongeBob.

But the ghosts never came until after dark. And to Davie, the ghosts were the point of visiting Grandma and Grandpa Walter in Gracetown during the summer.

The ghosts were why he put up with having to share a room with Neema, and the excruciating fact that Grandpa Walter and Grandma only had a huge old satellite dish, and every time they came to visit the number of channels had shrunk because all the networks were bailing to cable and DishNet or DirecTV or something invented in this millennium, so unless he was going to watch CNN or the History Channel or Lifetime—*get real!*—there was hardly anything on TV all summer long. And ghosts were definitely the reason he put up with mosquito-infested, broiling North Florida in the middle of hurricane season—yes, sometimes it rained every day—instead of just holding out for Christmastime.

In summer, it was *all* about the ghosts.

Large trucks carried away load after load of fallen pine trees, but the woods were still thick. *You see how they're cutting it all down?* Grandma always said on her way to this or that meeting to try to stop a new construction project. But while Gracetown had a shortage of virtually everything else—particularly in the movie theater department—there was no visible shortage of trees whatsoever. *Welcome to Gracetown—We've Got Trees!*

Grandma and Grandpa Walter had lived in Miami most of his life, but they had retired to Gracetown four years ago, on six acres of land shaped like a slice of pie—well, not a perfect piece, but it tapered to nothing at the V at the far fence. The single-story house was fenced in and set back from a two-lane road where traffic raced past on its way to more interesting places.

It didn't look anything like Davie would have imagined a haunted house should look—old and decrepit, or with an interesting feature like a balcony, or at least a veranda. Gracetown was full of plantation-style houses that looked like a reminder of the slavery Davie had seen with his own eyes when Dad showed him *Roots*, but Grandma and Grandpa Walter's house looked like they had ordered it over the Internet from Houses-R-Us. Just like any other house, except painted bright peach, a splash of Miami in the middle of the woods.

Grandma and Grandpa Walter were waiting for them in the yard when they drove up. The gravel driveway was a million miles long, so his grandparents needed plenty of notice to walk down to unlock the gate. Locking the gate was a Miami habit Grandma never gave up. Sometimes Grandpa Walter drove his car instead of walking because of his arthritis.

When Davie and his sister got out of the rental car, his grandparents fussed over them as if they'd been gone half a lifetime, like they always did. Tight hugs from Grandma. Playful punches from Grandpa Walter, who liked to remind Davie that he used to box when he was in the army in the 1950s. Promises of special outings and homemade sweets.

But it was different this time, too. Usually Dad just stood in the background and grinned, watching his parents. Davie's father had told him that when he was a kid, a psychic at a booth at a county fair told him that his parents would die when he was young—and he'd lived in fear of losing them since. Dad had never expected Grandma and Grandpa Walter to see him grow up, or to know his children. Dad said he finally figured out that the psychic wanted to scare him.

"But why would a psychic want to scare a little kid like that?" Davie had asked.

Dad had looked at him like it was the dumbest question in the world. "That was in 1976, Davie," Dad said. He waited a moment, as if the answer was hidden in the year, a code. Davie's blank face made him sigh. "Racist, that's all. What do you think?"

Dad's explanation for everything.

This time, Dad went straight to Grandma and hugged her almost as if he was too tired to stand, and she hugged him back with her eyes closed tight. *Did somebody die?* Davie thought.

The moment didn't last long—and Neema didn't even notice, because Grandpa was distracting her by pointing out a woodpecker in the oak tree—but Davie saw. Watching, Davie remembered that Dad hadn't always been a grown man. He'd been a little boy once, just like him, and he looked like a boy again, clinging to his mother in a way he always warned Davie not to cling to Mommy. *Mom.* Their faces captivated Davie, full of weary pain. Davie hadn't seen either of them look that tired before.

Then Grandpa Walter came over to pat Dad's shoulder, two solid taps, and the moment passed. Dad pulled away from his mother, and she turned her face toward the house, but not before Davie saw her wipe her eye.

Yep. Someone must have kicked the bucket. *Another one bites the dust*, he thought.

"Let's get the bags in," Grandpa said, even though Davie knew he couldn't lift heavy bags anymore because his joints hurt. He'd said it so Dad and Grandma would erase that hurting from their faces before Davie and Neema could see. Sometimes Davie wondered if he was psychic, too—a *real* psychic, not a county fair jerk who tried to scare little kids and maybe, just *maybe*, was a little bit racist. Davie could see things he couldn't see before.

Neema was in full whine, telling Grandma she wanted a nap, not even getting excited when they told her she would have *her own room* this time, and Davie couldn't bring himself to go inside yet to hear her complaining like a princess. There was a little sunlight left, and there was nothing to watch in the house, nothing to do. Not until after dark, anyway.

"Can I play outside?" Davie asked his father, an inspiration. They were in a foyer, walking carefully on the long rug so they wouldn't scratch Grandma's wood floor. There were a lot of rules in his grandparents' house, and sometimes it was easier just to sit and do nothing.

But outside! Outside as a whole different universe.

"Just watch for snakes," Grandma said. "And stay in the gate."

"Don't be silly, Mom," Dad said. "He's twelve now. Just don't go too far, Davie."

"Yessir."

Grandpa Walter always smiled when he called Dad "sir," so it was the quickest way to make sure Grandpa stayed in a good mood.

" . . . the way those drivers race past that fence," Grandma was saying, but the front door closed behind Davie and he flew down the steps, momentarily saved from having to answer yet more questions about how school was going.

If he was lucky, Ricardo might be around. Ricardo was a Mexican kid he met at Christmas, whose parents were migrants. Ricardo said he never stayed one place long, but he might get lucky. Or he could hang out with the Reed kids at the end of the street. The Reed twins were two years younger and obnoxious rednecks, but their older brother had *Rock Band* for PlayStation 3, so they were the most valuable friends Davie had, period. *Rock Band* was simply the coolest game ever invented, bar none.

The dirt in the area where his grandparents lived was called "red," but to Davie it looked more like a deep shade of orange. It was still called "Georgia clay," even though the Georgia border was a half hour's drive—which Davie knew because the closest movie theater was in Bainbridge, Georgia, not to mention the awesome Golden Corral buffet. The dirt didn't care which side of the border it was on, Georgia or Florida. The orange dirt was everywhere, right beneath the grass.

The orange dirt and gravel path ran through the center of the yard, presenting Davie with a clear choice—the gate and the road were on one side of the path, and the fence and the woods were on the other. Davie noticed that Grandpa still hadn't repaired the broken logs in one section of the ranch-style fence that separated his property from the woods. The same fence had been broken six months before. Telltale hoof-prints gathered around Grandma's fake deer near the driveway were evidence that woodland creatures were trespassing at night. *Dumb-butts can't tell the difference between what's real and what's not*, Davie thought.

Decision time: Hunting for snakes in the woods, or *Rock Band*?

Davie was about to take the path down to the road and head for the Reed house when he saw something move in the woods, beyond the broken fence. He heard dead leaves marking footsteps as it ran away, fast. Whatever it was, it was big. A deer? Another kid playing?

Davie's decision was made. He searched the castoffs from his grandparents' own personal forest of pine and oak trees until he found a sturdy dead branch as his walking stick. The stick was almost as tall as he was, and Davie liked the way it fit in his hand. He stripped away the smaller branches until it looked more like Mad-Eye Moody's staff from *Harry Potter*. He tapped the thick stick on the ground to make sure it would hold instead of breaking at the center. Satisfied, he headed into the woods.

Davie leaned on his stick for support when he climbed over the broken fence.

The woods behind his grandparents' house wasn't shady like the woods in movies. Most of the trees had thin trunks and not much shade to spare, but they were growing as far as he could see. Davie knew there were snakes, because Grandpa had told him he killed a rattler in the driveway only two weeks before. At the very least, he would go home with a story to tell.

Davie liked running in the underbrush, with obstacles every which way and snap decisions to be made. There—jump on the stone! There—watch out for the hole! He stumbled now and then, mostly just harmless scrapes. Acts of coordination and fearlessness were necessary for any ghost-hunter. Most ghosts were friendly, but how lame would it be to leave himself helpless if he met a hostile? Plan B was filed under R for Run.

Davie didn't have to run far. He'd gone only about thirty yards when he saw three boys huddled in a circle in a clearing. None of them were wearing shirts, only ragged-looking shorts of varying lengths. The three of them looked like brothers, each younger than the next. The eldest could be Davie's age.

Davie's feet made a racket crackling in the dead leaves, but none of the boys turned around to look at him. When the boys held hands, Davie understood why: They were praying over a huge hole someone had dug in the ground. As he got closer, Davie saw a large German shepherd sleeping beside the hole.

Not SLEEPING, crap-for-brains, Davie told himself. The big dog was dead. Its face and muzzle were matted with orange-brown mud.

He'd interrupted a funeral! Davie backed up a step and halfway hid himself behind a rare wide-trunked tree of pale, peeling bark, thin as paper. Davie had never had a dog—Mom thought keeping a dog inside the house was a disgrace, as did her whole family in Ghana, where dogs apparently were not considered man's best friend by a long shot—but he understood how sad it was when a pet died. He'd had a rat once, Roddy, like in the movie *Flushed Away*.

Roddy was an awesome rat. Lay across Davie's shoulder while he walked around, no problem. Rats were as smart as dogs, people said, but rats definitely got screwed in the life-span department. His rat had lived only two years. When Roddy died, Davie had cried himself to sleep for two nights, and hadn't wanted a pet of any kind ever since. He, Dad, Mom, and Neema had buried Roddy in the back yard, just like these boys.

But Roddy's hole in the ground hadn't been nearly so big, like a tunnel. The mountain of Georgia clay dirt beside the hole was as tall as the oldest boy. Someone had done some serious digging, Davie realized. Maybe their dad helped, or someone with a jack. It would have taken him all day to dig a hole like that. Or longer. Davie noticed that all of the boys were caked in red clay dust just as the setting sun intensified in a bright red-orange burst the color of a mango, turning the boys into shadowed silhouettes. Watching their vigil, Davie made up an epitaph: *Here lies Smoky, a Hell of a Dog / Crossed McCormack Road in the Midnight Fog—*

Suddenly, the youngest boy turned and stared him in the eye, whipping his head around so fast that Davie's rhyme left his mind. The boy was standing only ten yards from him, but his eyes were his most visible feature.

The whites were, anyway. That was all Davie could see, a white-eyed stare vivid against dark skin.

"Sorry about your dog," Davie said. No need to be rude. The oldest boy looked about twelve, too. Maybe he knew somewhere to play basketball. This clan could be a valuable find.

None of the others looked at Davie. The youngest, who might be six, turned away again.

It seemed best to leave them alone. Davie had never been to a funeral, thank goodness—Mom couldn't afford to bring him and Neema when her father in Ghana died, so she and Imani had gone alone—but he figured funerals weren't a good place to make friends. If the boys lived nearby, he'd find them later. If not, whatever. Kids in Gracetown weren't always nice to him, as if he didn't meet their standards. He talked funny and liked weird things, from a Gracetown point of view, so he never knew what kind of reception to expect.

Davie left and turned for home, digging his stick into pockets of soft soil as he walked. He didn't run, this time. It was getting dark, harder to see, and there was no reason to take a chance on breaking his leg. It would be ghost time soon.

Davie didn't realize how relieved he was to leave the woods until he saw the welcoming broken fence in the shadow of his grandparents' huge oak tree, which was covered in moss like Silly String. Home! The underbrush had seemed unruly, and he was glad to find his shoes back on neatly cropped grass. He felt a strange wriggling sensation in his stomach. Until he climbed back over the fence, he hadn't let himself notice he was a little scared. Just a little.

But the real scare didn't come until he got to the house.

Davie decided to go to the back door instead of the front because his shoes might be muddy, and Grandma would have a fit if he tracked dirt on her hardwood floors. As he was climbing the concrete steps to the back door, he glimpsed the kitchen window.

What he saw there made his stomach drop out of him.

Grandpa Walter stood by the fridge, arms crossed and head hanging; he might have been studying his shoes, except that his eyes were closed.

Grandma was clearing away dishes from the table, where Dad was sitting alone. Muted through the window, Davie heard Grandma saying, " . . . It's all right, baby. It's all gonna work out. No court in the country will let her take them all the way over there, I don't care if she's the mother or not. What's she gonna do, steal them? If she wants a fight, well, she's got one. We have money put away. You'll get a good lawyer, and that's that. Don't you worry."

His father sat at the table, forehead resting against the tabletop, his arms wrapped around his ears. His father was crying.

ALL NIGHT, Davie lay in bed trying to unhear and unsee it. Every time he saw the snapshot of that kitchen window, remembering Grandma's words and Dad's grieving pose, his stomach ate him. Now he knew what people meant when they said Too Much Information: It wasn't about stuff being too gross, or none of your business. Some information was too big for a single brain. Each time Davie remembered what he'd seen and heard, the enormity grew exponentially, with new and more terrible realizations.

His parents were definitely getting a divorce. Check. Hadn't seen *that* coming, since they never argued or raised their voices in front of him. They snapped at each other sometimes, but who didn't? Okay, so Mom thought Dad worked too much. She'd never made that a secret. And Dad definitely liked spending time alone. There was no denying it. And Mom's bad moods probably got on his nerves. So now, after twenty years, they were getting a divorce?

Divorce. That nuclear bomb should have been enough for one night— hell, one *lifetime*—but there was layer after layer, and it unspooled slowly as Davie stared at his grandparents' popcorn ceiling, seeing only visions of the kitchen window.

As if the D-word wasn't enough, Mom wanted to take them to Ghana. Dad didn't want them to go. Grandma and Grandpa were Dad's war-chiefs, and they were about to go to war.

Against Mommy. And Mommy against Daddy, Grandma, and Grandpa. And no matter what happened, he and Neema and Imani were FUBAR. Effed Up Beyond All Recognition.

The only tiny morsel of comfort Davie could take from The Worst Moment of His Entire Life was the knowledge that Grandpa Walter, Grandma and—*Thank you, God*—Dad himself had not seen him at the window. He'd had the good sense to duck away before a wandering pair of eyes found him and waved him inside to take his seat at the Oh-Crap table.

"Davie, we're glad you finally know the truth . . . You'll need you to be a man now . . . "

The very thought of that conversation with Dad made Davie want to vomit. He kept his palm clamped across his mouth, just in case of a surprise puke attack. He felt it in his throat.

As long as he ignored their sad eyes, went on with his life and pretended he hadn't heard, they would have to keep pretending, too. All of them would be putting on a show for each other, like a reality TV show called "FUBAR," but at least then Neema wouldn't find out. Or Imani, who couldn't possibly know, because she'd been in *way* too good a mood when she left for Evanston, Illinois, to meet her future as an incoming freshman in a minority summer program.

Let them have their lives a while longer, anyway. For the summer, anyway.

Ignorance was the only mercy he could still do for them. He only wished his father had his S-H-I-T together and could have kept him out of the loop a little longer, too. How the hell would he get through the next month?

Davie was on the verge of crying himself to sleep the way he had after Roddy the Rat died, but his unborn sob caught in his throat when he heard the footsteps padding against the hallway floorboards.

He thought he'd imagined it, so he sat up and didn't move, not even to get his flashlight. His ears were his most important tool: He listened.

Click-click-click. This time, he heard not only the footsteps, but clicking nails. Like a dog's paws. A heavy dog—about the size of the big German shepherd.

Davie had accidentally been holding his breath, and he needed to breathe. He took a long gasp of air, louder than he'd meant to, and stopped breathing again.

The dog's feet padded closer to his closed bedroom door. Davie stared toward the crack between the door and the frame in the moonlight, and he saw a shadow cross from one side to the other. About the size of a dog's nose.

Sfffff sfff fffff. Sniffing at the door.

"Holy effing S-H-I-T," Davie said, but only after the sniffing noise stopped and the sound of footsteps had padded away to silence.

Davie's plan was to lie absolutely still and do everything in his power to convince the dog that there was no reason to try to get into his room. Good dog, bad dog, whatever, Davie didn't want a ghost encounter with a dog. His central plan in case of a hostile entity—Communication and Negotiation—wasn't worth crapola with a dog.

The first ghost he met up close should definitely be human.

But the ghosts were tracking *him* already.

THE NEXT MORNING, Neema was gone.

He heard her chattering to herself in her room through her closed door when he came to tell her breakfast was ready. Grandma had a thing about eating breakfast before nine, so there was no sleeping in at Grandma's house, not if you wanted to eat.

" . . . And this one . . . and this one . . . and *this* one . . . " Neema was saying, probably for no particular reason. The eight-year-old girl's brain was truly the nonsense wonder of the world.

He knocked on her door twice. "Breakfast."

" . . . and thi—"

Neema went completely silent, in mid-word. When Davie opened her door, the bed was empty. The covers were turned back as if she'd just gotten up, and Neema's Raggedy Ann doll lay in her place, her wild black-thread pigtails fanned across the pillow. The doll's face was painted with a deformed triangle nose and a mental patient's smile. Dolls went from looking ridiculous to sinister in a blink. Davie took note: weird.

"Neema?" he said.

Neema's room had been Grandma's doll room until this summer, since Grandma decided Davie was too old to share a room with her. Finally! Grandma had cleared out only enough space for the bed and a small desk. Other than that, the room was filled with shelf after shelf of brown and black and white dolls, most of them babies dressed like it was baptism day, frozen in infancy. There were dozens of sets of little eyes in the room— none of them Neema's.

Davie waited for her giggle, or a surprise lunge from behind, or a rustle as she tried to hide. Neema sucked at hide-and-seek.

Nothing. An empty bed. An empty room with too many dolls.

Definitely weird.

"Neema, you're not funny. Breakfast," he said. He glanced inside the open closet door, which was full of nothing but boxed dolls, collector's items, except for Neema's one Sunday dress and a wicker hamper with its lid piled with folded clothes.

Under her bed, Davie found nothing but dust.

The window was halfway open, Davie noticed, raised at least eight inches. Ten, maybe. Could a girl Neema's size have squeezed out of so small a space?

Davie ran to the window to peer outside. Neema's room overlooked the back yard, so he saw the bed of dried pine needles and pine cones that lay scattered across the grass. This side of the house was closer to the woods than the living room, shaded by the taller nearby trees.

The broken fence was only twenty strides from Neema's window. The fence mesmerized Davie, as if it were a key to a puzzle. Neema had been here one second, and now she was gone.

But why the hell would Neema climb out of a window to go the woods? Since when? *Wouldn't.*

But this room was too small to hide in.

Davie scanned the doll shelves, almost expecting to find her there, as if she could have shrunk herself down to doll size. Row after row of unblinking brown, blue and green eyes gazed back. And little taunting pink-lipped smiles.

"Neema, quit playing," he said, poking at her bedcovers to make sure she hadn't disguised her bulk somehow. The bed was empty.

Davie picked up Raggedy Ann—who truly *was* raggedy, since she'd belonged to their Aunt Evie when she was a little girl, special-made by a black dollmaker—and and even looked under Neema's pillow, for no particular reason. "I mean it. Dang, you're such a baby."

Steely, eerie silence.

But I heard her. It was Neema. She was saying "And this one and this one . . ."

Just in case some law of physics or the space-time continuum had been violated, Davie checked the bathroom across the hall, too. And his own room. No Neema. There was always the front of the house, but how could she have gotten past him? No way.

You were standing right here in front of her door. YOU HEARD HER VOICE.

For the first time, Davie realized that the tears he thought he'd fought off soon before he heard the ghost dog hadn't been banished very far. They were still there, just beneath his eyeballs, waiting for the slightest reason to peek out. Neema being gone made him want to cry.

How could he tell Dad?

"Please, Neema?" he said to her empty room, his voice small.

That did it—his appeal to her charity. Conceding his helplessness.

The closet rustled, and the lid to the clothes hamper opened, revealing Neema's round face inside. She grinned. "I tricked you! I kept the clothes on top."

Davie was so relieved to see her that he couldn't get as mad as he wanted to be. "Good one. Seriously," he said, and helped her climb out. "I'll get you back, though."

"Not-uh."

"You wish, freak-girl."

Just like that, life was normal again. Now there would be no exhaustive explanations (*"See, this ghost dog was here, and I think he dragged Neema into another realm . . . "*), no looks of disappointment, and then concern, and then yawning horror.

Reality check.

Yeah, the divorce would be bad. But not as bad as losing Neema.

IN DAYLIGHT, armed with his new glass-half-full outlook, Davie couldn't believe his luck: a ghost encounter his very first night! This house was like a lake brimming with catfish. If he hadn't chickened out, he might have followed that dog to God-knew-what ghost rally, chock full of chances to capture the manifestation on video and audio for YouTube.

In daylight, Davie chastised himself for his crisis in faith in the power of communication. If he could say, "I don't want to hurt you" to a human ghost, then "Good boy, good boy" should do for a dog. He'd let himself fall prey to species bigotry, and he'd lain there like a lump while his chance at ghost-hunting stardom had trotted down the hall.

He'd need to man up by nightfall. He was so determined that he walked to the Handi Mart at the corner and paid way too much for a bag of dog biscuits, just to be on the safe side.

"Yes, I'm sure it was a dog," he told Neema in his room while he made his preparations, when she demanded the full story of why he had dog biscuits alongside his ghost-hunting supplies out on his bed.

"How do you know?"

"Because I saw some kids bury a dog yesterday. Right outside the back fence."

I hoped I hadn't blown Neema's mind badly enough to give her nightmares.

"*Cool!*" she said. "I wanna see the dog too!"

"*Shhhhhh,*" I shushed her. That was the main problem with Neema: She couldn't keep quiet. With Neema tagging along, living room recon was a nightmare. She could wake up an entire house without trying. Between that and her inability to sit still longer than five minutes, Neema was pretty much useless. Stealth and patience were the only two qualities that mattered in ghost-tracking. So far, at least, his baby sister had neither.

But if she was going to get trained, he had to train her now.

Imani said she heard the ghosts the first year she came to the Gracetown house in summer, but not after she was thirteen. She said it was as if the channel had changed, or she'd unplugged somehow. Grandma and Grandpa said they never noticed noises either except for occasional creaking, just like Mom and Dad. Maybe only kids could really hear the ghosts.

This might be his last chance. After this summer, Neema would be on her own.

"You have to take a nap so you won't be tired tonight, 'cuz we're gonna be up late," I said. "If I hear any whining—and I mean *any* whining about *anything*—I'm gonna go back to bed and do it alone some night when you're sleeping."

"No you won't. I'll stay awake every night too."

"I mean it, Neema. Either it's my rules or you don't play."

That shut her up quick. He didn't often have leverage over Neema, but he had big-time leverage now. She'd been begging him to let her track with him since she was three. Her face was longer every year, more like Mom's, and the thin cornrows Mom had slaved over for hours before she left still looked fresh and flawless on Neema's scalp, the ends anchored by a swarm of white barrettes shaped like tiny butterflies. She looked like a princess too.

"Why's Daddy sad?" Neema said. Changing the subject was her specialty.

He decided on the *nothing's-wrong-here* approach. "He's sad?"

She nodded, certain. "Yeah."

"I guess he misses Mommy."

"Yeah, me too," Neema said. Dad's sadness was contagious.

"We'll see her soon."

"Not-uh," she said. "A month's not soon. A month is a long time."

Neema often sounded certain of herself, but never more than now. She understood there was significance to it. She knew that Mom's time away meant something.

It might be harder to keep the secret than he'd thought.

At six o'clock, just when Davie thought he would lose his mind waiting for the sun to go down, Grandma excused herself from *The Game of Life*. She had a meeting, she said. The community was trying to stop another construction project. The "community" was busy.

"Why don't you want more houses, Grandma?" Neema said.

Davie wanted to kick her under the dining table. *Now* they were in for a whole tutorial on infrastructure and sewer lines. But instead, Grandma sighed and glanced at Dad, who shrugged. Dad barely listened to any of them; his conversations were in his head.

Grandma fixed her hairnet in an egg-shaped mirror on the wall. "I wasn't gonna say anything to you kids—but there's bodies buried over on that land across the street, out beyond Tobacco Road. McCormack's land.

They found an old burial site, the bones of people who lived 'round here a hundred years ago. And not a cemetery neither—this has been McCormack land for generations. But the university folks say they were black. Nobody knows how many bones there are, or how far they're spread out . . . so if they keep building up these houses, we'll never learn the full story about who they were, or how many people died."

It was the coolest thing Grandma had ever said. Davie was captivated.

Grandpa Walter spoke up, half-limping from the kitchen. His joints hurt worse at night. "If it was Indians, see, there's special laws about that. It's a burial ground, so it's sacred. But not for *us*. Nothing that's got to do with *us* is sacred. "

"Our family?" Neema asked. She hadn't figured out yet that whenever Dad and Grandpa said "us," they meant "black people."

"Everybody wants it buried," Grandma went on. "So I'm going to a meeting to try to stop the people from building more houses on top of the bones. In case there are more."

Neema looked at Davie with wide, gleeful eyes. Even Neema knew that the fresh unearthing of bones meant heightened ghost activity. What luck!

"How many skeletons did they find?" Davie said.

"Twelve," Grandma said.

"So far," Grandpa added. "Could've been a slaughter, like Rosewood. Hundreds of people hunted down like animals, a whole town."

Dad looked up at his parents, as if he'd just noticed the turn of conversation. "Thanks a whole hell of a lot. This is a great goddamn topic for my *eight-year-old*." He nearly roared Neema's age, and Neema jumped as if he was yelling at her. It was the maddest Davie had ever heard his father. Cussing at his parents! And blasphemy too, which Grandma couldn't stand.

Davie thought better of his next question, which was: *Were there any dogs?*

Instead, they all stopped talking about the bodies. Grandma went to her meeting, and Grandpa kept coaxing Neema to spin the wheel and help him read the cards while Davie and his father only pretended to play the board game. (More like a *bored* game, David told himself.) He and Dad were both happy to miss their turns if they were forgotten. Life was not the product as advertised.

Bedtime was a relief beyond words.

Thanks to a consistent campaign at every birthday and holiday, Davie had decent ghost-hunting gear. No EMF or motion detectors yet—but he had a lantern-style flashlight, an old 8mm video camera with night vision (a hand-me-down from Dad), a mini-cassette recorder he wore around his neck, and the digital camera his mother had given him for Kwanzaa. He kept it all inside his old army-green knapsack, alongside the extras: protein bars, water bottle (Mountain Dew would spray him, alas), a small notebook. And now, dog biscuits.

Be Prepared, the Boy Scouts said.

Waiting for Grandma and Grandpa to go to bed was always a breeze—they were down by nine-thirty, tops. Dad was the problem, usually. Dad liked to stay up late on his computer or watching TV, but on this trip Dad was sleeping late and going to bed early, with naps in-between. His laptop hadn't come out of its case once.

"Are you sick, Daddy?" Neema asked him after dinner. Dad hadn't even heard her.

Waiting for quiet was the hardest part. No TVs, no bathroom breaks, no refrigerator raids. Pure, uninterrupted quiet. Davie called it the Golden Hour, and it came at a different time every night. That night, the Golden Hour was ten-thirty. Quiet.

Davie leaped out of bed, unplugged his video camera (a dead video camera battery would be the difference between fame and obscurity), and strapped his ghost kit across his shoulder. Then he crossed the hall to Neema's room.

Neema's Raggedy Ann doll was propped up against Neema's closed door. The doll didn't look like it had been lain there gently, as Grandma would; Raggedy Ann looked thrown against the door, head lolling, legs akimbo. Her black-thread hair was wild, pulled of out its ponytails, or braids, or whatever she used to have. For the first time, Davie noticed the doll's faded red gingham dress, a relic. The doll looked a hundred years old, not just from the seventies.

What did girls *see* in dolls? After scooping up the doll, Davie opened Neema's door.

Neema was sitting at the foot of her bed, waiting for him. Still as a doll herself.

"What are you doing to her?" She said it as if Raggedy Ann were real.

He chuckled. "I'm not doing anything to your dumb doll." To put the doll in its place, he tossed Raggedy Ann to Neema, who caught the doll mid-air and clicked her teeth, irritated.

"Stop! Then why'd you take it?" Neema said.

"I have more important things to think about. It was outside the door, Brainiac."

"Liar."

"Whatever. Let's go."

Neema didn't get up. Instead, she hugged the Raggedy Ann to her chest, gazing across the room at the doll shelf. "I don't like all the dolls in here. It's like they're looking at me."

Davie glanced at the dolls' unblinking rows of eyes, and they gave him the creeps, too. But this wasn't the time to worry about a bunch of old dolls.

"If you're a scaredy-cat, stay in here," Davie said. "Ghosts aren't for scaredy-cats."

"I'm not a scaredy-cat."

"Then come on. And *no noise*."

Davie had recorded ghost activity all over his grandparents' house: a salt shaker that fell down on the kitchen table by itself, a faucet dripping backward in the bathroom (hard to prove, but he had seen it), and the egg-shaped mirror skewed slightly to one side in the foyer (Grandpa, seeing Davie's footage, had just said, "So the mirror's crooked—so what?")

But the living room was Davie's favorite place to camp. The living room was his grandparents' museum, the place for their old black-and-white photographs, old books, old paintings on the wall, old everything. Even the furniture had been in Grandma's family forever, shaky antique legs and upholstery that smelled like a dark closet. Ghosts liked the old and familiar. The living room was definitely the first place *he* would go.

"What now?" Neema whispered. She couldn't keep quiet to save her life.

"*Shhhh*. We camp out and we wait."

"I'm thirsty."

Davie closed his eyes and counted to five. Dad's trick to keep from getting too mad.

"Davie? I'm thirsty."

He reached inside his ghost kit and pulled out the water bottle. "Don't spill it on the wood, or Grandma'll freak out. Now just sit and be still. They won't come unless it's quiet."

Bringing Neema was a mistake, he decided. Fine: They'd camp out in the living room for an hour, she'd mess it up with her complaining and whining, and he'd go to bed. Tomorrow, he'd wait until she was asleep for sure. Tomorrow, he'd wait until midnight if he had to.

But Neema surprised Davie. After he chose their ideal camping spot behind Grandpa's recliner, right near the bookshelf full of musty-smelling books, Neema sat as still. Sometimes she hummed a little, but she caught herself and covered her mouth. Like him, she just stared into the darkness and cupped her ear to listen. Davie couldn't believe how much older Neema seemed since last summer, or even Christmas.

He'd tried ghost-tracking at Christmastime, but nothing happened, of course.

Ghosts only came in summer.

It was amazing how much noise even a quiet house could produce. When he was younger, Davie used to think he heard ghosts in every creak of the ceiling, every whir of the central air-conditioning, and every cyclic hum from the refrigerator. He used to jump when the automatic sprinklers went on outside and sprayed the windows with water.

Now, of course, Davie was an expert listener. And since he'd already heard a ghost the night before, he knew what he was listening for: click-click-click. The dog's paws. He kept a dog biscuit in his hand, a ready peace offering. The sweat on his palm was making it gummy.

They sat and listened for a solid hour. No clicking.

Beside him, Neema was nodding to sleep with her head against the recliner. Just as well, Davie thought. With Neema asleep, he could wait another hour, no problem. After that, he'd take her back to bed.

Davie felt a cramp from sitting in the same position with his hip bone against the hard floor, so he shifted until he was sitting criss-cross applesauce. When he did, he felt something wet seep into the seat of his pajama pants. Wet and *cold*.

He touched his pajama pants, and they were soaked. His hand splashed into a shallow puddle of cold liquid. "*Hey,*" he said, nudging Neema. "You spilled your water."

Neema blinked her eyes open, alert, and held up her half-empty water bottle, tightly capped. The light through the window allowed him to see her in the moonlight. "Not-uh," she said. "The top's on."

But before Neema had said a word, Davie realized the water couldn't have come from Neema's water bottle. No way had Neema's water been this cold. And there was too much. Water was all around them.

"Crap-o-la," Davie whispered, and rushed to take off his pajama top. He started wiping the floor as fast as he could, because Grandma would have a serious meltdown if her floor got spotted with water. Who else would she blame but him?

Davie's pajama top soaked through as soon as it touched the floor. Davie saw a shimmering sheen of water across the entire living room, from the foyer all the way to the kitchen, toward the back hall. *The floor was completely covered in water!*

A scent had been faint at first, but now he realized it filled up the entire room. The living room smelled like the water in the fish-tank where his third-grade teacher, Miss Richmond, kept the class's frogs and turtles. Sour. Like old, rotting plants and leaves.

Neema was sleepy, but she was getting the picture too. "My clothes are *wet—*" she said, raising her voice, but Davie clamped her mouth quiet.

"*Shhhhh,*" he said. His heart was a jackhammer in his chest. "Ghosts, Neema. Ghosts."

"In the water?"

"Yes," Davie said, because he didn't have time to explain. The ghost *was* the water—that was why it was so cold. The water was real, but it wasn't. He hoped not, anyway, because it was getting deeper. Maybe an inch deep already.

Davie pulled Neema to her feet, and he stood at a crouch, pulling his ghost kit higher so it wouldn't get wet. The dog biscuit fell out of his hand, forgotten, as he flipped his tape recorder to ON and opened the video camera's eye. He switched on night vision.

Through the viewfinder, the room was almost too bright. The moonlight exaggerated the gleam in the mirror on the wall and the screen on the TV, washing them in whiteness. His hand slightly unsteady, Davie lowered the camera toward the floor. Toward the water.

SPLASH

He saw bands of ripples, as if he'd tossed a handful of pebbles into the water.

Neema made a whimpering sound, clinging to Davie's hand. Without moving the camera, he turned his head to look at her, and Neema's wide, delighted eyes met his.

Did You Hear That? Neema mouthed.

Davie nodded, grinning. Neema grinned back.

If Neema had been scared, or crying, he would have whisked her back into her room and locked the door. But Neema *wasn't* a scaredy-cat, just like she said. Good girl! Neema was a ghost-hunter after all. Starting this young, she might be one of the best.

SPLASH SPLASH

Davie saw the water ripple again, synchronized with the sound. The sound was retreating. Someone—or some *thing*, like a dog—was walking toward the kitchen.

Davie held tight to Neema's hand, kept his camera trained on the ripples, and carefully began walking to follow the splashing sound. Immediately, a sensation of cold water seeped up to Davie's ankles, startling him. Behind him, Neema only giggled.

Weird, Davie realized. *We feel the water, but it doesn't splash when we walk.*

The water only splashed for the ghosts.

SPLASH SPLASH SPLASHSPLASHSPLASH

The splashing sound was faster, from more than one direction. It sounded like several people, or dogs, splashing at once. It sounded like . . . running.

Suddenly, water spattered to Davie's chest from the splashing. He felt something bump against his arm, knocking him off-balance for a step, and it was gone. Not a dog, then. Too big for a dog. Something as tall as him.

"Who are you?" a stranger's adult-sounding voice said. "I'm Davie Stephens."

It was only him. But his mouth was doing all the work, because Davie's mind was frozen shut. Sure, he'd seen a salt shaker fall, and he'd seen water dripping backward and a mirror suddenly askew, but he'd never *felt* a ghost touch him before. In movies, ghosts always walked through people, weightless.

But that one had pushed up against him. That one could have knocked him on his ass.

"*Run!*" a child's husky voice said in the dark, up ahead.

Not him. Not Neema. Someone else. A boy he didn't know.

From somewhere very far away, Davie thought he heard the sound of barking.

Davie realized only then that he was struggling to breathe, because fear and surprise had clotted his throat. Warm liquid seeped through his pajamas now; he had wet himself for the first time since he was Neema's age.

"He said, 'Run,'" Neema said.

Davie's lips only bobbed.

The boy's voice came again, from the kitchen doorway: "*Follow me!*"

"He said 'Follow me'!" Neema said, an urgent whisper.

Davie's body had forgotten how to move. Neema tugged on his hand, pulling him ahead toward the kitchen. One or two steps were enough to freeze Davie again, because the water felt higher now, up to his shins.

From his new vantage point in the center of the living room, Davie saw that the back door was wide open in the kitchen. Grandma and Grandpa Walter would never leave their back door open, especially with the mosquitoes in summer. The door definitely had not been open before.

Davie remembered his camera. Somehow, he had let it drop to his side, but he raised it. In night vision, the doorway looked like it was bathed in a spotlight.

And Davie saw a silhouette framed there—a boy turning to look at Davie over his shoulder. He was wiry, like Davie. He reminded Davie of the oldest boy he'd seen burying the dog. The fuzzy black silhouette in the light motioned his hand toward Davie.

"*Hurry!*" His voice was fainter.

"I heard something else," Neema said. "Something . . . "

Davie raised his eyes to peek at the doorway—but it was all empty dark. He could only see the ghostly figure when he raised the camera to his eye again. Still there!

Davie's instincts were at war. One part of him wanted to run back to his bedroom as fast as he could. The other part of him wanted to follow the boy calling to him from the doorway. Neema tugged on his hand, toward the kitchen. Neema wasn't just a ghost-hunter—Neema, it turned out, was a kamikaze.

Davie allowed himself to be pulled for two more steps, but then they both stopped.

Davie felt water above his knees now, and had to be higher to Neema. He took a startled step back. Walking in ghost water was one thing—but swimming was something else. Neema was a good swimmer because Mom made her take lessons at the Y every summer, but Davie's lessons hadn't stuck. Davie never liked water above his knees, and the way this water steepened, it would be above his *waist* soon.

"No," Davie told Neema, holding fast. "Stay here."

The dark image framed against the doorway's light hesitated. Turned his head to look outside, then back toward Davie. Then back outside again.

Then, he ran. And he was gone. As the boy ran, the splashing sound faded to nothing.

It took Davie a minute to realize there were tears running down his face.

It would take Davie Stephens several hours, until almost daylight, to realize *why* he had cried in that moment, standing with Neema in the living room. He wasn't crying because the ghost had sounded so scared—even though he surely had, and the ghost was just a kid, like him. And Davie wasn't crying because he knew that only his fear had held him back from following, and maybe the water *wouldn't* have gotten any deeper.

No, Davie was crying for one simple reason: For all the summers he had come to Grandma and Grandpa's house, with the strange noises in the hall and objects falling down, he had never actually *seen* a ghost. He had never seen a human being who had come to visit from somewhere far away; actual proof that dying wasn't forever.

That ghost was the most beautiful sight of his life.

When a sight like that crosses your eyes, Davie learned, there is nothing to do but cry.

"YEAH, I SEE the dark spot, Davie. What I *don't* see is a little boy." From Dad's voice, Davie knew that was the last time Dad would look into the viewfinder to see last night's footage. "And I've told you about staying up late. Look at you: Did you get any sleep?" Dad swiped at the camera as if to knock it from the kitchen table. Davie pulled it out of his reach just in time.

"What you got there, Davie?" Grandpa said. "Show me."

Neema was bouncing in her seat, dying to say what she'd seen, but Davie had made her *promise* that she wouldn't tell anyone she'd been up late with him. If Dad knew that, Davie would be locked in his room all night the rest of the summer.

The water didn't show in the camera, of course. Davie hadn't expected it to. Anyone knew that even infrared cameras couldn't pick up manifestations with any reliability; the energy field was too fragile. But he'd lucked out and captured actual evidence—the image in the doorway, silhouetted by the light. He *could* see it! There was no denying the shadow.

Davie leaned close to Grandpa while he gazed into the tiny viewfinder. Grandpa smelled like after-shave. Old Spice. An old man's smell.

"So . . . that's your ghost?" Grandpa said.

"I heard him, Grandpa. He said 'Run!' and 'Come on!' There was a splashing sound when he ran across the floor."

"*Lots* of splashing," Neema broke in. "And water up to here." She motioned up to her belly button. Then she caught herself, remembering her promise. "Davie told me."

"Well, that's a strange story, all right," Grandpa said, and turned his attention to his coffee cup. At least Grandpa pretended to be interested, which was more than Dad had done, but who wants to drink coffee when they believe they've seen a ghost?

What was wrong with grown-up eyes? *Will I go blind like them too?*

Grandma looked at Davie over her shoulder from the stove. "Well, there's no sign of water now, thank goodness. One time the A.C. broke, and our bedroom was flooded. Those floorboards warped and cracked—"

"But it wasn't *real* water, Grandma. It's like . . . old. Like ghosts."

Grandpa chuckled. "Well . . . you know what, Doris?"

Grandma shook her head. "Don't encourage him, Walt. He needs his rest at night."

"What's the harm?" Grandpa put his coffee cup back down and leaned over to look Davie in the eye. What he said sent a bolt of lightning through Davie's spine: "You know . . . All this land out here, before the developers came, it was nothing but swamp. Water all around."

Davie's heart was pounding as hard as when the ghost called out to him, beckoning.

Dad got up from the table and walked out of the kitchen. Probably to take a nap, Davie guessed, even though he'd just gotten out of bed.

"Swamp?" Davie said, remembering the smell of the water; almost a living smell.

"Shoot, yeah. They had to drain it. There's still some swampy patches out back, probably a hundred yards beyond the gate."

Grandma set a plate of pancakes down in front of Davie loudly enough to stop the conversation. "All these crazy stories about Gracetown in summer. You ought to be ashamed of yourself, Walt," she said. Then she took up the conversation in her own way: "They're trying to build back there now. You can bet they wouldn't tell anyone who buys those houses it's only swampland underneath. Just like they won't tell them there's no hospital for thirty miles. The land's not fit! And where's the sewage gonna go?"

Grandma could have gone on, but luckily the phone rang then. It was Imani, so her call was a big production. Everyone wanted their turn to talk to her. Even Dad came back to grab the portable kitchen phone to say hello.

Davie waited last to take his turn. Talking to Imani might mean lying, and he didn't like to start out any day with a lie. If she asked *How is everything?* he'd be lying right from the start.

When it was Davie's turn on the phone, he took it in his own room to tell her about his adventure with the ghost. For a while, Imani seemed interested, especially the part about the water. She talked to him like a real person, not her little brother, for a change. She didn't try to rush him off the phone to be with her friends, or to watch her favorite anime, *Death Note*, or to do her work. She said things like "Wow" and "Cool!" She said she couldn't wait to see his video. *Couldn't wait*, she said.

But then she asked a question that had nothing to do with ghosts: "How's Dad?"

Davie's stomach, suddenly, was a knot.

"Sleeps a lot," Davie said. "All the time."

"People sleep when they're depressed," Imani said.

She knows, Davie realized. *She wants to know if I know too.*

"Well," Davie said, heart pounding again—but this time from a deeper place, a more dangerous place, "I guess he's got a lot to be depressed about."

For a long time, neither of them said anything.

Then Imani said, "Did he tell you?"

And Davie said, "I heard him talking to Grandma."

And they were quiet for a while again. Davie's hand with the phone was trembling.

"It may not be for sure," Imani said finally. "You know how Mom is. Dramatic. She calls me every other day. I'm trying to talk her out of it. And Dad's stubborn, as usual. I know you don't want to live in Ghana. Neema either."

"No." Davie could barely speak over the lump in his throat. He'd been to Ghana once, when he was little, and all he remembered about that trip was heat and a man with no teeth his grandmother had haggled with at an open-air market. Africa didn't feel familiar to him, with too many differences—and it would be too far away from Dad. Too far away from his whole world.

"But if you do end up in Ghana, it wouldn't be all the time," Imani went on. "You'd go back and forth. And remember: Her dad worked for the government, so they have a nice house with a swimming pool. And there's an American school nearby, like where diplomats and people send their kids. You wouldn't be out in some village somewhere. You can't blame Mom,

Davie. Yeah, she's dramatic, but look at Dad too. He works all the time. Mom says he used to laugh and have more faith in life. She feels isolated. When they got married, he promised her they could live in Ghana for a while—and it's been almost twenty years. He always says *no*. What's she supposed to do?"

Davie had no idea what Imani was talking about, but the details of his life had already been decided. All he knew was that it felt wrong for Mom to talk to Imani like one of her girlfriends, not like her mother. Imani was on Mom's side, Davie realized. So that was how it would line up: Mom and Imani against Dad, Grandma, Grandpa Walter, him, and Neema. Those would be the camps.

Davie blinked. His eyes stung, but they were dry. Tears weren't enough for the feeling.

He suddenly hated his sister for her breeziness and her dorm room that felt safe to her, a haven she had claimed for herself. No wonder she'd been in such a good mood at the airport—she was escaping just in time, and she knew it. She had left him and Neema to fend for themselves.

"Anyway . . . " Imani went on. "Like I said, I'm trying to talk her out of it. A month's a good break for them. It'll all be okay. Don't worry. You'll see."

A sudden, loud knock on Davie's door ended their conversation.

"Davie—unlock this door!" It was Dad.

Davie hadn't realized he'd locked his door, thereby breaking the number-one house rule. He told Imani he had to go, clicked off the phone, and bounded from his bed to let Dad in. He hoped his unshed tears wouldn't show too much. He didn't want Dad to start talking to him about Mom and how dramatic she was (*"Don't you agree, ol' buddy?"*), patting Davie's knee and asking him to see things from his side. Davie already felt like he might puke.

Dad looked like he had aged ten years in two days. He hadn't shaved, and his stubble was more white than black.

"Did you leave this in my room?" Dad said. "Under my pillow?"

Davie looked at the object in his father's palm for at least five seconds before his brain allowed him to understand what he was seeing: a gummy-looking dog biscuit.

Gnawed at both ends.

DAVIE WANTED to go outside to the woods and find the place where the kids had buried the dog. That was his whole afternoon's plan, a no-brainer. But as soon as he got outside, he saw his father standing at the back fence, near the broken log, almost like he was guarding it. Dad's foot rested on the surviving lower log rail as he stared into the woods.

Davie walked beside him and stared, too, wondering if he would see the boys from there. He would enjoy a long conversation with them, all right. At first, Dad didn't hear Davie beside him. There were too many crickets and bugs of endless varieties singing up a storm. But when Davie's foot snapped a twig with a sharp crack, Dad turned around.

"I should fix this," Dad said, squeezing the broken log, which crossed the next fencepost like an X instead of lying down flat. The break was a tangle of wire and splinters.

"Why?" Davie said. "It lets the deer come in."

And maybe the ghosts too. Davie didn't know why he thought so, but he did.

Besides, if the fence was fixed, he'd have to find another way to get back there. He couldn't let the opportunity pass him by.

But if he couldn't find the kids, or the place they buried their dog, he could cross the street to look for the construction site where the bodies had been found. He didn't know if it was marked or anything—Grandma said the bodies had been dug up for weeks already—but it might be. There might be yellow tape strung up, like a police crime scene.

Dad sighed. "They expect me to fix it." He was probably talking about the fence, but his voice had sounded so faraway that suddenly David wasn't sure.

"Do you know how?" Davie said. He could answer that question either way. Dad could organize a whole documentary crew, but at home he could barely change a light bulb. That's what Mom said.

Dad's face snapped to look down at Davie, surprise in his eyes. Maybe he'd sounded too much like Mom. Or maybe he wondered what they were talking about, too.

"Neema's shopping with Grandma," Dad said. "We should go somewhere. Us two."

Davie didn't want to go anywhere with his father, but Dad needed him. "How 'bout the library?" Davie said.

That time, his father even smiled.

"KID, YOU'RE a genius," Dad whispered, setting up his laptop on the long library table. "I'm a week behind on this grant proposal, but there's something about a library, right? Makes you want to work. You gonna be all right?"

To Dad, "doing something together" meant being in the same room at the same time. Davie had figured he would be able to peel off on his own if he brought Dad to a library, so he could kill two birds with one stone. The library in Gracetown was hardly bigger than the library in Davie's elementary school, without the fun posters on the walls.

Dad was way too excited to be in a library. His knees bounced beneath the table, his eyes flitting around like every shelf was sprinkled with fairy dust. Davie wanted to ask his father if *he* was all right, but what was the point? Or course he wasn't.

"I'll go see what's in the sci-fi section," Davie said.

Dad winked at him. "Good man." He clapped his hands, ready to work. "Good man."

Davie made an appearance in Science Fiction/Fantasy/Horror, noting that with the entire Harry Potter series was checked out except for *Chamber of Secrets*. Lame. A quick peek at Dad, who was typing like a fiend, and Davie hustled over to the Research desk. The woman who sat there was old, of course, but weren't all librarians old? Maybe it was a job requirement. She was a black woman with silver hair she had cut very short, and her face was dotted with what looked like freckles from a distance, but were really big moles. If the woman's eyes weren't so bright, it would have been hard not to stare at her moles.

"Help you, young man?" she said.

"Uh . . . " Davie tried to think about the best way to put it. He had learned that mentioning the word *ghost* was a sure way to lose an adult's attention. He didn't discuss his hunts with strangers. "I live near the place where those bodies were found."

"You do, huh?" She was instantly interested, taking off her reading glasses. Her eyes were suddenly intense. "How do you feel about that?"

Davie was confused by the question. "Okay . . . I guess."

"What I mean is . . . does it upset you that so many people were buried there?"

"Nah. It's kinda' cool. I just wonder who they were. Did they live in the swamp?"

The librarian looked at him with a smile, as if he'd said the magic words. "So you want to know the history of the area?"

Davie nodded. "Right."

Apparently, librarians get excited when kids come up to them and ask about history. The librarian even called her boss over, a reedy white man, and he recommended a book too. Before Davie knew it, she had a stack in her hands.

"By the way," the librarian said, "my name is Mrs. Mabel Trawley. I'm from the Trawleys who live here in Gracetown, out near Trawley Hill. My great-grandfather was born on a tobacco plantation not far from the Stephenses. Are you their grandson?"

Davie nodded, but what did that have to do with anything? Just because he'd asked about the land didn't mean he wanted to hear the history of the world. Or tell her his life story.

"Well, you just tell your grandmamma that Mabel Trawley said hello. That's how people like to do here in Gracetown. We want to know how people's families turned out. See, it didn't start out so well for most of us. Our ancestors were slaves here. Did you know that?"

"Yeah. I know about slavery."

Davie was glad his father had shown him *Roots*, or he wouldn't have known what "slaves" really meant. Sure, he'd learned about Abraham Lincoln and the Civil War in school—and it had something to do with slaves—but only *Roots* had shown him how Kunta Kinte lost his foot trying to run for freedom. And how people's babies got sold away. The librarian pulled out a book called *Black Seminoles*. "There were lots of runaways who lived in the swamps. Met up with the Indians, all of them hiding out together."

"What about dogs?"

The librarian pursed her lips and flipped a book open to a drawing of black man, woman and young boy dressed in tatters, running through a swamp—chased by barking dogs. The dogs looked like ferocious monsters, with coats of fur so thick at their necks that they seemed to have manes. "Most times, tracking was the only way a slave master could bring his runaways back. Pieces of them, anyway."

Davie's neck felt ice-cold when he remembered the splashing water in the living room. The photo of the tracking dogs cast a very different light on the past two nights. *Tracking.* As in looking for him. Would he and Neema end up in pieces if they kept hunting for the ghost dog?

"Can I check out those books?" Davie said.

"What's got you so interested?"

What the heck? "Ghosts," Davie said.

"Oh, so you're seeing spirits," she said. Her voice made it sound everyday, like *Oh, so you had chicken for dinner last night?*

"That's right," she went on. "Summer."

"What about summer?"

She pursed her lips. "Come on, now. You wouldn't be seeing them otherwise."

Aside from Mom, who talked about ghosts singing in trees, Davie had never met another adult who would hold still and listen when he talked about ghosts. Even so, this woman's eyes were only half engaged; from time to time, she glanced down at a stain on her white blouse.

"What do you know about the ghosts?" he said.

"You tell me," she said. "I haven't seen any since I was your age."

Davie's heart fluttered. "It's true you don't see them when you're older?"

"Not in Gracetown. Nope." She brushed at the stain.

That afternoon, while Davie's father worked on his computer to forget his problems, Mabel Trawley shelved books and told Davie the history of Gracetown, Florida. Founded in 1845 by James Grace, who would later fight as a Confederate officer in the Civil War. The town started out prosperous because of tobacco farming, since people who smoked rarely quit the habit, and there were plenty of new people to take it up—and slaves to bring in the harvests. ("No tobacco, no Gracetown. No slaves, no tobacco. Plain facts," she said.) The huge tobacco barns, where the leaves were hung out to dry, still stood up and down the roads. ("There's a tobacco barn out back there somewhere behind your grandmama's house, for a fact.")

There was one Really Bad Thing that happened right after the turn of the century, she said. The year was 1909.

"In summer?" Davie said.

"Course it was summer."

Mabel Trawley told the story:

"Most black folks in Gracetown didn't have two dimes to rub together since slavery, but there were a handful of Negroes here and there who did all right. Men farmed and hired themselves out to the growers, or sharecropped, women took in wash, and babies made up of all their parents' hopes and dreams.

"One such family was the Timmons family. Isaiah Timmons and his wife, Essie, had three sons. He'd planned to stay in Gracetown only another year or so, just long enough to pay his debts and save enough money for train tickets to New York, where his brother could help them settle in a boarding house. He had it all planned out. Isaiah Timmons left behind his journal and notes. Otherwise, we might note have know much about him.

"Well, the Timmons family had to be mindful of all manner of trouble. All black folks back then lived under terrible rules with unthinkable consequences, so you best believe Isaiah Timmons was the most polite, gentle-mannered and kind-hearted Negro these white folks had ever seen. It was said he might have helped foil a riot or two in Gracetown; depending on the point-of-view, he was peacemaker or race traitor, or maybe both.

"Despite all of Isaiah Timmons' unending politeness, he gained powerful enemies in Gracetown for the simple reason that he was doing all right. If white folks saw that Isaiah Timmons had a hog, why, their first thought was, "Well, how come that nigger's got a better hog than me?" ("Sorry to use that word, but that's how folks talked back then. Calling black folks *nigger* was the same as calling them by name.") Instead of shaking their heads to marvel that a black man could put a roof over his families' heads, they begrudged him every tiny victory.

"If there was one man he hated most, and who was happy to return the sentiment, it was Virgil McCormack. He was a grower whose father had been a genuine slaveholder, and Old Virgil McCormack had never gotten used to the idea that the Negroes who worked for him weren't slaves. And that anyone with dark skin might have any rights to speak of.

"Isaiah Timmons worked for Virgil McCormack from time to time—a task he hated more than any other—and they also had the misfortune of sharing a border, right out where Tobacco Road is right now. Come to think of it, your grandparents' house used to be McCormack land, of course, so you're living right by the very spot where Isaiah Timmons and Virgil McCormack argued over whose land was whose.

"Well, the whole argument came to a head one summer when, in plain daylight, someone set fire to Isaiah Timmons' barn. The barn wasn't fifty yards from the house, and it burned straight to the ground. Well, that put the writing clear on the wall—Isaiah Timmons decided he and his family would head up north to New York whether they had train tickets or not. He packed up everything he could in a wagon, working the whole night through, and was ready to leave by dawn. Isaiah wasn't a coward, but he also wasn't a fool. Disputes with neighbors never ended well for black folks. Isaiah Timmons figured the sheriff would come next with an accusation of rape or some other charge to get rid of him—if he didn't string him up in a tree outright—and he wasn't going to wait around to see how creative his death would be.

"The three boys, it was said, had been helping their father pack that wagon . . . but when it was time to go, Isaiah and Essie Timmons called up and down the road, but they couldn't find a sign of those boys anywhere. The way Essie Timmons would tell the story later, it was as if they vanished into the air itself! Friends and neighbors helped him search—even the white man who ran the general store, whose great-great grandson is the mayor of Gracetown today—and they searched through and through. But those boys never turned up.

"Well, Isaiah Timmons was sick at heart and mad as hell, no doubt out of his mind with grief. It was one thing to try to hurt him, but what kind of people would hurt children? He took his shotgun and walked across the road to McCormack's land. Virgil McCormack lived in the same antebellum house his family lives in today. Isaiah Timmons found McCormack washing his automobile—the McCormacks were among the first in Gracetown to have a car—and Timmons aimed that shotgun right at McCormack's head, demanding to know what happened to his boys.

"I can tell you no white man in Gracetown had ever been spoken to by a Negro that way; not one who lived, anyway. They say Isaiah Timmons fired a warning shot into the air and just about made McCormack jump out of his skin. Got him to crying and begging. McCormack swore to God's Heaven he didn't know where those boys were, and Isaiah Timmons let him live only because he was too heavy-hearted to pull the trigger.

"You remember this: He could've killed him, but he didn't. And it wasn't about trying to save his own skin, 'cause confronting a white man with a shotgun was gonna look like a murder to white folks whether the white man lived or died. Isaiah Timmons' fate had been decided from the moment he walked up behind McCormack with a gun and too much manhood in his voice. But he lay that shotgun on his shoulder and walked away. That's the part everyone forgets.

"Well, that night the fireworks went off in Gracetown.

"All those folks who'd been held off from rioting, and all those scared whites who were sure the blacks were planning to slit their throats, built a bonfire of hate and fear that night. "Did you hear what happened to the Timmons boys?" on one side, and "Did you hear a nigger tried to shoot McCormack?" on the other, and everybody all worked up in a frenzy.

"There's always blood in a frenzy like that, and the side with the most manpower and the best weapons always wins. Isaiah Timmons was easy to find: McCormack and the police found him looking for his boys, and he probably didn't live long enough to tell his side. He died first. But lots of other black men in Gracetown got held to account for Isaiah Timmons and his shotgun. Anyone who looked like they were in a bad mood got rounded up, especially if they didn't have family in town. It's said a bunch of black men were rounded up and taken to McCormack's place and questioned. Somebody must not have liked their answers, because they got shot down right there in the muck. ('Are those the people the bones came from? The ones the builders are digging up?' Davie asked, and Mabel Trawley nodded slowly. 'That's what we think. The bodies from the Gracetown riot. It looks like they were dumped in the same plot.')

"There's bad blood between the McCormacks and the Timmonses to this day—they say McCormack stole those three Timmons boys, probably killed them outright, and that's what started it all. They had a sister, born not long after they died, and she later wrote a book about those boys and the Gracetown riot. *Three Brothers*, I think she called it. I haven't seen a copy of it, but people mention it from time to time. Isaiah Timmons probably ended up in that mass grave with the bones from the construction site— but I hear his widow told the story until the day she died: "McCormack took my boys. My three precious boys."

"*I saw them,*" Davie said, his heart banging in his chest. The library felt like a church chapel, as if they were talking about something holy.

"You saw who?"

"The boys. The three Timmons boys. They were burying a dog. I didn't know they were ghosts. I thought they were real, 'cuz it was still light outside. I forgot that . . . "

" . . . sometimes you can see them at dusk," Mabel Trawley said, with a nod and a smile.

"That used to fool me too."

Davie hadn't realized his father was listening from the next row until he and Mabel Trawley rounded the corner and almost ran into him. There was a thunderstorm on Dad's face.

"Are you the one who's been filling his head with these ghost stories?" Dad said to the librarian. Davie was so embarrassed by his father's anger, he wanted to melt into the floor.

"No, sir. I've just met this young man today. He's the one filling *my* head."

Dad's face softened. He shuffled his feet, unsure. "Sorry. I thought I heard you say . . . "

"You're Darryl Stephens, aren't you? Your father's the Stephens who enlisted in the Army, went to Korea, settled in Miami. You didn't grow up here in town at all, did you?"

Dad looked at the librarian as if he were almost afraid of her, like she was the psychic at the county fair of his youth. "How'd you know that?"

"Everyone knows everything in a small town. Bet you never even spent a summer here."

"Once. When I was about . . . fifteen."

"Too late," she said.

"Too late for what?"

Mabel Trawley looked at Davie and winked. "You and your son should have a talk, Mr. Stephens," she said. "He can show you what you missed. And while he's at it, Davie might be able to answer a question that's given a whole lot of folks in Gracetown a whole lot of grief."

Summer 1909

THE TIMMONS BOYS were, in order of birth, Isaac, Scott, and Little Eddie. Isaac, the eldest, was twelve, and each brother was separated by almost two years to the day, ending with Little Eddie, who had just turned eight the day before the barn burned down.

Isaac had never been afraid of fire. He'd mastered fire when he was younger than Little Eddie, and he'd been using it ever since for cooking, heating water for bathing and washing clothes, melting lye, sharpening blades, and any number of other tasks for which fire came in handy. Fire, to Isaac, was just another tool. He had forgotten how destructive it could be.

The fire that burned down the barn had actually started *outside* of the barn, where the boys were roasting themselves yams while their father was out in McCormack's field and their mother was pounding clothes at the creek. Isaac had gotten some honey from his gal Livvy's mother, and yams with honey were his favorite treat. He and his brothers were roasting yams in secret because they were supposed to be hanging clothes up to dry, but the Timmons boys found ways to do what they wanted when no one was watching them.

One call from Mama waving in the distance was enough to get them on their feet and running. They didn't notice the change in the wind, and they didn't realize the barn wall's wood was so dry because it hadn't rained a drop all summer. They never actually *saw* the cloud of sparks from their cook-fire that flew against the barn wall and came alight almost immediately. They were nowhere near the barn when it happened. What they did see an hour later, however, was roiling smoke carrying bad news. As soon as Isaac Timmons smelled smoke, he knew.

Their family's two horses and milking cow were safely clear of the barn when the fire broke out, but everything else was lost, charred and black. The barn was still standing, but two of its walls had burned clean away, and it was nothing but a big, ugly ruin. It was as if God was laughing at his father, telling him he would never have a farm of his own. He would be working for Old Man McCormack forever.

The older boys, in quick conference, tried to decide on the best way to tell Papa how they started the fire. Confession would mean consequences, of course: Their father had been raised on a razor strap *his* father had learned to wield like a long-dead overseer once wielded his cow-hide, so a confession would mean marks, welts and blood for Isaac. But he was the eldest, and it was his fault anyway—he'd told Scotty to put out the fire, but he hadn't seen him put it out with his own eyes—so a man had to take a punishment like a man.

He planned out how he'd say it: *Papa, we didn't mean it, but we burned down the barn*. He said it over and over again, marching outside to where Papa was assessing the damage.

"Papa?" Isaac said.

"Goddamn crackers," Papa said.

The idea came from Papa's own mouth.

To Isaac, his stroke of luck was too good to be true: Papa thought white folks had burned down the barn—probably McCormack and his sons. From the conversations Isaac had overheard when his parents thought he was sleeping, Papa already had plenty of reasons to be mad at the McCormacks. They were cheats, one thing. Never wanted to pay Papa what he was owed, like Papa was too dumb to count. And if Mama worked her hands raw to make Isaac a new shirt, one of the McCormack boys would go and tattle, and Ole Mr. McCormack would tell Papa, "Well, your boy just got a new shirt, so I reckon ya'll doin' better'n most niggers." And then he paid Papa even less. Mama hated Ole Missus McCormack so much that she could hardly make herself smile when she passed her on the road.

And McCormack, who had more land than he knew what to do with, was trying to say his plot bordering Papa's land was beyond the old oak, rather than just shy of it. He was planning on calling out surveyors and putting up a fence, since he knew Papa couldn't afford to pay anyone to say what *he* wanted them to say—not that any surveyor would side with him over McCormack. That McCormack was a thief to his bones, Mama always said.

And McCormack had the biggest, meanest dog in the county, trained to snap at black folks on sight. Papa had told him it was called a German shepherd dog, ordered special from up north, but Davie was sure that big dog was part wolf. It had wolf eyes and wolf teeth. Sometimes Isaac had nightmares about being chased by that dog. He never went anywhere close to McCormack's place without a big, heavy stick in his hand.

All in all, Isaac Timmons figured the only reason Ole Mr. McCormack *hadn't* burned down the barn was because he hadn't thought of it first.

"It was McCormack, huh Papa?" Isaac said to his father, outside the charred barn.

Papa looked at him good and long. At first, Isaac was afraid his father had seen straight through his lie, but there was something new and terrible in his father's eyes—it wasn't there long, but Isaac would never forget how his father's face chilled the blood in his veins. Papa was *afraid*! Isaac wanted to tell the truth as soon as he saw how scared his father was of McCormack, but he couldn't make his mouth work.

And so the story was born.

After that, the truth just got harder and harder to utter. And by the time all of them had been up for hours loading the wagon, with Papa trying to cheer them up with stories about the north while Mama pretended she wasn't crying, he had almost forgotten what the truth was.

Little Eddie would have told on them for sure, but Little Eddie hadn't figured out that the barn burned down because their makeshift cook-fire was too close to the wall where they were hiding from sight. Scott was usually the fastest tattle in town, but this time he kept the truth to himself, too—especially given his role in not putting out the fire properly. Scott was thinking about that razor-strap and how Papa had promised that the next time he and his older brother messed up, Isaac wasn't the only one who would take the blame. So Isaac and Scott cast each other miserable looks by lamplight all night long, folding Mama's quilts and blankets neatly into crates, carting out cooking utensils, and packing up the few farming supplies that weren't burned beyond usefulness.

Maybe it wouldn't be so bad to move, they thought. Mama was always afraid someone would come burn their whole house down with everyone inside, not just the barn. It had happened to a family in Quincy just a month ago. Besides, Papa was always in a bad mood after a day's dealings with McCormack, and Mama was worried Papa might say something to get them all killed. Papa did have a mouth on him.

Maybe, in fact, the barn burning down was something like Rev. Crutcher had said in church on Sunday, about how *ad-ver-si-ty* is a blessing in disguise.

The secret weighed heavier with each passing moment.

But the Timmons boys carried it. They were stronger than anyone could have imagined.

"SO . . . YOU HEARD a dog . . . and then a little boy?" Grandma said.

After a half-dozen repetitions, she finally had it right. At dinner, Davie had told the whole story, even admitting that Neema had been up with him. He'd started with the sniffing dog at his door and ended at the library. Mabel Trawley's information made his story seem that much more worth telling, so he had left nothing out.

"Right," Davie said. "A dog and a little boy."

"The boy said, 'Run! Follow me,'" Neema added.

"Pass the meat loaf," Grandpa Walter said. He was usually quick to play along, but not this time. Maybe his arthritis was hurting, Davie thought. He had noticed that Grandpa Walter laughed less and less because of pain.

Dad, though, was suddenly so interested that he was resting his cheek on his elbow as he listened. His elbow was planted beside his plate on the table. *No elbows on the table*, Grandma always said, but she was probably so glad to see Dad talking for a change that she kept quiet.

"But slave-catchers with dogs were before their time," Dad said. "Those boys, I mean."

"You think tracking dogs went away after slave times?" Grandma said. "The point is, maybe we can find an argument to stop the construction in all this, since those Timmons boys were never found. There weren't any children's bones at that first dig. I'll need to talk to that librarian myself."

Davie knew that Grandma couldn't care less about ghosts—she was just happy to have new ammunition in her anti-construction arsenal. Grandma reminded Davie of the mother in *Mary Poppins*, Mrs. Banks, who only truly came to life when she talked about her protests.

Davie noticed that both Dad and Grandma had red plastic cups instead of regular water glasses. A quick glance over, and Davie saw foam in his father's cup. He smelled it then: both Grandma and Dad were drinking beer. Davie had never even heard of, much less seen, his grandmother drinking beer—but Dad drank a lot of beer between projects. He drank more than Mom knew, because Dad took his bottles out for recycling late at night. Davie had seen him do it once and hadn't understood why until they were sitting at the dinner table a year later. Dad was used to hiding his drinking. It was a habit.

The mashed potatoes in his Davie's mouth suddenly tasted like paste. He missed his mother so much he wanted to cry, maybe because he was thinking about the three missing boys. He only had a very tiny idea of what being lost from his parents might feel like, one at a time, and already he could tell it might be a feeling that never got better.

"Tell me again what you saw out back," Dad said. "In the woods."

Dad's eyes were dancing like they had at the library, and Davie didn't like those eyes. Dad didn't believe in ghosts either; he was just trying to lose himself in something else. Davie felt like he was wearing X-ray glasses and could see down to his father's bones.

"I saw three boys burying a dog," Davie said. "There was a deep hole. *Really* deep."

Dad snapped his fingers. "Stop right there. Look at that image like a filmmaker would. You're looking at it too literally—it's a symbol. If these are ghosts, their appearance doesn't have to be some kind of literal recreation of an event from their lives. It might be more like a dream instead. That deep hole is a visual symbol for you. A message."

Grandma grinned, her eyes sparking. "Evidence in a town mystery buried right smack in the middle of Lot Sixty-five!" she said, giggling with glee. "You wait 'til I call Alice and tell her! What are those fat cat lawyers gonna say when we roll poor old Miss Timmons up in her wheelchair? Bet they won't be throwing up any more models after that."

"Who's Miss Timmons?" Davie said.

"She's ninety-some years old now," Grandma said. "She was kin to those boys, a sister born not long after they died. I think their mama was the only one who survived. How she didn't lose her mind after her whole family died, I just don't know. Maybe having the baby helped. And the geography checks out, doesn't it, Walt? We're right near the McCormack land."

Grandpa Walter grunted, fascinated by his cornbread. "Half the town's McCormack."

"You know what I mean. The plantation's still there."

"That really, really big one?" Neema said. "The really, really big white one?"

"Pass it by every day," Grandpa Walter said.

"I know which one," Dad said. "I see it through my bedroom window."

Maybe there *had* been fairy dust at the library, Davie realized. No one else in his family had cared about the ghosts he'd seen, and now everyone cared except Grandpa Walter. Neema grinned at Davie with rare admiration. She was wondering how he'd done it too.

Davie's father nudged his grandfather. "You sure you never saw ghosts, Dad?" Joking.

"I went through all that," Grandpa Walter said. "During the day, I watched my father catch hell from folks who couldn't stand the sight of a black man who wasn't stooping. At night, it was bumps and creaks. I loathed Gracetown. I was glad to be through with all of it."

Loathed was a strong word, and Davie hadn't heard his grandfather say it before. Grandpa Walt *had* seen ghosts as a child! He just hadn't liked it.

But maybe it could be different now.

"Will you stay up with us and hunt for ghosts, Grandpa Walter?" David said. Across the table, Grandma only laughed and shook her head. He'd known better than to ask her, beer or no beer. Ghost-hunting wasn't Grandma's style.

"*Please*, Grandpa?" Neema said.

"I'll stay up," Dad said instead.

Grandpa Walter shrugged. That was how it was decided.

That night, all four of them sat huddled behind the easy chair, not just him and Neema.

Davie heard Grandma watching TV in her bedroom, so it didn't feel like the Golden Hour, not exactly. But with Neema, Dad, *and* Grandpa Walt with them, Davie figured that whatever beacon he sent out to the ghost world was in Overdrive tonight.

"I didn't know you felt that way about Gracetown, Dad," Dad said in the quiet.

"Why do you think I didn't want to raise you here?" Grandpa said.

"Why'd you come back, then?"

"Times are different now," he said. "Mostly. And your mom wanted to go to the country. Home is home. Even if it doesn't always feel good, it's the only home you've got. You find a way to make it work."

"We're not talking about *that*," Dad said, voice clipped and low.

"We need to," Grandpa said.

Silently, Davie groaned. The real world couldn't intrude on their hunt! Davie had learned a long time ago that he never heard ghosts if he brought a book, or tried to do Sudoku puzzles. A ghost hunter's mind had to be quiet, even on the verge of sleep. *That* was when they came.

So Davie was afraid the spell would be broken. Dad would sigh and say they were being silly, or Grandpa would complain that his knees were aching. Neema might trigger the collapse by purring to Dad that she wanted something to drink. Davie could hear the foundation cracking.

But miraculously, for five minutes, they were quiet in the dark.

And then, just like that, the water was back.

Neema was so startled that she let out a little yelp, which scared Dad enough to jump.

"The floor's wet!" Neema shouted. Yes, *shouted*. (Ghosts, FYI, do not like shouting.)

"*Shhhhhhh*," I whispered, shaking her arm. "You'll scare it off."

"Davie, let go of your sister," Dad said. "And I don't feel any water."

"Me neither," Grandpa said. "We were promised ghost water, and I expect ghost water."

"You have to be a kid," Neema and I said together.

Dad and Grandpa looked at each other, practically winking.

Even with all of the distractions, Davie's mind was on the hunt. In a flash, he'd switched on his video camera, and his eyes were armed with night vision. Seeing in the dark was like being a superhero. Tiny snakes of light wriggled across the living room floor.

"It's all shimmery, like in moonlight," Davie said.

Neema wrestled over his shoulder. "Let me see."

Neema had pointed out that she hadn't been allowed to look through the night vision even once the previous night, so he gave her the camera. He pointed the lens toward the coffee table; the light hitting the glass-top table made it easier to see the water underneath.

"Whoa," Neema said.

"Before, we heard splashing," I whispered to Dad and Grandpa. "I don't hear any splashing yet. We need to be still and listen."

"Yessir, yessir," Grandpa said, and saluted.

So, they sat. While they waited, the water felt deeper. And colder. Neema and Davie rose to their feet because the floor felt so wet. Dad and Grandpa watched with fascination while Davie and his sister shook invisible droplets of water from their fingers, patted down wet clothes. Both Dad and Grandpa looked like they could hardly keep a straight face.

Then, Davie heard barking.

It was distant, but very distinct. And getting closer. Moving fast.

"The dog . . . " Neema said.

"It's coming." Davie said.

The barking didn't sound friendly. It was jabbering, persistent. Angry.

"Is it a good dog or a bad dog?" Dad said.

Davie's hands shook as he reached into his ghost kit for his doggy biscuits, wishing he had a better plan.

"Wait a minute," Dad said. "You *did* put that biscuit in my bed, Davie."

"No I didn't," I said.

"The ghost did it," Neema said.

"That's not funny, Davie. Playing games is one thing, but I when I ask you a question, I expect a truthful answer."

"Relax, Darryl," Grandpa said, sounding tired. "Let's be ghost-hunters."

Most ghosts run off lickety-split when there's too much talking. Davie had read countless stories about it on the ghost-hunter message boards on the Internet. But all in all, that angry dog scared him enough that maybe he hoped the dog would turn and run the other way. Maybe he wished the dog would do just that.

But the barking was louder. The dog was still coming.

Davie thought he'd been snapped into the dog's jaws when his father grabbed his arm and yanked him closer. It almost hurt. Maybe it did, a little. Dad's breath smelled like beer. "Davie, you promise me you had nothing to do with that doggy biscuit getting into my bed. You swear it wasn't you."

"Dad, I swear. It wasn't me."

"Me neither, Daddy," Neema said, although of course Dad would never get mad at her.

It was too dark for Davie to see his father's face, and Davie decided that using the night vision on Dad would get his camera broken. A painful instinct told him to expect a blow, maybe a slap. His father had never slapped him before, but there was always a first time. Dad was breathing fast, as if he had been running.

"You still hear a dog barking?" Dad said.

"Yessir," Davie said. He always called Dad "sir" if he was in trouble.

"And you and Neema feel water on the floor? Both of you?"

"Actually," Neema said, "it's up to my ankles."

"Shhhhh," I said.

Splashing!

Davie heard the chaotic sound of feet splashing in the water in uneven patterns, staggering. A boy shrieked like Davie had never heard anyone shriek, much less a child. The shriek wiped the grin off of Neema's face. It was the kind of shriek it was best to hear from a distance, because it might tear a hole in you up close.

But the shrieking was getting louder. Crying children were getting closer, splashing and stumbling. The three boys.

Davie's knees stopped working. His legs could barely support him.

"I'm scared," Neema said. She was crying too, joining their chorus.

When Grandpa turned the lights on, all the noises went away.

GRANDMA CALLED a family meeting at breakfast. After she heard Neema's crying the night before, she was in a bad mood about the whole ghost business. Neema had been too scared to sleep in the room full of dolls, so she had slept with Daddy. While the eggs and bacon got cold, Grandma spent the morning telling everyone she thought it was foolish for two grown men to be fed a children's fantasy about ghosts chased by a dog. And she had some choice words for Davie, too: He was too old—too *old*, she kept saying—to behave that way. He was supposed to be an example to Neema, and he needed to start acting his age.

"It was just some fun that went too far," Grandpa Walter said.

But that didn't satisfy Grandma. Dad tried next, telling her it was a valuable exercise in imagination, and how working through the scenario would help them understand the region's history—in fact, he said, the whole history of black America. Dad made it sound like something boring from a classroom, but that was Dad.

"It helps them process their history in terms they'll relate to," Dad finished.

Grandma gave him a dirty look.

Davie sighed, raising his hand. "Grandma . . . " he said. "If we don't listen to them, nobody else can. We can follow their voices. Maybe even find out if they died out back where I saw them with the dog. If their bones get dug up, you can stop the builders."

"Get an injunction . . . " Grandpa Walt cooed. He blew on his coffee to cool it.

But Grandma didn't fall for it right away. Not this time. "It's not good for Neema!"

"I won't cry this time," Neema said. "Davie told me to remember we're not hearing *real* screaming. It's old, so it's not really there. And they're not hurting anymore."

Well, that last part wasn't exactly true, Davie thought. If the three boys weren't hurting, they wouldn't be trying so hard to be heard. But Neema didn't need to have that spelled out. Like all ghosts, they just wanted their story known.

Grandma stared from one face to face, shaking her head. "Everyone in this house has lost their doggone mind. That includes me."

And so it was decided. Again.

That night, Grandma made special ghosts packs for everyone: extra flashlights, including the powerful hurricane flashlight that could light up the night like a spotlight. Packages of cheese and crackers. ("In case you're up late and get hungry.") Bengay for Grandpa. ("You know how your joints get, Walt.") Even boots and raincoats! ("Real water or not, I don't want you all getting wet.") For good measure, she handed Dad a shovel. ("Just in case you can get the digging started . . . ") Then she wished them luck and went to her bedroom to watch TV, closing her door tight so Lifetime wouldn't be too loud.

That night, Davie felt more like a ghost soldier than a mere ghost hunter. He had better supplies *and* reinforcements! And now that all of them knew what to expect, they wouldn't be surprised by the shrieking. The pain might not bother them so much.

He hoped not, anyway.

That night, the ghosts made them wait.

The excitement Davie had felt all day—really, every day since he'd first heard the dog sniffing at his door—burned into exhaustion. By nine o'clock, an hour after their vigil began, his eyelids were heavy and he was bothered by the hot raincoat. He felt a little silly wearing a raincoat inside the house. In the quiet, it was hard to remember the past few nights at all.

"Daddy?" Neema said in the hush.

"What's that, Pumpkin?"

Davie hoped they would keep their voices low.

"Are you and Mommy mad at each other?"

As scary as the barking and shrieking had been, Davie was more afraid to hear his father tell Neema a lie. Or worse, to tell her the truth.

"We shouldn't be talking now," Davie whispered.

"No, let's talk," Dad said. "It's all right."

But then Dad paused so long that Davie thought he'd changed his mind. After a few seconds, Dad took a deep breath. "Your mom and I love you very much . . . "

Oh crap, here it goes, Davie thought, his heart pounding. His hands trembled like they had when the ghost dog ran toward them with that angry bark. " . . . And we love each other very much. God knows that's true. But Mommy misses her family in Ghana—her mother is sick—and she wants to live closer to them. But I have a job where I can't just pack up and move. I work in Hollywood. So right now we're having a disagreement about where we're going to live. And where you're going to live."

It didn't sound as terrible as it had seemed when Dad was crying on the kitchen table. It didn't even sound like a divorce, not for sure.

Neema squirmed, moving to her father's lap. He was sitting cross-legged in front of the bookshelf behind the big recliner. Their lucky spot.

"You mean . . . we can't all live together?" Neema said.

"Maybe not right now."

"But . . . " Neema fought to put it all together. " . . . where would *we* live? Me and Davie?"

"With Mommy," Dad said, and Davie heard his voice crack. "Probably."

Grandpa's sigh was the only sound in the silence.

Until the scream.

The scream sounded like it was from right across the room, as close as the living room window. So loud that the windowpane cracked. All of them jumped and gasped. Neema wrapped her arms around her father's neck.

Grandpa's flashlight switched on. He bobbed the light near the window. The curtain was open, revealing veins of broken glass. "What the . . . Who broke that?"

"*No light*," Davie whispered. "Shut it off, Grandpa. Ghosts like the dark."

Muttering and cursing to himself, Grandpa turned off his flashlight. When he did, the brightness in Davie's night vision dimmed enough for him to gaze through the lens without squinting. This time, he didn't see any shadowy figure framed against the light from the window. Whoever had screamed was gone.

But the water was back, creeping higher while he hadn't been paying attention. This time, he saw currents swirling in the water, tiny rapids. Cold water crept into his boots, numbing his toes. Davie switched on the tape recorder around his neck. Back-up evidence.

"Water!" Neema said.

"I know. Watch out—it's getting higher."

"I can't believe that damn window broke," Grandpa said. "That thing cost . . . "

"*Shhhhh.*" This time, it was Davie's father. "Don't break the spell, Dad."

Sixty seconds passed. The scream sounded again, as if it were a movie that had been on Pause. Sounds crashed into the room: Splashing. Yelling. Barking and growling. Chaos.

"*Git 'im off! Git 'im off!*" a child's voice screamed.

Davie's mouth dropped open. His hands were unsteady, but he trained the camera back toward the window, toward the noise. This time, he saw several shadowy figures against the moonlight, arms flailing in a struggle. The tallest shadow—the oldest boy, Davie figured—was holding what looked like a giant stick. He raised it high and stabbed it like King Arthur's sword.

This time, the scream wasn't human. It was a dog's.

Another window cracked. Glass tinkled to the floor.

Grandpa Walt came to his feet. "*God*damn it," he said, sounding almost as scared as he was mad. He spoke to the darkness. "You stop breaking those windows!"

"The noise is doing it, Grandpa," Neema said. "Can't you hear it?"

Maybe Grandpa Walter was lucky he couldn't hear it. One, two, three, boys were sobbing. One was outright wailing, as if he was in the worst pain of his life.

"*Is he dead?*" one of the boys said.

"*Ithurtsithurtsithurtsithurts . . .*"

"*Hurry up and help me grab 'im. Let's go!*"

In Davie's viewfinder, the shadowy figures were gone. But he heard the splashing of several sets of footsteps running toward the kitchen again. Where the water would be deeper.

"They're moving," Davie said.

"The kitchen," Neema said, on Davie's heels.

While the rest of them scrambled to grab their supplies and follow, Grandpa only shook his head. "I'm not chasing nobody nowhere," Grandpa said.

"You sure, Dad?" Davie's father said. "It may turn out to be something."

Davie barely heard them over the sloshing of water as he ran to the kitchen doorway; he ignored the terrible feeling of cold water rising as high as his thighs. The back door was wide open again, just like he'd known it would be. When Davie looked through the viewfinder, he saw the taller boy beckoning in the doorframe.

Beckoning to them? To his brothers? Davie didn't know.

"We have to hurry!" Davie said, forgetting not to shout. "Before they're gone!"

The recliner hissed when Grandpa plopped himself down to sit. "My chasing days are over. But I'ma sit right here, and *nobody* better break no more of my damn windows."

Grandpa was talking to the ghosts.

"The water's too deep for me!" Neema said at Davie's side. "Over my waist!"

"Here, Pumpkin," Dad said, and hoisted her to his shoulders.

All three of them were breathing fast.

This was as far as Davie had ever followed the three boys. He didn't know what would come next. The dark kitchen suddenly looked strange and forbidding, full of shadowy hazard.

Still, Davie waded into deeper water, one step on the linoleum at a time.

Summer 1909

IT WAS AN HOUR before dawn, and Isaac Timmons was supposed to be resting. That was what his mama had told him to do. She'd made all three of them curl up on the living room rug under the oak tree, where the grass was soft. Mama had moved her favorite rug out of the house to keep it from getting muddy tracks, and she was planning to roll it up to pack last. She said they'd worked hard all night, so they deserved some sleep. "There's a long journey ahead," she'd said. Then she'd given them each a kiss and said, "And then we'll be away from Gracetown forever!" As if she'd come up with the plan to leave all on her own, and it had nothing to do with the barn. Mama had always considered Gracetown cursed, especially for Negroes.

His brothers were asleep, but Isaac Timmons wasn't. He was thinking about his best gal, Livvy, and how sad it was he would never see her again. Livvy's mom had just given him the honey he'd taken home to his brothers, which started the whole business with the barn, but Isaac couldn't blame Livvy for that. Hadn't Livvy only said last Sunday that she was *his* gal? And what kind of man would abandon his gal without so much as a goodbye?

No kind of man, Isaac thought. That's what Papa would say.

He would slip away and come right back. He'd be gone a half-hour at the most, if he ran. He couldn't ask Mama and Papa, because he knew what they would say. Livvy lived out McCormack's way, and he should never go that way. Not ever.

But Livvy was his gal. Once, she'd held his hand. Papa said he could expect to get married in three or four years, and Isaac decided he would come back for Livvy when he could. But for now, he had to tell his gal goodbye. *Had* to.

Isaac wasn't planning to wake his brothers, but each one nudged the next when he rolled off the rug. Even Little Eddie woke right up with bright eyes, ready to play.

"Where you goin'?" Scott said.

"Nowhere. Just stay here. I'll be back."

"*No*, Isaac," Scott said, sitting straight up. "He'll blame me."

"Pretend you're sleeping. Use your head." Papa used that phrase a lot.

"You goin' to Livvy's?" Scott said. "I wanna go too."

So all three of them snuck away from the rug, through the pines in back, beyond the creek and over to the McCormack side of the road, which had a fence. The long fence stretched as far as they could see. It was still half-dark, so it was quiet and still. Isaac took a long look at Gracetown as he walked— the long grass, cotton patches and pine trees—and wondered what New York would look like. He had never even seen a picture in a book.

All of the lights were still off in the McCormack house, which stood on the hill. That house looked like a castle, which he *had* seen in a book. He wondered if the McCormacks would ever find out his father thought he'd burned down the barn. Maybe they would never even know. Isaac hoped not. He didn't want to give Mr. McCormack the satisfaction.

"We gotta go faster," Isaac said. "Or they'll see we're gone for sure."

"You think Livvy's mama's gonna give us more honey?" Little Eddie said.

"You think Livvy'll give you a big sloppy kiss?" Scott teased.

Instead of getting mad, Isaac enjoyed the quiet around him. McCormack's land was on one side of the red clay and gravel road, swampy land on other. Walking with his brothers on the empty road toward Livvy's, it was hard to believe Mama and Papa were packing up everything they owned in a wagon to drive farther than Isaac's mind could imagine. Two days' journey was a long way away. If you married someone two days away, your parents might not see you for years. Papa had said New York was weeks away, by wagon. Papa didn't even think the wagon could make the trip.

A dead pine had toppled over and knocked out the logs to the McCormack fence. Most of the fence was intact, but one entire section had been crushed, and the fence was gaping open.

That was why he'd felt so peaceful, Isaac realized. Quiet. He should have known.

Isaac tugged on Little Eddie's shirt to keep him from walking ahead. He held up his hand to hush his brothers' tittering. The dawn was as silent as a tomb.

"Where's the dog?" Isaac whispered.

The boys looked up and down the road, dreading the sight of the dog sprinting toward them, freed from its prison. In their imaginations, the dog was three times its normal size, a monstrous beast. A Negro man in town missing three of his fingers told stories about McCormack's dog. McCormack trained his dog to bite niggers, the man said.

No dog was in sight. On McCormack's land, only a few chickens stirred. On the swamp side, there was no sound except from insects and reptiles; the swamp's constantly trilling song.

"We gotta go back," Isaac said. He held tight to Little Eddie's hand.

"What about the honey?" Little Eddie said.

"Mama say they treat that dog like family," Scott said. "Maybe it sleeps in the house."

It was a tempting thought, for a moment. Surely the dog was somewhere close to the house. The dog wouldn't be roaming on the road or the swamp, would it? Issac hated to lose his honor by leaving Livvy without a word of explanation. What would she think of him?

"Yeah . . . maybe," Isaac said. "Maybe."

Then they heard the barking.

"*You hear that? Run!*" the shadowy figured in the kitchen doorway said. He waved furiously, as if their lives depended on it.

"He's telling us follow him," Neema said from her perch on her father's shoulders.

"Then . . . let's follow," Dad said.

Davie waded farther into the kitchen, until he felt the water at his mid-chest. The sensation of fighting against the water to walk made it feel like he couldn't breathe. He was shaking all over. But the door was so close! The shadow was almost within his reach.

Water converged around the base of Davie's throat, a collar of ice. But the cold liquid didn't feel like clean water: it was heavier, more viscous, a slime of sweet-sour dead marine life and vegetation. The smell of the old, dead swamp made Davie want to vomit.

"I can't go anymore," Davie gasped. "The water's too high."

"Just to the door, Davie," Dad said. "If you can't after that, you can't."

"You can do it, Davie!" Neema said. Easy for *her* to say, Davie thought.

Davie gulped at the air. He didn't want to know what the water tasted like, but he wasn't going to turn back. With his next step, he held his breath in case he wouldn't touch bottom.

But he did.

The next thing Davie knew, he was standing outside on the back porch. Dad was one step below him, still carrying Neema. Staring toward the woods. The water had receded dramatically, only as high as Davie's ankles. Davie gasped two or three times at the clean air, remembering the awfulness of the water he'd waded through. He reeked of it.

"What now?" Dad said.

Neema pointed. "That way. I hear splashing."

His bearings returned, Davie raised the camera, using night vision to follow her finger. Whether she knew it or not, Neema was pointing straight toward the broken fence. With every step, Davie better heard the urgent whisper ahead in the darkness.

"*We'll lose 'im in the water! Run!*"

More splashing. Sets of feet in a hurry.

"Yeah, this way," Davie said.

They trotted off together, following Neema's finger and the splashing. They didn't run in a straight line, but they eventually ended up at the broken fence. Even with night vision, the woods were nearly pitch through the viewfinder. His only clear view was of the broken fence post, a jagged log toppled down.

The sight of the broken fence in the frame scared Davie. Once they left the backyard, all of the light would be behind them. "Official ghost-hunting audio journal," Davie said in a shaky voice to his tape recorder, remembering his protocols. "We've reached the broken fence. We still hear the splashing on the other side."

"Hurry, Davie!" Neema said. "They're going too far."

"Hold on," Dad said. "I can't carry Neema on my back in the woods."

Thank goodness. Dad was predictable, and suddenly Davie was glad.

"How's the water?" Dad asked me.

The water was like cold claws grasping his ankles, even with oversized boots on.

"Fine," Davie said. "It's lower now."

Dad grunted, lowering Neema to the ground. Then, Dad bent over to be closer to her eye-level. Neema giggled and danced when her feet touched the water.

"All right, listen, you two," Dad said. "We'll go to the woods. I'll allow this. But we'll have rules, and I'm only gonna say them once."

"Daddy, just say them *fast*," Neema said. The broken fence didn't scare her at all. She sounded like she was ready to wet herself from excitement.

"Stay close. Come when I call. *Watch* where you're walking," Dad said. "Davie?"

"Yessir." The splashing had veered right, up ahead. "The splashing is softer and softer," he said, speaking his audio journal. "But I still hear it."

Neema pointed again. "That way!" she said.

"Let's do it," Dad said, raising his shovel high.

As he stepped over the fallen log, Davie's heart pounded so hard that the blood rushing his ears drowned out the splashing. He couldn't believe Dad was letting them do this! There were snakes in the woods. There were coyotes and bears too, not just deer, and there were ghosts for an absolute fact. And Neema was with them, the one he babied to death over nothing!

Something was different about Dad. Something had changed, and Davie didn't know if the change was good or bad. Davie wondered if *he* should be the reasonable one tonight, just in case Dad had forgotten how. Maybe Dad had snuck more than one beer after dinner.

Dad flicked on the hurricane flashlight, and a precious circle of the woods before them turned as bright as midday. Every twig, leaf and stump threw a shadow.

Behind them, in the dark, came the sound of barking. The dog's splashing was directed, more disciplined. Like a guided missile.

"The dog!" Davie said.

"*Run!*" the boy up ahead yelled.

They ran awkwardly, more like jogging, careful with their speed to avoid tripping. Up ahead, the splashing sounded more and more frantic. The younger boys were crying, or maybe all of them were. Their cries filled the woods.

"Faster," Davie huffed.

"No," Dad said. "Too dangerous."

"No, Dad, it's too dangerous *not* to." Davie ran ahead, just to set a good example.

"Get out your doggie biscuits," Dad sad.

"That won't work!"

"How do you know?"

The dog was very large, and its bark sounded slobbery. Hungry.

"Because I can *hear* him! That. Won't. Work."

Neema wasn't saying anything by then. Neema could hear the dog's hunger too. She was proud she had made it past the first shrieks this time, but Neema was good and ready to go home. Lesson learned. She wasn't old enough to be a ghost-hunter. Like with Grandpa, the idea had lost all of its attraction.

Davie's father, who couldn't hear the barking, tugged on Davie's raincoat to slow him down. "Keep this up, Davie, and we'll go home."

"Yeah, Dad, we *should* go home, but now I don't know if we can." Maybe Dad would have understood if he'd waded through that muck. They had crossed to another side. It might not be easy to cross back. "Let's just go faster."

"Kofi David Stephens . . . *Slow down.* Someone could break a leg out here."

The barking and splashing behind them grew impossibly loud just before it fell silent. Davie held his breath.

Neema screamed.

For a blink, Davie's brain shut down: His baby sister was screaming?

Water thrashed as Neema writhed beside their father, still screaming. "*Something bit me!*" Neema cried, all childhood stripped out of her voice. "*It bit me,* Daddy! *My leg!*" And she screamed again, her horror renewed at the retelling.

There was more splashing when Dad bent over to pick her up. Vaguely, Davie wondered when their feet had started making the water splash, too. If the splashing water was real now, was the dog real now too? In his flashlight beam, Davie saw something wet glisten on Neema's leg. The dark wetness startled him so much that his hand shook, nearly dropping the flashlight, and the terrible image went away. Not water. Blood.

"Oh, babydoll, you're okay. *Shhhh.* You're okay." Even while Dad comforted Neema, he sounded petrified. Davie didn't have to wonder if he had imagined the blood. He knew the blood was there from the tremor in his father's voice. Davie hadn't seen the blood long, but he knew it was more than a little. Davie felt steaming water in his pants as he pissed on himself.

"Davie," Daddy said, in a soldier's voice Davie hadn't heard before. The tremor was gone, as if it hadn't been there at all. "Grab Neema."

Davie couldn't say anything. Couldn't move, at first.

"Davie, grab her. Something bit her, it's big, and it's still out here."

Davie grabbed Neema's hand, and Neema sobbed because she didn't want to be away from her father. Dad was the solver of all of Neema's problems, and now he had pushed her aside. Davie had to physically restrain her to keep her from clinging to their father. Using his muscles helped Davie shut off the panic ruling his mind.

Dad grabbed his shovel and picked it up, testing its weight in its hand.

Splashing came from behind them.

Davie grasped, diving away from the splashing, yanking Neema with him. Neema screamed, clinging to him with so much strength that Davie nearly staggered to his knees.

Dad whirled, his eyes following his flashlight beam. Nothing visible but brush. Davie tried to help with his own flashlight, but his beam kept zigging into the treetops because he couldn't hold his hand steady, especially with Neema pulling on him so hard.

"Can't see it . . . " Dad was whispering to himself. "I can't fucking see it . . . "

Davie remembered his audio journal: "Something just bit Neema," he said. Neema wailed, hearing the horror repeated.

"Davie, *be quiet*," Dad said.

But Davie couldn't be quiet. He was screaming too.

First, he felt a tug on the back of his raincoat. Then, something raked through clothes and skin on the back of his thigh, with the precision of knives. Davie had never known his body could feel so much pain. Davie fell to his knees, stunned by the fire in his nerves. As he fell, slimy water splashed his face.

Not cold anymore. Warm.

Inches in front of him, more water splashed, some of it stinging his eyes. The dog was probably staring him dead in the face.

"*IN FRONT OF ME!*" Davie screamed, and Dad took a wild swing with his shovel at the air in front of Davie's face. Dad only threw himself off-balance.

But Dad's second swing hit something. There was a *ping* sound, a watery thud, and the sound of an animal's yelp. Dad stabbed the shovel down like a stake, and a shriek flew from the nothing under Dad's shovel. A beast, invisible.

"Is it dead?" Neema said.

Dad jabbed his shovel into the land around him, and water splashed.

"I hear that," Dad said, amazed. "Jesus. I hear it."

"Why can't-can't we-we see it?" Neema said, wrapped so hard around Davie that he could barely breathe. He screamed out again. The pain was truly dazzling.

By then, all three of them might have been crying.

"Okay," Dad said, trying to find a place for it in his mind. "Okay. Okay. I know it's here, but we can't see the dog. We can't see it. Okay."

"Is it dead?" Neema said again.

Dad jabbed at the ground. More splashing. "I don't know. I don't know where it is. I don't know if it's dead. It's not here. It's not here." Dad's voice sounded far away, from California. Dad was fading too.

Davie felt his father's hands patting him, examining his injury. His father's touch made him cry out again.

"Davie? Listen to me."

Davie tried to listen, but Dad's voice kept melting. Slipping under the world.

Water splashed on Davie's cheeks, and his eyes jolted open. Dad's nose was nearly touching him. "Davie, I know you're hurt, but you need to listen to me: Can you walk?"

Davie tried to stand up, and the pain made him vomit. Dad patted his shoulder.

"Davie, I can't carry both of you. Do you hear me?" Dad said. His voice was shaky, almost pleading. "Neema's ankle's hurt, so she can't walk. But I think you can."

"I can't!" he said. The back of his thigh was on fire. "Dad, it *hurts.*"

"I can't leave you here. So that means we all have to go—*now,*" Dad said, breathing in his face. This time, Davie didn't smell beer; he smelled his father's perspiration, the smell of horsey rides and swinging from Dad's arms in the back yard. The memories made Davie cry out, worse than the pain from his bite. Dad was panting. "This one time, Davie. I need you to grow up very fucking fast."

Davie gasped out a sob, but then he lost interest in crying. He was in pain in every way, but the pain wasn't as bad as knowing the dog was still out there. They were in big trouble, and crying wasn't going to change it.

"I need a stick," Davie said. He sniffed, and snot churned in his nose. "A weapon."

"Good boy." Dad's flashlight swept the forest floor, and the stick appeared as if by miracle. "Grab that one, fast. Then we'll go back the way we came. Did you get enough for YouTube?"

Davie tried to laugh, but it only came out like crying. He grabbed the fallen branch, which was thick, but not too thick for his palm. A perfect fit. It reminded him of the same stick he'd used when he saw the boys in the woods, already free of excess twigs and dead leaves. But it couldn't be way out here. Could it? *My magic staff,* Davie thought, hopeful. Desperate.

When Davie shifted his weight to his good leg, his injured leg screamed at him. He didn't know how much he was bleeding, but he could feel the fabric of his jeans knotted up in his bloodied parts. Every movement was agony. Panic tangled his breaths in his lungs. He was gasping suddenly.

"Stay calm. We're gonna get out of here, Davie. I promise. I'll get you a doctor."

"Me too?" Neema whispered from the safety of Dad's arms.

"You too, Pumpkin. You ready, Davie?"

Davie nodded, catching his breath, but his lips were shaking. He gripped his stick tightly with one hand, trained his flashlight ahead with the other. He couldn't use night vision now—it limited his scope too much. He would have to trust his own eyes for the walk back to the fence.

"Let's go," Dad said, just before they heard the barking behind them again.

Angry barking. *SPLASHSPLASH*

Davie just kept thinking *No.* It wasn't possible. It couldn't be. It wasn't fair.

"I heard that," Dad said, amazed and frightened. "I hear something coming."

"*Run!*" said a boy's voice from ahead of them.

"I heard that," Dad said. His voice was dazed.

They had no choice but to run; the boy's urgent voice only confirmed their instincts. Dad's feet made heavy splashes as he staggered under Neema's extra weight. Tree trunks appeared suddenly in their flashlights, almost too late to avoid colliding with them, so running took all of Davie's concentration—at first. Then he realized they were following the voices, keeping ahead of the dog's splashing behind them, running the wrong way. The fence back to his grandparents' house was *behind* them.

Where were the ghosts taking them?

Davie ventured a quick glance through night vision for a long view—and he saw a huge, looming structure up ahead and toward the right, blocking the moonlight.

"A tobacco barn," Davie said.

He had never seen it in daylight. He doubted that it was real, but it was there. At the edge of the swamp. *The Timmons boys crossed a swamp to lose the dog*, Davie realized. He thought he said it aloud for his audio journal, but he was only whispering.

"*Come on, we'll close the barn door*," the boy's husky voice ahead said, full of reason.

"The barn door!" Dad said. "We'll close the door."

Consensus.

The barking was getting closer again.

Davie and his father must have caught up to the others, because the splashing of the ghost boys blended with theirs. He heard their sobs and whispers close to his ear. They were running together, all of them. Combined, their feet sounded like an army, and Davie hoped they were.

Like Davie, they were crying and in pain. They understood. But still they ran.

Davie thought his lungs would burst. The meat of his back thigh hurt so much that he was convinced it was falling apart, unfurling flesh with every twig he brushed against. He couldn't tell the difference between his sobs and his hitching breaths, but he checked his night vision lens again. Part of his head was still working.

Were they moving at all? The tobacco barn was too far. Too far. They wouldn't make it, he realized. The barking behind them was gaining too fast. The dog was too loud, too close.

They needed another plan.

"We can't . . . we can't . . . " Davie wheezed.

A shriek sounded, to Davie's left. The bottom fell out of his world until he saw that neither Dad nor Neema was shrieking. Dad froze in his tracks, lowering lowered Neema to the ground so he could wield his shovel as a weapon. Neema sobbed, clinging to their father's legs, staring wide-eyed toward the place where the shrieking had come. Dad was wide-eyed too.

Beside them, there was a frenzy of splashing in the water.

"*Ithurtsithurtsithurtsithurtsithurts!*"

Davie didn't know whose voice it was. It could be any of them.

"Where is it?" Dad said, ready with his shovel.

Davie looked through night vision and saw the whorls of water dancing about ten yards ahead of them. There was a great commotion. "There! By that stump!"

Dad had only lunged ahead one step when a beast let out a terrible sound. For an instant, right before he blinked, Davie thought he saw water splash as if a boulder had just been tossed inside, framing the dead dog like a chalk drawing. The dog was big. He could have killed them.

"*I got it!*" The oldest boy said.

"*Is it dead?*"

"It's not dead!" Davie said. He had heard the dog felled three times and counting, but the dog always came back. Davie had learned that much. As soon as his legs started pumping again, he heard a splash behind him—and a sound like a shower as the dog shook off water.

The barking started right away.

"*Run!*"

Davie no longer knew whose voice he heard. Dad scooped Neema up into his arms and followed Davie's lead, racing toward the barn. Neema clung to Daddy so she wouldn't hit her head on tree branches, but Dad still had to run slowly with Neema in his arms. Too slow!

The dog would catch them again. The dog always caught them.

"*Run!*" the voice said ahead.

Then, even worse, an urgent scream: "*STOP!*"

But Davie couldn't stop his legs in time. Suddenly, there was no ground beneath Davie's feet. His feet plunged downward to nothingness, like stepping off of a sand bar at the beach.

He was drowning in soft earth. Mud.

Even before Davie fully realized he had fallen into some kind of hole—and a large one, since the earth yawning around him—he began scrabbling to try to pull himself out. His slide was slow, a taking-its-time kind of terror, and Davie screamed, grasping for a twig or a rock, anything to hold him above ground.

"Be still!" Dad said. Davie had heard that same terror in Dad's voice when Neema screamed, except now Dad's voice was more hollowed out, like he was witnessing a death. He had dropped Neema just short of the hole, or they all might have fallen. "Davie, don't move! Please don't move, Davie."

As Dad reached for him—his hand still a good six inches off—something cracked beneath Davie, old damp wood aged beyond its time, and Davie plunged downward again. Suddenly, Dad's hand was gone.

Dad and Neema both yelled his name, as if he could will his fall to stop.

Davie screamed and sobbed, panicked by the taste of bitter mud in his mouth. His legs jerked, kicking and there was nothing but air beneath him. Below, there was a long fall. As mud slid down around him, gathering speed and resolve, Davie couldn't understand why mud had risen to his chin and no farther. Or why he hadn't fallen yet.

His clothes pinched at the nape of his neck, as if he were dangling on a hook. Something was holding him up from behind.

The ghost?

His jaw trembling, Davie turned around to see with his own eyes.

A stubborn tree branch had snagged his raincoat, he saw from the corner of his eye. Grandma's raincoat had saved him from falling.

"I said *be still*," Dad said, grabbing his arm. "It's like a . . . well . . . or something. It's a long drop down, Davie."

Davie last brave act that night was to train his night vision down to the hole below his dangling feet. He thought he saw the flare from the whites of a small boy's eyes. No, two, then three, pairs of terrified eyes! Davie heard three boys yelling beneath him, and then only a horrible silence.

They had fallen. All three boys had fallen, just like he, Neema, and Dad almost had.

Davie could only breathe again once Dad had pulled him far clear of the hole, when he was sure all four limbs were on solid ground. He was afraid to walk anywhere, afraid of falling again. "You're okay," Daddy said, stroking Davie with one arm and Neema with the other. Davie could hear his father's heart thundering in his chest. "You're okay. It's all okay."

"Is it gone?" Neema said.

Davie wondered if she was talking about the dog or the hole, or both. No barking, but it could be hiding. Waiting.

"I don't know," Dad said. "We're going to the barn. Where is it, Davie?"

"What if it's not real?" Davie said.

"It's real enough."

They were only forty yards away from the barn, but it was a long forty yards. Davie realized he didn't hear splashing when he walked anymore. The barn was on dry land.

By the time they got to the barn door, Davie's body was drenched in perspiration. He felt like he was swimming in his clothes. But he helped Dad pry the barn door loose from its mooring, and they slammed the heavy door shut. Dad used his shovel to lock it in place, since there was no other way to secure it.

By then, Davie was lying on the barn floor, his face pressed against the scratchy wood. The barn smelled of sweet tobacco leaves, a smell that burned his throat. "The dogs chased them to the swamp," Davie said. "They killed the dog. But they fell in a hole."

Dad barely heard him, too consumed with comforting Neema. As much as Davie craved comfort himself, he didn't mind. He would have died to keep Neema safe. He still might.

"Maybe a . . . storm cellar," his father panted. "Maybe a well. Probably no way out."

Maybe they had fallen and broken their necks right away. Or been buried alive. Maybe they had died waiting for someone to find them. And all the while, the town was going to hell because they were gone. Davie could only cry about the whole sad mess.

The Timmons brothers never made it to the barn. They fell when the barn was just within sight. It wasn't fair, after what they'd been through. It wasn't fair.

While Davie cried, Dad undressed him and Neema, examining their wounds by flashlight, washing them with bottled water. He looked relieved. There was blood, but the bleeding had already stopped. He divided the packet of Extra Strength Tylenol he kept in his wallet between them. The pain was still at a roar, but having a pill to take made him feel better.

"You're fine," Dad promised them, and they hoped he wasn't lying.

The tobacco barn was cavernous. When Dad walked to the other side of the barn to make sure there were no other doors to lock, his absence seemed eternal. Davie thought he would faint waiting for his father to come back to their corner, where Dad had spread out their coats to make a cushion for them to rest. If Davie hadn't been stroking Neema's hair and telling her everything was fine, just like Dad, he might have started crying again.

But his father did come back, and he brought good news.

"We're locked tight as a drum," he said. "I checked every corner. Nothing's getting in."

And that was that. By silent agreement, they knew they weren't going to open the door until morning. Ghosts don't like the light.

They ate cheese and crackers and drank bottled water. They talked about favorite characters from television, movies and books to keep from thinking about their world.

That was when Davie heard it from the slats in the wooden wall, a foot from his ear:

Snnnnfffff snnfff snnffffff

The dog was sniffing at the door.

A LOUD BARK woke Davie, a roaring in his ear. Daylight blinded him when he opened his eyes. He blinked, his limbs frozen by a sight so improbable that he forgot his pulsing pain: The towering tobacco barn around him was no more than a shell, most of the wall planks stripped away, its rooftop lost among the pines, its floor overgrown with generations of underbrush.

A German shepherd's face lunged toward Davie, pink tongue caressing sharp teeth.

He's followed us to daytime, Davie thought. That thought whitened out anything else that tried to come into his mind, until he couldn't remember where he was. Or who.

Neema's scream pulled Davie out of his trance.

Davie let out his own yell, pinwheeling his arms as his only weapon against the dog.

"Calm down, Davie!"

"Son, it's all right. Whoa there. Whoa."

"Neema, it's Grandma! It's all right."

"Can't you see, Sheriff? They're scared of the *dogs*."

Once the police tracking dogs were well out of sight, the world came back to Davie in slow bits and pieces. But it took a while.

Davie's next fully formed memory was sitting on a yellow police blanket slurping apple juice from a juice box; the best apple juice he'd ever tasted. Neema, slurping her own juice box across from him, was sharing the exact same feeling as she gazed at him. Both of them almost smiled. That was the first hint Davie felt that maybe they were all right. Maybe.

Davie couldn't hear what his father was saying to the sheriff over the hood of the sheriff's huge SUV, the sheriff nodding and taking notes. Davie couldn't imagine what kind of story Dad could tell someone who hadn't been there.

Davie gasped. He patted his side for this gear, but everything except his shirt had been stripped off by the paramedics. "My camera!" he said. More like a croak.

Grandpa held his ghost kit high up in the air. "Got everything here, Davie. Just relax." Grandpa was using his cane, Davie noticed. He had never seen him use his cane outside before.

"Grandpa, it *bit* us," Davie said. "Even though we couldn't see it."

Grandpa nodded, gesturing for him to hush. "*Shhhh*. You just relax right now. No need to get excited. It's gone now."

Grandma's eyes were tired. Davie realized his grandparents must have both been up all night, worried sick when they never came back from the woods. Davie didn't know how far they had traveled, but it had taken a long time to find them. Davie felt terrible for giving his grandparents the same awful suffering Isaiah and Essie Timmons had, even for a night.

When Grandma stroked Davie's head, he held her wrist tightly. "Grandma, I know what happened to the Timmons boys," he whispered.

"Hush, Davie," Grandma said. "Walt's right. Forget about that, baby."

"There's a hole—over there! A dog was chasing them, and they fell in. I know it. I almost fell in, too!"

Grandma sent a withering look Dad's way. She was so mad at Dad for taking them out into the woods at night, she probably could barely think of anything else.

"Somebody has to find the bodies," Davie said. "Or it's all for nothing. Just tell them to dig. Tell Miss Timmons her brothers are here. If she wants to find them, she's got to dig."

THE PARTICULARS are unnecessary. All three Timmons boys eventually died, though not at once. Isaiah Timmons died never knowing that his sons lay trapped in the abandoned cellar of a house knocked over in a twister in '02. That house had crumbled like toothpicks, but the barn beyond it hadn't had a scratch. Such is the way with twisters.

The boys' mother, Essie, would walk the ground within a stone's throw of her sons' burial place on three separate occasions in the fifty years before she died. She never knew, not even a hunch.

All Old Man McCormack ever knew was that someone had killed his dog. The dog was found, at least.

There was no justice in it. All four of the deceased thought so.

AFTER DAVIE and Neema were released from their night's stay at Tallahassee Memorial, Dad moved them to the new Quality Inn that had just opened off of the 10, only ten minutes from Davie's grandparents but safely across Gracetown's boundary. Technically, out of town.

Neema wouldn't hear about sleeping at the house another night, even when Grandma promised to put the dolls away. But Davie wasn't ready to go home to California yet.

Not until he *knew*.

Grandpa Walter and Grandma were sweetness and spice around Davie, but Davie knew they were furious with Dad for taking his two children into the dark woods. *What were you thinking?* Mom was on her way, too. Dad had tried to sound happy when he told Davie she was coming, but the dread on Dad's face had been hard to ignore.

So Davie knew there was really nothing in the way of it now. So much for their month apart. So much for Imani's plans to change Mom's mind. The future was here, a month early.

To take his mind off of the impending disaster, Davie checked his video footage.

The footage of the living room only showed the broken windows—not the *breaking* windows, a key distinction—and conversations between him, Neema, Dad, and Grandpa Walter. No splashing or shrieking on the video. Same old same old. Nothing new. Even the shadow of the Timmons boy in the kitchen doorway wasn't as distinct as it had been the first time, and the first time it had been pretty sucky.

The footage got better in the woods, but Davie had to stop the tape when he heard Neema scream. Out of nowhere, he suddenly heard all of it: Barking. Voices. Water. Not as loud as it had been, but undeniably there—true ghost phenomena, when he was ready to show it. He just wasn't sure when. Maybe soon, maybe not. Maybe tomorrow. Maybe never.

Davie found that it was hard to know anything anymore.

Dad quietly let himself into the hotel room and motioned Davie over. Grandma had dozed off in the hotel room's recliner and Neema was curled up sleeping at the foot of the bed, where she'd been watching the Disney Channel at a low volume. Hopping with his crutch, Davie followed Dad into the hotel room's bathroom. The bright lights made Dad look older.

"So . . . they're digging," Dad said, out of the blue.

"Right now?"

"Started this morning. Mom and Dad didn't think I should say anything, but I thought you deserved to know, Davie."

Dad said it as if it was something to think about.

"I have to go," Davie said.

Dad's face flinched, a tic that almost closed his right eye. "How's your leg?"

Davie's back thigh radiated pain, flaring with every step, but that was irrelevant. "Painkillers," Davie said. "It's fine."

"Davie, they might not find anything. Or, maybe they will. Either way, it'll be hard."

If Dad hadn't been there . . .

The thought began as a constant refrain in his mind, but it never finished itself. That thought didn't need finishing, because he would be dead if his father hadn't been there. Davie knew that as well as he knew his name. But they hadn't talked about it yet. Dad had never told Davie what he thought had happened in the woods. Maybe they didn't need to.

"Is Mom coming to take us now?" Davie said.

Dad didn't blink. "Looks that way." He made a fist before slowly fanning his fingers.

They stood in the bathroom, quiet. Dad's fingers drummed on the sink's fake marble counter. Dad didn't seem like man who had been crying in the kitchen anymore.

"I'll tell her it's not your fault," Davie said.

"It has nothing to do with that. Or you. That's the truth, Davie."

Davie believed him, but he also remembered the animal terror and loathing on his father's face when he was swinging his shovel at the invisible thing chasing him and Neema. He wondered if Dad would feel that about Mom one day, or if maybe even *he* would. He wished a fight weren't coming. He would have to choose sides.

"What time is Mom getting here?"

"Late. Seven."

There was still time for things to stay the same. Just for a while.

"Don't you want to see the bones too, Dad?"

"I just . . . want to be careful about it. I'm on thin ice around here, Davie."

Davie hoped Dad wasn't convinced there had never been a dog, that maybe they had been attacked by a hungry bear in the dark. He hoped Dad wouldn't start forgetting.

"But you want to, don't you?" Davie said. "Don't you want to see?"

Dad bit his lip and nodded.

So, they left a note for Grandma on Quality Inn stationery—and they went.

THE DIG for the bones of Isaac, Scott, and Little Eddie Timmons had begun quietly, without fanfare. The attorneys for the warring parties—the developer, Stellar Properties Inc., and a group of residents calling themselves the Gracetown Citizens Action Council, of which Miss Essie Timmons was an honorary chair—exchanged phone calls and reached a compromise.

The digging had begun only a day after the missing family told its ghost story.

At dawn.

Despite the instability at the surface, much of the old abandoned cellar had filled with debris and soil over time, so it wasn't as easy as finding a ready tunnel. The dig took time.

As the day wore on, a bulldozer and small scooper wound their way down the newly worn path to the abandoned tobacco barn developers would have razed the week before, if town politics hadn't hung them up. They would have found the hole themselves the hard way, so it was best it was found before someone got killed.

The company CEO, who'd approved the dig personally, thought it was a win-win: His company could demonstrate goodwill to the superstitious, rustic locals, and symbolically lay the whole issue of corpses to rest. ("You see?" he could say. "This proves it for once and for all: No more bodies here!" It wasn't exactly the ideal slogan for a housing development, but it was an improvement over their current PR standing.)

Neighborhood Watch, which had transformed into a satellite of the Gracetown Citizens Action Council, had volunteers up and down McCormack Road who called multiple numbers on their phone trees when they saw construction trucks on the move. The movement of workers and equipment to Lot 65 gained more attention on a Saturday than one might think.

By mid-morning, a good crowd had gathered at the edge of the dig.

In fairness to the Timmons family, the excavation was eight feet by eight feet, which Stellar had argued was more than enough of a safety margin for finding the bones. A square block of the soil would be dug up, bit by bit, and the dig wouldn't end until it was twenty yards down. Almost like digging for oil, some onlookers thought.

While one set of workers hauled up the soil, another sifted through for bone fragments on blankets with students from the anthropology department at the college. Adults shooed children away from the sifters, and police officers shooed adults and children alike away from the growing hole, which looked more deadly as the day wore on.

Before noon, there were three occasions of great excitement at the dig on Lot 65.

The first was when a green van from Gracetown Glen Retirement Home came bouncing along the path, and two uniformed workers wheeled out ninety-one-year-old Essie Timmons, named for her mother, who had spent her lifetime drowning in her mother's grief about her three lost sons. Essie Timmons had been raised in the shadow of her dead brothers, and her mother's obsession with finding out the exact how and why of their vanishing had been bequeathed to her. In the 1940s, she had written a book on the subject, *Three Brothers: The Timmons Family and the Gracetown Riots*. (She owned the only three remaining copies, and she never allowed anyone to touch their pages.) She had always given talks at the elementary school on the subject until her stroke a decade before. But while her body was diminished, her mind was sharp.

Essie Timmons' dark face was deeply webbed by her age lines, but her cheekbones were still a carbon copy of her dead brother Isaac's. She wore a mound of white hair so vivid that it was visible from a distance. She never left her wheelchair and had trouble holding her head upright, so she looked more dead than alive. But no matter. While a uniformed worker stood over her with an umbrella, Essie Timmons sat out in the sun and watched the workmen dig.

Every once in a while, a well-meaning citizen came up to the old woman to offer her a cold drink, or to ask her if she was hungry. Essie Timmons just raised her hand to motion them away. Her eyes were an eagle's, never distracted from the rising clumps of Georgia clay soil.

Watching and waiting.

The second event of great excitement was heralded by a murmuring through the onlookers that spread from one end of the gathering to the next: *McCormack's here.*

Frank McCormack was a slightly-built man of seventy-two whose face looked much older. He owned the land where the first bodies had been found, and his grand old house on the hill was visible from the Stephens' windows.

In the wake of that ill-fated dig on his property, nearly two miles from this one, word had spread that his great-great-grandfather sanctioned the burial—on his own land—of twelve black men killed in the Gracetown riots. A different reporter called him about it every other week, the latest from as far as California. As if that wasn't enough to make his stomach ache at night, Frank McCormack had lost a million dollars so far when the construction on his lots came to a halt, and much of that money had been lost because of Essie Timmons.

Although they technically weren't in sight of each other yet, it was rare to see Frank McCormack and Essie Timmons in the same company. Their families hadn't spoken for generations. And there they both were, at the dig.

The third unexpected thing was when the boy and his father came.

By that time, the number of onlookers at the dig had swelled to at least sixty, maybe more, with yet more planning to come watch the spectacle on their lunch breaks. No one had wondered before why the Stephens children weren't there, given their ordeal, so the boy's arrival was that much more a surprise. He was so small! And so brave.

A crutch was the only visible sign of whatever had happened to the boy in the woods. Both the father and son had the haunted look of war veterans, and they stayed close to each other, but far from everyone else, standing in the shade of a live oak as old as the tobacco barn. Their shyness was understandable, after what they'd been through. (And the Stephens clan could be standoffish, so it was to be expected.)

Some of the onlookers speculated that Davie Stephens had dreamed it, and he'd found the burial site sleepwalking. Others were sure that the ghost of the Timmons boys had taken him by the hand and led him to the collapsed cellar. As for the reports of a wild animal attack, no one gave that much credence. ("That's just crazy talk.")

In any case, the Stephens boy's presence made the dig seem even more significant—perhaps, in a way, even historic. A few people grumbled about poor taste when Hal Lipcomb showed up selling roasted ears of corn and bags of pecans from a basket, but he sold plenty. If it felt more like a town fair, so be it. This wasn't something that happened every day.

"Don't you get your hopes up, Miss Essie," said the man with the old woman's umbrella. His name was Lee, and he loved his work; every old woman reminded him of his grandmother, who had raised him and whom he missed every day. He didn't want any more heartaches for Essie Timmons. He had warned her not to come. Not being from Gracetown, he didn't understand all the excitement about somebody claiming they'd seen a ghost.

Essie Timmons nodded, barely hearing him. Her eyes on the clods of falling dirt.

"The boy said so," she said.

One of Frank McCormack's sons, Sam, who had driven to the dig from his tax attorney's office in Tallahassee, sighed and ran his fingers through his sandy hair. Tobacco squirted from his teeth to the soil below. He noticed that he and his father were only two of a handful of white people at the gathering; his wife said that noticing such things made him a racist, but he noticed all the same. Lately, race was all anyone wanted to talk about, and Sam McCormack was so sick to death of it that he didn't care if he was racist or not.

"Reckon they'll find anything?" Sam McCormack asked.

Old Man McCormack shielded his eyes from the sun with his palm. He ventured a quick glance at Davie Stephens before his eyes went back to the dig. "He's the right age," he said. "For seeing 'em."

"Yeah, just right," his son said. "And it's summer."

Essie Timmons, far across the plot, whispered to her attendant: "He saw them. They're down there. He says they fell."

DAVIE HADN'T REALIZED how much he was considered a celebrity until he and his father arrived at the dig and people stepped aside to make way for them. He'd never experienced so many eyes on him, like a movie star. The hush following his every step felt as dreamlike as the shouts and screams he'd heard in the night.

Davie took his father's hand as he walked, like Neema would have. He felt eight years old again. Davie hadn't expected so *many* people either, like someone had sold tickets.

What if everyone ended up thinking he was a fool?

A hydraulic shovel was set up over a gaping hole, which reminded Davie of the hole he thought the Timmons boys had dug, with the dead dog lying beside it.

Thoughts of the dog made Davie shiver. He blocked the memory by watching the people picking through clumps of soil, and his heart caught when a young woman in a white college T-shirt pulled up something big enough to be a leg bone.

But it was just a heavy stick.

Davie's heart pummeled him. Maybe it hadn't been a good idea to come.

"We're here in Gracetown, Florida, at a most unusual community event," Dad said. Davie thought his father was talking to him, but when he looked up he saw that his father was shooting the video camera, panning across the crowd. "Three young boys have been missing for nearly one-hundred years, and these Gracetown residents believe the bones of those boys will be found. Here. Today. And they believe it because of ghosts."

"Hope you're not recording over mine," Davie said. Part of him knew he wouldn't care, in some ways. The video of that night only showed part of what had happened.

"Fresh tape. Yours is safely labeled, in the drawer."

Davie smiled. Dad was right: It felt safer to look at everything through a lens. Like someone else. His eyes followed his father's camera to the shell of a tobacco barn, nearly hidden within the trees. Next, two young boys buying roasted corn from a vendor. Girls climbing a tree. An old black woman sitting in a wheelchair under a caretaker's umbrella.

Dad put the camera down. "That's Essie Timmons, Davie," Dad said. "Those boys were her brothers. Do you want to go over and . . . ?"

Davie shook his head, mortified. He wouldn't be able to talk to her about the boys.

"That's okay," Dad said. "I only said it in case you wanted to. You've done plenty."

"Are you making a documentary?" Davie said.

Dad nodded. "Actually, *we* are, if that's okay with you. Forget a grant—we can get investors. A ghost story. Then I could take some time off."

"What for?" Davie said. He hoped Dad wasn't going to go off to hide in his work.

"To go to Ghana."

Davie was afraid he had heard wrong. "I thought you didn't want to go."

"Shouldn't we all be in one place?"

Davie nodded, blinking to keep his tears away. "Does Mom want you to come?"

"I think so," Dad said. The tic squinted his eye again. "We'll see."

That answer was a kick in the stomach, far from the assurances Davie had hoped for. But that was growing up, Davie figured. Gloves off. The bites are real.

The truth would have to do.

A workman wearing a red helmet popped up above ground to wave his flashlight frantically. *"Hold up!"* he said. His voice tremored with excitement. "Look at this!"

By then, in the middle of lunchtime, the crowd numbered more than a hundred.

The woods went silent as the machinery stopped. Miss Essie Timmons sat up straighter in her wheelchair than she had in years. Old Man McCormack began reciting the Lord's Prayer. Both of them were begging God for relief.

A faraway dog was barking, mostly yapping, but Davie and his father were probably the only two who noticed the sound. The barking raked across Davie's memories, sharp as teeth. Davie closed his eyes, feeling a lightheadedness he knew might make him faint.

That's not him. He's not real. He won't come out in daylight.

Slowly, Davie's heart slowed. His breath melted in his throat so he could swallow.

A sound traveled through the crowd Davie would never forget. A chorus of gasps first, almost one collective breath, then a continuous hum from one throat and chest to the next, some high, some low, a sound of depthless grief and boundless wonder. Davie felt his father's hands squeeze his shoulders hard, clenching so tight it hurt.

"God," his father said.

Davie opened his eyes to see what the people of Gracetown had found.

The workman climbed to the surface gingerly, cradling a calcified child's frame. The corpse was curled in rigor mortis, but intact. Muddied bones dangled, but didn't break. He was small. Maybe the youngest.

"Little Eddie!" Essie Timmons said, rising to her feet. Two miracles, side by side.

An old white man wearing a suit and tie walked to the old woman's wheelchair and leaned close to her ear. She nodded. He put his hand on her shoulder, and she patted it. Then the man walked away, toward a younger man who might be his son.

Dad kept his camera trained on Essie Timmons for a long time. When the worker brought the bones to her and she wiped away a tear, Davie heard his father suck in his breath.

It took two more hours to find the other two sets of bones, and they weren't intact like the smallest child's had been. Instead, they came up in pieces.

All Davie ever saw of Isaac was his skull, every tooth in place. Smiling, in a horrible way.

By that time, Davie was almost sorry he'd come. He would rather remember the Timmons boys as living, at least. Running. Trying to save each other.

Davie's thigh was killing him. He needed more pills. Besides, he noticed, it was three o'clock. Three was a long way from dusk, but he didn't want to take any chances. No way did he want to be in these woods anytime even close to dark.

"I'm ready," he told his father.

"You okay?"

"Yeah, just tired," Davie said, but that was a lie. He didn't know yet if he was okay. That would depend on whether Neema would ever again sleep through the night without screaming and crying. Or if either of them would ever pet a dog. Being okay depended on Dad. Or Mom. Or maybe all of them.

When he and his father started walking toward Dad's rental car parked at the edge of the orange Georgia clay road, everyone stopped what they were saying and doing, even the workers. Someone started clapping, and soon everyone was, a few of them hooting. Their applause rose into treetops that had been filled with screams so soon before. The prettiest girl Davie had ever seen—tall and dark, about thirteen, with a face like a girl from TV—grinned at him as if she had met him in her daydreams. Davie felt his face blush for the first time in his life.

His heart almost didn't give a cold shudder when he heard the faraway sound of the yappy dog's barking. He almost didn't wonder how he would ever sleep again.

⌐

This story and the previous one, "Summer," are a kind of odd prophecy: In 2013, I received a call from the Florida Attorney General's office informing me that my late mother, Patricia Stephens Due, had an uncle, Robert Stephens, who probably was among dozens of children buried on the grounds of the Dozier School School for Boys, a reform school in Marianna, Florida, where boys were tortured and killed for generations. I had never heard of the Dozier School, buried children, or Robert Stephens, my great-uncle who died there in 1937, at fifteen. But months later, my father, husband, son, and I would go to the excavation site in the woods in Marianna where University of South Florida researchers sifted through soil in search of bones—just like I had written in "Ghost Summer" five years earlier. Even my nine-year-old son, Jason, wore gloves and helped search the excavated soil. Jason was just the right age to help out, after all.

The eeriness of the coincidence makes me think it isn't a coincidence in the slightest.

The story was first published in The Ancestors, *edited by Brandon Massey. It received a Kindred Award from the Carl Brandon Society.*

The Knowing

But the hardest, the worst, was yet to come.
Letitia just knew it.

Free Jim's Mine

May 1838
Dahlonega, Georgia

"HE OUT YET?" Lottie's husband William breathed behind her, invisible in the dark.

Lottie's heart sped, a thumping beneath her breastbone that stirred the child in her belly.

"Don't know," Lottie said. "Hush."

She stared from her hiding place behind the arrowwood shrubs, heavy belly low to the soil. They had slipped past the soldiers at Fort Dahlonega, and now they were twenty yards west of the mine's gate, which stood open wide as miners escaped the cavern's mouth for the night. Shadowy figures ambled toward them, unaware.

Would she know her Uncle Jim in the dark? Lottie had not seen her father's brother in five years. Until then, he'd come to see mama two or three times a year after Lottie's father died. But now he was a freeman—the only free Negro she knew. Free Jim, everyone called him.

Mama said God shined light into his massa's heart one day and he wrote up Uncle Jim's freedom papers after church. But most said Uncle Jim bought a mojo and poured a powder with calamus, bergamot, and High John the Conqueror root in his massa's morning tea.

As tiny feet kicked at her, Lottie vowed she would name William's baby Freedom. If only she could find Uncle Jim and survive the night, they could all change their names.

A few white miners remained huddled at the gate while she waited and hoped to see Uncle Jim's beard or his shock of white-splashed hair. One by one, the miners untied their horses. About a dozen colored men emerged last, but they did not have horses. Instead, they shuffled down the road as fast as they seemed able, lanterns swinging. Uncle Jim, born a slave, had slaves working for him? *What makes you think he'll help you?* The forlorn call of a bullfrog hidden somewhere nearby reminded Lottie of swinging from a rope on a rotting oak branch, slowly to and fro.

They would not make it without Uncle Jim. Would not make it to the state line, or to the farmhouse in North Carolina where the Quakers would come fetch them. The last few days' horrid rain had stopped at last, but they would be cold tonight. Lottie couldn't remember when her clothes last had been dry.

"Go to 'em, William," Lottie said to William. "Say you lookin' for a few days' wages. Say you wanna talk to Free Jim." Panic made her voice sound twelve instead of seventeen.

"They'll know that's gum," William said.

Without the wagon, they had been forced to go to Uncle Jim in Dahlonega, where William had been reared. Cherokees weren't welcome since the Army started marching families off. William said he'd rather die running with her than let the white man choose his home.

"Whatever you gonna say, hurry and say it, Waya," she told him.

William's mother had given him a Cherokee name, Waya, though he used William outside of his boyhood home to set white men at ease. William pressed his palm to the side of her belly, head bowed. Then he stood and crept past the brush and up the road toward Lot 998—Free Jim Boisclair's mine.

The chatter at the mine entrance went quiet when William walked up. Lottie tried to hear, lying so still that she didn't brush away the insects that tickled her ankles and calves. But she couldn't hear a word over the bullfrog's warble, vexing her like a haint.

A sign, it was. A bad sign.

Then she heard the low, snapping bark that followed her into her dreams. Dogs were on their trail again! "Damn, damn, damn," she whispered to the dark.

Next, the men came. On the road, two white riders trotted north, their *clop-clopping* steady and loud. If not for the brush, she would be in plain view. The angry barking drew closer, crisper. And William was surer with his knife!

Lottie's frightened heartbeat shook the earth.

They would be found! Her eyesight dimmed. She would beg mercy from the slave-catchers. She was carrying a child, plain as day. One of them might have brains enough to realize that cow-hiding her might kill the child—and then what would they tell Marse Campbell about his lost property? She would never see William again; he would be sent away with his people. But he would not be alone. She'd wanted freedom, but at least she and her baby would live.

The plan was hard, but anything was better than dogs.

The riders stopped in the road, barely six strides from where she hid.

Two shadows walked from the mine's gate to meet the men, one carrying a lamp. Lottie saw the paunch of a man's middle beneath a brightly colored vest, pocket watch swinging. She had seen that pocket watch before. Please, Jesus, was he the one?

"Evenin'." Uncle Jim's voice! His pocket watch winked in the lamplight.

"Evenin'." The lead rider spoke in a manner reserved for other white men.

"Need you at the ice house. Injun'll stand watch here."

The riders circled Uncle Jim and William on their horses. Uncertain, it seemed.

"All right, then," the lead rider said after a long while. He made a kissing sound for his horse, and the second man followed him up the road. Lottie had never seen white men do what a nigger told them. Uncle Jim had a mojo for sure! *Had* to.

Uncle Jim thrust the lamp into the brush, his wide nose nearly pressed to hers. "You're damn fools. 'Specially *you*, Lottie."

Uncle Jim's first words to her in five years.

Five years ago, he'd told Mama he would keep his promise to his dead brother. He'd gone to the back door of Marse's house and tried to talk to him, even offered him a bank note, but Marse Campbell had turned him away. Lottie and mama both had cried themselves hoarse. Lottie had not, could not, forget Uncle Jim's last words to her.

Don't you fret, Lottie. I'll come back for you.

• • •

UNCLE JIM cursed a fury as he led her and William around a bluff on the brick-lined path to a wooden door. A preacher should know better than to blaspheme, and wasn't he a preacher? Wasn't he the one who'd taught her to read Scripture? Wasn't he the one who had left her in Augusta when he'd promised to buy her freedom?

Once the door was closed behind him, they walked a narrow corridor on a wood plank floor until Uncle Jim stopped at a door made half of glass. JAMES BOISCLAIR, the glass read in script so fancy she could barely make out the lettering.

Inside, he lit lamps and brought daylight to the small room. The desk buried in papers, bookshelves stuffed with books. Lottie hadn't realized she was shivering until Uncle Jim laid a warm blanket across her shoulders, and her trembling stopped.

"Look at you," Uncle Jim said. He'd fussed away his anger; now he only sounded sad. "You thought you'd get to the state line?"

"Got this far," Lottie said.

Uncle Jim's eyes lashed fire at William. "What are you going to do for her and a baby? *You?* She has kin in Augusta."

"Ain't his fault," Lottie said. "I wanted to come. Had to. I couldn't wait no more."

Marse Campbell had refused to let her take William as her husband. When her belly showed, he told her he would drown her half-breed baby if she gave him trouble. Drown her baby! William had been telling her she should run all along. He knew the roads and the woods. The first day she'd seen William, he'd sat perched in his driver's berth with the promise of faraway places.

"I saw a runaway notice in town!" Uncle Jim said, fingers twisting his beard. "Someone will piece it together. Those men you saw were not stupid men."

"We saw those crackers do what you told 'em," Lottie said. "Jumped right quick."

"Those," Uncle Jim said, "are white men who would turn in a stray Cherokee and his nigger runaway for a whole lot less than Campbell's reward. For shillings!"

Outside, the rain started its cruel pounding.

Uncle Jim went silent when William took a step to him. She hoped Uncle Jim would not lay hands on him. Her husband would show his knife.

"Jim Boisclair's a big man," William said. "The mercantile. Eating house. Ice house. And this gold mine. Jim Boisclair's got his name, Lottie. No time to fool with you. My uncle was a big man too—had a dozen slaves. Now where is he?"

"I know you," Uncle Jim said. "Injun Willie the driver. You've hauled for me. My men were wondering why you're not on your way to Ross's Landing with the rest. Or Tennessee. Where you gonna hide in Dahlonega?"

"It's *talon-e-ga*, not Dahlonega," William said. "You steal the word and destroy it."

"I ain't stole a damn thing," Uncle Jim said.

"Stealing from our grandfathers' mountain is nothing? Stealing land is nothing?"

Their words sounded like blows. It was all going terribly wrong.

"William, please," Lottie said.

"You're big enough to move the mountain," William said. "To take the gold. We ask a small thing from a big man."

When William glanced her way, Lottie begged him with her eyes: *Stop vexing him.*

"We jus' need a roof for the night," Lottie said. "We move on at daylight. William had a wagon, but we had to leave it cuz of the paddyrollers and all the soldiers on the road. We'll walk if we gotta, but if'n a body could ride us up closer to North Carolina . . . "

"Then why don't I snap my fingers and make pigs fly?" Uncle Jim said. "Didn't you hear me? I can't be seen with—"

"We could sleep in the mine."

Lottie wondered who'd said it, but it was her own tiny voice. From Uncle Jim's face, she might have said they should light themselves afire.

Uncle Jim shook his head. "It ain't fit, Lottie."

"Fit?" Lottie said. "What I care 'bout that? You think I'd rather be drug through the woods by dogs? Me an' my baby?" When she said *baby*, Uncle Jim cast his eyes to the floor.

William brushed his fingertip across the colorful book spines on Uncle Jim's shelf. "You afraid we're gonna steal your gold, big man?"

"Git away from there and mind your business," Uncle Jim said.

William reached up to a higher shelf, which was empty except for a small sack of burlap bound with twine. William took the sack and weighed it in his hand.

"*Don't touch that*," Uncle Jim said. He tripped over his rug rushing to William, knocking books to the floor as he snatched the sack away. He hid it beneath his shirt, his whole body shaking. "That's not for anyone but me to touch!"

Lottie had never laid eyes on a bag of luck before, but she was sure William had found Uncle Jim's. He kept his mojo in plain sight. He might have feathers or bones in the sack, or powders, or strands of his old massa's hair. She knew people who'd bartered food or shoes to heal maladies and turn a beau's head their way, or to wish ill luck on their masters, but she had never imagined such a mighty mojo. With so much power, could the creature who'd sold it to Uncle Jim be called human?

"What that cost you, Uncle Jim?" Lottie whispered.

Uncle Jim looked at her with tears, bottom lip quavering. "I can't help you, Lottie," he said. "It's not I don't want to, girl—I *can't*. Every time I do . . . when I try . . . it goes wrong. You hear me? *I'm* free. Just me. I can't share it with nobody else—even you. Especially you, girl. Don't you see?"

"You turnin' us away?" Lottie said. "To the dogs and patrollers?"

"Might be better," Uncle Jim said. "You hear? Might be better'n staying with me."

Lottie had seen survivors of dogs with rent limbs, missing eyes and ruined faces. She didn't want to believe dogs could be better than anything, even death, but the mine's stink seeped beneath the closed door; sour water full of rot.

"Told you he wouldn't help us," William said. He'd been wiping his hands on the seat of his pants since Uncle Jim took the bag of luck, as if his palms were sticky from its touch.

Lottie raised herself to her feet so fast that she felt dizzied.

"We gotta leave this place," Lottie said.

Uncle Jim's heartbroken eyes said, *Yes, thank the Lord you understand, child.* But his lips twitched, as if against his will, and his mouth said, "Into the cold night? The rain? How can I?"

That was how the plan was settled.

Before the first miners arrived at dawn, Uncle Jim would hire a wagon master he knew, an Irishman named Willoughby who had no fondness for slavery or the Cherokee relocation. Willoughby would drive them to the train—"I'll be up the whole night to devise the papers and think of a pretense!"—and try to ride with them as far as Charlotte. Uncle Jim would pay Willoughby handsomely for his silence and peril, greater than the advertised reward.

But arrangements would take until morning. A long night lay ahead.

"Tonight," Uncle Jim said, "you must sleep in the mine."

UNDER THE GROUND, Lottie met the purest lack of light she had ever known. Every step, it seemed, was blacker than the last.

Lottie steadied herself against the pocked wall, which felt as damp and slimy as a water snake. William stayed close to her, offering his hand, but instinct made her hold his arm instead. William wiped his unclean palms still, as if they itched from the bag of luck.

Uncle Jim's lamp was a poor defense. A flickering, sickly light.

"With the storms, the whole mine was flooded," Uncle Jim said. "Where we're going, water's still as high as your ankles. Higher, in some places. Lottie, mind where you walk. Don't get that dress wet."

Lottie's dress had been wet for two days. She would have laughed if she hadn't been so desperate to run back up the narrow steps as quickly as she could. She almost stepped on the dead, bloated rat at her feet, halfway under the water, a flash of light fur against the void.

"At least the flood killed the rats," Uncle Jim said. "But they're raising a stench."

"Water is good," William said. "It fools the dogs' noses."

Nothing was good about this water. No rainwater or creek bed carried the stench of the water in the mine. Lottie thought she might bathe for days and never be clean of it. She hoped the smell couldn't reach William's baby inside her, but it seemed all too certain her unborn could smell it too.

"Well . . ." Uncle Jim said. "You needn't worry about dogs down here." He huffed a breath when he said *dogs*.

"What, then?" Lottie said.

Uncle Jim looked back at her, his face and eyes invisible.

"Breaking your necks," he said. "Blowing yourselves to bits. Touch *nothing*, hear?"

The narrow cavern opened to release them to a wider space where a mining car smaller than a wagon sat on the tracks, empty and still. If only the Underground Railroad were truly underground, she thought. If only they could ride to freedom unseen by any human eyes.

"Where's the gold at?" Lottie said. The walls did not look golden.

"Deep in the rocks. T'ain't plain to the eye."

Black water pooled just beyond the mining car, shimmering tar in the light. Dripping echoed around them endlessly. Again, Lottie fought the urge to run.

"We ain't gonna drown down here, is we?" Lottie said.

"Not so long as you do as you're told and don't wander," Uncle Jim said. "Come on."

As he led them past the mining car, water seeped into her worn shoes, cold enough to tingle her toes. Water dripped just beyond her nose, and Lottie looked up: sharp rock formations like swords above them stood poised to fall and slice them in two. The next water droplet caught her eye, and she panicked as the cold stung and blinded her. With a gasp, she wiped her eyes clear. Her lungs locked tight until she could see Uncle Jim's lamp again.

William pointed to a narrow enclave, a shelter to their right. "Here?"

"No," Uncle Jim said. "Not far enough in. That's where the men crouch during the blasts. We'll find you another like it."

The corridor forked, and Lottie tried to map their location the way she did in the woods, but by the next fork she was confused. No landmarks guided her here.

The sloshing grew deafening as the floodwater rose to their shins. Lottie gathered her dress at her waist to try to avoid soaking it in stink. Mama had warned her not to stay wet, that she could get sick and die. But even though both she and Mama knew death might await her, Mama had said, *Yes, let*

William take you and that baby away. There ain't nothing for you here. Go see Jim at his gold mine. At least it's a chance.

But the longer Lottie walked, the less it seemed like any kind of chance. Death above or death below, it didn't matter—dying was dying. And Lottie felt death down here.

William gave a start, staring into the water near his feet. "Ya'll see that?"

"What?" Lottie said.

William probed the water with his foot. "I saw . . . something."

"Quit your daydreaming," Uncle Jim said, but he sounded frightened. He still had the bag of luck snugly beneath his shirt. Holding it tight.

The water was higher now, at her knees. The damp fabric she carried was a heavy load. Her shins hurt from walking downhill, and the baby's bulk nearly toppled her with each step.

"What that bag do, Uncle Jim?" Lottie said. She raised her voice to be heard over their steady wading. "How you get it? Can I get one too?"

Uncle Jim faced her. The lamplight aged his face, made his eyes appear to burrow into his skin. His transformation startled her. "Stop that talk."

"You say when you try to help, it always go wrong," Lottie said. "How it go wrong?"

"You got to sell your heart for freedom, Lottie," Uncle Jim said. "Just like me."

"We're not like you," William said.

"Sure you are, red man. I've been watching them round up your people. Soldiers come knocking at the door, don't give nobody time to gather clothes. Everything you had is gone. They take the children in one wagon, the parents in the other, just to make sure nobody runs. You think they dreamed that up special for you? The ones who run—well, they don't listen to their hearts, do they? Their hearts are cold as ice."

Lottie blinked away tears. She tried not to think of Mama getting lashed because Marse Campbell would never believe she didn't know where her daughter had run to. Tried not to think about how Mama would never see her first grandchild. And that was just the best of what might come. Lottie's shaking started again, her knees knocking like clapping hands. In a few steep footsteps, the water reached above her thighs; dark slime in her most unwanted places.

"How it gonna go wrong for us, Uncle Jim?" Lottie said.

When Uncle Jim was silent for a time, she gave up on having an answer. And when he spoke, she wished he hadn't.

"It always goes wrong, girl," Uncle Jim said. "Don't get it in your heads you'll both make it up to North Carolina—and then what? Philadelphia? You're fools if you think this ends well. You never should've come. Think of the last words you want to say to each other, and be sure to say 'em quick. You won't both survive the night."

THEY HAD TO stoop to enter the boxy blast enclave.

In the far back corner, the water didn't creep as high. A narrow, uneven ledge was raised enough for them to sit out of the stinking muck. Lottie hoped the water would drop by morning. Uncle Jim had said it might—if the rain let up. She couldn't tell if it was raining outside, but it was surely raining *inside*. The only sounds were the chorus of dripping water and Uncle Jim's sing-song prayer as he walked back up to the world above.

" . . . Lord, take pity on your poor servants on this long night . . . " she heard his voice echo through the passageway. The words collided and faded, but she could make them out well enough to feel the prayer move her spirit. "Do not punish this poor shepherd, Lord, for we all have suffered enough. Do not punish the innocent, Lord, for all they desire is the freedom to serve you better . . . "

Every few words, his voice hitched in a sob. He was the very sound of despair.

Then it was a faraway whisper.

Then he was no voice at all.

All around her, the dark.

Uncle Jim had given them two lamps, but the two-hundred miles since Augusta had taught them to save kerosene for dire necessity. They had checked their matchsticks before blowing out the lamps, and while Lottie's had gotten wet in her pouch somehow, William had kept his dry. Lottie had fewer possessions now than ever. Before this night, she had never wanted for moonlight or air to breathe.

But Lottie was glad for the dark, since she didn't want William to see her tears. He was helpless to soothe her, so why should they punish each other? She huddled against the best man she knew, hearing Uncle Jim's prayer in her mind, rubbing her belly.

Uncle Jim had said that in the morning he would give them a treasure chest in the Irishman's wagon: dry clothes, a packed traveling bag, food, boxes of matches, a new compass. And money—how much she could only guess, if Uncle Jim's hired man didn't steal it first.

Neither of them had a timepiece, but she thought it had to be ten o'clock. At least.

In seven hours, Uncle Jim would come back for them. Seven hours. Seven years, it might as well be. But he would come. He *would* come, this time.

Seven hours, Lord. Let them last seven hours.

Don't let her mother's lashes be for nothing. Don't let William's grandmother's cries in her sickbed when the soldiers came be for nothing. Let it all matter for something.

Unless he means to drown you both here. For your own good.

And didn't he? Hadn't she heard his soul's guilt in his weepy prayer?

Lottie couldn't swallow away her sob, and William slid his palm against her hot cheek, all tenderness. Did he know it too? Did he know Uncle Jim had sent them into the mine to die?

Loud splashing flew toward them. Gone as soon as they heard it.

They sat closer, their bodies hard as stone. The splashing had come from directly outside the mouth of their enclave. Had Uncle Jim come back so soon? No more than half an hour could have passed.

"Uncle?" she whispered.

William covered her mouth with the palm. His heartbeat pulsed through his skin.

The next splash sounded like two limbs colliding. Then an undulating motion, one spot to the next. And sudden, impossible silence. They could be back out in the forest, jumping at bears and bobcats.

"That ain't a man," William said. "Didn't I say I saw somethin'? He saw it too."

"What it look like?" Lottie said. "A snake?"

"Too big for a snake," William said. "Too wide. Can't say what it looked like, but it wasn't no fish or snake. It looked 'bout as long as me."

"It's a man, then," Lottie said. "Somebody chasin' us."

"No," William said. "Not a man."

William calmly struck a match and lit his lamp. In the brightness, colored circles danced across Lottie's eyes.

Her vision snapped to focus when she heard the splash again. The creature was beyond the poor reach of their lamp, but she could hear its size—the front end slapping the water first, then the back. Like William said, as long as a man. But maybe wider. Beyond reason, she expected a bloodhound to come flying from the water, teeth gnashing.

William sucked in a long breath.

"You see it?" Lottie said.

William shook his head, waving his lamp slowly back and forth across the water.

Lottie's heart tried to pound free of her. "Maybe it's a gator!"

"No," William breathed. He stayed patient with his lamp's spotlight, which showed only brown flecks floating in the murk.

"What, then?" Lottie said.

"As a boy," he said quietly, "I heard stories about Walasi. A giant frog. My mother told me, her mother told her, her mother's mother, through time. To the beginning."

Ain't no damned frog that big, Lottie's mind tried to tell her, but she remembered the bullfrog's call she'd heard outside. An omen after all.

William pointed left. "Look there," he said, calm beyond reason.

Ripples fluttered in the lamplight. Then a frothy splashing showered them. Lottie screamed, but did not close her eyes. She wanted to see the thing. A silhouette sharpened in the water, like giant fingers stretching, or a black claw. Her hands flew to cover her eyes, but she forced her fingers open to peek through.

The creature churned the water, tossing its massive body. A shiny, bulging black eye as large as her open palm broke the water's plane, nestled by brown-green skin. Lottie screamed.

The creature flipped, its eye gone. Was this its belly? Pale beneath the water, smooth as glass. Too big to be anything she could name. The mine's thin air seared her lungs.

"Did you see it?" William's grin made him look fevered. His eyes seemed as wild and wide as the water creature's. "The frog?"

It can't be, she tried to say, arguing with her eyes. But her mouth would not move.

Lottie was whimpering, a childish sound she hadn't made since the day Marse Campbell turned Uncle Jim away. She sat as far back as she could from the water, her arms locked around her knees. Her bones trembled as she rocked.

William whipped off his tattered shirt. His readied knife gleamed.

"Leave it be!" she said.

"Any child knows about Walasi, but no one has seen him. And now . . . here he is!" William's excitement unsettled Lottie. "Walasi tries to kill everyone in the village. But a warrior slays him."

Lottie felt a fear deeper than the mine's darkness. Maybe Uncle Jim's mojo had confused his mind. Had that come of touching it?

"Waya . . . " She called him by his mother's name, hoping he would hear her.

William clasped her upper arm and squeezed. His face wore an eerie grin. "When the warrior kills Walasi, it turns to little frogs. Harmless. They scatter. The village is saved."

"All your people is gone far away," Lottie said. "You ain't got no village. Ain't nothin' you can do!"

"What else should I do, dear Lottie?" he said. "Should I run and hide like a boy?

He laid his head across her belly, and she breathed him up and down. Lottie tried to summon words to bring sense to him, but she had no strength to speak.

Then he slipped from her, holding tight to his knife. He dove into the black water.

Lottie screamed. "*Waya!*"

Endless silence, except for the dripping water.

Every evil Lottie could dream felt certain: The creature was pulling strips of her husband's flesh with its teeth, far worse than any dog. And it would come to take her next. It would tear the baby from her and scatter its limbs. Uncle Jim had bargained his freedom with a curse. He had sacrificed them.

The world spun, the mine's darkness fighting to take her thoughts too. She felt dizzy enough to faint, but she could not. Could *not*. Lottie kept her mind awake by counting off in her head as she waited for William to pop up from the water. . . . *eleven . . . twelve . . . thirteen . . . fourteen . . .*

William could hold his breath a long time. He swam like a fish in the pond near the road where he drove past Marse Campbell's farm once a month. Showing off for her.

Thirty-five . . . thirty-six . . . .thirty-seven . . . thirty-eight . . .

Lottie stood as close to the water's lapping edge as she dared, using William's lamp to try to see. She tried calling both of his names. After a time, fingers shaking, she lit the second lamp too. His absence only grew brighter. The water lay still and silent.

Ninety-one . . . ninety-two . . . ninety-three . . .

"No . . . " Lottie whispered. "No . . . "

At five hundred, she stopped counting.

She felt too breathless to sob. Even tears shunned her misery.

How could she have let William go? Why hadn't she let him drag her down with him How dare he go to freedom without her!

Time passed uncounted. Lottie only realized she had slept when the water woke her with a start.

Just beyond her haven, something was moving—a steady gliding from one side to the next, back and forth. But even bleary-eyed, confused and sick with sorrow, Lottie knew the sound was not from William. No man could glide so quickly or make such a sound.

Her lanterns made no impression on the water's void, showing her nothing.

"*Git on away from me!*" she shrieked at the dark, as if monsters heeded commands.

The water's splashing told her that the creature still lurked. Watching her? Preparing to make her and her baby its next meal?

"You give me my husband back!"

She tried to shout again, but her throat's tatters produced only a whisper, more frightened than angry.

How had she forgotten her knife? She prized the ivory-handled penknife William had given her as a wedding gift, of sorts, when they decided they would run. Their time in the woods had dulled the blade from too much hacking and cutting, but she still had it. The knife was all that remained of William now.

Lottie grasped her knife and held it out like a sword toward the churning water. Like her, the blade was weak and small, but she wielded it as if they both had greater power.

"You hear me?" she said, and this time her voice was stronger too.

The thing in the water did hear. It swam closer to her, splashing water over the ledge in its huge wake. Lottie had not believed she could feel greater terror, but the advancing creature awakened such a childlike fear in her that she wanted to cover her eyes.

But she did not. Arm outstretched with her knife, she watched. And waited.

The bulbous eye appeared again before the water swallowed the sight of it, much closer than it had been before. Gone before she could lunge at it. Then came a wet slapping on the stone as the creature hoisted itself nearer to her with shiny green-brown skin. It was not a claw, nor a human hand, but a large and sinister blending of the two that fanned across the ledge as if to reach for her.

Lottie had no time to scream. She stabbed at the closest—digit?—and hacked at it, feeling euphoria when a piece of the creature fell separate from the rest. The creature howled, muffled under the water, and the limb retreated to escape her, snatched away. Lottie kicked the cursed tendril away from her, back into the black pool.

Her laughter was not true laughter—just a desperate, gasping cackle—but the sound of it filled the cave. Then Lottie collapsed into sobs that joined the chorus of falling water droplets from above.

Drip-drip. Drip-drip.

A plan came to Lottie. With a plan, she stole shallow breaths. Her sobbing eased.

She would stay away from the water.

Drip-drip.

She would teach their child his father's Cherokee name. *Drip-drip.*

She would teach their child that Waya's family had lived in peace along the Etowah River before soldiers took them away. *Drip-drip.*

She would feed their child the corn and hickory nuts Waya loved so much, alongside Mama's corn cakes. *Drip-drip.*

Minutes passed, then hours, while Lottie made her plans for freedom that she would win at such an unfathomable cost.

"Lottie? You still here?"

When a voice came, Lottie shrieked. Hope swelled in her. But, no.

Not William. Not Waya.

Had she slept again? Her body was stiff against the stone.

Hours must have passed. Lamplight swayed in the passageway. The water had receded to a thin sheet. She smelled pipe tobacco. Her uncle's shadow floated on the wall.

"We got to hurry, girl."

Uncle Jim did not ask about William. He was not surprised her husband was gone.

"Waya," she whispered to the ravaged cave.

"Come on, Lottie—my man's outside waiting."

As Free Jim reached for her, his two gold rings flared like droplets from the sun.

His pinkie finger, a bloodied crust, was freshly sliced away.

~~

I wrote this for a former student, Daniel José Older, and Rose Fox for the wonderful anthology Long Hidden: Speculative Fiction from the Margins of History. *The story was inspired by a trip to a gold mine in Dahlonega, Georgia, where I first heard that a black man had owned a local gold mine. The mine was called Free Jim's Mine, and he was indeed named James Boisclair. During my research, I learned that the little-known Georgia gold rush displaced the Cherokee people and set them on the Trail of Tears. The rest is entirely fiction.*

The Knowing

OUR TEACHER said one day that knowledge is power, and I had to raise my hand even though I don't like to; I like to sit and be quiet and watch people and wait for lunchtime. But I had to ask him if he was sure about that, or if maybe knowledge isn't just a curse. He asked me what I meant by that, and I said, Hey, that's what my mama always says. Knowing is her curse, she whispers, touching my forehead at night softly with her long fingers, like spiders' legs. Sometimes I wake up in the middle of the night and she's there whispering and rocking me. But I didn't tell my teacher that part. I could tell from the way my teacher looked at me sideways and went on with his lesson that he thought I was trying to be a smart-ass. People always think you're something you don't want to be. Mama says that, too.

I like this school in Chicago all right because my math teacher is real pretty, with long legs and a smile that means what it says. But me and Mama won't be here long. I know that already. I was in six different schools last year. It's always the same; one day I walk into wherever we're staying and she looks up at me through her cigarette smoke and says, "Throw your things in a bag." That must mean the rent hasn't been paid, or somebody got on her nerves, or maybe she's just plain sick of being wherever we are. I don't say anything, because I know if she stays unhappy too long, she'll start throwing things and screaming at the walls and the police might come and put me in foster care like that time in Atlanta. I was gone six months, staying with these white people who were taking care of six other boys. Mama almost lost me that time. When the judge said she could take me back, I smiled in the courtroom so he wouldn't see how mad I was at Mama, but I hate it when she acts like she's the kid instead of me. I didn't speak to her for a whole week, and when I did, I said to her, "Damn, Mama, you gotta do better than that." I meant it, too.

And she promised she would. She really tries. Things will be really cool for a while, better than cool, and then I walk through the door and see that look on her face and those Marlboro Lights or whatever she smokes when she's in a smoking mood, and I know we're moving again. I guess she feels like she'll be all right if she just runs away from it, as if you could run away from your own head.

I wish Mama wouldn't smoke dope. It freaks her out. She goes up and down the stairs and walks through the halls wailing and sobbing, pounding on people's doors and shouting out dates. March 12, 2003. September 6, 2006. December 13, 2020. I have to find her and bring her back to the apartment to listen to Bob Marley or Bunny Wailer, something that calms her down. I hug her tight and, when she sobs, I can feel her shaking against me. Those are the times I have to be the grown-up. It's all right, Mama, I say.

"Nicky," she says to me in a little girl's voice, "I ain't only telling. I make it happen. When they ask me, I say, okay, you're October fifteenth, you're February eighth. I'm doin' the deciding, Nicky. It's me. Ain't it? Ain't it?"

She gets like that on dope, thinking she's God or something. I have to keep telling her, "Mama, it ain't you. Knowing ain't the same as deciding. *TV Guide* don't decide what's on TV."

Then, if I'm lucky, she'll get a smile on her face and go to sleep. If I'm unlucky, she'll keep crying and go back running through the halls and one of the neighbors will call the police. That's what happened in Atlanta. They thought she was crazy, so they locked her up and took me away. Lucky for her, the doctor said nothing was wrong with her.

But he didn't know what she knows.

In Miami Beach, the last place we lived, our apartment was upstairs from a botanica, which is where the Cubans go to find statues of saints and stuff like that, trying to make magic. Mama took one look at that place and almost busted out laughing. She doesn't believe in statues, she says. But she was real nice to the owner, Rosa, who mostly spoke Spanish. Mama told Rosa what she does, what she knows. It took the lady three or four times to understand Mama, and then she didn't want to believe her. "El día que la gente van a morir?" Rosa asked, frowning. You could tell she thought Mama was trying to scam her.

Mama sucked on her teeth, getting impatient. She looked back toward an old lady in the back of the shop who was checking out some oils in small glass bottles on a shelf. The lady was breathing hard, walking real slow. Mama can smell sick people, no lie. Mama leaned close to Rosa's ear. "You know that lady?" Mama asked her.

Rosa nodded. "Sí. My aunt," she said. "Está enferma."

"She's gonna die soon. Real soon."

Rosa looked offended, her face glowing red like a dark cherry. She turned away from Mama, straightening up some of the things on her shelves. You should have seen all that stuff; she had clay pots and plates and cauldrons and beads and tall candles inside glasses with holy people painted on them, even a candle that's supposed to burn fourteen hours. And there were teas labeled Te de Corazón and Te de Castilla. I always pay attention when I'm in a new place. I like to see everything.

"Listen," Mama said to Rosa, trying to get her attention. "You know your days of the week in English? Remember Friday. That lady back there gonna die on Friday." Mama held up two fingers. "Friday in two weeks. Viernes. Nicky, how you say two weeks in Spanish?"

"Dos . . . " I had to think a few seconds " . . . semanas."

Rosa stared at me, then at Mama's two fingers, then dead into Mama's eyes. From her face, it was like Rosa couldn't tell if she wanted to me mad, scared, or sad. People always look like at Mama that way.

"Then you come upstairs and get me," Mama said. "I want to work here."

I had forgotten all about Rosa and her botanica when someone knocked on our door on a Sunday morning. Mama was out getting groceries and I was watching cartoons on the black-and-white TV Mama had bought from a thrift shop for twenty dollars. It only got two channels, but one of the channels showed the Road Runner on Sundays, and that's my favorite. Rosa was standing there in our doorway, dressed up in black lace. I almost didn't recognize her because she was wearing lipstick and had her face made up to look nice even though her eyes were sad. It took me a second to remember she must be on her way to her aunt's funeral.

"Mama's not here," I said.

"When she come, you tell her for me, no?" Rosa said. "Tell her she say truth. She say truth."

I wanted to close the door. I was missing the best part, where Wile E. Coyote straps the rocket to his back so he can fly. He always crashes in the end, but at least he flies for a little while. "So, does she have a job or what?" I asked her.

Rosa nodded.

Cool, I thought. Whenever Mama has a job, there's always a little extra money for candy bars and T-shirts and movies and stuff. Mama only works because of me, because she likes to buy me things like other kids. I felt a little guilty, though. In Miami Beach, I knew I'd better enjoy Mama's new job while it lasted. She could never work long before she had to run away.

At the botanica, Rosa put a sign up in the window saying she had a psychic inside, and she told people they could go back into the storeroom, past the colorful curtain, to talk to Mama. The thing is, Rosa got it all wrong at first. She was saying Mama could tell people if their husbands were cheating or if they would get a raise at work, the kind of lame stuff they see on TV commercials. Mama just shakes her head and tells people she knows one thing, one thing only—and when she says what it is, some of them really do turn pale, like ghost-pale. Then they stand up as if she smells bad and they're afraid to stand too close to her.

At Rosa's botanica, Mama didn't get too many customers at first. But it was still kind of nice because she and Rosa started becoming friends, even though they could barely talk to each other. I like Mama to have friends. When Mama wasn't helping at the cash register, most of the day she'd sit back there watching TV or playing cards with me. Sometimes, when there weren't any customers, Rosa would come back with us and watch Spanish-language soap operas. I liked to watch them, too, because you don't need to know Spanish to understand those. Someone's cheating on somebody. Somebody's pissed about something. Mama and Rosa would laugh together, and Rosa would explain some parts to Mama: "He very bad man," she would say in her sandpapery voice, or "That woman no married to him." But Rosa didn't need to do that, because most things don't need words. Most things you can see for yourself.

So one day there was a thunderstorm, and Rosa was shaking her head as stood in front of her store window staring out at the dark clouds. Lightning turned on the whole sky with a flash, then it was black again, and the thunder sounded like a giant boulder being rolled across the clouds. Miami Beach has the best storms I've ever seen, but Rosa was only letting herself see the scary parts.

"I get killed to drive in that," Rosa said.

Mama grinned. "No you won't. Not today." Mama's grin was so big, Rosa looked at her real close. I could see Rosa's face change, the corners of her lips lying flat.

"Ain't nothin' to worry about. You got a long ways. You want to know?" Mama said.

"No," Rosa said through tight lips. All of a sudden, she didn't sound like Mama's friend anymore; she sounded like her boss-lady. She waved her hand in Mama's face. "No. No."

Mama shrugged, trying to pretend she wasn't hurt. She was just trying to be nice. But that's how it is, because nobody wants the only thing Mama knows how to give away.

It took a week at the botanica before even one customer decided to hear what Mama had to say. I liked that lady. She was brown-skinned and young, and she touched me on my shoulder when she passed me in the doorway instead of looking right past me like most people do. Maybe if I'd been older, I would have wanted to ask her out on a date. Or she could have been my sister, maybe.

"Are you the psychic?" she asked Mama. She had some kind of island accent, who knows what. Everyone in Miami was like us, from somewhere else.

Mama wasn't in a how-can-I-help-you-today kind of mood. "You want a psychic? Then you need to call one of them stupid-ass telephone services and waste your money to hear what you want. I only got one thing to tell." Then Mama told her what her specialty was.

But the woman didn't run away, and she didn't look scared. She just made her eyes narrow and stared at my mother like she couldn't quite see her. "Are you telling the truth?"

"I ain't got time for lies," Mama said.

"Then I want to know. How much?"

The price is usually twenty dollars for people Mama likes, a hundred for people she doesn't. She asked this woman for twenty, exact change. You always have to pay first. That's the rule. Then Mama makes you sit across from her at the card table, she takes an index card from her pile, and she scribbles a date in pencil, just like that. She doesn't have to close her eyes or hold your hand or whisper to Jesus. It's nothing like that at all.

"Now," Mama said, holding the card up so the woman couldn't see what she'd written, "I'ma tell you from experience, this ain't the best time to look at this, not right now. Some folks like to go where there's lots of light, or nice music, or where you got somebody you love. This ain't nothin' to share with strangers. That means me, too. Save it for when you're ready."

But when Mama gave her the card, the woman held it in her palms like a shiny seashell and stared down, not even blinking. I saw her shoulders rise up, and she let out a breath that sounded like a whimper. I wished she'd listened to Mama, because it makes me feel bad when people cry.

But this woman, when she stood up to leave, she was smiling. A smile as long as a mile. This time, when she walked past me, she pressed her palm against my cheek. She made me smile, too.

When she was gone, Mama clapped her hands twice and laughed. "Look at that! That girl is something else." Mama is always so happy when she doesn't make people afraid.

"She's gonna be an old-timer, huh?" I said. Mama shook her head. "No, child. Ten years almost to the day. May fourth," she said, her face bright like it hadn't been in a long time.

I didn't get it at first. The woman was so young, like in her twenties. How could she be happy to have ten years left? But then I thought, maybe she was sick with something really bad, and she thought she was a goner already. To her, maybe ten years was like a whole new life.

It's weird. I've seen grown men with gray hair and deep lines in their faces drop to their knees and cry after Mama told them they had twenty-five years. No lie. Maybe they thought they had forever, and Mama's telling them the day, month, and year just made it real. And then there are people like this lady, so young and pretty, with no time left at all, and they walk out smiling like it's Christmas. Those people are my favorite kind.

• • •

MAMA SAYS she wasn't born knowing. She says she just woke up one morning when she was sixteen, looked at her family at the breakfast table, and knew. She knew her father was going to drop dead of a heart attack in January, in three years, after giving a Sunday sermon. She knew her mother was going to live to be ninety just like her great-aunt. She knew her brother, Joe, was going to get killed in an Army accident in 1987, and her sister was going to get shot to death by her boyfriend in 1999. She says she just ran to her room and cried, because all that knowing hurt her heart.

Then, it started coming true. Mama says her father dropped dead of a heart attack after giving the sermon the first Sunday after New Year's, in January, and her mother treated Mama like it was her fault. Same when the phone call came about Mama's brother, my dead uncle Joe.

Mama wanted to hide her knowing, but right after her father died like she said he would, people started coming to the house to see her. Because some people—maybe they're just weird, or they're less scared than other people—think knowing is power. Just like my teacher said. But Mama doesn't feel that way, not at all. A curse, she calls it. She has all this knowing, but there's nothing she can do to stop it once she knows. Even if she prays and fasts, it doesn't change anything. My dead uncle Joe never even joined the Army because Mama begged him not to, but he got run over by a car on the exact day she said in 1987 anyway, the same year I was born.

Nobody can cheat it, except maybe the other way. Mama knew a boy in high school who got her to tell him how old he would be on the day it would happen, and she said he would be seventy-two. Then, he decided to act stupid and jump off the top bleacher at the football stadium like he was Superman, and he broke his neck. Mama saw it happen, and he was dead on the spot when he was only eighteen. That was the only time Mama was wrong.

Mama told me she had to think about that a long, long time. That was when she left home for good, and she spent more than a year thinking about how she got the date wrong for that one boy. Then, she decided on an answer: Maybe it'll happen faster if you make it happen on purpose, but it never happens later. The day is the day, and that's all there is to it. That's what Mama says.

Mama never had a boyfriend or anything, not the kind of boyfriend who gives you flowers on your birthday or takes you to the movies. She never even knew my Daddy's name. Some people might not tell their children something like that, but Mama will say all kinds of things. She tells me she was an ugly child coming up, always sassing back and running around where she wasn't supposed to be, sticking her nose in grown folks' business, and the knowing came as her punishment. God don't like ugly, she always tells me. She says that to scare me into acting right so I won't get punished the way she did, but that doesn't scare me. I wouldn't mind knowing the way she knows. I'd find a way to get rich from it instead of letting it drive me crazy like Mama does.

Grandmama is sixty-eight now. She still lives in the same house in Macon, all alone, and most of the time she won't return Mama's calls, not since Auntie Ree got shot by her boyfriend. Everyone tried to warn Auntie Ree because her boyfriend used to beat her up, but then again, it wouldn't have made a difference anyway, just like with my dead uncle Joe. Mama saw how it would all happen.

I always call Grandmama collect once a month, no matter where we are. She picks up the phone if she hears my voice on her answering machine, but she won't talk to Mama except by accident. The way I see it, Grandmama's husband is dead and two of her children are gone, too, so I think she's only mad because Mama told her she still has so long to wait.

THE DAY we had to move from Miami Beach, I'd just aced a math test, no lie. I had the second-highest score in the class—answers come to me easy if I think hard enough—and on the way home from school, I was looking at the palm trees through the school bus window, thinking it would be snowing if we were still living in Detroit like we did last winter. And when I walked through the door, Mama was sitting there on the sofa with a Marlboro Light. Damn.

"We're moving on," she said. "Pack a bag."

Her face was damp, and there were little wads of toilet paper all over the floor, like if there had been a parade. She'd been crying all day while I was in school again. "You ain't working today?" I asked her, hoping it wasn't what I thought. I like new places, but I didn't want to leave that time. Not already.

"I been fired. So we're moving."

"Rosa fired you, Mama? How come?"

Mama's face turned hard, and she dragged on her cigarette, sucking it like reefer smoke. "We had a fight," Mama said. She blew the smoke out while she talked. "She didn't have no right to say what she said. 'Bout how I need help to take care of you right, I need to call Big Brothers or some mess, how I can't give you things like you need. You ain't none of her goddamn business."

The funny thing is, I always wondered what it would be like to be in Big Brothers, to have some dude who wears a suit to his job every day come play ball with me on weekends. It's not the same as a daddy, but it's better than nothing. But it's too bad for Rosa that she said that, because Mama gets pissed when people say she can't take care of me, especially after Atlanta. And she always has the last word in a fight. Once she gets mad, there's no keeping her quiet.

"So you told her?"

"Just go throw your things in a bag, Nicky."

"I don't want to leave here, Mama. Dang," I whined. I sounded like a baby, but I didn't care. "Tell her you lied, you're sorry. Tell her you just made it up."

I could see her hand holding the cigarette was shaking. Whenever Mama smokes a cigarette, she always seems like she's about to drop it. New tears were running down her face. "I don't know why I said that to Rosa. That wasn't right. Maybe she didn't mean nothin' by it, but she made me so mad, talking about you."

I sat next to her on the couch and reached for her hand. She wouldn't squeeze back. "Tell her it didn't mean nothing. We don't have to move just because of that. That ain't nothing."

"No, Nicky . . . " Mama whispered. "Telling to hurt somebody is the worst thing a person can do. Even the devil couldn't do nothing worse."

I'd seen Mama acting crazy for sure, running around in her underclothes, screaming at anybody who could hear, but I'd never seen her quiet. That scared me more than it would have if she'd been throwing pots and pans on the floor. She sounded different.

I got mad all of a sudden. "Shoot, Mama, forget Rosa. Who does she think she is, trying to say you can't take care of me? Nobody asked her."

Mama laughed a little and stared at the floor.

"You are taking care of me, Mama. Better than anybody."

"Sure am . . . " Mama said, still not looking up at me. "I got to . . . until May twelfth."

"Two thousand five," I said, squeezing her hand again, and Mama just closed her eyes.

Until right then, when I heard myself say it, the date had seemed so far away. I'd always known I would be fifteen that year, but I'd never stopped to think it was only three years away. It wasn't so far off anymore.

We left Miami Beach, which is too bad because it's so alive there. There are so many people who sing and dance and laugh and act like every day is the only one left. I wish we could have stayed there. Even in November, it's already freezing in Chicago, and people are dressing warm, walking fast, waiting for spring to come. In a cold place, there's no such thing as today, just tomorrow. Will it snow tomorrow? Will it be sunny tomorrow? But Mama said she couldn't face Rosa, so we jumped on a bus and stopped riding when we got bored. This time, we stopped in Chicago. But there's never really anywhere to go.

I guess Mama felt so bad about what she said to Rosa because it reminded her of all the times before when she'd lost her temper and said what she doesn't mean to say. I don't think she can help it. I was only six when she did it to me, even though I don't remember what I did that made her so mad in the first place. I was little, but I never forgot what she said: "I'll be through with your foolishness on May twelfth, 2005, because that's your day, Nicky. You hear?"

I told a friend once, a kid named Kalil I had just started hanging out with at my school in Atlanta, after he told me about something bad that had happened to his family in the country where they came from. We were just standing on the playground, and we told our worst stories. His story had soldiers; mine was only about Mama and May 12, 2005.

That was the only time anyone ever looked at me the way people always look at Mama. But the thing I like most about kids is that even though they get scared like anybody else, they can forget they're scared pretty fast. Especially kids like Kalil, who know there's more to the world than video games and homework. I guess that made us alike. He hardly waited any time at all before he said, "Does that bother you?" Just like that.

I'd never thought about that before. We were both ten then, so fifteen was five years off, half my whole life, and by that time, I'd be in high school, nearly a man. A whole different person. I told him I didn't think it bothered me. When you grow up around someone like Mama and you hear about it all the time, you know everybody has a turn, and you just try to find something interesting every day to make you glad it hasn't happened yet.

That's why I didn't mind it in Miami Beach when the TV only got two channels—see, I don't need more than two channels, as long as there's something I can watch. I'll watch the evening news and soap operas in English or Spanish or even golf, if Tiger Woods is playing. Hell, I don't even mind when we don't have a TV, which we usually don't. I read comic books and books from the library and take walks and watch people. Kalil said he wouldn't go to school if he were me, but I don't mind. There's always something interesting somewhere, even at school. Like the way my math teacher smiles, when you can see her whole heart in it. I don't think anyone in my class has noticed that except me.

"You're really brave, Nicky," Kalil told me in Atlanta. I don't feel brave but I do think about it sometimes. I wonder how it'll go down, if it will hurt when it happens, or if I'll be crossing the street and a car will come around a corner all of a sudden like with my dead Uncle Joe. Or maybe I'll see someone getting robbed and I'll get shot like Auntie Ree when I try to stop the bad guy, and someone will say I was a hero. That would be best. I wonder if it'll happen even if I stay in bed that day and never leave my room, or if I'll just get struck by lightning while I'm staring out of my window at the greatest storm I've ever seen. I never get sick, so I don't think it'll be that. I think it'll be something else, but I'm not sure what.

Even Mama says she doesn't know.

⌒

This was originally published in Gumbo: A Celebration of African American Writing, *co-edited by the dear, late E. Lynn Harris and Marita Golden to benefit the Hurston/Wright Foundation whose mission is to discover, mentor, and honor black writers. This story speaks to the fear of mortality that underlies much of my work. Nicky's mature perspective on his own brief life gives me strength.*

After all, we are not here nearly long enough . . . and each of us is waiting for our Day.

Like Daughter

I GOT THE CALL in the middle of the week, when I came wheezing home from my uphill late-afternoon run. I didn't recognize the voice on my computer's answer-phone at first, although I thought it sounded like my best friend, Denise. There was no video feed, only the recording, and the words were so improbable they only confused me more: "Sean's gone. Come up here and get Neecy. Take her. I can't stand to look at her."

Her words rolled like scattered marbles in my head.

I had just talked to Denise a week before, when she called from Chicago to tell me her family might be coming to San Francisco to visit me that winter, when Neecy was out of school for Christmas vacation.

We giggled on the phone as if we were planning a sleepover, the way we used to when we were kids. Denise's daughter, Neecy, is my godchild. I hadn't seen her since she was two, which was a raging shame and hard for me to believe when I counted back the years in my mind, but it was true. I'd always made excuses, saying I had too much traveling and too many demands as a documentary film producer, where life is always projected two and three years into the future, leaving little space for here and now.

But that wasn't the reason I hadn't seen my godchild in four years. We both knew why.

I played the message again, listening for cadences and tones that would remind me of Denise, and it was like standing on the curb watching someone I knew get hit by a car. Something had stripped Denise's voice bare. So that meant her husband, Sean, must really be gone, I realized. And Denise wanted to send her daughter away.

"I can't stand to look at her," the voice on the message was saying again.

I went to my kitchen sink, in the direct path of the biting breeze from my half-open window, and I was shaking. My mind had frozen shut, sealing my thoughts out of reach. I turned on the faucet and listened to the water pummel my aluminum basin, then I captured some of the lukewarm stream in my palms to splash my face. As the water dripped from my chin, I cupped my hands again and drank, and I could taste the traces of salty perspiration I'd rubbed from my skin, tasting myself. My anger and sadness were tugging on my stomach. I stood at that window and cursed as if what I was feeling had a shape and was standing in the room with me.

I think I'd started to believe I might have been wrong about the whole thing. That was another reason I'd kept some distance from Denise; I hadn't wanted to be there to poke holes in what she was trying to do, to cast doubts with the slightest glance. That's something only a mother or a lifelong friend can do, and I might as well have been both to Denise despite our identical ages. I'd thought maybe if I only left her alone, she could build everything she wanted inside that Victorian brownstone in Lincoln Park. The husband, the child, all of it. Her life could trot on happily ever after, just the way she'd planned.

But that's a lie, too. I'd always known I was right. I had been dreading that call all along, since the beginning. And once it finally came, I wondered what the hell had taken so long. You know how Denise's voice really sounded on my answering machine that day? As if she'd wrapped herself up in that recorder and died.

"Paige, promise me you'll look out for Neecy, hear?" Mama used to tell me. I couldn't have known then what a burden that would be, having to watch over someone. But I took my role seriously. Mama said Neecy needed me, so I was going to be her guardian. Just a tiny little bit, I couldn't completely be a kid after that. Mama never said exactly why my new best friend at Mae Jemison Elementary School needed guarding, but she didn't have to. I had my own eyes. Even when Neecy didn't say anything, I noticed the bruises on her forearms and calves, and even on Neecy's mother's neck once, which was the real shocker. I recognized the sweet, sharp smell on Neecy's mother's breath when I walked to Neecy's house after school. Her mother smiled at me so sweetly, just like that white lady Mrs. Brady on reruns of *The Brady Bunch* my mother made me watch, because she used to watch it when she was my age and she thought it was more appropriate than the "trash" on the children's channels when I was a kid. That smile wasn't a real smile; it was a smile to hide behind.

I knew things Mama didn't know, in fact. When Neecy and I were nine, we already had secrets that made us feel much older; and not in the way that most kids want to feel older, but in the uninvited way that only made us want to sit by ourselves in the playground watching the other children play, since we were no longer quite in touch with our spirit of running and jumping. The biggest secret, the worst, was about Neecy's Uncle Lonnie, who was twenty-two, and what he had forced Neecy to do with him all summer during the times her parents weren't home. Neecy finally had to see a doctor because the itching got so bad. She'd been bleeding from itching between her legs, she'd confided to me. This secret filled me with such horror that I later developed a dread of my own period because I associated the blood with Neecy's itching. Even though the doctor asked Neecy all sorts of questions about how she could have such a condition, which had a name Neecy never uttered out loud, Neecy's mother never asked at all.

So, yes, I understood why Neecy needed looking after. No one else was doing it.

What I didn't understand, as a child, was how Neecy could say she hated her father for hitting her and her mother, but then she'd be so sad during the months when he left, always wondering when he would decide to come home. And how Neecy could be so much smarter than I was—the best reader, speller, and multiplier in the entire fourth grade—and still manage to get so many F's because she just wouldn't sit still and do her homework. And the thing that puzzled me most of all was why, as cute as Neecy was, she seemed to be ashamed to show her face to anyone unless she was going to bed with a boy, which was the only time she ever seemed to think she was beautiful. She had to go to the doctor to get abortion pills three times before she graduated from high school.

Maybe it was the secret-sharing, the telling, that kept our friendship so solid, so fervent. Besides, despite everything, there were times I thought Neecy was the only girl my age who had any sense, who enjoyed reciting poems and acting out scenes as much as I did. Neecy never did join the drama club like I did, claiming she was too shy, but we spent hours writing and performing plays of our own behind my closed bedroom door, exercises we treated with so much imagination and studiousness that no one would ever guess we were our only audience.

"I wish I had a house like yours," Neecy used to say, trying on my clothes while she stood admiring herself in my closet mirror, my twin.

By fall, the clothes would be hers, because in the summer Mama always packed my clothes for Neecy in a bundle. For my other little girl, she'd say. And beforehand Neecy would constantly warn me, "Don't you mess up that dress," or "Be careful before you rip that!" because she already felt proprietary.

"Oh, my house isn't so special," I used to tell Neecy. But that was the biggest lie of all.

In the years afterward, as Neecy dragged a parade of crises to my doorstep, like a cat with writhing rodents in her teeth—men, money, jobs; everything was a problem for Neecy—I often asked myself what forces had separated us so young, dictating that I had grown up in my house and Neecy had grown up in the other. She'd lived right across the street from my family, but our lives may as well have been separated by the Red Sea.

Was it only an accident that my own father never hit me, never stayed away from home for even a night, and almost never came from work without hugging me and telling me I was his Smart Little Baby-Doll?

And that Mama never would have tolerated any other kind of man? Was it pure accident that I'd had no Uncle Lonnie to make me itch until I bled with a disease the doctor had said little girls shouldn't have?

"Girl, you're so lucky," Neecy told me once when I was in college and she'd already been working for three years as a clerk at the U Save Drugstore. She'd sworn she wasn't interested in college, but at that instant her tone had been so rueful, so envy-soaked, that we could have been children again, writing fantastic scripts for ourselves about encounters with TV stars and space aliens behind my closed bedroom door, both of us trying to forget what was waiting for Neecy at home. "In my next life, I'm coming back you for sure."

If only Neecy had been my real-life sister, not just a pretend one, I always thought. If only things had been different for her from the time she was born.

I CALLED DENISE a half hour after I got her message. She sounded a little better, but not much. Whether it was because she'd gathered some composure or swallowed a shot or two of liquor, this time her voice was the one I've always known: hanging low, always threatening to melt into a defeated laugh. She kept her face screen black, refusing to let me see her. "It's all a mess. This place looks like it was robbed," she said. "He took everything. His suits. His music. His favorite books, you know, those Russian writers, Dostoyevsky and Nabokov, or whatever-the-fuck? Only reason I know he was ever here is because of the hairs in the bathroom sink. He shaved first. He stood in there looking at his sorry face in the mirror after he'd loaded it all up, and he . . . " For the first time, her voice cracked. "He left . . . me. And her. He left."

I couldn't say anything against Sean. What did she expect? The poor man had tried, but from the time they met, it had all been as arranged as a royal Chinese marriage. How could anyone live in that house and breathe under the weight of Denise's expectations? Since I couldn't invent any condolences, I didn't say anything.

"You need to take Neecy." Denise filled the silence.

Hearing her say it so coldly, my words roiled beneath my tongue, constricting my throat. I could barely sound civil. "The first time you told me about doing this . . . I said to think about what it would mean. That it couldn't be undone. Didn't I, Neecy?"

"Don't call me Neecy." Her words were icy, bitter. "Don't you know better?"

"What happens now? She's your daughter, and she's only six. Think of—"

"Just come get her. If not, I don't . . . I don't know what I'll do."

Then she hung up on me, leaving my melodramatic imagination to wonder what she'd meant by that remark, if she was just feeling desperate or if she was holding a butcher knife or a gun in her hand when she said it. Maybe that was why she'd blacked herself out, I thought.

I was crying like a six-year-old myself while my cab sped toward the airport. I saw the driver's wondering eyes gaze at me occasionally in his rearview mirror, and I couldn't tell if he was sympathetic or just annoyed. I booked myself on an eight-forty flight with a seat in first class on one of the S-grade planes that could get me there in forty minutes. Airbuses, I call them. At least in first class I'd have time for a glass or two of wine. I convinced the woman at the ticket counter to give me the coach price because, for the first time in all my years of flying, I lied and said I was going to a funeral. My sister's, I told her, tears still smarting on my face.

If you could even call that a lie.

THREE MORE MONTHS, just ninety days, and it never would have happened. If Denise had waited only a few months, if she'd thought it through the way I begged her when she first laid out the details of her plan, the procedure would not have been legal. The Supreme Court's decision came down before little Neecy was even born, after only a couple hundred volunteers paid the astronomical fee to take part in the copycat babies program. To this day, I still have no idea where Denise got the money. She never told me, and I got tired of asking.

But she got it somehow, somewhere, along with two hundred thirty others. There were a few outright nutcases, of course, lobbying to try to use DNA samples to bring back Thomas Jefferson and Martin Luther King; I never thought that would prove anything except that those men were only human and could be as unremarkable as the rest of us. But mostly the applicants were just families with something left undone, I suppose. Even though I never agreed with Denise's reasons, at least I had some idea of what she hoped to accomplish. The others, I wasn't sure. Was it pure vanity? Novelty? Nostalgia? I still don't understand.

In the end, I'm not sure how many copycat babies were born. I read somewhere that some of the mothers honored the Supreme Court's ban and were persuaded to abort. Of course, they might have been coerced or paid off by one of the extremist groups terrified of a crop of so-called "soulless" children. But none of that would have swayed Denise, anyway. For all I know, little Neecy might have been the very last one born.

It was three months too late, but I was moved by the understated eloquence of the high court's decision when it was announced on the News & Justice satellite: Granted, what some might call a "soul" is merely an individual's biological imprint, every bit as accidental as it is unique. In the course of accident, we are all born once, and we die but once. And no matter how ambiguous the relationship between science and chance, humankind cannot assign itself to the task of re-creating souls.

I'm not even sure I believe in souls, not really. But I wished I'd had those words for Denise when it still mattered.

She actually had the whole thing charted out. We were having lunch at a Loop pizzeria the day Denise told me what she wanted to do. She spread out a group of elaborate charts; one was marked HOME, one FATHER, one SCHOOL, all in her too-neat artist's script. The whole time she showed me, her hands were shaking as if they were trying to fly away from her. I'd never seen anyone shake like that until then, watching Denise's fingers bounce like rubber with so much excitement and fervor. The shaking scared me more than her plans and charts.

"Neecy, please wait," I told her.

"If I wait, I might change my mind," Denise said, as if this were a logical argument for going forward rather than just the opposite. She still hadn't learned that doubt was a signal to stop and think, not to plow ahead with her eyes covered, bracing for a crash.

But that was just Denise. That's just the way she is. Maybe that's who she is.

Denise's living room was so pristine when I arrived, it was hard to believe it had witnessed a trauma. I noticed the empty shelves on the music rack and the spaces where two picture frames had been removed from their hooks on the wall; but the wooden floors gleamed, the walls were scrubbed white, and I could smell fresh lilac that might be artificial or real, couldn't tell which. Denise's house reminded me of the sitting room of the bed and breakfast I stayed in overnight during my last trip to London, simultaneously welcoming and wholly artificial. A perfect movie set, hurriedly dusted and freshened as soon as visitors were gone.

Denise looked like a vagrant in her own home. As soon as I got there, I knew why she hadn't wanted me to see her on the phone; she was half dressed in a torn T-shirt, her hair wasn't combed, and the skin beneath her eyes looked so discolored that I had to wonder, for a moment, if Sean might have been hitting her. It wouldn't be the first time she'd been in an abusive relationship. But then I stared into the deep mud of my friend's irises before she shuffled away from me, and I knew better. No, she wasn't being beaten; she wouldn't have tolerated that with Neecy in the house. Instead, my friend was probably having a nervous breakdown.

"Did he say why he left?" I asked gently, stalling. I didn't see little Neecy anywhere, and I didn't want to ask about her yet. I wished I didn't have to see her at all.

Answering with a grunt rather than spoken words, Denise flung her arm toward the polished rosewood dining room table. There, I saw a single piece of paper laid in the center, a typewritten note. As sterile as everything else. In the shining wood, I could also see my own reflection standing over it.

"Haven't you read it?" I asked her.

"Neecy's in the back," Denise said, as if in response.

"Shhh. Just a second. Let's at least read what the man said." My heart had just somersaulted, and then I knew how much I didn't want to be there at all. I didn't want to think about that child. I picked a random point midway through the note and began reading aloud in the tone I might have used for a eulogy: " . . . You squeeze so hard, it chokes me. You're looking for more than a father for her, more than a home. It isn't natural, between you and her—"

"Stop it," Denise hissed. She sank down to the sofa, tunneling beneath a blanket and pulling it up to her chin.

I sighed. I could have written that note myself. Poor Sean. I walked to the sofa and sat beside my friend. My hand felt leaden as I rested it on the blanket where I believed Denise's shoulder must be. "So you two fought about it. You never told me that," I said.

"There's a lot I didn't tell you," Denise said, and I felt her shivering beneath the blanket. "He didn't understand. Never. I thought he'd come around. I thought—"

"You could change him?"

"Shut up," Denise said, sounding more weary than angry.

Yes, I felt weary, too. I'd had this conversation with Denise, or similar ones, countless times before. Denise had met Sean through a video personal on the Internet where all she said was, "I want a good husband and father. Let's make a home." Sean was a nice enough guy, but I had known their marriage was based more on practical considerations than commitment. They both wanted a family. They both had pieces missing and were tired of failing. Neither of them had learned, after two divorces, that people can't be applied to wounds like gauze.

And, of course, then there was little Neecy. What was the poor guy supposed to do?

"She's in her room. I already packed her things. Please take her, Paige. Take her." Denise was whimpering by now.

I brushed a dead-looking clump of hair from Denise's face. Denise's eyes, those unseeing eyes, would be impossible to reach. But I tried anyway, in hopes of saving all of us. "This is crazy. Take her where? What am I going to do with a kid?"

"You promised."

Okay, Mama. I will.

"What?"

"You promised. At the church. At the christening. You're her godmother. If anything happened to me, you said you would."

I thought of the beautiful baby girl, a goddess dressed in white, her soft black curls crowned with lace—gurgling, happy, and agreeable despite the tedium of the long ceremony. Holding her child, Denise had been glowing in a way she had not at her wedding, as if she'd just discovered her entire reason for living.

Tears found my eyes for the first time since I'd arrived. "Denise, what's this going to mean to her?"

"I don't know. I don't . . . care," Denise said, her voice shattered until she sounded like a mute struggling to form words. "Look at me. I can't stand to be near her. I vomit every time I look at her. It's all ruined. Everything. Oh, God—" She nearly sobbed, but there was only silence from her open mouth. "I can't. Not again. No more. Take her, Paige."

I saw a movement in my peripheral vision, and I glanced toward the hallway in time to see a shadow disappear from the wall. My God, I realized, the kid must have been standing where she could hear every hurtful word. I knew I had to get Neecy out of the house, at least for now. Denise was right. She was not fit, at this moment, to be a mother. Anything was better than leaving Neecy here, even getting her to a hotel. Maybe just for a day or two.

I couldn't take care of both of them now. I had to choose the child.

"Neecy?" The bedroom door was open only a crack, and I pressed my palm against it to nudge it open. "Sweetheart, are you in here?"

What struck me first were the books. Shelves filled with the colorful spines of children's books reached the ceiling of the crowded room, so high that even an adult would need a stepladder. Every other space was occupied by so many toys—costumed dolls, clowns, stuffed animals—that I thought of the time my parents took me to FAO Schwarz when I was a kid, the way every square foot was filled with a different kind of magic.

The bed was piled high with dresses. There must have been dozens of them, many of them formal, old-fashioned tea dresses. They were the kind of dresses mothers hated to wear when they were young, and yet love to adorn their little girls with; made of stiff, uncomfortable fabrics and bright, precious colors. Somewhere beneath that heaping pile of clothes, I saw a suitcase yawning open, struggling uselessly to swallow them all.

"Neecy?"

The closet. I heard a sound from the closet, a child's wet sniffle.

Neecy, why are you in the closet? Did your daddy beat you again?

She was there, inside a closet stripped of everything except a few wire hangers swinging lazily from the rack above her head. I couldn't help it; my face fell slack when I saw her. I felt as if my veins had been drained of blood, flushed with ice water instead.

Over the years, I'd talked to little Neecy on the telephone at least once a month, whenever I called Denise. I was her godmother, after all.

Neecy was old enough now that she usually answered the phone, and she chatted obligingly about school and her piano, acting and computer lessons, before saying, Want to talk to Mommy? And the child always sounded so prim, so full of private-school self-assuredness, free of any traces of Denise's hushed, halting—the word, really, was fearful—way of speaking. It wasn't so strange on the phone, with the image so blurry on the face screen. Not at all.

But being here, seeing her in person, was something else.

Neecy's hair was parted into two neat, shiny pigtails that coiled around the back of her neck, her nose had a tiny bulb at the end, and her molasses-brown eyes were set apart just like I remembered them. If the girl had been grinning instead of crying right now, she would look exactly as she'd looked in the photograph someone had taken of us at my sixth birthday party, the one where Mama hired a clown to do magic tricks and pull cards out of thin air, and we'd both believed the magic was real.

Denise was in the closet. She was six years old again, reborn.

I'd known what to expect the whole time, but I couldn't have been prepared for how it would feel to see her again. I hadn't known how the years would melt from my mind like vapors, how it would fill my stomach with stones to end up staring at my childhood's biggest heartache eye-to-eye.

Somehow, I found a voice in my dry, burning throat. "Hey, sweetie. It's Aunt Paige. From California."

"What's wrong with my mommy?" A brave whisper.

"She's just very upset right now, Neecy." Saying the name, my veins thrilled again.

"Where'd Daddy go?"

I knelt so that I could literally stare her in the eye, and I was reminded of how, twenty-five years ago, Neecy's eyelids always puffed when she cried, narrowing her eyes into slits. China-girl, I used to tease her to try to make her laugh. Here was my China-girl.

I clasped the child's tiny, damp hands; the mere act of touching her caused the skin on my arms to harden into gooseflesh. "I'm not sure where your daddy is, sweetie. He'll come back."

Hey, Neecy, don't cry. He'll come back.

Staring into Neecy's anguish, for the first time, I understood everything.

I understood what a glistening opportunity had stirred Denise's soul when she'd realized her salvation had arrived courtesy of science: a legal procedure to extract a nucleus from a single cell, implant it into an egg, and enable her to give new birth to any living person who consented—even to herself. She could take an inventory of everything that had gone wrong, systematically fix it all, and see what would blossom this time. See what might have been.

And now, gazing into Neecy's eyes—the same eyes, except younger, not worn to sludge like the Neecy quivering under a blanket in the living room—I understood why Denise was possibly insane by now. She'd probably been insane longer than I wanted to admit.

"Listen," I said. "Your mom told me to take you to get some pizza. And then she wants us to go to my hotel for a couple of days, until she feels better."

"Will she be okay?" Neecy asked. Her teary eyes were sharp and focused.

Yes, I realized, it was these tears ripping Denise's psyche to shreds. This was what Denise could not bear to look at, what was making her physically ill. She was not ready to watch her child, herself, taken apart hurt by hurt. Again.

Neecy was dressed in a lemon-colored party dress as if it were her birthday, or Easter Sunday. Did Denise dress her like this every day? Did she wake Neecy up in the mornings and smile on herself while she reclaimed that piece, too? Of course. Oh, yes, she did. Suddenly, I swooned. I felt myself sway with a near-religious euphoria, my spirit filling up with something I couldn't name. I only kept my balance by clinging to the puffed shoulders of the child's taffeta dress, as if I'd made a clumsy attempt to hug her.

"Neecy? It's all right this time," I heard myself tell her in a breathless whisper. "I promise I'll watch out for you. Just like I said. It's all right now, Neecy. Okay? I promise."

I clasped my best friend's hand, rubbing her small knuckles back and forth beneath my chin like a salve. With my hand squeezing her thumb, I could feel the lively, pulsing throbbing of Neecy's other heart.

⌒

I wrote this story for Sheree Renée Thomas's groundbreaking anthology Dark Matter: A Century of Speculative Fiction from the African Diaspora, *which featured works by luminaries such as Octavia E. Butler, Samuel Delany,*

W. E. B. DuBois, Steven A. Barnes, Nalo Hopkinson, Charles R. Saunders, and too many others to name. This anthology was a watershed in helping to define black speculative fiction, now commonly known as Afrofuturism.

When I wrote this story, there was much discussion about the cloning of a goat. I have always been puzzled by the public fascination with cloning, since people are so much more than their genes. This story answered my question: "Why would someone want to clone herself?"

Aftermoon

AT SIX-THIRTY, the moon was already faintly visible in the waning daylight, patiently awaiting its turn to light up the streets in pale blue and gray. The After-Moon, Kenya always called it. It wasn't the real Moon, the full moon; it only looked like it, except chewed smaller at the rims. The After-Moon was startling and nearly as beautiful, but it ultimately held no more allure for Kenya than it would if she were any other city-dweller tossed suddenly into its sight.

Kenya ignored the moon as she walked from the Clark Street subway stop toward her building, vanishing inside the purposeful stream of twilight home-goers. She felt it watching her—she always did—but she refused to look up. She'd decided a long time ago that just because the moon tried to talk to her didn't mean she had to listen. Her grandfather had felt differently about that; but, then again, he was different in a lot of ways. Kenya was especially proud that she didn't allow ghosts and memories to steer her life.

Kenya's stomach growled. At dinnertime, especially during the summer, Brooklyn Heights always smelled like the sidewalks had been basted with butter, pine nuts, and garlic. All the take-out places had their doors propped open, trying to tantalize people like Kenya, who never planned their meals in advance.

But tonight, she knew exactly what she wanted, because she'd withheld it from herself the night before, when she'd wanted it most: a barely-seared, blood-red steak. The meat was waiting for her in her freezer at home, so she'd thaw it and cook it, maybe twenty seconds in the pan on each side. This was the only time of month Kenya knew exactly what she wanted to eat. Not a need, she reassured herself, just an appetite. Her grandfather might even be proud of her, if he'd still been living and could have shared a moonlight meal. Except, she reminded herself, he would have been

173

irritated with her for the ritual of cooking the flesh at all. Not to mention how absurd he would think it was not to have hunted for her food first, making her own kill.

Kenya's mind was on her hunger, so it was only an accident when she walked past a basement office she must have passed every day for nearly a year, dwarfed beneath the Indian/Chinese video store and a Northern Italian restaurant, Giovanni's, that all the people in her building raved about. Today, the glint of the buffed brass sign caught her eye because it so perfectly complemented the day's last light. The bold letters were embossed into the shiny plate in black: JACK REEVES, DERMATOLOGY. And beneath that, following Dr. Reeves' mumbo-jumbo of degrees and licenses, it said in script: LYCANTHROPY.

Kenya's first thought was to go in and give this quack a piece of her damned mind.

She wasn't offended easily, but the sign set off sparks that made her teeth tighten. Maybe it was only because of the time of month, she tried to reason with herself, but the nerve of this guy, this so-called doctor, poking such callous fun in a sign posted on a public street!

She wasn't sure why she found herself descending the cracked concrete steps leading to the office door, because a doctor wouldn't keep hours this late, and what was she going to do if he did? Still, sparks didn't need reason; they improvised just fine. Maybe she'd slide a nasty note beneath his door. Maybe she'd write down his telephone number and lodge an anonymous complaint on his voice-mail. Ignorant fool, she thought. Before she realized it, she was fantasizing about the pleasure of ripping his face into—

The light was on, illuminating a waiting room beyond the glass door. A small, hand-written list of office hours taped inside proclaimed that Dr. Jack Reeves, Dermatology, was open until 7:00 p.m. on all weekdays except Wednesdays. Which meant he was still there. Good, she thought, and flung the door open to a cacophony of jangling chimes.

Inside the office, though, her mood softened, retreating from the unseemly places it had been trying to lure her. There was nothing unusual about the appearance of the doctor's office. The light inside was bright, welcoming, making the waiting room and the gaily-colored magazines neatly fanned on the coffee table feel like part of a life-sized display case. Very familiar. And yet . . .

Thinking about it later, she wondered if maybe she had first been arrested by the smell. Her nostrils smarted for a moment from the thick scent of burning incense, before she relaxed and allowed herself to breathe in the luxurious smell. Part campfire, part lavender, part . . . cedar closet? Oh, it was something, that smell! It was a smell to bottle and steal whiffs from in the middle of the night.

But the office's scent was nothing compared to the music. As soon as Kenya heard it, she spun around to search for the speakers, as if seeing the music's source would somehow help her own it. She could not distinguish between voice and instrument—in fact, she could not say with certainty that the music was composed of either, just as it seemed to have no discernible melody—but she knew that it was music, meaning it was the very definition of music. Barely loud enough to hear, it thrilled against her ears.

Standing frozen in the waiting room, Kenya forgot why she had been angry. Or why she had come in. Or even where she was.

"That music's something, isn't it?" a man's voice said from her left.

Released from the spell, Kenya turned to see a hulking figure standing behind a half-open glass partition, wrapped inside an ill-fitting doctor's coat. He was only partially visible, the rest of his bulk muddied behind the misted glass. She saw his enormous wiry beard, one curious brown eye, and half of his round spectacles staring out at her like a Moon.

"It's . . . " Kenya searched her mind for words, avoiding not only clichés but words that were unworthy. But her search was fruitless; her mind was empty of words.

"Are you hungry?" the man behind the partition asked.

The question was odd, a non sequitur, a muted part of Kenya's brain realized, but her mouth nonetheless flooded with saliva. She saw the man fling something toward her at an arc, and her nose recognized long before her eyes could focus that it was a small strip of raw beef. To her own astonishment, she snatched the meat out of the air with a decisive snap of her teeth.

• • •

"I THOUGHT your sign outside was a joke," Kenya told him later, when the music was gone and she felt more like herself. Now, sitting primly on the leather sofa in the waiting room, the woman who'd heard the music was a stranger to her. Only her satisfied stomach, and tiny bits of raw beef caught between her teeth, reminded her of who she'd been. Embarrassed, she worried at the food fragments with a peppermint-flavored toothpick the doctor had offered her.

"Sure, right. Most people think it's a gag. That's the beautiful part."

Dr. Jack, as he insisted on being called, had fixed a pot of coffee that he served himself in a mug that read, wryly, WHAT A HAIRY SITUATION. He offered a cup to Kenya, but she refused. Caffeine in any form, even a minuscule amount, made her crazy, she told him. Especially right after the Moon, she thought, noting that last part only to herself.

"To some people, crazy is good," Dr. Jack told her, winking. "But you're smart to keep your distance. Coffee's my vice."

Kenya tried to assess Dr. Jack the way her grandfather had taught her, looking for signs. He had a mane of intricately curled dark hair that spilled onto his face in the form of a neatly combed beard, which rode high on his cheeks and grew all the way to his mid-chest before tapering away. From what she could see of his neckline above his white smock, the hair grew freely there, too. Dr. Jack, yes, was one hairy guy.

But there was always more to it than the hair, she knew. She tried to hold his eyes, to see what she could find there, that arcane quality that had informed her grandfather's brown-eyed gaze. Dr. Jack's eyes were set back deep beyond his bearded pudgy cheeks, and they told her nothing except that he might be kind. She decided, in that instant, to trust him.

"How did you know about me?" she asked

He shrugged. "The music. If you didn't have the genes, all you'd hear was Muzak. An ocarina and strings playing 'Black Dog' by Zeppelin."

She regarded him blankly. She didn't know the song.

"That's a joke," he said, grinning. She tried to assess his teeth, but the grin vanished too quickly. "But seriously, the music gives you away. Only my very special patients hear it at all." He said this with tremendous warmth, a little too much. Kenya didn't like his eagerness; it glowed from him like the bright, giddy energy of first dates with the kind of men who typically had too many chips and dents just beneath the surface to warrant any more of her time.

"When did your condition manifest?" he asked, suddenly sounding like a doctor again.

"I don't think I want to talk about that." The awful episode right before her ninth birthday tried to goad its way to consciousness, but she refused to open that window. Not now.

"Right. I forget, you're not a patient yet. So you do the asking, then."

"How many . . . I mean . . . "

"I have thirteen special patients, a very small part of my practice. All from the Tri-State area except for one guy from DC. He takes the train in for group night, once a month. Last night, matter of fact. You missed it."

Thirteen! This doctor was the first person she'd met in New York who seemed to share her condition. There were other men, too? Kenya imagined the commuter from DC in a tailored suit with a briefcase in his hand, probably a lawyer, scanning the *Washington Post* or the *Times* while he rode in. She liked that picture. The image of the man on the train re-awakened her hopeless adolescent yearnings for a mate who would accept her. She'd been so certain that no man like that would exist that she'd sat for hours on the back porch with her grandfather, allowing him to fill her head with nonsense and cynicism, only to escape the ache of her daydreams. Had hopelessness also driven her to accept the marriage proposal from Lee, a man who was funny and good-hearted, but who lived three-thousand miles away and whom she honestly had yet to really know. And, more to the point, a man who could never know her.

Dr. Jack's faceless commuter on the train saddened Kenya in ways she couldn't explain. And to think he'd been here only yesterday! Perhaps in this very room.

"That many? Just in New York?" she said.

"Give or take. I have to account for a few strays, pardon the expression. But you're the first new face I've seen in two years."

"You have . . . " Kenya stumbled over the word, momentarily lapsing into the desperation of a fifteen-year-old's mind. " . . . treatments?"

"Mostly cosmetic. I'm a dermatologist, understand, so I'm—"

"The hair," she said, her voice shrill and urgent. Had that really been her voice at all? "You have treatments for the hair?"

"Sure, right." He nodded, the grin floating back across his mouth. This time, unless she imagined it, she did notice a slight extra sharpness to his incisors. Just like her grandfather's. "That's my specialty. I'll have you smooth as a baby's bottom."

Kenya stared at him. She could feel the steadily rising pulsing of her heartbeat in her fingertips, surging with blood that warmed her face in a flare. She didn't speak. She was afraid that strange, helpless voice would fly from her mouth again.

"Yeah, I know," Dr. Jack said, as if responding to her thoughts. "Sometimes you don't even know what you're looking for until you've found it."

"Sheep don't live lives, they live lies," Gramp always told her. "Your mama's hell-bent on tryin' to raise you in the world of sheep. But you damn sure ain't no sheep, girl. Are you?"

There were never real answers to Gramp's questions. When Kenya was twelve and began thinking for herself, she'd tried to pose logic against him, but his questions always writhed and twisted like snakes that could change their shape and size depending on the point he wanted to make. Not that the point ever changed.

Summers with Gramp were always more fun to anticipate than they were to actually spend, because by the third day of her two-month visit Kenya always figured out there was no one but Gramp to talk to and even less to do. He had a seventy-year-old wood-frame house that had never heard a whisper about the invention of air-conditioning in a tiny Oregon town called Fortune, which was not big enough to be a true town. The six buildings that made up what Kenya supposed was "downtown" Fortune were a saloon, a market that served hot and cold sandwiches, a barber shop that doubled as a post office, the two-room First Church of the Living Christ, a drugstore, and a tack and feed. The entire patch of buildings went dark after nine, so no one driving by could even see Fortune at night. Most people never saw Fortune at all. There, Kenya disappeared, and so did the world outside.

Mostly, timber families lived in Fortune. Houses dotted the hilltop tree-lines on large parcels of land, but the precious few neighbors never ventured near Gramp's house, and Kenya had never been able to identify any families with children her age. Which left her and Gramp. Two months, each year, felt like a lifetime. She'd tried to complain to her parents that Gramp was a bad influence on her, but either they didn't believe her or Gramp's bad influence was exactly what they were counting on, especially her mother, with her secretive gazes each summer as she waved goodbye.

The only nights at Gramp's she truly enjoyed—the nights that, given her circumstances, were more incredible and long-awaited than Christmas Day—were the Moon nights. One night each month. And every night until the Moon, he told her, was preparation. He told her there was only one night each month when she truly existed at all.

"It's like any other gift. You don't pay attention to something long enough, you forget," Gramp used to say, gazing out from his back porch across his unkempt property, where wild tiger-lilies grew in quilt patterns in the crabgrass. "And don't be afraid of that word 'monster.' That's a word invented by conventional folk either too stupid or too scared to follow their own souls. Too scared to create nothin' of their own."

"Monsters don't create anything," Kenya might have argued, or something like it.

"What's wrong with you, girl? Of course they do. They create fear, and there ain't nothing more powerful on this planet Earth." Gramp gave her headaches from so much confusion.

But the confusion vanished on Moon nights. The Moon gave her experiences that defied memory, that had no place for discussion at her parents' dinner table or among the classmates who sat in the neatly-lined desks at her school: Bare feet descending nearly weightless across beds of sharp twigs that could not hurt her. Wind tickling and stroking the hairs across her naked back. Foreign songs emerging from her throat, screeching across the treetops.

And twice, when she was very fast and very lucky, the opportunity to kill. Once, it had been a squirrel. Another time, a raccoon. Caught, startled, in her hands. Killed with instinctive swiftness, fur raking against her teeth.

Only on Moon nights did it make any sense at all. Only then did Kenya truly understand why Gramp lived in Fortune, secluded as a forest creature himself. And why the neighbors never once came to call.

Every year, despite the prospect of hot boredom of summer nights that made her want to scream herself to sleep, Kenya couldn't wait to go see her grandfather. When she wasn't with him, Moon nights were almost like any other. The forgetting always began right away.

Dr. Jack's office seemed much less inviting when Kenya came back for her first official appointment. The lovely incense was still in the air, so it calmed her nerves; and she could hear traces of the music, even more faint than before. It was harder to hear now, of course, because the Moon had been nearly a week ago, and her senses had faded considerably.

But she was put off when she saw his examining room. There was a framed eight-by-ten photo of Lon Chaney, Jr. in elaborate costume placed prominently on the wall, alongside a full-sized movie poster, which jarred Kenya so much in its cartoonish menace that she could taste bile in her throat. Seeing the images, she could very nearly smell her grandfather's pipe tobacco and the perfume of the pine needles of the Christmas trees that had grown wild on his property. Gramp had kept film reels of classic horror movies, and she'd watched them with him late at night for lack of anything else to do, all the while feeling slightly sick to her stomach. Now, seeing Gramp's favorite movie celebrated again, Kenya felt a prickling in her marrow that couldn't have been deeper if she'd been staring at a poster of a handkerchief-bound Mammy or a fat-lipped, watermelon-slurping pickaninny.

Why in the world had she come here? This coarse, trivial man had nothing to teach her.

But it was too late now. Already, she had bared herself to her midriff, and his fingers were traveling up and down her spine, following the trail of hair.

"Geez, this isn't bad at all," he said. "Is this your typical growth?"

"Pretty much. I never get much facial hair, thank God. Just very fine hair on the cheeks, and it falls out after a few hours," she told Dr. Jack, yanking her eyes away from the movie poster's glare. "My back and chest are the problem."

"Let's see the chest," he said, walking around the table to face her. There, she knew, he had a perfect view of the triangle-shaped thatch of black fur between her breasts. Only a select few people had ever seen it, mostly technicians at hair-removal salons who clucked with shock and pity at how a hormonal condition could go so badly awry. Not even her mother had seen what grew on her chest. But Gramp had, of course. Her hair had delighted him, and he promised her that if she followed the diet he taught her, she'd grow a lot more like it once she was older. Of course, she had done nothing of the sort.

"This is nothing," Dr. Jack said.

It hadn't seemed like nothing to Terrell Jordan, who'd slipped his hand beneath Kenya's blouse while they were necking in the back row of a movie theater when they were both in high school. He'd been so quick, she hadn't even seen it coming; and if she'd expected a maneuver like that from bookish Terrell, she'd never have made out with him at all. When his fingers met the hair, he didn't say anything or make a sound. His fingers just twitched and flew away as if he'd been burned. He pulled his lips back and stared at her, his eyeglasses reflecting the light from the movie screen. That was all she could see of his face.

No more making out after that, or movies either. But at least, as far as she knew, he never told anyone. She very nearly loved him for that.

"It doesn't feel like 'nothing' when I'm getting it pulled out, believe me," she said.

"How do you do that?"

"Well, creams don't work and electrolysis is a waste of time. Waxing, usually."

"Oh, for God's sake, are you kidding me?" Dr. Jack said, gazing at her with the abhorrence and concern she had come to expect from everyone who had tried to tend to her hair. He sucked his teeth. "Don't do that. Not ever again. You'll damage your skin that way, believe me. See these dark spots . . . ? That's why I'm here." From his coat pocket, he produced a white jar of unlabeled paste. He unscrewed it and showed her the texture, which was the color of peanut butter not quite as thick. It had a sweet scent.

"This is a combination of flowers, herbs and enzymes," he said. "Apply it to the affected area the day before the Moon, and keep applying it every six hours for the next forty-eight hours. You'll see a difference right away, if the hair grows in at all. Within a day or two, any hair you do get should wash right off. If it doesn't, we can try something else. But this works great in ninety percent of my cases, and your growth is so mild you shouldn't have a thing to worry about. I have patients who need vats of the stuff, but it works."

Con-artist, Kenya thought. It couldn't be that easy.

"Money-back guarantee," Dr. Jack added. "But it ain't cheap, I'm afraid. Fifty bucks a jar. Most of the ingredients are imported."

"That's all there is to it?"

"Modern times," Dr. Jack said. "Modern solutions."

Kenya took the jar and stared at the brown paste. She wondered what Gramp would have thought of it. Or her parents, for that matter. Perhaps, armed with the paste, they might not have sent her to spend her summers with Gramp at all. What in the world had they been trying to prepare her for?

Dr. Jack pulled up a wooden chair and sat in front of Kenya with a slate. He seemed so much more conventional now than he had that first night, when he was tossing her raw meat across the room. "Since you're my patient now, how about a few questions?"

Kenya shrugged, then nodded.

"Tell me when your condition manifested."

"Uhm . . . When I was a toddler, my mother says. I had mood swings . . . "

"On Moon nights?"

"Yes."

"And your parents?"

"No. I don't even think my father knows, not the whole thing, and my mother pretty much pretended it wasn't happening," Kenya said, momentarily despising their smooth skin and predictable temperaments the way she had as a child. "But my grandfather, yes. I got the genes from my mother's father. They barely talked to each other, but she knew about him."

"That's it? No aggravating circumstances?"

"A bite," she said softly. "More like a nip, I guess. From a wild dog." Her first and only camping trip with her parents, and it had been a disaster. Out of her parents' sight for only a few minutes, she'd offered some food to the underfed, haggard-looking animal sniffing their campsite out of a child's natural pity. The dog had bitten her instead, drawing pricks of blood. Her right hand still bore the scar, although it was so faded that only she could still see it was there.

"A dog? That's an old wives' tale," Dr. Jack said.

"Still . . . it got worse after that. I was eight. That's when the hair started coming."

"Average age of onset is about twelve, thirteen, so you were definitely accelerated," Dr. Jack said. "Certain sun-blocks aggravate it. And a high-protein diet. But dog-bites? Nah."

"That's what happened to me. Maybe it wasn't all dog, then."

Dr. Jack's pen paused as he considered this. His shaggy eyebrows climbed, then fell at rest. "Okay, I'll give you the benefit of the doubt on that one. What about symptoms?"

Kenya did not want to tell him about Gramp and the woods. He'd died when she was thirteen, and she'd long ago discarded those experiences as though they had never been. "Uhm . . . irritability. I get a little jittery. A few appetite changes. Mostly, it's just the hair."

"So it's a cosmetic problem," he said.

She smiled. She wished she'd learned to think of it that way before now. "Yes," she said, at ease for the first time since her arrival. "I like that."

"You wouldn't believe how much of life is semantics." Dr. Jack put his metal slate aside. "I tell people to think of it as an allergy, if that helps."

To what? she almost said, before she realized that, of course, she knew: the Moon.

"I like that, too," Kenya said. "I'll take that over my grandfather telling me I was a freak. Oh, and that I should have pride in my freakishness because it makes me superior."

Dr. Jack shrugged. "I hear that too. Works for some people, doesn't for others. Listen, I offer more comprehensive services here, if that interests you. Moon-feasts. Hunting nights and retreats upstate, up by the

Adirondack Mountains. Great woods up there. A van-load of folks from Canada join us there twice a year, and they're a wild bunch. And we do group meetings, like I think I mentioned before."

For an instant, something inside Kenya turned sharp and glistening. She'd spent the past few days, and fitful nights, contemplating whether or not she would like to meet any of the others, particularly the commuter from Washington, DC. Even thinking about the stranger made her feel disloyal to Lee, who was almost the same mysterious phantom. She'd never known any others except Gramp, after all, and she'd grown comfortable with the assumption that she never would. She didn't trust the part of herself that craved their fellowship. Besides, it was too late for that. She had chosen Lee, and she would make a life with him. She would be done with it.

Perhaps if she had met Dr. Jack and his peculiar circle sooner. But she hadn't.

"I have a few singles . . . " Dr. Jack went on, trying to entice her.

"I'm engaged," Kenya said. "I'm getting married in three months."

"Is he family?"

The word "family" confused Kenya for an instant, before she allowed herself to enjoy its reassuring quality. Are you family, Dr. Jack? she wanted to ask, because she really wasn't sure. Gramp would have known by a scent or something in this man's gaze, but Kenya's instincts felt dull and unreliable, so all she could rely on was his hairiness, which could be explained in so many other ways. She'd conveniently used those other explanations herself.

She thought of Lee's cherubically hairless chest, his bare back that gleamed with massage oil. He was a vegetarian, but aside from that obvious flaw, he was a painfully good person, and he loved her with great zeal. So far, anyway. Kenya fought a sudden constriction of her throat, as if someone were strangling her.

"No, he's not family," she said. "And he doesn't know. He lives in L.A., and we only see each other every couple months. Usually I leave the hair alone until right before I see him."

"What about after you're married?"

"I don't know," she said. "Maybe I'll tell him one day."

"That's brave," Dr. Jack said, staring at her with naked admiration.

In the end, that was what gave Dr. Jack away. Not his scent or the shape of his teeth, but his envy. She wondered how much time he spent importing his ingredients, making his paste, conducting his group sessions, planning his Moon-feasts. Between that and his regular practice, she surmised, he must not have time for much else, and maybe he liked it that way, basking in the image of Lon Chaney, Jr. Exalting his own strangeness.

She wondered if he secretly scorned her for being a sheep. The way Gramp would.

"Good luck with your fiancé," Dr. Jack said. "That's a tough disclosure for people to swallow. At least you know we're here if you get any ugly surprises."

Ugly surprises. Nope, Kenya thought, the biggest surprise she might get from Lee would be a spontaneous hug or some profound gesture of his devotion. The ugliness was what she expected; revulsion, surliness, fear. Then, if she was very lucky, gradual acceptance. If Dr. Jack's hair paste actually worked, that would make her task so much easier with Lee—he might not have to see it, not ever. She had to hope so, anyway.

She hoped for something much more than the way Terrell Jordan, by the end of their senior year, gave her only wistful half-waves in the hallway as evidence that he had once laughed at her jokes, or that she'd ever made his palms sweat. She'd taken those waves home with her and replayed them in her giddy imagination as if they mattered, as if they were so much more than reminders of Terrell's cowardice. When she lay very quietly on her made-up bed and closed her eyes, hugging her book-bag to her chest, she could even imagine that Terrell had stroked and kissed that thick patch of hair between her budding breasts instead of pulling his hand away.

I wrote this for Sheree Renée Thomas's Dark Matter: Reading the Bones (2004), *the second anthology in the series. This volume, just as the first in 2001, was honored with the World Fantasy Award for Best Anthology in 2005.*

Trial Day

LETITIA WAS a few months shy of ten the summer Brother was scheduled to stand trial.

Brother was only her half-brother, and his name was Wallace Lee, but Letitia had always called him Brother because, to her, the warmth and strength of that word suited him best. In turn, he'd always called her Lettie, the sassier nickname she preferred, instead of the prissier and cumbersome "Letitia" that Daddy and her stepmother insisted on calling her by. Her stepmother thought nicknames were low-class, and Daddy usually went by whatever her stepmother said, so Brother called her Lettie in secret.

Brother lived with his mama in Live Oak, which was a day's drive south in Daddy's shiny new 1927 Rickenbacker, farther than most people she knew had traveled in their lives, so she didn't see him as often as she wanted to. During the summers, and sometimes for Thanksgiving, Brother took a train to stay with them for as long as two weeks, arranging his long limbs into knots so he could sleep on the living room couch. Brother was only fifteen now, but he'd always been tall. Letitia had never met Brother's mother, but Daddy was tall enough for two. Letitia and Brother had different mamas in different towns—although Daddy had never been married to either woman—and her stepmother told Letitia the whole thing was a disgrace and a ought to be a source of personal shame to her, as if Letitia could be responsible for any of the doings in the world before she was born. By studying Brother, Letitia decided that his mama must be dark-skinned like her own, and probably pretty too, judging by Brother's long, thick eyelashes. When he visited them last summer, Brother had been nearly as tall as Daddy and his voice had dropped to a lower register. Letitia had listened to the two of them laughing on the front porch late at night, having a conversation she wasn't allowed to listen to, and they had sounded to Letitia like two grown men having a gay old time, not a father and son.

She still remembered the way they'd laughed, barking out into the night wind. Listening to that sound, which seemed to surround the house, Letitia had fallen asleep with a smile, rocking in their happy noise.

Even her stepmother, Bernadette, stayed out of the way when Brother was here. Bernadette didn't talk to Brother with her voice shrilled high the way she talked to Daddy, and sometimes Brother could make her laugh, too. When he did, she'd hide her mouth behind a napkin or her hand as if she didn't want anyone to witness a smile on her face. Most times, no one did. Bernadette's smiles were hard to come by, and always accidental. Letitia had long ago given up trying to think up ways to bring out Bernadette's smiles. But Brother could. Laughter and smiles of any kind were hard to come by during Brother's impossibly long absences, when Letitia began to wonder if she would see him again or if she'd just dreamed him. Of all the reasons Letitia had to love him—and his kindness toward her was unlike anyone else's except her father's and poor Mama's—perhaps she loved Brother most for bringing the laughter and smiles.

So it came as a shock to Letitia when she learned that Brother was in jail. Bernadette told as if she were discussing a stranger she'd read about in the newspaper. "Got himself thrown in jail for armed robbery! That's what these young boys get for being so wild. They'll probably give that foolish boy the chair, robbing a white man like that," she told Letitia. "Your daddy took up with every tramp and hoodoo woman who looked his way, so what else can he expect?"

Letitia was too scared for Brother to be angry about Bernadette's insults. She knew what The Chair was. The Chair was the electric chair at Raiford State Prison, where colored men were sent to grow old—or to die, if they were destined to take their seat on The Chair. As much as Letitia had heard about Raiford and The Chair in her tender nine years of life, she had never imagined she could know someone who got sent there. Those were the hard-luck stories from people with hard-luck lives.

Daddy was Richard Reaves. He had his own grocery store and a cotton farm. He had a house with two stories and three bedrooms on a thirty-acre parcel of land that had once been owned by slaveholders. Daddy and Cecil Johnson, who owned the colored mortuary, were the two most envied men in the county—and Daddy was most envied of the two because Bernadette was so much more light-skinned than Mr. Johnson's wife. (Daddy and Bernadette looked like twins, with their straight hair and honey skin.) When daddy installed the new upstairs bathroom, neighbors flocked to the house because they were still using outhouses and they wanted to see with their own eyes how a colored man right there on Percival Street had a working toilet and bathtub upstairs in his house, in addition to the one downstairs.

Letitia's daddy did not have hard luck, so Brother could not have been sent to Raiford.

"That's just a misunderstanding, and it's being worked out. I'm sure Wallace Lee's home by now," Daddy said when she asked him, mussing her hair. But he never looked her in the eye when he said it, and Letitia felt a growing, heavy pool of disdain in her belly when it occurred to her that Daddy was lying to her. She had never thought of her father as the kind of man who would lie to a stranger, much less to his daughter. To her.

That summer, suddenly, everything in Letitia's world began to feel all wrong. Hearing about Brother's arrest was the first thing. Hearing the lie in Daddy's voice had been the next. But the hardest, the worst, was yet to come. Letitia just knew it.

Letitia knew many things, mostly things she wished she didn't. Her teacher called her unusually perceptive, which sounded like a grand thing, but Bernadette instead accused Letitia of mischief and lies, helpless to find anything but wickedness in her. Despite Letitia's efforts to behave as well as she could at all times to make her presence less burdensome, she knew that Bernadette considered her the very living image of everything was wrong with her life. Letitia had known this about Bernadette when she was as young as five, the first time Daddy had brought her to live with him because Mama was too poor. Bernadette hated her right away, at first glance. Letitia had not known exactly why, but the hatred had been as plain as the moon in the sky. In later years, Letitia had come to realize that Bernadette hated her because she was proof that Daddy had known other women before her, and because she hated mothering a strange woman's daughter when she could not have children herself.

But knowing why hadn't made Letitia feel any more welcome in her father's house. She only felt welcome when Daddy came home at night, when Bernadette locked most of her hatred for Letitia away and concentrated on finding things to dislike about Daddy. Letitia was afraid to enjoy anything about her father's beautiful house, because none of it was really hers. She could be sent away at any time, and she would hardly ever see Daddy if that happened, like it was before. When Letitia brought powders from Mama to slip into Berndatte's bathwater, she only wanted her stepmother to stop hating so much.

Bernadette never said these things aloud like an evil stepmother in a fairy-tale, but she didn't have to. Letitia knew words were only part of who people were, and usually the least important part. Sometimes, she felt she could just see through people, as if they were standing before her naked. She could see into people's hearts.

At church, people who were stealing from their bosses, cruel to their children, or wooing someone other than the person they were married to avoided locking eyes with Letitia, for fear she might tell on them. When she was younger, she'd blurted things out that made adults gasp, and once a minister had plain slapped her face from the shock of hearing his business told. Now, she'd learned to keep quiet. Letitia's aunties and neighbors near Mama's house had theories about why Letitia had her gift: It was said that she had been born with a caul covering her face, which gave her the seeing-eye, the third-eye. Others thought it was because Mama was a roots-woman, and she had tied a piece of High John the Conqueror root around Letitia's neck the moment she was born. She knew things, and usually knowing brought her only disappointment and trouble, so speculating over the reasons why brought her no joy.

And there would be no joy for some time. That much she knew, too.

This problem with Brother was going to change everything. The problem with Brother was going to make every other problem seem small from now on. The problem with Brother would be up to her to fix, in the end.

One afternoon when Daddy was at his store and Bernadette was taking a nap because she'd overheated herself working in her garden, Letitia went to the corner of the parlor Daddy used as his office, with his oak roll-top desk and electric lamp and stacks of papers in different piles. Letitia climbed up into Daddy's leather chair and surveyed the desk. Before she could decide exactly what she was looking for, or where to begin, the return address typed on a piece of mail caught her eye: LIVE OAK, it said.

The letter had been opened with a letter-opener's neat incision across the top. Letitia brought it out to read by the sunlight stealing in beneath the drawn shade. The whole letter was typed, which told Letitia it must be important.

Dear Mr. Reaves,

Regarding the matter of Wallace Lee Hutchins, I cannot impress upon you enough how urgent it is that you appear at the County Courthouse at 1:00 p.m. Friday, July 20. Many cases like this one are disposed of in the blink of any eye, to the defendant's disadvantage. As an attorney for the National Association for the Advancement of Colored People (NAACP), I am investigating the rising number of very troubling capital cases in this county. Your son's case is one of an alarming pattern.

Please allow me to be frank: Two eyewitnesses, including the shopkeeper, have told police they saw the two boys with a .22-caliber pistol at the time of the robbery. The witnesses and the defendants have quarreled in the past, so one party's word goes against the other's—but since the witnesses are white, I don't have to tell you which version will have more credibility. Mrs. Kelly is fighting the charges against her son with all her soul—she was the one who contacted the NAACP—but I'm afraid she is in a similar position to your own son's mother. Both ladies are ill-respected in this community.

Again, Mr. Reaves, it is vital that you contact me as soon as possible to help me prepare your son's defense. My resources in this matter are limited, but I believe if the jury heard the testimony of a respected colored business-owner in his son's defense, we may get a lesser sentence. You are his best chance. My great fear, sir, is that the prosecutor will seek execution. Two young men were executed earlier this year after being tried in very similar circumstance, where a robbery was committed, but there were no injuries or fatalities. Armed robbery, it seems, is a capital offense for colored boys.

Plainly put, I am asking you to help me save your son's life. I think we can both agree that if these two young men committed an armed robbery—and although they both maintain their innocence, it's very possible that they did—they deserve a severe punishment in the eyes of the law. They will go to jail for a long time, as is only proper.

But these are sixteen-year-old boys, and neither deserves to die for the ignorant work of one night, especially not under a legal system that is a sham, in a county where hunting colored men is virtually legal. (There was a lynching not a mile from where I'm lodging the night I arrived—my first exposure to the heinous phenomenon. But it is your son's case that has been sent to the top of the docket.)

Please help me in this matter. I am trying to prevent another lynching, this one in a courtroom.

The letter was the most important thing Letitia had ever found. It seemed to howl in her hands. She held it so tightly she was afraid she might rip the neat paper it clean in two, reading it and re-reading it, until she'd memorized the words that mattered. She knew she would want to draw upon the memory of this letter for a long time to come, because there was so much to think about. So much to ponder. She wanted to steal the letter and lie about its disappearance, but she couldn't steal from Daddy.

Letitia understood it all, now: Brother and a friend had been charged with robbing a store with a gun. The shopkeeper and another witness who didn't like Brother claimed Brother and his friend had a gun, and it was Brother's word against theirs. The court was rushing to take the case to trial, and they would probably ask for The Chair. A lot of colored people have been getting The Chair lately, and the problem is so bad that a national association for colored people came to see about it. And if Daddy didn't go, Brother might die. It was all so plain to Letitia, it was as if she'd known the whole story the first time Bernadette mentioned that Brother was in jail.

The letter said the trial was going to start on July 20. Letitia hadn't thought about what day of the month it was because there was no reason to track time in the summers, but she checked the kitchen wall calendar and learned it was Tuesday, July 17.

Brother's trial was in less than three days.

"You're going, aren't you, Daddy?" Letitia said at dinner, when she finally dared.

Bernadette looked angry before she knew if she should be. "Going where?" she said in a suspicious tone. She expected to find wrong everywhere. "What are you talking about?"

Daddy's face became stone. He looked at Letitia quickly, then his eyes passed over to Bernadette's. "She ain't talking about nothing," Daddy said.

"Aren't you going to Brother's trial?" Letitia said.

When she said the word *trial*, Daddy's shoulders hunched as if a huge weight had suddenly been hoisted upon them.

"Richard . . . Washington . . . Reaves," her stepmother said. Her voice whispered, but her face was shouting, changing colors in the queer way it often did.

"Now, come on, Bernadette . . ." Daddy said, pushing himself away from the table. He stared at the floor. "Don't start up again. We're sitting to a pleasant meal."

"We settled that, Richard. You promised." Her voice was creeping toward a shout now.

"Yes, we settled it," Daddy said. "Of course we did. Pay Letitia no mind."

"But you are going, aren't you, Daddy? If you don't, Brother could die."

Daddy started cursing under his breath then, something he rarely did. He stood up from the table quickly, throwing his napkin onto his plate. Then he took Letitia's arm in a way that felt nearly rough, bringing her to her feet. "That's enough, Letitia," he said, thundering. Letitia's heart seemed to rock backward and then fall still. "You come on with me right now."

Letitia was nearly in tears by the time Daddy took her to her room and closed the door behind them. Daddy had only beaten her with his belt once before, when she'd sassed at Bernadette, and she'd cried for two days straight. Letitia couldn't imagine she'd earned another whipping just for asking about Brother. Midnight, Letitia's stocky black cat, mewed softly from the bed, and the sight of his curious green eyes comforted her. On days like this one, Midnight was her only friend. He rarely left her room the whole day long.

"Have you been into my mail?"

"Yessir," Letitia said. "But I only wanted to know about Brother."

"Well, I'm very sorry you did that, Letitia, because that letter was not for your eyes. That letter was from a lawyer from New York who's just trying to scare us so we'll do what he says. He hasn't lived down here, and he doesn't understand my position. He's asking me to do something I can't do, and I want you to put it out of your head. Your brother got himself in some trouble, so he'll probably go to jail. But I sent some money, and he'll be just fine."

Letitia did not remember any part of the letter that said Daddy should send money.

"Daddy, he says you have to go, or Brother will get The Chair."

Letitia's father was perspiring now, and Letitia didn't think it was just because the upper floor was stifling after so many daylight hours of rising heat beneath the angry summer sun. Daddy looked nervous. No, not nervous—he looked scared, the way he looked when he brought his hunting rifle out of the closet because a strange car was driving slowly past their house at night. Some people were jealous of him, he said—some white people—and jealousy was apparently something to fear. There was a bead of sweat on the bulb at the end of his nose, and he could barely make himself keep his brown eyes fixed on hers.

"You're too young to take all this in, Letitia," Daddy said, his voice sad and gentle. "You can't believe everything somebody says just because it's typed on a piece of paper. That lawyer's job is to help your brother. But I'm not a lawyer, and I'm no help to him. And besides that, there's no chance they'll give Wallace Lee the chair. He didn't kill nobody."

"The letter said—"

He shook her, just enough to make his words sink in. "What did I just tell you about believing everything that's typed on a piece of paper? That's a spook story he wrote in that letter. That's so I'll do what he says."

"But why won't you, Daddy? You have a car. You could drive there."

Daddy sighed, and his breath smelled like pipe tobacco. "Nothing's that simple, little princess. Wallace Lee's mother and me knew each other a long time ago. She's shamed herself in that town in ways that have nothing to do with me, and if I get all tangled in this mess, running off to a courtroom where there's newspaper reporters and such, then I'll be shamed too. A businessman can't afford to be shamed. All a colored man has in this world is his name, Letitia. And besides that, there's no use me going trying to stir up trouble. The Klan runs that county, and there's Klan in this county, too. People in a place to make life very hard for all of us. Now, my heart aches for Wallace Lee—but I've seen how such things come out in the end, and it wouldn't do any good for any of us. I would just make this situation worse. Far worse."

For the first time, Letitia realized that Daddy had a whole list of reasons why he was not going to Live Oak to save Brother, one having little to do with another. As she stared up at him in that instant, he shrank in her eyes, although he was still three feet taller, with thick arms and thighs as solid as the trunk of an oak. He began to look very small, the way he looked to her when Bernadette chased him from one corner of the house to the other with her sharp tongue, his shoulders wincing with every blow.

"It's 'cause of Bernadette, isn't it?" Letitia said. "She don't want you to go."

Daddy was not the slapping sort, but Letitia realized from the stewing cloud that crossed her father's eyes that he had probably come as close as he ever had to slapping her in the mouth. She had learned long ago that the truth made people angry, and to speak of it was considered evil. If she hadn't been so upset about Brother, she would have known better.

Letitia's room was directly across the hall from Daddy's, and even when their door was closed, she knew what went on in there when she wasn't trying. She knew how Bernadette expected Daddy to account for his whereabouts every minute of every day. She knew how Bernadette told him no when he said he was thinking about buying more land or expanding his store, because she preferred him to buy pretty things for the house. And worst of all, Letitia knew how Daddy had to beg—how he had to make his voice sound silly and ask a dozen times or more, each time sounding sillier than before—just to convince Bernadette to lie in his bed with him like a man lies with his wife. Most times, begging or no begging, her answer was no. Letitia did not know much about the private things men and women did together, but she knew that the sound of her father's begging made her feel sick to her stomach.

If Daddy understood how much she really knew, he would have slapped her for sure.

"Letitia," Daddy said, a low thunder still roiling in his voice. "Don't you dare put that magic-eye on me, gal. You best learn to stay out of grown people's business. I've made my decision, and that's the last I have to say about it."

You're so weak, Daddy, Letitia thought. You look big and strong, but you're weak through and through. And she began to cry. Daddy left her to sort out her tears for herself instead of kissing them from her cheeks the way he usually did. Letitia cried late into the night, stroking her cat, wondering how the whole world could have gone so wrong in so little time.

The next day, as she always did when she had nowhere else to turn, Letitia walked the half-mile's distance on an unpaved road to see Mama. Whenever Letitia went to Mama and cried about how mean Bernadette was to her, she knew how to fix it. She knew which powders, which doll, and which combinations of roots, bone and blood would make Bernadette more humble, more tolerable, more kind. Bernadette never got completely quiet—something Letitia had wished for often—but after a good ritual or two, Letitia noticed she had two or three weeks in a row when Bernadette did not say a single unkind thing to her. That was all the proof she needed that Mama's magic worked.

After she heard the story, Mama clucked her tongue in the space where she'd lost three of her front teeth in a riding accident when she was a very young woman. The work of a curse, people said. Everyone considered the lost teeth a great tragedy, since Mama would be very pretty otherwise, but Letitia knew that Daddy must not have minded. Maybe he hadn't loved Mama because she had no teeth, but he had thought she was pretty enough to court.

"That man, that man," Mama sighed. "Well, don't nothin' change. Always too skeered of what people think." It was rare that Mama said anything bad about Daddy in her presence.

"I think it's 'cause of Bernadette."

"Well, shoot, we know that," Mama said. "What ain't the fault of that devil-woman?"

"Do a spell, Mama. Make it so Bernadette will say Daddy can go save Brother. Make her go out her head, or get her real sick." Or kill her. That was what Letitia really wanted to say. Once, when Mama had made a little rag-doll of Bernadette when she was being more unpleasant than ever, Letitia's fingers had itched to tear the doll's tiny head clean off. Instead, Mama had given the doll's leg a good twist, and Bernadette had been laid up in bed for two weeks because she hurt her knee after falling in a near Daddy's tomato patch ditch.

But this time, instead of consulting her doll or her large leather pouch where she kept vials of powders, or gathering herbs from the woods alongside the roadway, Mama sighed and shook her head. "Cain't, Letitia. We hexed that woman five, six times. I told you that kinda' magic comes back on you. She got protection, and she's comin' back strong now. Naw, chile, we mess with any bad juju now, and yo' brother's gon' die."

Brother's gon' die. Meeting Letitia's ears, those three words turned her blood cold. Tears appeared in her eyes, but froze there. Her entire world felt frozen.

"The spirits is playin' tricks," Mama said, running her hand across her tightly-braided hair. Her bracelets of shells and cheap metals tinkled together. "Somebody got a curse on that house, and we got to do a higher ceremony. I think it's got to be you, 'cause you're blood kin to your brother. You need a sacrifice ritual, Lettie. You seen me bleed chickens, and that's what you got to do. But if you want the message to get across, don't use a chicken. That might not get what you want quick enough. Use your black cat."

Letitia had been filled with horror since her mama said the word sacrifice, because no matter how important the cause, she hated to see animals killed. For that reason and that reason alone, Letitia considered it a lucky thing she'd moved away from Mama's house, because people came for favors and Mama routinely slaughtered chickens, goats and pigs, for rituals or for meals, or usually for both. Letitia had been mortified enough at the idea of killing her first chicken, but nothing compared to her horror of hearing her Mama mention her cat.

Although Letitia didn't speak, Mama saw it in her eyes.

"Lettie, I know you love that cat. But you'll make the spirits listen if you bleed something you love. You see how I keep my bleeding chickens apart from my stewing chickens? I treat 'em special. And I had to do this, too, when I was your age."

"I won't," Letitia said.

"Then you don't wanna save your brother then, do you?"

Letitia's stomach hurt as she thought of Brother's row of smiling teeth. Brother was in a cage somewhere, and soon he would go to The Chair.

"Daddy will go see about him," Letitia said.

"Chile, yo' daddy ain't goin' nowhere. I know yo' daddy. I know him. If he was gonna go, he'd'a gone from the start. He woulda been there an' back. Nothin' can't keep that man from somethin' he wanna do, and nothin' can't change his mind, neither. Bernadette's got him stuck bein' wrongheaded, to let his own boy die. There's ways for women to get ahold of men until they can't fight, an' that's how Bernadette's got him. An' she was too strong for me, chile. Else, you an' me both would be livin' in yo' Daddy's fine house, wouldn't we?"

That was true, too. Letitia had always known it, but it hurt to hear Mama say it. The idea that Bernadette was more powerful than Mama terrified her. But of course she was! By now, Letitia's her tears had freed themselves, glistening across her face. She hitched back a sob.

"This is one o' them times you got a choice, Letitia. You can do what you want and hope things don't turn out wrong, or you can do what you know will make things right."

Letitia's next sob escaped throat fully formed. She suddenly wished that her parents had never met for the secret Sunday-afternoon meetings Mama had told her about, because then she would never have been born.

"If you gon' do it, do it clean and quick, like you seen me. When the blood's spilt, say this prayer: Spirit, release my daddy an' give him strength to fight the curse. An' do it at midnight. See how you named that cat? Like you known it from the start. Mama'll come bring you a new cat someday."

That was a lie, too, in its own way. Mama could not afford to bring her hardly anything.

"By myself?" Letitia heard herself ask.

"Just take the cat out back, to yo' Daddy's barn. Do it quick." With that, she handed Letitia a slender, shiny knife from the pocket of her stained old apron. Just the size for Midnight.

Letitia did not remember her walk home, nor did she remember most of the day. She told Bernadette she didn't feel well—which wasn't the least bit untrue—and she sat on her bed stroking Midnight's velvet-soft fur, rubbing her chin against the top of his head while his purr's roar seemed to fill her ears. As much as she hated to believe Mama's words, she knew their truth. Daddy had made up his mind, and he would not go see about Brother on his own. And Brother, most certainly, would die without Daddy's help. If there was a curse on her house, like Mama had said, then the curse on the town where Brother was in jail was a hundred times bigger. A hundred times stronger. It was a curse that had touched many families already.

And the trial day would ruin everything, Letitia knew. If Brother went to The Chair, Daddy would be a changed man. The bourbon bottle he kept hidden in the pantry for special occasions would become his constant companion. Bernadette, full of her own guilt, would be more hateful than ever. And Letitia would grow to despise them both. For all her life, she would judge men as weak and act accordingly, learning from the lesson of Daddy and Bernadette. She might hate them, but she would imitate them all the same. She knew these things as sure as she knew her name. Letitia felt her future unfolding like a clear-minded dream. It was so imminent, poised with terrible ease, that she marveled that Daddy and Bernadette couldn't see it, too.

But they couldn't. If they could, Daddy would have left for the trial by now.

Midnight's green eyes shined up at her like two perfect marbles, and he mewed at her. In Sunday school, Letitia had studied Judas Iscariot, the Betrayer, and the thought made her cry harder. Midnight wasn't the same as Jesus, of course, but he trusted her. For the past year, since Daddy said she could keep the cat who had planted himself on their doorstep, she had taken care of Midnight, and he had taken care of her. How could she kill a creature that loved her?

But then Letitia remembered Abraham and Isaac from the Old

Testament. God told Abraham to sacrifice his son—which she had thought was very mean of God when she'd heard the story, to tell the truth—but in the end it was only a test. Just like Abraham, she only had to show her willingness to do what Mama said, and God would provide another way to save Brother. Or maybe this was the only way, and she and Midnight were making a sacrifice like Jesus had, to save another's soul.

By sunset, Letitia made up her mind with a deep, ragged breath. She would do it. Just before midnight, she would take the cat to the barn. She would bring Daddy's catalog-ordered gold pocket-watch, which he kept on his desk at night, and as soon as the tall hand and short hand pointed to midnight, just like Mama said, she would . . .

She would . . .

"I have to do it, Midnight," Letitia whispered to her cat, who was curled in her lap with none of Jesus's inkling at The Last Supper that his sacrifice was waiting. "Maybe God will save you. But even if He doesn't, you can save Brother. I know you can."

And it seemed to Letitia, miraculously, that the cat mewed a tiny Yes, the way a cat would say yes if it could speak, as if Midnight understood it all and it was perfectly fine with him.

Midnight was happy to be in the barn because Letitia had brought out a dish of milk first. He found the dish and crouched comfortably beside it, lapping it up. She watched him drink, enjoying the slurping sound he made and the sloppy droplets of milk dotting his whiskers. Midnight was two parts cat and one part hog, Daddy always said. That thought made her smile through her tears.

Then, she felt her resolve melting. Watching Midnight, she felt frozen with disbelief at the very thought of what she planned to do, and she and wanted nothing more than to scoop Midnight into her arms and run back to bed before she got caught outside the house. Then, she remembered that wonderful sound of Daddy and Brother laughing on the porch, how that sound had lulled her to sleep. How he called her Lettie. How he hugged her and said he loved her every time he came to stay, never tugging on her hair or teasing the way her friends' older brothers did.

Only two minutes until midnight. How had the time gone so fast?

Quickly, watching Midnight drink his milk, Letitia said a series of prayers. God, please let Midnight forgive me for what I'm about to do . . . and please let this just be a test, so you will stop my hand at the last moment . . . and please don't let Midnight die . . . but if Midnight has to die, please let his sacrifice stop the curse so Daddy will go look after Brother and keep him safe.

Her prayer gobbled a full minute. With as heavy a heart as she had ever known, nearly choking off her breath so that her head felt light, Letitia realized it was time. Time to take out the shiny knife Mama had given her. Time to hold Midnight tight and feed his blood to the spirits.

Midnight had once gotten himself covered in mud and Bernadette had demanded that she fill up a tin tub and bathe him or else he could not come into the house—so Letitia knew from experience that it was hard to hold Midnight still for something he didn't want to do. She knew to watch out for his claws, especially those powerful back claws, and she would have to hook her arm tightly around him. And she knew she would have to keep no space between her knees, because he would back up against her as far as he could.

Now, just like then, she told herself she would think of the task, not of Midnight himself, or else with all his thrashing and complaining, she might feel sorry and forget what was at stake. Daddy was weak, so she had to be strong, and that was that.

Sure enough, Midnight put up a fight. Even if he didn't know what she was planning, he was angry to be pulled away from his milk, and he was wriggling from the start. Letitia was startled when she felt razor-thin stripes of pain across her forearm from Midnight's claws, and then she felt angry. The anger helped. She clamped her knees around him and hooked one arm around his middle, tight. Despite the perspiration dampening her palm, she kept a firm grip on the knife and raised it to Midnight's throat. Mama always used the throat.

Letitia wanted to close her eyes, but she couldn't. She poked and then slashed with the knife, quickly, and even though the cut wasn't nearly deep enough, she was amazed to see a ribbon of blood seep through Midnight's fur, right above his tiny collarbone. While Midnight screeched and renewed his escape attempt, Letitia watched, fascinated, as two fat, crimson drops of blood fell to the dusty barn floor at her feet.

She kept her grip around the cat. Until the very last second, she almost forgot the prayer, but then she began, reciting it as well as she could remember: "Spirit, please help lift the curse and make my Daddy strong so he will go see about Br—"

"What in great red hell are you doing?"

It sounded like it might be God's voice at first, albeit not as kindly as she'd thought God might sound, but when she gathered her senses above her racing heart, Letitia realized it was only Daddy's voice. She looked up and she saw him standing in the doorway of the barn, wearing only his trousers. She saw his chest heaving up and down with his breathing. His expression was a combination of rage and shock she had never seen on her father's face, and it seared her. The sight of him made her drop the knife, and Midnight scrambled from her arms, scratching her chest through her nightgown as he launched himself from her with his powerful hind legs. Letitia did not know if the blood on her gown was hers or Midnight's.

"Letitia, what are you doing?" Daddy said.

"Mama said . . . she said . . . " But Letitia couldn't finish, because she felt too overcome.

Abraham and Isaac, she remembered. God had stepped in and sent Daddy.

Daddy fumbled for his belt, before he realized he wasn't wearing it. His sleep-wrinkled face was growing more alert, more angry. He wanted to beat her, she saw. He wanted to beat her in a way he had never beaten her before.

"Mama said if I sacrificed Midnight, I'd break the curse and you would go see about Brother," Letitia said, finally finding the words. She pointed to the droplets of blood that spattered the floor. "See, Daddy? I had to bleed Midnight, but I did it for Brother, Daddy. I did it so you'd go to the trial."

Daddy stared at her pointing finger, then back at her face, than back at her finger, and his own face seemed to transform. The only light was the dim lantern she'd brought with the bowl of milk, but Daddy's face wasn't the same anymore. The only word for it, really, was haunted. He cradled his abdomen, as if a grown man had kicked him in the stomach hard.

"We have to save Brother, Daddy," Letitia said, a whisper.

Daddy rocked in place, like he did when he'd had too much to drink. Then, he took a lurching step until he was no longer facing her. One step at a time, he walked away. He did not look at her or speak to her. She saw him climb the steps of the back porch, and he was back inside the house. He left the back door wide open. Bernadette wouldn't like that, Letitia thought. All the mosquitoes could come in.

For a long time, Letitia called for Midnight outside. She finally heard him growling somewhere out in the bushes near the cotton patch, but he would not come to her. Maybe he would never come back, she realized.

But this time, she did not cry.

Letitia quietly washed her bloody scratches clean in the kitchen sink, blew out the lamp and climbed the stairs to go into her room. Daddy's door was closed, but she could hear Bernadette's voice through the door, wide awake. "Richard, what's into you? I said to talk to me, goddammit. You put that suitcase down, you hear me? Do you know what time it is?"

Quickly, Letitia stole into her own room and shut the door. She suddenly needed to tear off every piece of clothing she was wearing, even though her body was shaking. She climbed into her bed, under her covers, seeking sanctuary while her breathing came hard and deep from her lungs. She had a headache. The memory of Midnight's blood on the knife made her stomach twist, and she was afraid she would be sick.

She had left Daddy's pocket-watch lying on the barn floor, she remembered. And Bernadette's bowl from the kitchen. They would be mad about that, she thought. She thought she'd best get out of bed and go fetch them, but she couldn't move from where she lay.

Letitia heard the door to Daddy's room open across the hall, followed by his heavy footsteps. She couldn't see him, of course, but somehow she knew he was wearing his best brown suit and white shirt, with his brown Sunday derby. He was wearing the clothes that told everyone that he was Richard Reaves, a business-owner, and he was not a hard-luck sort of man.

Bernadette had given up shouting, but now she was outright begging instead, the way she liked to hear Daddy beg. "Richard . . . you aren't thinking clearly. Do you know what they'll do to an uppity yellow nigger who thinks he can just walk in there and have a say? Think of it, Richard! Don't be a fool. Don't get your name mixed up in this mess. That boy's gonna be all right. You aren't thinking. What about your family? What about me and Letitia? I swear to Jesus, if you don't stop this foolishness, I won't be here when you come back."

Bernadette's voice trailed the heavy footsteps down the stairs. Through her open window, Letitia heard the front door open, and the sound of Bernadette's voice in the night, suddenly shrieking like a woman in pain. "Richard, don't do this—I love you!"

But Bernadette's professed love, to Letitia, just sounded like the same old hatefulness. No matter, though. She had bled Midnight, and the curse was broken. Daddy's ears belonged to himself again and he had his strength back.

Letitia heard the engine to Dad's choke and sputter, than roar to life. Letitia closed her eyes, smiling. The sound of that purring engine as it drove away was as sweet as the memory of Daddy's laughter with Brother on the porch that night. As sweet as Christmas morning and as gentle as the stinging of Mama's loving hands when she pulled her hair into tight plaits between her knees, the way only Mama really knew how.

For once, Letitia's third eye—what Daddy called her magic eye—wasn't working. Brother's future was very blurry and far away, not for her to know. All she knew for sure was that Richard Reaves was on his way to the trial in his good suit to try to save Brother. And that knowledge would last her as long as she would live.

⌒⌒

Nalo Hopkinson invited me to submit a short story to her anthology Mojo: Conjure Stories. *I wanted to "fix" a broken piece of my family history—my grandmother, the late Lottie (Powell) Sears Houston, clearly remembered her half-brother being on trial for his life, and her father was too intimidated to testify on his behalf, which she considered cowardly for the rest of her life— though I can only imagine the institutional racism standing in his way. Her brother died on Death Row.*

Did Brother die in this story? Maybe, maybe not.

But at least Lettie gave her father strength enough to try.

CARRIERS

I know Dr. Ben was very worried
I might make somebody sick.

Patient Zero

THE PICTURE CAME! Veronica tapped on my glass and woke me up, and she held it up for me to see. It's autographed and everything! For you, Veronica mouthed at me, and she smiled a really big smile. The autograph says, *To Jay—I'll throw a touchdown for you.* I couldn't believe it. Everybody is laughing at me because of the way I yelled and ran in circles around my room until I fell on the floor and scraped my elbow. The janitor, Lou, turned on the intercom box outside my door and said, "Kid, you gone crazier than usual? What you care about that picture for?"

Don't they know Dan Marino is the greatest quarterback of all time? I taped the picture to the wall over my bed. On the rest of my wall I have maps of the United States, and the world, and the solar system. I can find Corsica on the map, and the Palau Islands, which most people have never heard of, and I know what order all the planets are in. But there's nothing else on my wall like Dan Marino. That's the best. The other best thing I have is the cassette tape from that time the President called me on the telephone when I was six. He said, "Hi, is Jay there? This is the President of the United States." He sounded just like on TV. My heart flipped, because it's so weird to hear the President say your name. I couldn't think of anything to say back. He asked me how I was feeling, and I said I was fine. That made him laugh, like he thought I was making a joke. Then his voice got real serious, and he said everyone was praying and thinking about me, and he hung up. When I listen to that tape now, I wish I had thought of something else to say. I used to think he might call me another time, but it only happened once, in the beginning. So I guess I'll never have a chance to talk to the President again.

After Veronica gave me my picture of Marino, I asked her if she could get somebody to fix my TV so I can see the football games. All my TV can play is videos. Veronica said there aren't any football games, and I started to get mad because I hate it when they lie. It's September, I said, and there's always football games in September. But Veronica told me the NFL people had a meeting and decided not to have football anymore, and maybe it would start again, but she wasn't sure, because nobody except me was thinking about football. At first, after she said that, it kind of ruined the autograph, because it seemed like Dan Marino must be lying, too. But Veronica said he was most likely talking about throwing a touchdown for me in the future, and I felt better then.

This notebook is from Ms. Manigat, my tutor, who is Haitian. She said I should start writing down my thoughts and everything that happens to me. I said I don't have any thoughts, but she said that was ridiculous. That is her favorite word, ridiculous.

Oh, I should say I'm ten today. If I were in a regular school, I would be in fifth grade like my brother was. I asked Ms. Manigat what grade I'm in, and she said I don't have a grade. I read like I'm in seventh grade and I do math like I'm in fourth grade, she says. She says I don't exactly fit anywhere, but I'm very smart. Ms. Manigat comes every day, except on weekends. She is my best friend, but I have to call her Ms. Manigat instead of using her first name, which is Emmeline, because she is so proper. She is very neat and wears skirts and dresses, and everything about her is very clean except her shoes, which are dirty. Her shoes are supposed to be white, but whenever I see her standing outside of the glass, when she hasn't put on her plastic suit yet, her shoes look brown and muddy.

Those are my thoughts.

September 20

I HAD A QUESTION today. Veronica never comes on Fridays, and the other nurse, Rene, isn't as nice as she is, so I waited for Ms. Manigat. She comes at one. I said, "You know how they give sick children their last wish when they're dying? Well, when Dr. Ben told me to think of the one thing I wanted for my birthday, I said I wanted an autograph from Dan Marino, so does that mean I'm dying and they're giving me my wish?" I said this really fast.

I thought Ms. Manigat would say I was being ridiculous. But she smiled. She put her hand on top of my head, and her hand felt stiff and heavy inside her big glove. "Listen, little old man," she said, which is what she calls me because she says I do so much worrying, "You're a lot of things, but you aren't dying. When everyone can be as healthy as you, it'll be a happy day."

The people here always seems to be waiting, and I don't know what for. I thought maybe they were waiting for me to die. But I believe Ms. Manigat. If she doesn't want to tell me something, she just says, "Leave it alone, Jay," which is her way of letting me know she would rather not say anything at all than ever tell a lie.

October 5

THE LIGHTS in my room started going on and off again today, and it got so hot I had to leave my shirt off until I went to bed. Ms. Manigat couldn't do her lessons the way she wanted because of the lights not working right. She said it was the emergency generator. I asked her what the emergency was, and she said something that sounded funny: "Same old same old." That was all she said. I asked her if the emergency generator was the reason Dr. Ben took the television out of my room, and she said yes. She said everyone is conserving energy, and I have to do my part, too. But I miss my videos. There is nothing at all to do when I can't watch my videos. I hate it when I'm bored. Sometimes I'll even watch videos I've seen a hundred times, really a hundred times. I've seen *Big* with Tom Hanks more times than any other video. I love the part in the toy store with the really big piano keys on the floor. My mom taught me how to play "Three Blind Mice" on our piano at home, and it reminds me of that. I've never seen a toy store like the one in Big. I thought it was just a made-up place, but Ms. Manigat said it was a real toy store in New York.

I miss my videos. When I'm watching them, it's like I'm inside the movie, too. I hope Dr. Ben will bring my TV back soon.

October 22

I MADE VERONICA cry yesterday. I didn't mean to. Dr. Ben said he knows it was an accident, but I feel very sorry, so I've been crying too. What

209

happened is, I was talking to her, and she was taking some blood out of my arm with a needle like always. I was telling her about how me and my dad used to watch Marino play on television, and then all of a sudden she was crying really hard.

She dropped the needle on the floor and she was holding her wrist like she broke it. She started swearing. She said Goddammit, goddammit, goddammit, over and over, like that. I asked her what happened, and she pushed me away like she wanted to knock me over. Then she went to the door and punched the number code really fast and she pulled on the doorknob, but the door wouldn't open, and I heard something in her arm snap from yanking so hard. She had to do the code again. She was still crying. I've never seen her cry.

I didn't know what happened. I mashed my finger on the buzzer hard, but everybody ignored me. It reminded me of when I first came here, when I was always pushing the buzzer and crying, and nobody would ever come for a long time, and they were always in a bad mood when they came.

Anyway, I waited for Ms. Manigat, and when I told her about Veronica, she said she didn't know anything because she comes from the outside, but she promised to find out. Then she made me recite the Preamble to the Constitution, which I know by heart. Pretty soon, for a little while, I forgot about Veronica.

After my lessons, Ms. Manigat left and called me on my phone an hour later, like she promised. She always keeps her promises. My telephone is hooked up so people on the inside can call me, but I can't call anybody, inside or outside. It hardly ever rings now. But I almost didn't want to pick it up. I was afraid of what Ms. Manigat would say.

"Veronica poked herself," Ms. Manigat told me. "The needle stuck through her hot suit. She told Dr. Ben there was sudden movement."

I wondered who made the sudden movement, Veronica or me?

"Is she okay?" I asked. I thought maybe Ms. Manigat was mad at me, because she has told me many times that I should be careful. Maybe I wasn't being careful when Veronica was here.

"We'll see, Jay," Ms. Manigat said. From her voice, it sounded like the answer was no.

"Will she get sick?" I asked.

"Probably, yes, they think so," Ms. Manigat said.

I didn't want her to answer any more questions. I like it when people tell me the truth, but it always makes me feel bad, too. I tried to say I was sorry, but I couldn't even open my mouth.

"It's not your fault, Jay," Ms. Manigat said.

I couldn't help it. I sobbed like I used to when I was still a little kid. "Veronica knew something like this could happen," she said.

But that didn't make anything better, because I remembered how Veronica's face looked so scared inside her mask, and how she pushed me away. Veronica has been here since almost the beginning, before Ms. Manigat came, and she used to smile at me even when nobody else did. When she showed me my picture from Dan Marino, she looked almost as happy as me. I had never seen her whole face smiling like that. She looked so pretty and glad.

I was crying so much I couldn't even write down my thoughts like Ms. Manigat said to. Not until today.

November 4

A LONG TIME AGO, when I first came here and the TV in my room played programs from outside, I saw the first-grade picture I had taken at school on TV. I always hated that picture because Mom put some greasy stuff in my hair that made me look like a total geek. And then I turned on the TV and saw that picture on the news! The man on TV said the names of everyone in our family, and even spelled them out on the screen. Then, he called me *Patient Zero*. He said I was the first person who got sick.

But that wasn't really what happened. My dad was sick before me. I've told them that already. He got it away on his job in Alaska. My dad traveled a lot because he drilled for oil, but he came home early that time. We weren't expecting him until Christmas, but he came when it was only September, close to my birthday. He said he'd been sent home because some people on his oil crew got sick. One of them had even died. But the doctor in Alaska had looked at my dad and said he was fine, and then his boss sent him home. Dad was really mad about that. He hated to lose money. Time away from a job was always losing money, he said. He was in a bad mood when he wasn't working.

And the worse thing was, my dad wasn't fine. After two days, his eyes got red and he started sniffling. Then I did, too. And then my mom and brother.

When the man on TV showed my picture and called me Patient Zero and said I was the first one to get sick, that was when I first learned how people tell lies, because that wasn't true. Somebody on my dad's oil rig caught it first, and then he gave it to my dad. And my dad gave it to me, my mom, and my brother. But one thing he said was right. I was the only one who got well.

My Aunt Lori came here to live at the lab with me at first, but she wasn't here long, because her eyes had already turned red by then. She came to help take care of me and my brother before my mom died, but probably she shouldn't have done that. She lived all the way in California, and I bet she wouldn't have gotten sick if she hadn't come to Miami to be with us. But even my mom's doctor didn't know what was wrong then, so nobody could warn her about what would happen if she got close to us. Sometimes I dream I'm calling Aunt Lori on my phone, telling her please, please not to come. Aunt Lori and my mom were twins. They looked exactly alike.

After Aunt Lori died, I was the only one left in my whole family.

I got very upset when I saw that news report. I didn't like hearing someone talk about my family like that, people who didn't even know us. And I felt like maybe the man on TV was right, and maybe it was all my fault. I screamed and cried the whole day. After that, Dr. Ben made them fix my TV so I couldn't see the news anymore or any programs from outside, just cartoons and kid movies on video. The only good thing was, that was when the President called me. I think he was sorry when he heard what happened to my family.

When I ask Dr. Ben if they're still talking about me on the news, he just shrugs his shoulders. Sometimes Dr. Ben won't say yes or no if you ask him a question. It doesn't matter, though. I think the TV people probably stopped showing my picture a long time ago. I was just a little kid when my family got sick. I've been here four whole years!

Oh, I almost forgot. Veronica isn't back yet.

• • •

November 7

I HAVE BEEN staring at my Dan Marino picture all day, and I think the handwriting on the autograph looks like Dr. Ben's. But I'm afraid to ask anyone about that. Oh, yeah—and yesterday the power was off in my room for a whole day! Same old same old. That's what Ms. M. would say.

November 12

Ms. MANIGAT is teaching me a little bit about medicine. I told her I want to be a doctor when I grow up, and she said she thinks that's a wonderful idea because she believes people will always need doctors. She says I will be in a good position to help people, and I asked her if that's because I have been here so long, and she said yes.

The first thing she taught me is about diseases. She says in the old days, a long time ago, diseases like typhoid used to kill a lot of people because of unsanitary conditions and dirty drinking water, but people got smarter and doctors found drugs to cure it, so diseases didn't kill people as much anymore. Doctors are always trying to stay a step ahead of disease, Ms. Manigat says.

But sometimes they can't. Sometimes a new disease comes. Or, maybe it's not a new disease, but an old disease that has been hidden for a long time until something brings it out in the open. She said that's how nature balances the planet, because as soon as doctors find cures for one thing, there is always something new. Dr. Ben says my disease is new. There is a long name for it I can't remember how to spell, but most of the time people here call it Virus-J.

In a way, see, it's named after me. That's what Dr. Ben said. But I don't like that.

Ms. Manigat said after my dad came home, the virus got in my body and attacked me just like everyone else, so I got really, really sick for a lot of days. Then, I thought I was completely better. I stopped feeling bad at all. But the virus was already in my brother and my mom and dad, and even our doctor from before, Dr. Wolfe, and Ms. Manigat says it was very aggressive, which means doctors didn't know how to kill it.

Everybody wears yellow plastic suits and airtight masks when they're in my room because the virus is still in the air, and it's in my blood, and it's on my plates and cups whenever I finish eating. They call the suits hot suits because the virus is hot in my room. Not hot like fire, but dangerous.

Ms. Manigat says Virus-J is extra special in my body because even though I'm not sick anymore, except for when I feel like I have a temperature and I have to lie down sometimes, the virus won't go away. I can make other people sick even when I feel fine, so she said that makes me a carrier. Ms. Manigat said Dr. Ben doesn't know anybody else who's gotten well except for me.

Oh, except maybe there are some little girls in China. Veronica told me once there were some little girls in China the same age as me who didn't get sick either. But when I asked Dr. Ben, he said he didn't know if it was true. And Ms. Manigat told me it might have been true once, but those girls might not be alive anymore. I asked her if they died of Virus-J, and she said no, no, no. Three times. She told me to forget all about any little girls in China. Almost like she was mad.

I'm the only one like me she knows about for sure, she says. The only one left.

That's why I'm here, she says. But I already knew that part. When I was little, Dr. Ben told me about antibodies and stuff in my blood, and he said the reason him and Rene and Veronica and all the other doctors take so much blood from me all the time, until they make purple bruises on my arms and I feel dizzy, is so they can try to help other people get well, too. I have had almost ten surgeries since I have been here. I think they have even taken out parts of me, but I'm not really sure. I look the same on the outside, but I feel different on the inside. I had surgery on my belly a year ago, and sometimes when I'm climbing the play-rope hanging from the ceiling in my room, I feel like it hasn't healed right, like I'm still cut open. Ms. Manigat says that's only in my mind. But it really hurts! I don't hate anything like I hate operations. I wonder if that's what happened to the other little girls, if they kept getting cut up and cut up until they died. Anyway, it's been a year since I had any operations. I keep telling Dr. Ben they can have as much blood as they want, but I don't want any more operations, please.

Dr. Ben said there's nobody in the world better than me to make people well, if only they can figure out how. Ms. Manigat says the same thing. That makes me feel a little better about Virus-J.

I was happy Ms. Manigat told me all about disease, because I don't want her to treat me like a baby the way everybody else does. That's what I always tell her. I like to know things.

I didn't even cry when she told me Veronica died. Maybe I got all my crying over with in the beginning, because I figured out a long time ago nobody gets better once they get sick. Nobody except for me.

November 14

TODAY, I ASKED Ms. Manigat how many people have Virus-J.

"Oh, Jay, I don't know," she said. I don't think she was in the mood to talk about disease.

"Just guess," I said.

Ms. Manigat thought for a long time. Then she opened her notebook and began drawing lines and boxes for me to see. Her picture looked like the tiny brown lines all over an oak-tree leaf. We had a tree called a live oak in our backyard, and my dad said it was more than a hundred years old. He said trees sometimes live longer than people do. And he was right, because I'm sure that tree is still standing in our yard even though my whole family is gone.

"This is how it goes, Jay," Ms. Manigat said, showing me with her pencil-tip how one line branched down to the next. "People are giving it to each other. They don't usually know they're sick for two weeks, and by then they've passed it to a lot of other people. By now, it's already been here four years, so the same thing that happened to your family is happening to a lot of families."

"How many families?" I asked again. I tried to think of the biggest number I could. "A million?"

Ms. Manigat shrugged just like Dr. Ben would. Maybe that meant yes.

I couldn't imagine a million families, so I asked Ms. Manigat if it happened to her family, too, if maybe she had a husband and kids and they got sick. But she said no, she was never married. I guess that's true, because Ms. Manigat doesn't look that old. She won't tell me her age, but she's in her twenties, I think. Ms. Manigat smiled at me, even though her eyes weren't happy.

"My parents were in Miami, and they got it right away," Ms. Manigat said. "Then my sister and nieces came to visit them from Haiti, and they got it, too. I was away working when it happened, and that's why I'm still here."

Ms. Manigat never told me that before.

My family lived in Miami Beach. My dad said our house was too small—I had to share a room with my brother—but my mother liked where we lived because our building was six blocks from the ocean. My mother said the ocean can heal anything. But that can't be true, can it?

My mother wouldn't like it where I am, because there is no ocean and no windows neither. I wondered if Ms. Manigat's parents knew someone who worked on an oil rig, too, but probably not. Probably they got it from my dad and me.

"Ms. Manigat," I said, "Maybe you should move inside like Dr. Ben and everybody else."

"Oh, Jay," Ms. Manigat said, like she was trying to sound cheerful. "Little old man, if I were that scared of anything, why would I be in here teaching you?"

She said she asked to be my teacher, which I didn't know. I said I thought her boss was making her do it, and she said she didn't have a boss. No one sent her. She wanted to come.

"Just to meet me?" I asked her.

"Yes, because I saw your face on television, and you looked to me like a one-of-a-kind," she said. She said she was a nurse before, and she used to work with Dr. Ben in his office in Atlanta. She said they worked at the CDC, which is a place that studies diseases. And he knew her, so that was why he let her come teach me.

"A boy like you needs his education. He needs to know how to face life outside," she said.

Ms. Manigat is funny like that. Sometimes she'll quit the regular lesson about presidents and the Ten Commandments and teach me something like how to sew and how to tell plants you eat from plants you don't, and stuff. Like, I remember when she brought a basket with real fruits and vegetables in it, fresh. She said she has a garden where she lives on the outside, close to here. She said one of the reasons she won't move inside is because she loves her garden so much, and she doesn't want to leave it.

The stuff she brought was not very interesting to look at. She showed me some cassava, which looked like a long, twisty tree branch to me, and she said it's good to eat, except it has poison in it that has to be boiled out of the root first and the leaves are poisonous too. She also brought something called akee, which she said she used to eat from trees in Haiti. It has another name in Haiti that's too hard for me to spell. It tasted fine to me, but she said akee can never be eaten before it's opened, or before it's ripe, because it makes your brain swell up and you can die. She also brought different kinds of mushrooms to show me which ones are good or bad, but they all looked alike to me. She promised to bring me other fruits and vegetables to see so I will know what's good for me and what isn't. There's a lot to learn about life outside, she said.

Well, I don't want Ms. Manigat to feel like I am a waste of her time, but I know for a fact I don't have to face life outside. Dr. Ben told me I might be a teenager before I can leave, or even older. He said I might even be a grown man.

But that's okay, I guess. I try not to think about what it would be like to leave. My room, which they moved me to when I had been here six months, is really, really big. They built it especially for me. It's four times as big as the hotel room my mom and dad got for us when we went to Universal Studios in Orlando when I was five. I remember that room because my brother, Kevin, kept asking my dad, "Doesn't this cost too much?" Every time my dad bought us a T-shirt or anything, Kevin brought up how much it cost. I told Kevin to stop it because I was afraid Dad would get mad and stop buying us stuff. Then, when we were in line for the King Kong ride, all by ourselves, Kevin told me, "Dad got fired from his job, stupid. Do you want to go on Welfare?" I waited for Dad and Mom to tell me he got fired, but they didn't. After Kevin said that, I didn't ask them to buy me anything else, and I was scared to stay in that huge, pretty hotel room because I thought we wouldn't have enough money to pay. But we did. And then Dad got a job on the oil rig, and we thought everything would be better.

My room here is as big as half the whole floor I bet. When I run from one side of my room to the other, from the glass in front to the wall in back, I'm out of breath. I like to do that. Sometimes I run until my ribs start squeezing and my stomach hurts like it's cut open and I have to sit down and rest. There's a basketball net in here, too, and the ball doesn't ever touch the ceiling except if I throw it too high on purpose. I also have comic books, and I draw pictures of me and my family and Ms. Manigat and Dr. Ben. Because I can't watch my videos, now I spend a lot of time writing in this notebook. A whole hour went by already. When I am writing down my thoughts, I forget about everything else.

I have decided for sure to be a doctor someday. I'm going to help make people better.

November 29

THANKSGIVING WAS GREAT! Ms. Manigat cooked real bread and brought me food she'd heated up. I could tell everything except the bread and cassava was from a can, like always, but it tasted much better than my regular food. I haven't had bread in a long time. Because of her mask, Ms. Manigat ate her dinner before she came, but she sat and watched me eat. Rene came in, too, and she surprised me when she gave me a hug. She never does that. Dr. Ben came in for a little while at the end, and he hugged me too, but he said he couldn't stay because he was busy. Dr. Ben doesn't come visit me much anymore. I could see he was growing a beard, and it was almost all white! I've seen Dr. Ben's hair when he's outside of the glass, when he isn't wearing his hot suit, and his hair is brown, not white. I asked him how come his beard was white, and he said that's what happens when your mind is overly tired.

I liked having everybody come to my room. Before, in the beginning, almost nobody came in, not even Ms. Manigat. She used to sit in a chair outside the glass and use the intercom for my lessons. It's better when they come in.

I remember how Thanksgiving used to be, with my family around the table in the dining room, and I told Ms. Manigat about that. Yes, she said, even though she didn't celebrate Thanksgiving in Haiti like Americans do, she remembers sitting at the table with her parents and her sister for Christmas dinner. She said she came to see me today, and Rene and Dr. Ben came too, because we are each other's family now, so we are not alone. I hadn't thought of it like that before.

December 1

NO ONE WILL tell me, not even Ms. M., but I think maybe Dr. Ben is sick. I have not seen him in five whole days. It is quiet here. I wish it was Thanksgiving again.

January 23

I DIDN'T KNOW this before, but you have to be in the right mood to write your thoughts down. A lot happened in the days I missed.

The doctor with the French name is gone now, and I'm glad. He wasn't like Dr. Ben at all. I could hardly believe he was a real doctor, because he always had on the dirtiest clothes when I saw him take off his hot suit outside of the glass. And he was never nice to me—he wouldn't answer at all when I asked him questions, and he wouldn't look in my eyes except for a second. One time he slapped me on my ear, almost for nothing, and his glove hurt so much my ear turned red and was sore for a whole day. He didn't say he was sorry, but I didn't cry. I think he wanted me to.

Oh yeah, and he hooked me up to IV bags and took so much blood from me I couldn't even stand up. I was scared he would operate on me. Ms. Manigat didn't come in for almost a week, and when she finally came, I told her about the doctor taking too much blood. She got really mad. Then I found out the reason she didn't come all those days—he wouldn't let her! She said he tried to bar her from coming. Bar is the word she used, which sounds like a prison.

The new doctor and Ms. Manigat do not get along, even though they both speak French. I saw them outside of the glass, yelling back and forth and moving their hands, but I couldn't hear what they were saying. I was afraid he would send Ms. Manigat away for good. But yesterday she told me he's leaving! I told her I was happy, because I was afraid he would take Dr. Ben's place.

No, she told me, there isn't anyone taking Dr. Ben's place. She said the French doctor came here to study me in person because he was one of the doctors Dr. Ben had been sending my blood to ever since I first came. But he was already very sick when he got here, and he started feeling worse, so he had to go. Seeing me was his last wish, Ms. Manigat said, which didn't seem like it could be true because he didn't act like he wanted to be with me.

I asked her if he went back to France to his family, and Ms. Manigat said no, he probably didn't have a family, and even if he did, it's too hard to go to France. The ocean is in the way, she said.

Ms. Manigat seemed tired from all that talking. She said she'd decided to move inside, like Rene, to make sure they were taking care of me properly. She said she misses her garden. The whole place has been falling apart, she said. She said I do a good job of keeping my room clean—and I do, because I have my own mop and bucket and Lysol in my closet—but she told me the hallways are filthy. Which is true, because sometimes I can see water dripping down the wall outside of my glass, a lot of it, and it makes puddles all over the floor. You can tell the water is dirty because you can see different colors floating on top, the way my family's driveway used to look after my dad sprayed it with a hose. He said the oil from the car made the water look that way, but I don't know why it looks that way here. Ms. Manigat said the water smells bad, too.

"It's ridiculous. If they're going to keep you here, they'd damn well better take care of you," Mrs. Manigat said. She must have been really mad, because she never swears.

I told her about the time when Lou came and pressed on my intercom really late at night, when I was asleep and nobody else was around. He was talking really loud like people do in videos when they're drunk. Lou was glaring at me through the glass, banging on it. I had never seen him look so mean. I thought he would try to come into my room but then I remembered he couldn't because he didn't have a hot suit. But I'll never forget how he said, They should put you to sleep like a dog at the pound.

I try not to think about that night, because it gave me nightmares. It happened when I was pretty little, like eight. Sometimes I thought maybe I just dreamed it, because the next time Lou came he acted just like normal. He even smiled at me a little bit. Before he stopped coming here, Lou was nice to me every day after that.

Ms. Manigat did not sound surprised when I told her what Lou said about putting me to sleep. "Yes, Jay," she told me, "For a long time, there have been people outside who didn't think we should be taking care of you."

I never knew that before!

I remember a long time ago, when I was really little and I had pneumonia, my mom was scared to leave me alone at the hospital. "They won't know how to take care of Jay there," she said to my dad, even though she didn't know I heard her. I had to stay by myself all night, and because of what my mom said, I couldn't go to sleep. I was afraid everyone at the hospital would forget I was there. Or maybe something bad would happen to me.

It seems like the lights go off every other day now. And I know people must really miss Lou, because the dirty gray water is all over the floor outside my glass and there's no one to clean it up.

February 14

6-4-6-7-2-9-4-3

   6-4-6-7-2-9-4-3

   6-4-6-7-2-9-4-3

I remember the numbers already! I have been saying them over and over in my head so I won't forget, but I wanted to write them down in the exact right order to be extra sure. I want to know them without even looking.

Oh, I should start at the beginning. Yesterday, no one brought me any dinner, not even Ms. Manigat. She came with a huge bowl of oatmeal this morning, saying she was very sorry. She said she had to look a long time to find that food, and it wore her out. The oatmeal wasn't even hot, but I didn't say anything. I just ate. She watched me eating.

She didn't stay with me long, because she doesn't teach me lessons anymore. After the French doctor left, we talked about the Emancipation Proclamation and Martin Luther King, but she didn't bring that up today. She just kept sighing, and she said she had been in bed all day yesterday because she was so tired, and she was sorry she forgot to feed me. She said

I couldn't count on Rene to bring me food because she didn't know where Rene was. It was hard for me to hear her talk through her hot suit today. Her mask was crooked, so the microphone wasn't in front of her mouth where it should be.

She saw my notebook and asked if she could look at it. I said sure. She looked at the pages from the beginning. She said she liked the part where I said she was my best friend. Her face-mask was fogging up, so I couldn't see her eyes and I couldn't tell if she was smiling. I am very sure she did not put her suit on right today.

When she put my notebook down, she told me to pay close attention to her and repeat the numbers she told me, which were 6-4-6-7-2-9-4-3.

I asked her what they were. She said it was the security code for my door. She said she wanted to give the code to me because my buzzer wasn't working, and I might need to leave my room if she overslept and nobody came to bring me food. She told me I could use the same code on the elevator, and the kitchen was on the third floor. There wouldn't be anybody there, she said, but I could look on the shelves, the top ones up high, to see if there was any food. If not, she said I should take the stairs down to the first floor and find the red EXIT sign to go outside. She said the elevator doesn't go to the first floor anymore.

I felt scared then, but she put her hand on top of my head again just like usual. She said she was sure there was plenty of food outside.

"But am I allowed?" I asked her. "What if people get sick?"

"You worry so much, little man," she said. "Only you matter now, my little one-of-a-kind."

But see I'm sure Ms. Manigat doesn't really want me to go outside. I've been thinking about that over and over. Ms. Manigat must be very tired to tell me to do something like that. Maybe she has a fever and that's why she told me how to get out of my room. My brother said silly things when he had a fever, and my father too. My father kept calling me Oscar, and I didn't know who Oscar was. My dad told us he had a brother who died when he was little, and maybe his name was Oscar. My mother didn't say anything at all when she got sick. She just died very fast. I wish I could find Ms. Manigat and give her something to drink. You get very thirsty when you have a fever, which I know for a fact. But I can't go to her because I don't know where she is. And besides, I don't know where Dr. Ben keeps the hot suits. What if I went to her and she wasn't wearing hers?

Maybe the oatmeal was the only thing left in the kitchen, and now I ate it all. I hope not! But I'm thinking maybe it is because I know Ms. Manigat would have brought me more food if she could have found it. She's always asking me if I have enough to eat. I'm already hungry again.

6-4-6-7-2-9-4-3

6-4-6-7-2-9-4-3

February 15

I am writing in the dark. The lights are off. I tried to open my lock but the numbers don't work because of the lights being off. I don't know where Ms. Manigat is. I'm trying not to cry.

What if the lights never come back on?

February 16

There's so much I want to say but I have a headache from being hungry. When the lights came back on I went out into the hall like Ms. M told me and I used the numbers to get the elevator to work and then I went to the kitchen like she said. I wanted to go real fast and find some peanut butter or some Oreos or even a can of beans I could open with the can opener Ms. M left me at Thanksgiving.

There's no food in the kitchen! There's empty cans and wrappers on the floor and even roaches but I looked on every single shelf and in every cabinet and I couldn't find anything to eat.

The sun was shining really REALLY bright from the window. I almost forgot how the sun looks. When I went to the window I saw a big, empty parking lot outside. At first I thought there were diamonds all over the ground because of the sparkles but it was just a lot of broken glass. I could only see one car and I thought it was Ms. M's. But Ms. M would never leave her car looking like that. For one thing it had two flat tires!

Anyway I don't think there's anybody here today. So I thought of a plan. I have to go now.

Ms. M, this is for you—or whoever comes looking for me. I know somebody will find this notebook if I leave it on my bed. I'm very sorry I had to leave in such a hurry.

I didn't want to go outside but isn't it okay if it's an emergency? I am really really hungry. I'll just find some food and bring it with me and I'll come right back. I'm leaving my door open so I won't get locked out. Ms. M, maybe I'll find your garden with cassavas and akee like you showed me and I'll know the good parts from the bad parts. If someone sees me and I get in trouble I'll just say I didn't have anything to eat.

Whoever is reading this don't worry. I'll tell everybody I see please please not to get too close to me. I know Dr. Ben was very worried I might make somebody sick.

Originally published in 2000 in The Magazine of Fantasy and Science Fiction—*five years after the publication of my first novel—"Patient Zero" was my first published short story. I vowed that I would continue writing short fiction, despite the demands of my life as a new novelist. It was included in two best-of-the-year science fiction anthologies and remains one of my most beloved short stories. Jay's loneliness and innocence still break my heart.*

Danger Word

(Written with Steven Barnes)

WHEN KENDRICK opened his eyes, Grandpa Joe was standing over his bed, a tall dark bulk dividing the morning light. Grandpa Joe's beard covered his dark chin like a coat of snow. Mom used to say that guardian angels watched over you while you slept, and Grandpa Joe looked like he might have been guarding him all night with his shotgun. Kendrick didn't believe in guardian angels anymore, but he was glad he could believe in Grandpa Joe.

Most mornings, Kendrick opened his eyes to only strangeness: dark, heavy curtains; wooden planks for walls; a brownish-gray stuffed owl mounted near the window with glassy black eyes that twitched as the sun set, or seemed to. A rough pine bed. And that *smell* everywhere, like the smell in Mom and Dad's closet. Cedar, Grandpa Joe told him. Grandpa Joe's big hard hands had made the whole cabin of it, one board and beam at a time.

For the last six months, this *had* been his room, but it still wasn't, really. His Spider-Man bedsheets weren't here. His G.I. Joes, Tonka trucks and Matchbox racetracks weren't here. His posters of Iron Man and Kobie weren't on the walls. This was his bed, but it wasn't his room.

"Up and at 'em, Little Soldier," Grandpa Joe said, using the nickname Mom had never liked. Grandpa was dressed in his hickory shirt and blue jeans, the same clothes he wore every day. He leaned on his rifle like a cane, so his left knee must be hurting him like it always did in the mornings. He'd hurt it long ago, in Vietnam.

"I'm going trading down to Mike's. You can come if you want, or I can leave you with the Dog-Girl. Up to you." Grandpa's voice was morning-rough. "Either way, it's time to get out of bed, sleepyhead."

Dog-Girl, the woman who lived in a house on a hill by herself fifteen minute's walk west, was their closest neighbor. Once upon a time she'd had six pit bulls that paraded up and down her fence. In the last month that number had dropped to three. Grandpa Joe said meat was getting scarce. Hard to keep six dogs fed, even if you needed them. The dogs wagged their tails when Kendrick came up to the fence because Dog-Girl had introduced him to them, but Grandpa Joe said those dogs could tear a man's arms off.

Don't you ever stick your hand in there, Grandpa Joe always said. *Just because a dog looks friendly don't mean he is. Especially when he's hungry.*

"Can I have a Coke?" Kendrick said, surprised to hear his own voice again, so much smaller than Grandpa Joe's, almost a little girl's. Kendrick hadn't planned to say anything today, but he wanted the Coke so bad he could almost taste the fizz; it would taste like a treat from Willy Wonka's Chocolate Factory.

"If Mike's got one, you'll get one. For *damn* sure." Grandpa Joe's grin widened until Kendrick could see the hole where his tooth used to be: his straw-hole, Grandpa Joe called it. He mussed Kendrick's hair with his big palm. "Good boy, Kendrick. You keep it up. I knew your tongue was in there somewhere. You better start using it, or you'll forget how. Hear me? You start talking again, and I'll whip you up a lumberjack breakfast, like before."

It *would* be good to eat one of Grandpa Joe's famous lumberjack breakfasts again, piled nearly to the ceiling: A bowl of fluffy eggs, a stack of pancakes, a plate full of bacon and sausage, and homemade biscuits to boot. Grandpa Joe had learned to cook in the Army.

But whenever Kendrick thought about talking, his stomach filled up like a balloon and he thought he would puke. Some things couldn't be said out loud, and some things *shouldn't*. There was more to talking than most people thought. A whole lot more.

Kendrick's eye went to the bandage on Grandpa Joe's left arm, just below his elbow, where the tip peeked out at the edge of his shirtsleeve. Grandpa Joe had said he'd hurt himself chopping wood yesterday, and Kendrick's skin had hardened when he'd seen a spot of blood on the bandage. He hadn't seen blood in a long time. He couldn't see any blood now, but Kendrick still felt worried. Mom said Grandpa Joe didn't heal as fast as other people because of his diabetes. What if something happened to him? He was old. Something could.

"That six-point we brought down will bring a good haul at Mike's. We'll trade jerky for gas. Don't like to be low on gas," Grandpa said. His foot slid a little on the braided rug as he turned to leave the room, and Kendrick thought he heard him hiss with pain under his breath. "And we'll get that Coke for you. Whaddya say, Little Soldier?"

Kendrick couldn't make any words come out of this mouth this time, but at least he was smiling, and smiling felt good. They had something to smile about, for once.

Three days ago, a buck had come to drink from the creek.

Through the kitchen window, Kendrick had seen something move—antlers, it turned out—and Grandpa Joe grabbed his rifle when Kendrick motioned. Before the shot exploded, Kendrick had seen the buck look up, and Kendrick thought *It knows*. The buck's black eyes reminded him of Dad's eyes when he had listened to the news on the radio in the basement, hunched over his desk with a headset. Kendrick had guessed it was bad news from the trapped look in his father's eyes.

Dad would be surprised at how good Kendrick was with a rifle now. He could blow away an empty Chef Boyardee Ravioli can from twenty yards. He'd learned how to aim on *Max Payne* and *Medal of Honor*, but Grandpa Joe had taught him how to shoot for real, a little every day. Grandpa Joe had a room full of guns and ammunition—the back shed he kept locked—so they never ran low on bullets. Kendrick supposed he would have to shoot a deer one day soon. Or an elk. Or something else. The time would come, Grandpa Joe said, when he would have to make a kill whether he wanted to or not. *You may have to kill to survive, Kendrick*, he said. *I know you're only nine, but you need to be sure you can do it.*

Before everything changed, Grandpa Joe used to ask Mom and Dad if he could teach Kendrick how to hunt during summer vacation, and they'd said no. Dad didn't like Grandpa much, maybe because Grandpa Joe always said what he thought, and he was Mom's father, not his. And Mom didn't go much easier on him, always telling Grandpa Joe *no*, no matter what he asked. *No*, you can't keep him longer than a couple weeks in the summer. *No*, you can't teach him shooting. *No*, you can't take him hunting.

Now, there was no one to say *no*. No one except Grandpa Joe, unless

Mom and Dad came back. Grandpa Joe had said they might, and they knew where to find him. They might.

Kendrick put on the red down jacket he'd been wearing the day Grandpa Joe found him. He'd sat in this for neverending hours in the safe room at home, the storage space under the stairs with a reinforced door, a chemical toilet and enough food and water for a month. Mom had sobbed, "*Bolt the door tight. Stay here, Kendrick, and don't open the door until you hear Grandpa's 'danger word'—NO MATTER WHAT.*"

She made him swear to Jesus, and she'd never made him swear to Jesus before. He'd been afraid to move or breathe. He'd heard other footsteps in the house, the awful sound of crashing and breaking. A single terrible scream. It could have been his mother, or father, or neither—he just didn't know.

Followed by silence; for one hour, two, three. Then, the hardest part. The worst part.

Show me your math homework, Kendrick.

The danger word was the special word he and Grandpa Joe had picked because Grandpa Joe had insisted on it. Grandpa Joe had made a special trip in his truck to tell them something bad could happen to them, and he had a list of reasons how and why. Dad didn't like Grandpa Joe's yelling much, but he'd listened. So Kendrick and Grandpa Joe had made up a danger word nobody else knew in the world, not even Mom and Dad.

And he had to wait to hear the danger word, Mom said.

No matter what.

By the time Kendrick dressed, Grandpa was already outside loading the truck, a beat-up navy blue Chevy. Kendrick heard a thud as he dropped a large sack of wrapped jerky in the bed.

Grandpa Joe had taught him how to mix up the secret jerky recipe he hadn't even given Mom: soy sauce and Worcestershire sauce, fresh garlic cloves, dried pepper, onion powder. He'd made sure Kendrick was paying attention while strips of deer meat soaked in that tangy mess for two days, and then spent twelve hours in the slow-cook oven. Grandpa Joe had also made him watch as he cut the deer open and its guts flopped to the ground, all gray and glistening. *Watch, boy. Don't turn away. Don't be scared to look at something for what it is.*

Grandpa Joe's deer jerky was almost as good as the lumberjack breakfast, and Kendrick's mouth used to water for it. Not anymore.

His jerky loaded, Grandpa Joe leaned against the truck, lighting a brown cigarette. Kendrick thought he shouldn't be smoking.

"Ready?"

Kendrick nodded. His hands shook a little every time he got in the truck, so he hid his hands in his jacket pockets. Some wadded-up toilet paper from the safe room in Longview was still in there, a souvenir. Kendrick clung to the wad, squeezing his hand into a fist.

"We do this right, we'll be back in less than an hour," Grandpa Joe said. He spit, as if the cigarette had come apart in his mouth. "Forty-five minutes."

Forty-five minutes. That wasn't bad. Forty-five minutes, then they'd be back.

Kendrick stared at the cabin in his rearview mirror until the trees hid it from his sight.

The road was empty, as usual. Grandpa Joe's rutted dirt road spilled onto the highway after a half-mile, and they jounced past darkened, abandoned houses. Kendrick saw three stray dogs trot out of the open door of a pink two-story house on the corner. He'd never seen that door open before, and he wondered whose dogs they were. He wondered what they'd been eating.

Suddenly, Kendrick wished he'd stayed back at Dog-Girl's. She was from England and he couldn't always understand her, but he liked being behind her fence. He liked Popeye and Ranger and Lady Di, her dogs. He tried not to think about the ones that were gone now. Maybe she'd given them away.

They passed tree farms, with all the trees growing the same size, identical, and Kendrick enjoyed watching their trunks pass in a blur. He was glad to be away from the empty houses.

"Get me a station," Grandpa Joe said.

The radio was Kendrick's job. Unlike Dad, Grandpa Joe never kept the radio a secret.

The radio hissed and squealed up and down the FM dial, so Kendrick tried AM next. Grandpa Joe's truck radio wasn't good for anything. The shortwave at the cabin was better.

A man's voice came right away, a shout so loud it was like screaming.

" . . . AND IN THOSE DAYS SHALL MEN SEEK DEATH AND SHALL NOT FIND IT . . . AND SHALL DESIRE TO DIE AND DEATH SHALL FLEE FROM THEM . . . "

"Turn that bullshit off," Grandpa Joe snapped. Kendrick hurried to turn the knob, and the voice was gone. "Don't you believe a word of that, you hear me? That's B-U-Double-L-*bullshit*. Things are bad now, but they'll get better once we get a fix on this thing. Anything can be beat, believe you me. I ain't givin' up, and neither should you. That's givin'-up talk."

The next voices were a man and a woman who sounded so peaceful that Kendrick wondered where they were. What calm places were left?

" . . . mobilization at the Vancouver Armory. That's from the commander of the Washington National Guard. So you see," the man said, "there *are* orchestrated efforts. There *has* been progress in the effort to reclaim Portland and even more in points north. The Armory is secure, and running survivors to the islands twice a week. Look at Rainier. Look at Devil's Wake. As long as you stay away from the large urban centers, there are dozens of pockets where people are safe and life is going on."

"Oh, yes," the woman said. "Of course there are."

"There's a learning curve. That's what people don't understand."

"Absolutely." The woman sounded absurdly cheerful.

"Everybody keeps harping on Longview . . . "—The man said *Longview* as if it were a normal, everyday place. Kendrick's stomach tightened when he heard it.—" . . . but that's become another encouraging story. Contrary to rumors, there *is* a National Guard presence. There *are* limited food supplies. There's a gated community in the hills housing over four hundred. Remember safety in numbers. Any man, woman or teenager who's willing to enlist is guaranteed safe lodging. Fences are going up, roads barricaded. We're getting this under control. That's a far cry from what we were hearing even five, six weeks ago."

"Night and day," the cheerful woman said. Her voice trembled with happiness.

Grandpa Joe reached over to rub Kendrick's head. "See there?" he said.

Kendrick nodded, but he wasn't happy to imagine that a stranger might be in his bed. Maybe it was another family with a little boy. Or twins.

But probably not. Dog-Girl said the National Guard was long gone and nobody knew where to find them. *Bunch of useless bloody shitheads*, she'd said, the first time he'd heard the little round woman cuss. Her accent made cussing sound exotic. If she was right, dogs might be roaming through his house, too, looking for something to eat.

" . . . There's talk that a Bay Area power plant is up again. It's still an unconfirmed rumor, and I'm not trying to try to wave some magic wand here, but I'm just making the point—and I've tried to make it before—that life probably felt a lot like this in Hiroshima."

"Yes," the woman said. From her voice, Hiroshima was somewhere very important.

"Call it apples and oranges, but put yourself in the place of a villager in Rwanda. Or an Auschwitz survivor. There had to be some days that felt *exactly* the way we feel when we hear these stories from Seattle and Portland, and when we've talked to the survivors . . . "

Just ahead, along the middle of the road, a man was walking ahead of them.

Kendrick sat straight up when he saw him, balling up the tissue wad in his pocket so tightly that he felt his fingernails bite into his skin. The walking man was tall and broad-shouldered, wearing a brick-red backpack. He lurched along unsteadily. From the way he bent forward, as if bracing into a gale, Kendrick guessed the backpack was heavy.

He hadn't ever seen anyone walking on this road.

"Don't you worry," Grandpa Joe said. Kendrick's neck snapped back as Grandpa Joe sped up his truck. "We ain't stoppin'."

The man let out a mournful cry as they passed, waving a cardboard sign. He had a long, bushy beard, and as they passed his eyes looked wide and wild. Kendrick craned his head to read the sign, which the man held high in the air: STILL HERE, the sign said.

"He'll be all right," Grandpa Joe said, but Kendrick didn't think so. No one was supposed to go on the roads alone, especially without a car. Maybe the man had a gun, and maybe they would need another man with a gun. Maybe the man had been trying to warn them something bad was waiting for them ahead.

But the way he walked . . .

No matter what, Mom said.

Kendrick kept watching while the man retreated behind them. He had to stop watching when he felt nausea pitch in his stomach. He'd been holding his breath without knowing it. His face was cold and sweating, both at once.

"Was that one?" Kendrick whispered.

He hadn't known he was going to say that either, just like when he asked for a Coke. Instead, he'd been thinking about the man's sign. *Still here.*

"Don't know," Grandpa Joe said. "It's hard to tell. That's why you never stop."

They listened to the radio, neither of them speaking again for the rest of the ride.

TIME WAS, Joseph Earl Davis III never would have driven past anyone on the road without giving them a chance to hop into the bed and ride out a few miles closer to wherever they were going. Hell, he'd picked up a group of six college-age kids and driven them to the Centralia compound back in April.

But Joe hadn't liked the look of that hitcher. Something about his walk. Or, maybe times were just different. If Kendrick hadn't been in the car, Jesus as his witness, Joe might have run that poor wanderer down where he walked. An ounce of prevention. That was what it had come to, in Joe Davis's mind. Drastic measures. You just never knew, that was the thing.

EREH LLITS, the man's sign said in the mirror, receding into a tiny, unreadable blur.

Yeah, I'm still here too, Joe thought. And not picking up hitchhikers was one way he intended to *stay* here, thanks a bunch for asking.

Freaks clustered in the cities, but there were plenty of them wandering through the countryside nowadays, actual packs. Thousands, maybe. Joe had seen his first six months ago, coming into Longview to rescue his grandson. His first, his fifth, and his tenth. He'd done what he had to do to save the boy, then shut the memories away where they couldn't sneak into his dreams. Then drank enough to make the dreams blurry.

A week later, he'd seen one closer to home, not three miles beyond the gated road, *not five miles from the cabin*. Its face was bloated blue-gray, and flies buzzed around the open sores clotted with that dark red scabby shit that grew under their skin. The thing could barely walk, but it had smelled him, swiveling in his direction like a scarecrow on a pivot.

Joe still dreamed about that one every night. That one had *chosen* him.

Joe left the freaks alone unless one came at him—that was safest if you were by yourself. He'd seen a poor guy shoot one down in a field, and then a swarm came from over a hill. Some of those fuckers could walk pretty fast, could *run*, and they weren't stupid, by God.

But Joe had killed that one, the pivoting one that had chosen him. He'd kill it a dozen times again if he had the chance; it was a favor to both of them. That shambling mess had been somebody's son, somebody's husband, somebody's father. People said freaks weren't really *dead*—they didn't climb out of graves like movie monsters—but they were as close to walking dead as Joe ever wanted to see. Something was eating them from the inside out, and if they bit you, the freak shit would start eating you, too. You fell asleep, and you woke up different.

The movies had that part right, anyway.

As for the rest, nobody knew much. People who met freaks up close and personal didn't live long enough to write reports about them. Whatever they were, freaks weren't just a city problem anymore. They were everybody's problem.

Can you hold on, Dad? My neighbor's knocking on the window.

That's what Cass had said the last time they'd spoken, then he hadn't heard any more from his daughter for ten agonizing minutes. The next time he'd heard her voice, he'd barely recognized it, so calm it could be nothing but a mask over mortal terror. *DADDY? Don't talk—just listen. I'm so sorry. For everything. No time to say it all. They're here. You need to come and get Kendrick. Use the danger word. Do you hear me, Daddy? And . . . bring guns. Shoot anyone suspicious. I mean* anyone, *Daddy.*

Daddy, she'd called him. She hadn't called him that in years.

That day, he'd woken up with alarm twisting his gut for no particular reason. That was why he'd raised Cassidy on the shortwave two hours earlier than he usually did, and she'd sounded irritated he'd called before she was up. *My neighbor's knocking on the window.*

Joe had prayed he wouldn't find what he knew would be waiting in Longview. He'd known what might happen to Cass, Devon, and Kendrick the moment he'd found them letting neighbors use the shortwave and drink their water like they'd been elected to the Rescue Committee. They couldn't even *name* one of the women in their house. That was Cass and Devon for you. Acting like naïve fools, and he'd told them as much.

Still, even though he'd tried to make himself expect the worst, he couldn't, really. If he ever dwelled on that day, he might lose his mind . . . and then what would happen to Kendrick?

Any time Joe brought up that day, the kid's eyes whiffed out like a dead pilot light. It had taken Kendrick hours to finally open that reinforced door and let him in, even though Joe had used the danger word again and again. And Kendrick had spoken hardly a word since.

Little Soldier was doing all right today. Good. He'd need to be tougher, fast. The kid had regressed from nine to five or six, just when Joe needed him to be as old as he could get.

As Joe drove beyond the old tree farms, the countryside opened up on either side; fields on his left, a range of hills on his right. There'd been a cattle farm out here once, but the cattle was gone. Wasn't much else out here, and there never had been.

Except for Mike's. Nowadays, Mike's was the only thing left anyone recognized.

Mike's was a gas station off exit 46 with Porta-Potties out back and a few shelves inside crammed with things people wanted: flour, canned foods, cereal, powdered milk, lanterns, flashlights, batteries, first aid supplies, and bottled water. And gas, of course. How he kept getting this shit, Joe had no idea. *If I told you that, I'd be out of business, bro*, Mike had told him when Joe asked, barking a laugh at him.

Last time he'd driven out here, Joe had asked Mike why he'd stayed behind when so many others were gone. Why not move somewhere less isolated? Even then, almost a full month ago, folks had been clumping up in Longview, barricading the school, jail and hospital. Had to be safer, if you could buy your way in. Being white helped too. They said it didn't, but Joe Davis knew it did. Always had, always would. Things like that just went underground for a time, that's all. Times like these the ugly stuff festered and exploded back topside.

Mike wasn't quite as old as Joe—sixty-three to Joe's more cumbersome seventy-one—but Joe thought he was foolhardy to keep the place open. Sure, all the stockpiling and bartering had made Mike a rich man, but was gasoline and Rice-A-Roni worth the risk? *I don't run, Joe. Guess I'm hard-headed.* That was all he'd said.

Joe had known Mike since he first built his cedar cabin in 1989, after retiring from his berth as supply sergeant at Fort McArthur. Mike had just moved down from Alberta, and they'd talked movies, then jazz. They'd discovered a mutual love of Duke Ellington and old sitcoms. Mike had always been one of his few friends around here. Now, he was the only one.

Joe didn't know whether to hope his friend would still be there or to pray he was gone. Better for him to be gone, Joe thought. One day, he and the kid would have to move on too, plain and simple. That day was coming soon. That day had probably come and gone twice over.

Joe saw a glint of the aluminum fencing posted around Mike's as he came around the bend, the end of the S on the road. Although it looked more like a prison camp, Mike's was an oasis, a tiny squat store and a row of gas pumps surrounded by a wire fence a man and a half tall. The fence was electrified at night: Joe had seen at least one barbecued body to prove it, and everyone had walked around the corpse as if it wasn't there. With gas getting scant, Mike tended to trust the razor wire more, using the generator less these days.

Mike's three boys, who'd never proved to be much good at anything else, had come in handy for keeping order. They'd had two or three gunfights there, Mike had said, because strangers with guns thought they could go anywhere they pleased and take anything they wanted.

Today, the gate was hanging open. He'd never come to Mike's when there wasn't someone standing at the gate. All three of Mike's boys were usually there with their greasy hair and pale fleshy bellies bulging through their too-tight T-shirts. No one today.

Something was wrong.

"Shit," Joe said aloud, before he remembered he didn't want to scare the kid. He pinched Kendrick's chin between his forefinger and thumb, and his grandson peered up at him, resigned, the expression he always wore these days. "Let's just sit here a minute, okay?"

Little Soldier nodded. He was a good kid.

Joe coasted the truck to a stop outside of the gate. While it idled, he tried to see what he could. The pumps stood silent and still on their concrete islands, like two men with their hands in their pockets. There was a light on inside, a super-white fluorescent glow through the picture windows painted with the words GAS, FOOD in red. He could make out a few shelves from where he was parked, but he didn't see anyone inside. The air pulsed with the steady burr of Mike's generator, still working.

At least it didn't look like anyone had rammed or cut the gate. The chain looked intact, so it had been unlocked. If there'd been trouble here, it had come with an invitation. Nothing would have made those boys open that gate otherwise. Maybe Mike and his boys had believed all that happy-talk on the radio, ditched their place and moved to Longview. The idea made Joe feel so relieved that he forgot the ache in his knee.

And leave the generator on? Bullshit.

Tire-tracks drew patterns in hardened mud. Mike's was a busy place. Damn greedy fool.

Beside him, Joe felt the kid fidgeting in his seat, and Joe didn't blame him. He had more than half a mind to turn around and start driving back toward home. The jerky would keep. He had enough gas to last him. He'd come back when things looked right again.

But he'd promised the kid a Coke. That was the only thing. And it would help erase a slew of memories if he could bring a grin to the kid's face today. Little Soldier's grins were a miracle. His little chipmunk cheeks were the spitting image of Cass's at his age.

Daddy, she'd called him on the radio. Daddy.

Don't think about that don't think don't—

Joe leaned on his horn. He let it blow five seconds before he laid off.

After a few seconds, the door to the store opened, and Mike stood there leaning against the doorjamb, a big ruddy white-haired Canuck with linebacker shoulders and a pigskin-sized bulge above his belt. He was wearing an apron, like he always did, as if he ran a butcher shop instead of a gas station. Mike peered out at them and waved. "Come on in!" he called out.

Joe leaned out of the window. "Where the boys at?" he called back.

"They're fine!" Mike said. Over the years, Joe had tried a dozen times to convince Mike he couldn't hear worth shit. No sense asking after the boys again until he got closer.

The wind skittered a few leaves along the ground between the truck and the door, and Joe watched their silent dance for a few seconds, considering. "I'm gonna go do this real quick, Kendrick," Joe finally said. "Stay in the truck."

The kid didn't say anything, but Joe saw the terror freeze his face. The kid's eyes went dead just like they did when he asked what had happened at the house in Longview.

Joe cracked open his door. "I'll only be a minute," he said, trying to sound casual.

"D-don't leave me. Please, Grandpa Joe? Let me c-come."

Well, I'll be damned, Joe thought. This kid was talking up a storm today.

Joe sighed, mulling it over. Pros and cons either way, he supposed. He reached under the seat and pulled out his Glock 9mm. He'd never liked automatics until maybe the mid-80s, when somebody figured out how to keep them from jamming so damned often. He had a Mossberg shotgun in a rack behind the seat, but that might seem a little too hostile. He'd give Kendrick the Remington 28-gauge. It had some kick, but the Little Soldier was used to it. He could trust Little Soldier not to fire into the ceiling. Or his back. Joe had seen to that.

"How many shots?" Joe asked him, handing over the little birder.

Kendrick held up four stubby fingers, like a toddler. So much for talking.

"If you're coming with me, I damn well better know you can talk if there's a reason to." Joe sounded angrier than he'd intended. "Now . . . how many shots?"

"*Four!*" That time, he'd nearly shouted it.

"Come on in," Mike called from the doorway. "I've got hot dogs today!"

That was a first. Joe hadn't seen a hot dog in nearly a year, and his mouth watered. Joe started to ask him again what the boys were up to, but Mike turned around and went inside.

"Stick close to me," Joe told Kendrick. "You're my other pair of eyes. *Anything* looks funny, you point and speak up loud and clear. Anybody makes a move in your direction you don't like, *shoot*. Hear?"

Kendrick nodded.

"That means *anybody*. I don't care if it's Mike or his boys or Santa Claus or anybody else. You understand me?"

Kendrick nodded again, although he lowered his eyes sadly. "Like Mom said."

"Damn right. Exactly like your mom said," Joe told Kendrick, squeezing the kid's shoulder. For an instant, his chest burned so hot with grief that he knew a heart attack couldn't feel any worse. The kid might have *watched* what happened to Cass. Cass might have turned into one of them before his eyes.

Joe thought of the pivoting, bloated freak he'd killed, the one that had smelled him, and his stomach clamped tight. "Let's go. Remember what I told you," Joe said.

"Yes, sir."

He'd leave the jerky alone, for now. He'd go inside and look around for himself first.

Joe's knee flared as boot sank into soft mud just inside the gate. Shit. He was a useless fucking old man, and he had a Bouncing Betty fifty klicks south of the DMZ to blame for it. In those happy days of Vietnam, none of them had known that the *real* war was still forty years off—but coming fast—and he was going to need both knees for the real war, you dig? And he could use a real soldier at his side for this war, not a little one.

"Closer," Joe said, and Kendrick pulled up behind him, his shadow.

When Joe pushed the glass door open, the salmon-shaped door chimes jangled merrily, like old times. Mike had vanished quick, because he wasn't behind the counter. A small television set on the counter erupted with laughter; old, canned laughter from people who were either dead or no longer saw much to laugh about. "EEEEEEE-dith," Archie Bunker's voice crowed. On the screen, old Archie was so mad he was nearly jumping up and down. It was the episode with Sammy Davis, Jr., where Sammy gives Archie a wet one on the cheek. Joe remembered watching that episode with Cass once upon a time. Mike was playing his VCR.

"Mike? Where'd you go?" Joe's finger massaged his shotgun trigger as he peered behind the counter.

Suddenly, there was a loud laugh from the back of the store, matching a new fit of laughter from the TV. He'd know that laugh blindfolded.

Mike was behind a broom, one of those school-custodian brooms with a wide brush, sweeping up and back, and Joe heard large shards of glass clinking as he swept. Mike was laughing so hard his face and crown had turned pink.

Joe saw what he was sweeping: The glass had been broken out of one of the refrigerated cases in back, which were now dark and empty. The others were still intact, plastered with Budweiser and Red Bull stickers, but the last door had broken clean off except for a few jagged pieces still standing upright, like a mountain range, close to the floor.

"Ya'll had some trouble?" Joe asked.

"Nope," Mike said, still laughing. He sounded congested, but otherwise all right. Mike kept a cold six months out of the year.

"Who broke your glass?"

"Tom broke it. The boys are fine." Suddenly, Mike laughed loudly again. "That Archie Bunker!" he said, and shook his head.

Kendrick, too, was staring at the television set, mesmerized. From the look on his face, he could be witnessing the parting of the Red Sea. The kid must miss TV, all right.

"Got any Cokes, Mike?" Joe said.

Mike could hardly swallow back his laughter long enough to answer. He squatted down, sweeping the glass onto an orange dustpan. "We've got hot dogs! They're—" Suddenly, Mike's face changed. He dropped his broom, and it clattered to the floor as he cradled one of his hands close to his chest. "*Ow! SHIT ON A STICK!*"

"Careful there, old-timer," Joe said. "Cut yourself?"

"Goddamm shit on a stick, shit on a stick, goddamn shit on a stick."

Sounded like it might be bad, Joe realized. He hoped this fool hadn't messed around and cut himself somewhere he shouldn't have. Mike sank from a squat to a sitting position, still cradling his hand. Joe couldn't see any blood yet, but he hurried toward him. "Well, don't sit there whining over it."

"*Shit on a stick, goddamn shit on a stick.*"

When Mike's wife Kimmy died a decade ago, Mike had gone down hard and come up a Christian. Joe hadn't heard a blasphemy pass his old friend's lips in years.

As Joe began to kneel down, Mike's shoulder heaved upward into Joe's midsection, stanching his breath and lifting him to his toes. For a moment Joe was too startled to react, the what-the-hell reaction stronger than reflex that had nearly cost him his life more than once. He was frozen by the sheer surprise of it, the impossibility that he'd been *talking* to Mike one second and—

Joe snatched clumsily at the Glock in his belt, and fired at Mike's throat. Missed. *Shit.*

The second shot hit Mike in the shoulder, but not before Joe had lost what was left of his balance and gone crashing backward into the broken refrigerator door. Three things happened at once: His arm snapped against the case doorway as he fell backward, knocking the gun out of his hand before he could feel it fall. A knife of broken glass carved him from below as he fell, slicing into the back of his thigh with such a sudden wave of pain that he screamed. And Mike had hiked up Joe's pant-leg and taken hold of his calf in his teeth, gnawing at him like a dog with a beef rib.

"Fucking *sonofabitch.*"

Joe kicked away at Mike's head with the only leg that was still responding to his body's commands. Still, Mike hung on. Somehow, even inside the fog of pain from his lower-body injury, Joe felt a chunk of his calf tearing, more hot pain.

He was bit, that was certain. *He was bit.* Every alarm in his head and heart rang.

Oh God holy horseshit, he was bit. He'd walked right up to him. They could make sounds—everybody said that—but this one had been *talking*, putting words together, acting like . . . acting like . . .

With a cry of agony, Joe pulled himself forward to leverage more of his weight, and kicked at Mike's head again. This time, he felt Mike's teeth withdraw. Another kick, and Joe's hiking boot sank squarely into Mike's face. Mike fell backward into the shelf of flashlights behind him.

"*Kendrick!*" Joe screamed.

The shelves blocked his sight of the spot where his nephew had been standing.

Pain from the torn calf muscle rippled through Joe, clouding thought. The pain from his calf shot up to his neck, liquid fire. Did the bastards have venom? Was that it?

Mike didn't lurch like the one on the road. Mike scrambled up again, untroubled by the blood spattering from his broken nose and teeth. "I have hot dogs," Mike said, whining it almost.

Joe reached back for the Glock, his injured thigh flaming while Mike's face came at him, mouth gaping, teeth glittering crimson. Joe's fingers brushed the automatic, but it skittered away from him, and now Mike would bite, and bite, and then go after the Little Soldier—

Mike's nose and mouth exploded in a mist of pink tissue. The sound registered a moment later, deafening in the confined space, an explosion that sent Mike's useless body toppling to the floor. Then, Joe saw Kendrick just behind him, his little birding rifle smoking, face pinched, hands shaking.

Holy Jesus, Kendrick had done it. The kid had hit his mark.

Sucking wind, Grandpa Joe took the opportunity to dig among the old soapboxes for his Glock, and when he had a firm grip on it, he tried to pull himself up. Dizziness rocked him, and he tumbled back down.

"Grandpa Joe!" Kendrick said, and rushed to him. The boy's grip was surprisingly strong, and Joe hugged him for support, straining to peer down at his leg. He could be wrong about the bite. He could be wrong.

"Let me look at this," Joe said, trying to keep his voice calm. He peeled back his pant leg, grimacing at the blood hugging the fabric to flesh.

There it was, facing him in a semi-circle of oozing slits: A bite, and a deep one. He was bleeding badly. Maybe Mike had hit an artery, and whatever shit they had was shooting all through him. Damn, damn, damn.

Night seemed to come early, because for an instant Joe Davis's fear blotted the room's light. He was bit. And where were Mike's three boys? Wouldn't they all come running now, like the swarm over the hill he'd seen in the field?

"We've gotta get out of here, Little Soldier," Joe he said, and levered himself up to standing. Pain coiled and writhed inside him. "I mean now. Let's go."

His leg was leaking. The pain was terrible, a throb with every heartbeat. He found himself wishing he'd faint, and his terror at the thought snapped him to more alertness than he'd felt before.

He had to get Little Soldier to the truck. He had to keep Little Soldier safe.

Joe cried out with each step on his left leg, where the back of his thigh felt ravaged. He was leaning so hard on Little Soldier, the kid could hardly manage the door. Joe heard the tinkling above him, and then, impossibly, they were back outside. Joe saw the truck waiting just beyond the gate.

His eyes swept the perimeter. No movement. No one. *Where are those boys?*

"Let's go," Joe panted. He patted his pocket, and the keys were there. "Faster."

Joe nearly fell three times, but each time he found the kid's weight beneath him, keeping him on his feet. Joe's heartbeat was in his ears, an ocean's roar.

"Jump in. Hurry," Joe said after the driver's door was open, and Little Soldier scooted into the car like a monkey. The hard leather made Joe whimper as his thigh slid across the seat, but suddenly, it all felt easy. Slam and lock the door. Get his hand to stop shaking enough to get the key in the ignition. Fire her up.

Joe lurched the truck in reverse for thirty yards before he finally turned around. His right leg was numb up to his knee—*from that bite, oh sweet Jesus*—but he was still flooring the pedal somehow, keeping the truck on the road instead of in a ditch.

Joe looked in his rearview mirror. At first he couldn't see for the dust, but there they were: Mike's boys had come running in a ragged line, all of them straining as if they were in a race. Fast. They were too far back to catch up, but their fervor sent a bottomless fear through Joe's stomach.

Mike's boys looked like starving animals hunting for a meal.

Kendrick couldn't breathe. The air in the truck felt the way it might in outer space, if you were floating in the universe, a speck too far in the sky to see.

"Grandpa Joe?" Kendrick whispered. Grandpa Joe's black face shone with sweat. He was chewing at his lip hard enough to draw blood.

Grandpa Joe's fingers gripped at the wheel, and the corners of his mouth turned upwards in an imitation of a smile. "It's gonna be all right," he said, but it seemed to Kendrick that he was talking to himself more than to him. "It'll be fine."

Kendrick stared at him, assessing: He seemed all right. He was sweating and bleeding, but he must be all right if he was driving the truck. You couldn't drive if you were one of them, could you? Grandpa Joe was fine. He said he was.

Mom and Dad hadn't been fine after a while, but they had warned him. They had told him they were getting sleepy, and they all knew getting sleepy right away meant you might not wake up. Or if you did, you'd be changed. They'd made him promise not to open the door to the safe room, even for them.

No matter what. Not until you hear the danger word.

Kendrick felt warm liquid on the seat beneath him, and he gasped, thinking Grandpa Joe might be bleeding all over the seat. Instead, when he looked down, Kendrick saw a clear puddle between his legs. His jeans were dark and wet, almost black. It wasn't blood. He'd peed on himself, like a baby.

"Are you sleepy?" Kendrick said.

Grandpa Joe shook his head, but Kendrick thought he'd hesitated first, just a little. Grandpa Joe's eyes were on the road half the time, on the rearview mirror the rest. "How long before your mom and dad got sleepy?"

Kendrick remembered Dad's voice outside of the door, announcing the time. *It's nine o'clock, Cass.* Worried it was getting late. Worried they should get far away from Kendrick and send for Grandpa Joe to come get him. Kendrick heard them talking outside of the door plain as day; for once, they hadn't tried to keep him from hearing.

"A few minutes," Kendrick said softly. "Five. Or ten."

Grandpa Joe went back to chewing his lip. "What happened?"

Kendrick didn't know what happened. He'd been in bed when he heard Mom say their neighbor Mrs. Shane was knocking at the window. All he knew was that Dad came into his room, shouting and cradling his arm. Blood oozed from between Dad's fingers. Dad pulled him out of bed, yanking Kendrick's arm so hard that it snapped, pulling him to his feet. In the living room, he'd seen Mom crouching far away, by the fireplace, sobbing with a red face. Mom's shirt was bloody, too.

At first, Kendrick had thought Dad had hurt Mom, and now Dad was mad at him, too. Dad was punishing him by putting him in the safe room.

They're in the house, Kendrick. We're bit, both of us.

After the door to the safe room was closed, for the first time, Kendrick heard somebody else's footsteps. Then, that scream.

"They stayed for ten minutes, maybe. Not long. Then they said they had to leave. They were getting sleepy, and they were scared to near me. Then they went away for a long time. For hours," Kendrick told Grandpa Joe. "All of a sudden I heard Mom again. She was knocking on the door. She asked me where my math homework was. She said 'You were supposed to do your math homework.'"

Kendrick had never said the words before. Tears hurt his eyes.

"That was how you knew?" Grandpa Joe said.

Kendrick nodded. Snot dripped from his nose to the front of his jacket, but he didn't move to wipe it away. Mom had said not to open the door until Grandpa Joe came and said the danger word. No matter what.

"GOOD BOY, Kendrick," Grandpa Joe said, his voice wavering. "Good boy."

All this time, Joe had thought it was his imagination.

A gaggle of the freaks had been there in Cass's front yard waiting for him, so he'd plowed most of them down with the truck so he could get to the door. That was the easy part. As soon as he got out, the ones still standing had surged. There'd been ten of them at least; an old man, a couple of teenage boys, the rest of them women, moving quick. He'd been squeezing off rounds at anything that moved.

Daddy?

Had he heard her voice before he'd fired? In the time since, he'd decided the voice was his imagination, because how *could* she have talked to him said his name? He'd decided God had created her voice in his mind, a last chance to hear it to make up for the horror of the hole his Glock had just put in her forehead. *Daddy?*

It had been Cass, but it *hadn't* been. Her blouse and mouth had been a bloody, dripping mess, and he'd seen stringy bits of flesh caught in her teeth, just like the other freaks. It hadn't been Cass. Hadn't been.

People said freaks could *make noises*. They walked and looked like us. The newer ones didn't have the red shit showing beneath their skin, and they didn't start to lose their motor skills for a couple days—so they could run fast, the new ones. He'd known that. Everybody knew that.

But if freaks could talk, could recognize you . . .

Then we can't win.

The thought was quiet in Joe's mind, from a place that was already accepting it.

Ten minutes, Little Soldier had said. Maybe five.

Joe tried to bear down harder on the gas, and his leg felt like a wooden stump. Still, the speedometer climbed before it began shaking at ninety. He had to get Little Soldier as far as he could from Mike's boys. Those boys might run all day and all night, from the way they'd looked. He had to get Little Soldier away . . .

Joe's mouth was so dry it ached.

"We're in trouble, Little Soldier," Joe said.

Joe couldn't bring himself to look at Kendrick, even though he wanted to so much he was nearly blinded by tears. "You know we're in trouble, don't you?" Joe said.

"Yes," the boy said.

"We have to come up with a plan. Just like we did at your house that time."

"A danger word?" Kendrick said.

Joe sighed. "A danger word won't work this time."

Again, Kendrick was silent.

"Don't go back to the cabin," Joe said, deciding that part. "It's not safe."

"But Mom and Dad might . . ."

This time, Joe did gaze over at Kendrick. Unless it was imagination, the boy was already sitting as far from him as he could, against the door.

"That was a story I told you," Joe said, cursing himself for the lie. "You know they're not coming, Kendrick. You said yourself she wasn't right. You could hear it. That means they got your father, too. She was out in the front yard, before I got inside. I had to shoot her, Little Soldier. I shot her in the head."

Kendrick gazed at him wide-eyed, rage knotting his little face.

That's it, Little Soldier. Get mad.

"I couldn't tell you before. But I'm telling you now for a reason . . ."

Just that quick, the road ahead of Joe fogged, doubled. He snapped his head up, aware that he had just lost a moment of time. His consciousness had flagged.

But he was still himself. Still himself, and that made the difference, right? He was still himself, and just maybe he would stay himself, and beat this damned thing.

If you could stay awake . . .

Then you might stay alive for another, what? Ten days? He'd heard about someone staying awake that long, maybe longer. Right now, he didn't know if he'd last the ten minutes. His eyes fought to close so hard that they trembled. *There'll be rest enough in the grave.* Wasn't that what Benjamin Franklin had said?

"*Don't you close your eyes, Daddy.*" Cass's voice. He snapped his head around, wondering where the voice had come from. He was seeing things: Cassie sat beside him with her pink lips and tight ringlets of brown hair. For a moment he couldn't see Little Soldier, so solid she seemed. "*You always talked tough this and tough that. Da Nang and Hanoi a dozen places I couldn't pronounce. And now the one damned time in your life that it matters, you're going to sleep?*" The accusation in her voice was crippling.

"*We trusted you, and you walked right into that store and got bitten because you were laughing at Archie Bunker? I trusted you Daddy.*"

Silence. Then: "*I still trust you Daddy.*"

Suddenly, Joe felt wide-awake again for the last time in his life.

"Listen to me: I can't give you the truck," Joe said. "I know we practiced driving, but you might make a mistake and hurt yourself. You're better off on foot."

Rage melted from Kendrick's face, replaced by bewilderment and the terror of an infant left naked in a snowdrift. Kendrick's lips quivered violently.

"No, Grandpa Joe. You can stay awake," he whispered.

"Grab that backpack behind your seat—it's got a compass, bottled water, jerky and a flashlight. It's heavy, but you'll need it. And take your Remington. There's more ammo for it under your seat. Put the ammo in the backpack. Do it now."

Kendrick sobbed, reaching out to squeeze Joe's arm. "P-please, Grandpa Joe . . . "

"*Stop that goddamned crying!*" Joe roared, and the shock of his voice silenced the boy. Kendrick yanked his hand away, sliding back toward his door again. The poor kid must think he'd crossed over.

Joe took a deep breath. Another wave of dizziness came, and his chin rocked downward. The car swerved slightly before he could pull his head back up. Joe's pain was easing and he felt stoned, like he was on acid. He hadn't driven far enough yet. They were still too close to Mike's boys. So much to say . . .

Joe kept his voice as even as he could. "There were only two people who could put up a better fight than me, and that was your mom and dad. They couldn't do it, not even for you. That tells me I can't either. Understand?"

His tears miraculously stanched, Kendrick nodded.

READ REVELATIONS, a billboard fifty yards ahead advised in red letters. Beside the billboard, the road forked into another highway. Thank Jesus.

The words flew from his mouth, nearly breathless. "I'll pull off when we get to that sign, at the crossroads. When the truck stops, *run*. Hear me? Fast as you can. No matter what you hear . . . don't turn around. Don't stop. It's twenty miles to Centralia, straight south. There's National Guard there, and caravans. Tell them you want to go to Devil's Wake. That's where I'd go. When you're running, stay near the roads, but keep out of sight. If anyone comes before you get to Centralia, hide. If they see you, tell 'em you'll shoot, and then do it. And don't go to sleep, Kendrick. Don't let anybody surprise you."

"Yes, sir," Kendrick said in a sad voice, yet still eager to be commanded.

The truck took control of itself, no longer confined to its lane, or the road, and it bumped wildly as it drove down the embankment. Joe's leg was too numb to keep pressing the accelerator, so the truck gradually lost speed, rocking to a stop nose down, its headlights lost in weeds. Feeling in his arms was nearly gone now, too.

"I love you, Grandpa Joe," he heard his grandson say. Or thought he did.

"Love you, too, Little Soldier."

Still here. Still here.

"Now, go. *Go.*"

Joe heard Kendrick's car door open and slam before he could finish.

He turned his head to watch Kendrick, to make sure he was doing as he'd told. Kendrick had the backpack and his gun as he stumbled away from the truck, running down in the embankment that ran beside the road. The boy glanced back over his shoulder, saw Joe wave him on, and then disappeared into the roadside brush.

With trembling fingers, Joe opened the glove compartment, digging out his snub-nose .38, his favorite gun. He rested the cold metal between his lips, past his teeth. He was breathing hard, sucking at the air, and he didn't know if it was the toxin or his nerves working him. He looked for Kendrick again, but he couldn't see him at this angle.

Now. Do it now.

It seemed that he heard his own voice whispering in his ear.

I can win. I can win. I saved my whole fucking squad. I can beat this thing . . .

Joe sat in the truck feeling alternating waves of heat and cold washing through him. *As long as he could stay awake . . .*

He heard the voice of old Mrs. Reed, his sixth-grade English teacher; saw the faces of Little Bob and Eddie Kevner, who'd been standing beside him when the Bouncing Betty blew. Then, he saw Cassie in her wedding dress, giving him a secret gaze, as if to ask if it was all right before she pledged her final vows at the altar.

Then in the midst of the images, some he didn't recognize.

Something red, drifting through a trackless cosmos. Alive, yet not alive. Intelligent but unaware. *He'd been with them all along, those drifting spore-strands gravitating toward a blue-green planet with water and soil . . . filtering through the atmosphere . . . rest . . . home . . . grow . . .*

A crow's mournful caw awakened Joe, but not as much of him as had slipped into sleep. His vision was tinged red. His world, his heart, was red. What remained of Joe knew that *it* was in him, awakening, using his own mind against him, dazzling him with its visions while it took control of his motor nerves.

He wanted to tear, to rend. Not killing. Not eating. Not yet. There was something more urgent, a new voice he had never heard before. *Must bite.*

Panicked, he gave his hand an urgent command: *pull the trigger.*

But he couldn't. He'd come this close and couldn't. Too many parts of him no longer wanted to die. The new parts of him only wanted to live. To grow. To spread.

Still, Joe struggled against himself, even as he knew struggle was doomed. *Little Soldier. Must protect Little Soldier. Must . . .*

Must . . .

Must find boy.

KENDRICK HAD BEEN running for nearly ten minutes, never far from stumbling, before pure instinct left him and his mind woke up again. His stomach hurt from a deep, sudden sob. He had to slow down because he couldn't see for his tears.

Grandpa Joe had been hunched over the steering wheel, eyes open so wide that the effort had changed the way his face looked. Kendrick thought he'd never seen such a hopeless, helpless look on anyone's face. If he had been able to see Mom and Dad from the safe room, that was how they would have looked, too.

He'd been stupid to think Grandpa Joe could keep him safe. He was an old man who lived in the woods.

Kendrick ran, his legs burning and throat scalding. He could see the road above him, but he ran in the embankment like Grandpa Joe had told him, out of sight.

For an endless hour Kendrick ran, despite burning legs and scalded throat, struggling to stay true to the directions Grandpa Joe had given him. South. Stay south.

Centralia. National Guard. Devil's Wake. Safe.

By the time exhaustion claimed Kendrick, rainclouds had darkened the sky, and he was so tired he had lost any certainty of placing his feet without disaster. The trees, once an explosion of green, had been bleached gray and black. They were a place of trackless, unknowable danger. Every sound and shadow seemed to call to him.

Trembling so badly he could hardly move, Kendrick crawled past a wall of ferns into a culvert, clutching the little Remington to his chest.

Once he sat, his sadness felt worse, like a blanket over him. He sobbed so hard he could no longer sit up straight, curling himself in a ball on the soft soil. Small leaves and debris pasted themselves to the tears and mucous that covered his face. One sob sounded more like a wail, so loud is startled him.

Grandpa Joe had lied. Mom had been dead all along. He'd shot her in the head. He'd said it like it hardly mattered to him.

Kendrick heard snapping twigs, and the back of his neck turn ice-cold. *Footsteps.* Running fast.

Kendrick's sobs vanished, as if they'd never been. He sat straight up, propping his shotgun across his bent knee, aiming, finger ready on the trigger. He saw a small black spider crawling on his trigger wrist—one with a bloated egg sac, about to give birth to a hundred babies like in *Charlotte's Web*—but he made no move to bat the spider away. Kendrick sat primed, trying to silence his clotted nose by breathing through his mouth. Waiting.

Maybe it was that hitchhiker with the sign, he thought.

But it didn't matter who it was. *Hide.* That was what Grandpa Joe said.

The footsteps slowed, although they were so close that Kendrick guessed the intruder couldn't be more than a few feet away. He was no longer running, as if he knew where Kendrick was. As if he'd been close behind him all along, and now that he'd found him, he wasn't in a hurry anymore.

"I have a gun! I'll shoot!" Kendrick called out, and this voice was very different than the one he'd used to ask Grandpa Joe for a Coke. Not a little girl's voice, this time, or even a boy's. It was a voice that meant what it said.

Silence. The movement had stopped.

That was when Grandpa Joe said the danger word.

Kendrick's finger loosened against the trigger. His limbs gave way, and his body began to shake. The woods melted away, and he remembered wearing this same jacket in the safe room, waiting. Waiting for Grandpa Joe.

There had never been a gunshot from Grandpa Joe's truck. Kendrick had expected to hear the gunshot as soon as he ran off, dreading it. Grandpa Joe always did what needed to be done. Kendrick should have heard a gunshot.

"Go back!" Kendrick said. Although his voice was not so sure this time, he cocked the Remington's hammer, just like he'd been taught.

Kendrick waited. He tried not to hope—and then hoped fervently—that his scare had worked. The instant Kendrick's hope reached its peak, a shadow moved against the ferns above him, closer.

"Breakfast," Grandpa Joe's watery voice said again.

⌒

After years of collaborating on film and TV pitches and projects, "Danger Word" was my first prose collaboration with my husband, science fiction writer Steven Barnes. We later expanded the premise and changed Kendrick's age and gender (to sixteen-year-old Kendra) for our YA zombie novels Devil's Wake *and* Domino Falls.

The short film we adapted from this story in 2013, directed by Luchina Fisher, can be viewed at www.dangerword.com.

Removal Order

TINY BLACK DOTS speckled Nayima's white-socked feet as she shuffled across the threadbare carpet in her grandmother's living room. Gram's four cats were gone, but the fleas had stayed behind. Nayima had learned to ignore the itching, but the sight of so many fleas made her sick to her stomach. The flea problem had seemed small compared to Nayima's daily ever-growing list of responsibilities, but she would not keep her Gram in filth.

"Shit," Nayima said to the empty living room, the fleas, and the slow, steady whistling of Gram's sleep-breathing in the next room.

Gray morning light beckoned her. Nayima flung the front door open and sat on the stoop, breathing fast to try to beat the nausea, which felt too much like death. Fledgling panic gnawed the rim of her stomach. She could make out the headline of the bright electric pink flier Bob the groundskeeper had dutifully posted on the community bulletin board across the green belt from Gram's house: REPORT TO THE NEAREST HOSPITAL IF . . . and the litany of symptoms. Stomachache and vomiting were high on the list, beneath persistent headache and double vision.

That had been a month ago. Bob was gone, and the hospital's doors were chained. Even the bright flier was nearly obscured in the gray-brown haze that had settled over her neighborhood like a sepia camera filter. The San Gabriel mountain range that stood a few blocks from Foothill Park was nearly hidden beneath a sheet of brown clouds. Sunlight bled through the sky in a fuzzy ball, but less light than yesterday. So much for Southern California sunshine. Nayima had gotten used to the smell, the eye and sinus irritation, the coughing at bedtime, but she hated the way the smoke had changed the daylight. Each morning she hoped the day would be a bit clearer and brighter, but the sky was always a little worse than before, like eyesight slowly going dim.

But she could manage the flea problem. *That* she could do.

The irony wasn't lost on her: she had only remained because she didn't want to move Gram. Now she would have to move Gram after all, without the help of neighbors, soldiers or police officers. The infestation was too far gone for insecticides—and she'd already emptied a can, making it harder to breathe in the house. Gram had taught her how hard fleas were to kill, with her menagerie of pets in the house Nayima had been raised in since she was four. Nayima had felt like just another of Gram's adopted creatures.

The street spread before Nayima with its alien coloring and emptiness, her neighbors' windows dark and sleeping. Most of the driveways were clear except for a few vandalized cars left behind. The week before, a daytime marauder had come through on a loud motorcycle, raising a racket and tossing clothes into the trees. Kids, she guessed, but she'd stayed out of sight, so she wasn't sure. A long-sleeved shirt and ratty blue jeans still hung from high fronds in the neat row of palm trees in front of the green belt.

Nayima used to walk her neighborhood for exercise, rounding the green belt and pool area, the basketball court, the rows of stucco exteriors in carefully matched paint. This day she scouted for a new home—testing the doorknobs, sniffing the air inside, assessing the space. She had visited them all before. Most had been damaged beyond usefulness by looters.

She chose the house on the opposite corner from Gram for its proximity and the bright yellow roses blooming in front, lovely and clueless. Mr. Yamamoto's house. Inside, its Spartan decor had given looters little to muss, although broken glass glittered in the kitchen. But the house had double doors large enough to push Gram's bed through. The lock was intact. No windows broken. No terrible odors. No carpeting to hide nests of biting fleas.

Sanctuary.

"Thank you, Mr. Yamamoto," she said.

Mr. Yamamoto had offered to drive her and Gram to the high desert in the back of his SUV, though she'd seen relief flicker in his hollowed eyes when she'd refused. He'd had a carload already, with his daughter and grandchildren from Rancho. Instead, he had given her a box of spices, most of them characteristically useless: every Halloween, he'd handed out clementine oranges instead of candy. Before Gram got sick, she and Mr.

Yamamoto had walked their dogs together. Like Gram, he was retired. Like everyone, he had left most of his belongings behind.

Gram's old digital wristwatch told her it was 7:30 in the morning. From the dark sky, it could be evening. The day had already wearied her, and the hard part had not yet begun.

Gram was asleep. She lay slanted on her side where Nayima had left her at 4:00 a.m., after her careful ritualistic padding of pillows to keep her from slumping on to her back. Studying Gram's quiet face, Nayima marveled again at how the cancer had stolen the fat from her cheeks, shrinking her grandmother to a smaller husk each day.

The usual thought came: *Is she dead?*

But no. Gram's chest moved with shallow breaths. In the early days, when cancer was new to them both, she had fretted over every moan, gasped at every imitation of a death mask on Gram's brown, lined face. Gram was nearly seventy, but she had never looked like an old woman until the cancer. Her white hair was still full and springy, but now her face looked like she would not last the day, which was how she always looked.

But Gram always did last the day. And the next.

The bell was on Gram's mattress, though she had not had the strength to ring it in a long time. The hospital-grade bed had cost a fortune, equipped with an inflated mattress that was gentler against Gram's breaking skin. It didn't work as well without its electric pump, but Nayima kept it inflated with an old bicycle pump. Not enough, maybe, but it was inflated. The county had shut off the power to the entire area after the evacuation.

Nayima felt the magnitude of her impending tasks. Should she dress and treat Gram's sores before or after the move? Damnation either way.

Later, she decided. She didn't want to face the sores with the move still waiting. The move would irritate Gram's sores with or without a cleaning and dressing first, but maybe after was best. She wished her cell phone worked, not that there was anyone to call for advice. An Internet search would have felt like a miracle. The lack of advice wearied her.

As if her loud uncertainty had awakened her, Gram's eyes flew open. Gram's eyes had once been the brightest part of her, though they were milky now.

"Baby?" Gram said.

Nayima stepped closer to the bed. She could smell that the wounds needed cleaning—the dead flesh odor she hated. She slipped her hand over Gram's dry palm. Gram squeezed, but did not hold on.

"I'm here, Gram," she said.

Gram stared with the same eyes that had probed Nayima when she came home late from "movies" with her first boyfriend smelling of weed and sex. But this time, the questions were too big and vast for words, with answers neither of them wanted to hear. Nayima hadn't let Gram watch the news or listen to the radio in weeks, so Gram didn't know how many others were facing illness. She didn't know the neighbors had left.

"We have to move to Mr. Yamamoto's house," Nayima said. "Too many fleas here."

"The . . . cats?" Gram said.

"They're fine," Nayima said. That was probably a lie. She had stopped feeding Gram's four cats and locked them out after the evacuation, so the cats had left too. She'd cried about it at the time, but at least cats could hunt.

"Tango too?" Gram's eyes grew anxious. Maybe Gram had heard the lie in her voice.

"Tango's still mean and fat," Nayima said.

Was that a smile on Gram's face? Gram had asked her to keep a single framed photo displayed on the table beside her bed, snapped the first summer Nayima came home from Spelman: the overfed black cat, Tango, was in Gram's lap while Nayima hugged Gram from behind in her powder blue college sweatshirt. Nayima's best friend, Shanice, had taken the photo. The glowing pride on Gram's face haunted Nayima now.

Gram's eyes started to flutter shut, but Nayima squeezed her hand and they opened again, alert. "I'm going to push you in the bed, Gram," she said, "but it will hurt."

"That's okay, baby," Gram said. That was Gram's answer to every piece of bad news.

Nayima had stockpiled pain pills with help from Shanice, who was an RN and had raided the meds as soon as she caught wind of how bad things were going to be. Thanks to Shanice—who had moved next door when they were both in the sixth grade—Nayima had a box of syringes, hundreds of oxy pills, saline packs for hydration, ointment and dressing for bedsores, bed pads, and enough Ensure to feed an army. But Gram hadn't been able to swallow anything on her own since before the neighbors left, so all Nayima could do was crush the pills in warm, sterile water and inject them. Gram's arms looked like a junkie's.

The smell was worse when Nayima leaned over Gram to inject her crushed pill. Nayima's throat locked. How would she clean her and scrape away Gram's dead skin later if she could barely stand the smell now?

Gram's eyes were flickering again, ready to close.

"Are you hungry?" Nayima asked.

Gram's lips moved, but she didn't say anything Nayima could hear.

Nayima didn't smell feces, so she would postpone the rest—the changing of the urine-soiled bed pad, the gentle sponge cleaning, the bedsores, the feeding. All of that would wait until they had moved to Mr. Yamamoto's flea-free home.

He always had been meticulous, Mr. Yamamoto. Even his roses were still on schedule.

"I love you, Gram," Nayima said, and kissed her grandmother's forehead. She allowed her lips to linger against the warm, paper-thin skin across the crown of Gram's skull.

Gram's breath whistled through her nose. She whistled more now, since the smoke.

Luckily, the cancer wasn't in Gram's lungs, so breathing had never been a problem. But breathing would be a problem for both of them soon. It hadn't occurred to Nayima to ask Shanice for oxygen, not back then. She hadn't known the fires were coming. Even the dust masks Nayima wore outside had just been in a box left untouched for years in Gram's garage. She wore them until they fell apart; she only had twenty-two more.

When Nayima fitted a new dust mask across her grandmother's nose and mouth, Gram didn't even open her eyes.

The first scream didn't come until they were well beyond the front door, when Nayima had lulled herself into thinking that the move might not be so bad. One of the wheels wandered off the edge of the driveway, rattling Gram's bed. Her scream was strong and hearty.

"Sorry," Nayima whispered, her mantra. "I'm sorry, Gram."

Gram's eyes, closed before, were wide and angry. She glared at Nayima, then turned her gaze to the sky. Even with pain lining her face, Nayima saw Gram's bewilderment.

"It's smoke," she said. "Brushfires."

The bewilderment melted away, leaving only the pain. Most of Nayima's life with Gram, there had been wildfires every other summer. They both had grown accustomed to the sirens and beating helicopters that were still Nayima's daily and nightly music. She heard a far-off helicopter now, and a choppy, angry voice from an indistinct loudspeaker. She braced for popping gunshots, but there were none. Not this time.

"Mr. Yamamoto took a trip with his grandchildren, so he said we could use his house," Nayima said, trying to distract Gram, but a bump elicited a shriek. "I'm sorry, Gram. I'm sorry."

At the edge of the driveway, it occurred to Nayima that she could pull the car out of the garage instead. She'd packed the passenger side and trunk solid, but she'd left the back seat empty for Gram, layered with blankets. She could wash, dress, and feed Gram right outside and then carry her into the car. Would the screams be any worse? What difference would it make if Gram was screaming in Foothill Park or screaming somewhere down the smoky interstate?

Nayima's tears stung in the smoke. She had to stop to wipe her eyes dry with a section of her thin shirt. When she looked at her clothing, she realized she was only wearing a black tank top and underwear, the clothes she slept in. And white socks. She had so much laundry to do.

Gram's shriek melted to a childlike, hopeless sob.

Nayima gave Gram's hand another squeeze and then carefully, very carefully, pushed the rolling bed across the bumpy asphalt, toward the beckoning yellow rose blossoms.

"Look, Gram," she said. "Mr. Yamamoto's roses are blooming."

Gram coughed a phlegmy cough behind her dusk mask. And screamed in pain again.

Gram was crying by the time Nayima finally brought the bed to rest in its new home beside Mr. Yamamoto's black sofa and artificial palm tree.

Nayima cursed herself. Why hadn't she found a way to kill the fleas at Gram's house instead? What had possessed her? A fierce headache hammered Nayima's temples, bringing paralyzing hopelessness as bad as she'd felt since the 72-Hour Flu took over the news. Nayima remembered how much she had hated riding in the car with Tango when Gram took him to the vet, the way the cat cried so plaintively from his cage, with true terror. And it would be so much worse with Gram on the road, facing whatever might jostle the car outside.

So they were both crying while Nayima pulled Gram's bandages away to reveal the black and red angry stink of her wounds, the yawning decay that cratered her back. Nayima could nestle a golf ball in the cavern that grew above her grandmother's right buttock. Infection had found the sores despite Nayima's steady cleanings.

"Fuck," she said. "Fuck."

Her hands were shaking as she debrided the wound in a clumsy imitation of what Shanice had tried to teach her—the cruel, steady scraping of Gram's most tender flesh.

And, of course, Gram screamed the whole while.

But Nayima carried on despite the lump clogging her throat, despite her smoke-stinging eyes. Then the infected flesh began to disappear, the smell turned more sterile, the ointments began their healing, the bandages sealed the mess from sight.

And Gram stopped screaming. Stopped whimpering. Only moaned here and there to signal she needed a moment to rest, and Nayima let her rest whenever she could.

Nayima retrieved her jug of boiled water, dipped her sponge in it, and gently washed Gram between her legs, water running in streams down the wrinkled crevices of her thighs. Washed Gram's downy, thin patch of pubic hair. Checked her for signs of skin irritation from urine, and was thankful to find none. That, at least, was going right.

Then it was time to feed her, so Nayima checked beneath the surgical tape that affixed Gram's gastric tube near her navel. No infection there either, nothing out of place. Then she filled a bag with Ensure, hung it from the waiting hook on the bed, and watched the tube fill with nourishment as it crawled toward Gram's stomach.

By then, Gram was already sleeping, as if the day had never happened. The smoke seemed to clear from the air.

"Thank you, God," Nayima said.

Mr. Yamamoto had running water, and a state-of-the art grill on the patio, if only she could find food worthy of it. He had cleaned out his kitchen cabinets before he left, she remembered; he hadn't left a mess. No rotting odors from his fridge, no toilets left unflushed.

And no fleas. Mr. Yamamoto's house was a vacation.

Nayima checked on Gram regularly, turning her every two hours. She moved her car to Mr. Yamamoto's pristine garage, which looters had overlooked. She even found a flashlight and an empty gas can, which she squeezed into her trunk. She turned and fed Gram again.

The sky was dark long before sunset.

The coyotes were fooled by the dark skies and the sirens. Just before five o'clock, a coyote chorus rose, sharp through the house's walls. There were more coyotes all the time. Maybe some left-behind dogs had joined the coyotes, howling their grief. They sang all around her, as if Foothill Park were ringed by wilderness.

Nayima decided she wasn't afraid. Not yet. Maybe one day. Maybe tomorrow.

She sat on the front porch of Mr. Yamamoto's house with a warm beer, her only indulgence, one of her last six in an eighteen-pack she'd found in a neighbor's rec room. She'd rather have weed, but beer still helped her forget what needed forgetting. A little. For a time. Nayima stared back at Gram's narrow two-story townhouse across the street. Their jacaranda tree had showered the driveway with purple buds. Would her tree survive the fires? Would she come back and find beauty in the ruins to show her children one day?

She was ready to go back inside when a siren squawked close by, and a police cruiser coasted in front of her, so mud-caked she could barely see its black and white paint. Unnecessarily, the red flasher came on in a light show against her the wall.

The man who climbed out of the car was stocky, not much taller than she was, with sun-browned skin and dark hair. She was glad when she saw his town police uniform, which seemed friendlier than a soldier's. He looked about her age, as young as twenty-one. She had seen him before, perhaps during the evacuation. Like most cops, he wasn't smiling. *Sanchez*, his name tag read. Yes, he had been here before.

She expected him to say something about her sitting outside in her underwear, but he didn't seem to notice. Maybe he saw people half naked on a regular basis.

"You cleaning this place up?" he said, incredulous.

A week ago, fast food wrappers and debris had covered the grass in the green belt, where she and Shanice and their friends had played until they were too old to play outside. She hadn't meant to clean it all, but a little each day had done it, her therapy. She hadn't risked hurting herself to climb the palm tree to take down the flapping shirt and jeans. But she might one day. Trash still hugged the fence around the pool. She hadn't gotten to that.

"I grew up here. I want it to look right."

"Don't you have anything better to do?" he said.

"My car is packed with everything I need."

"Then why are you still here?"

She suddenly remembered meeting him before. He had come with the team from the hospital that examined Gram to make sure she only had cancer and not the 72-Hour Flu. Mr. Yamamoto and other neighbors had reported that Gram had been sick for a long time. This cop might have said his grandmother had raised him too. Nayima couldn't quite remember. Her memories that day had been frozen out from her terror that they would take Gram away.

"My grandmother's got cancer," she said. "Remember?"

Gunfire crackled east of them. Sometimes the rounds were from soldiers, sometimes random rage. Looters might come tonight.

"You have a gun?" he said.

The earnestness in his voice made her anxious. "Of course."

"What kind?"

"A thirty-eight?" She tried not to say it like a question. It was Gram's Smith & Wesson she bought in her old neighborhood, where Nayima's mother had lived and died. A world away.

"Ammo?"

"A box. And what's in . . . the chamber?" She'd fumbled, trying to remember gun terms.

"You know how to shoot one?"

"Is this a test?"

She was sorry as soon as she'd said it. His face deflated; maybe he thought they'd been having a friendly conversation. "A gun's no good if you can't use it," he said. He ripped an orange page from his pad, stuck it to Mr. Yamamoto's window. Ugly and permanent.

REMOVAL ORDER, it read.

"Forty-eight hours," he said. "Anyone still here . . . it won't be pretty."

"Are they burning J next?" she said. The county had divided neighborhoods into lettered sectors. Foothill Park was in Sector J, or so all the notices kept saying.

"Yes. Anyone in J better be gone in forty-eight."

"Is it working?" she said. "Does burning stop it?"

"If it lives on things we touch, why not?" he said. "Don't ask me. I pass out stickers."

But that wasn't all he did. She noted the handgun strapped around his waist, the semi-automatic slung across his chest. She wondered how many people he had killed.

"I listen to the car radio," she said. "People say it's not working."

"So we should sit on our asses and do nothing?"

"Maybe you could teach me," she said. "How to shoot."

He stopped and turned slowly, profile first, as if his body followed against his will. A sneer soured one side of his face, but it was gone by the time he faced her. "Does it look like I have time for private lessons?"

"You brought it up."

"Are you playing rich princess out here?" he said. "None of the rules are for you?"

He'd been fooled by the mountains close enough to walk to and the estates lined up a quarter-mile up the street. He'd been fooled because Bob had made sure everyone kept the detached townhouses military neat, with matching exterior paint. But Foothill Park had been home to some of the county's poorest residents, the few who had dark skin or spoke Spanish at home. She and her friends used to call it "Trailer Park," although now she couldn't understand why.

"This is my grandmother's house," she said. "She moved into a tiny little two-bedroom she could barely afford so I could go to school here. I was her second chance to get it right, and she changed my life. Gram bought this house when they were cheaper. She never went to college, but I'm in grad school. When Gram got sick, I took a year off to move back in. Plain old cancer—nothing fancy. Old-fashioned dying takes time. So here I am."

He stared at her with pale brown eyes, the color of the houses' walls.

"Hold on a minute," he said.

He went back to his car, ducking out of sight. His sudden absence felt menacing, as if she should run and lock the door rather than waiting. But Nayima was not afraid of the cop, though she probably should be. What scared her more was the tasks waiting for her: the tedium and horror of her days.

He returned with a plastic shopping bag, heavy from its load. When he gave her the bag, she found two packages of whole chicken parts, frozen solid.

"Do you have electricity where you live?" she said.

He shook his head, a shadow across his brow. "Nah. Bunch of us were sweeping some houses on the hill. Guy up there had a generator and a subzero freezer. Food's hard as a rock."

The magnitude of the gift suddenly struck her: She had not had meat in a month, except a chunk or two in canned soup. She hoped the man on the hill had given up his food voluntarily, or that he had left long ago. But if he had left, why would his generator still be on?

"Thank you," she said. "I'm Nayima. What's your name? I mean . . . your first name?"

He ignored her question, just like he ignored her underwear.

"Don't ruin it," he said. "I don't have time to cook. I'll be back tomorrow for lunch."

After Nayima had cleaned and fed Gram in the morning, she grilled chicken on Mr. Yamamoto's patio Grillmaster instead of washing clothes like she'd planned. The chicken had mostly thawed overnight, so she started cooking first thing. She retrieved the spices from Mr. Yamamoto's gift box and rolled the chicken pieces in sage, garlic, and paprika the way Gram had taught her. She spent an hour looking for salt—and found it in a hidden, unruined corner of Shanice's kitchen. She'd had a memory of Shanice's mother keeping a box of salt in that exact spot. She could almost hear her friend's laughter.

Nayima hadn't had much practice on the grill—meat had disappeared fast, even before the supermarkets shut down—so she hovered over the chicken to be sure she didn't burn it. The patio smelled like a Fourth of July cookout. She didn't mind the new smoke.

She tested a wing too soon. It was too hot, meat bloody near the bone, but her mouth flooded with saliva at the taste of the spices. Such flavor! She wanted to eat the food half raw, but she waited, turning carefully, always turning, never letting the skin burn black.

At noon—the universal lunchtime—he still had not arrived.

Nayima's stomach growled as she turned Gram from the left side to the right, pulling her higher in the bed beneath her armpits, supporting her against the pillows. Gram moaned, but did not scream. Nayima changed the bag for Gram's feeding tube and kissed her forehead. "I love you, Gram," she said. But Gram was already sleeping.

By one o'clock, Nayima stopped waiting for the cop. She ate three pieces of the chicken: a thigh, a leg, and a wing, sure to leave plenty in case he brought friends.

He came alone at three-fifteen, coasting up to her curb in the same filthy cruiser. In brighter daylight, earlier in the day, his face looked smudged across his forehead and cheeks. He might not be bathing. All of him smelled like smoke.

"The chicken's ready," she said.

"J gets burned in twenty-four," he said, as if in greeting. His voice was hoarse. "You understand that, right?"

"I'll fix your plate," she said.

They ate at Mr. Yamamoto's cedar patio table beside the grill. Nayima offered him one of her precious beers, but he shrugged and shook his head.

She had found paper plates in the kitchen, but they ate with their fingers. It might have been the best chicken she'd ever cooked. She had another leg, stretching her bloated stomach. They studied their food while they ate, licking their fingers even though all the new protocols said *never* to put your fingers in your mouth. She hoped it wouldn't be too long before she would have chicken again.

"What's going on out there?" she said.

"Bad," he said mournfully. "All bad."

She knew she should ask more, but she didn't want to ruin their meal.

The question changed his mood. He wiped his fingers across his slacks, standing up. She wondered if he would try to make a sexual advance, but that thought felt silly as she watched him stride toward the glass patio door to the house. She was nearly invisible to him.

"Be right back," he said.

"Bathroom's the first left."

She decided she would explain herself to him, present her case: how a jostling car would torture Gram, how anyone could see the dying old woman only needed a little more time.

A gunshot exploded inside the house.

Nayima leaped to her feet so quickly that her knee banged against the table's edge.

Looters. Had looters invaded the house and confronted the cop? Her own gun was far from reach, hidden beneath the cushion on Mr. Yamamoto's sofa, where she'd slept. Her heart's thrashing dizzied her.

The glass patio door slid open again, and Sanchez slipped out and closed it behind him again. He did not look at her. He went to the grill to pick over the remaining chicken pieces.

"What happened?" Nayima said.

Sanchez's shoulders dropped with a sigh. He looked at her. His eyes said: *You know.*

Nayima took a running step toward the house, but her knee pulsed with pain. Instead, she plopped down hard on the bench. She held the edge of the table to keep her balance when the bench teetered, nearly falling.

Sanchez sat on the other side of the bench, righting it beneath his weight.

He planted both elbows on the table, stripping meat from the bones with his teeth.

The smell of his sweaty days, the smell of the smoky sky and the cooking bird, the smell of Gram's hair on hers from Gram's hairbrush, made Nayima feel sick. Her food tried to flee her stomach, but she locked her throat. Her grasping fingers shook against the picnic table's rough wood. She could not breathe this thick, terrible air.

"It'll be dark soon, so it's best to get on the road," Sanchez said. "The 210's pretty clear going east. Then you'll want to go north. They say the Five is still passable, for now. You don't want to be anywhere near here tomorrow."

She wanted to float away from his voice, but every word captivated her.

"Where?" she whispered.

"Anywhere but San Francisco. My family headed to Santa Cruz. I'll be going up there too when all this is done."

He reached into his back pocket and laid a smudged index card on the table, folded in half. She didn't touch it, but she saw a shadowed Santa Cruz address in careful script.

Then he ate in silence while Nayima sat beside him, her face and eyes afire with tears of rage and helplessness.

"Where's your car keys?" he said.

"In the car," she whispered past her stinging throat.

"You need anything in the house?"

The question confused her. Which house?

"My backpack," she said.

"Your gun in there too?"

She shook her head.

"Then where is it?"

She told him.

"I'll go get it," he said. "Thanks for the chicken. Real good job. I'll get your stuff. Just go around and wait in front of the house. Then I'll open the garage, and you can get in your car and drive away. One-two-three, it's done." His voice was gentle, almost playful.

Nayima was amazed when she realized she did not want to hurt Sanchez. Did not want to lunge at him or claw at his eyes. The index card on the table fluttered in a breeze. The air was so filled with smoke, she could almost see the wind.

"No," she said. "Just go. Please."

Any sadness in his eyes might have been an illusion, gone fast. He left her without a word, without hesitation. He had never planned to stay long.

When he left, Nayima ripped up the index card into eight pieces. Then, panicked at having nowhere to go, she collected the pieces and shoved them into her back pocket.

When a coyote howled, setting off the chorus, she heard the ghost of Gram's screams.

A sob emerged, and Nayima howled with the coyotes and lost dogs and sirens.

Then she stopped. She thought she'd heard a cat's mew.

A scrabbling came, and a black cat bounded over the wooden patio fence. The cat had lost weight, so she would not have recognized Tango except for the V of white fur across his chest. The sight of Tango made her scratch her arm's old flea bites.

Maybe it was a sign. Maybe Tango was a message from Gram.

Tango jumped on the patio table, rubbing his butt near her face as he sniffed at the chicken bones. Nayima cleared the bones away—chicken bones weren't good for pets, Gram always said. Instead, Nayima grabbed a chicken thigh from the grill and tossed it to the patio floor. Tango poked at it hungrily, retreated from the heat. Mewed angrily. Poked again.

"Hey, baby," Nayima said in Gram's voice, scratching Tango behind his ears. He purred loudly. Nayima stroked Tango for a long time while he ate. Slowly, her thoughts cleared.

Nayima went into the house, took a blanket from the sofa, and draped it over Gram in her bed. Nayima kept her face turned away, so she did not see any blood, although she smelled it. She wanted to say goodbye, but she had been saying goodbye for weeks. Months, really. She would have the rest of her life, however long or short that would be, to say goodbye to Gram.

Instead, Nayima gathered the remaining chicken, her gun, and her backpack. She didn't need the meds now, but they were in the car. They would be valuable later. She also had endless cans of Ensure, which would soon be her only food.

Tango followed Nayima to her car; she left the back door open for him while she packed the last of her things. If Tango jumped in, fine. If he didn't, fine.

Tango jumped into the car. She closed the door behind him.

As she pulled out of the driveway, she took one last drive around the green belt, although she purposely did not look at Gram's house and the jacaranda tree. The pool's blue waters were as placid as they'd been when she and Shanice lived in chlorine all summer, with Bob yelling at them to keep the noise down. She noticed a flat basketball at the edge of the court. The shirt and jeans still flapped in the tree.

Tango did not like the car. Nayima had not finished rounding the green belt before he began complaining, a high-pitched and desperate mew that sounded too much like crying. When he jumped to the large cooler on the front seat, she knew she'd made a mistake.

Nayima stopped the car. She opened her door. Tango bounded across her lap to get out of the car, running free. He stopped when he was clear of her and stared back from his familiar kingdom of grass, the only home he wanted to know. He groomed his paw.

Tango was Nayima's last sight in her rearview mirror before she drove away.

Her old life receded, tiny as a flea.

⌒

"Removal Order" is the first of three linked Nayima stories I wrote for an apocalypse trilogy edited by John Joseph Adams and Hugh Howey: The End Is Nigh, The End Is Now, *and* The End Has Come. *The caretaking imagery in the story comes from the experience of watching my late mother, Patricia Stephens Due, suffer the effects of bedsores late in her life. The horror of losing a loved one feels as terrible as watching the world fall apart.*

Herd Immunity

A MAN WAS far ahead of her on the road. Walking and breathing. So far, so good.

That he was a man, Nayima was certain. His silhouette against the horizon of the rising roadway showed his masculine height and the shadow of an unkempt beard. He pulled his belongings behind him in an overnight suitcase like a business traveler. Maybe she trusted him on sight because of the unmistakable shape of a guitar case slung across his back. She'd always had a thing for musicians.

"Hey!" she screamed, startling herself with her bald desperation.

He paused, his steady legs falling still. He might have turned around. She couldn't quite make out his movements in the quarter-mile or more that separated them. The two of them, alone, were surrounded on either side by the golden ocean of central California farmland, unharvested and unplowed, no trees or shade in sight as the road snaked up the hillside.

His attention gave her pause. She hadn't seen anyone walking in so long that she'd forgotten the plan that had kept her alive the past nine months: Hide. Observe. Assess.

But fuck it.

She waved and called again, so he would be certain she wasn't a mirage in the heat.

"Hey!" she screamed, more hoarsely. She tried to run toward him, but her legs only lurched a stagger on the sharp grade. She was dizzy from heat and modulated hunger. The sky dimmed above her, so she stopped her pathetic chase and braced her palms against her knees to calm the cannon bursts from her heart. The world grew bright again.

He walked on. She watched him shrink until the horizon swallowed him. She remembered a time when terrifying loneliness would have made her cry. Instead, she began following him at the pace her body had grown

269

accustomed to. He didn't seem afraid of her; that was something. He hadn't quickened. He was tired and slow, like her. If she was patient, she would catch up to him.

Nayima hadn't planned to stay on State Road 46 toward Lost Hills. She had wanted to follow the last highway sign—one of the few conveniences still in perfect working order—toward a town just ten miles east. But she decided to follow the man instead. Just for a while, she'd told herself. Not so far that she'd run too low on water or go hungry.

Nayima followed him for three days.

She wasted no energy or hope checking the scattered vehicles parked at odd angles for fuel or food, although most still had their keys. She was far too late for that party. Cars were shelter. Handy when it rained. Or when it was dark and mountain lions got brave, their eyes glowing white in her flashlight beam. ("Bad, bad kitty," she always said.)

The cars on SR-46 weren't battered and broken like the ones in Bakersfield, witnesses to riots or robberies. For a time, carjacking had been the national hobby. She'd jacked a car herself trying to get out of that hellhole—with a sprained ankle and a small mob chasing her, she'd needed the ride more than the acne-scarred drunk sleeping at the wheel. On the 46, the pristine cars had come to rest, their colors muted by a thin veil of burial dust.

Nayima missed her red Schwinn, but she'd hit a rock the day before she'd seen the man on the road—the demon stone appeared in her path and knocked her bicycle down an embankment. She'd been lucky only to bump her elbow hard enough to make her yell. But her bike, gone. Crumpled beyond salvage. Nayima didn't allow herself to miss much—but damn. And this man, her new day job, meant she didn't have time to peel off to look for tucked-away farmhouses and their goodies. Too risky. She might lose him. Instead, Nayima walked on, following her ghost.

She imagined how they would talk. Testify. Teach what little they knew. Start something. Maybe he could at least tell her why he was on the 46, what radio broadcast or quest had beckoned. She hadn't heard anything except hissing on radios in three months. She didn't mind walking a long distance if she might arrive somewhere eventually.

Each morning she woke from her resting place—the crook of a tree, an abandoned car that wasn't a tomb, in the cranny beneath the inexplicably locked cab of an empty eighteen-wheeler parked ten yards off the road like a beached whale—and wondered if the man had gone too far ahead. If he'd walked the whole night just to shake her. If he'd found a car that had sung him a love song when he caressed her and turned the key.

But each day, she saw signs that he was not lost. He was still walking ahead, somewhere just out of sight. Any evidence of him dampened her palms.

He left a trail of candy wrappers. Chocolate bars mostly, always the minis. Snickers, Twix, Almond Joy (her favorite; that wrapper made her stomach shout at the sight). Her own meals were similarly monotonous, but not nearly as colorful—handfuls of primate feed she'd found overlooked at a vet's office outside Bakersfield. Her backpack was stuffed with the round, brown nuggets. Monkey Balls, she called them. They didn't taste like much, but they opened up her time for walking and weren't nearly as heavy as cans.

On the third morning, when the horizon again stretched empty, and sinking dread bubbled in her stomach, the road greeted her with a package of Twizzlers, six unruined sticks still inside. The Twizzlers seemed fresh. She could feel his fingertips on the wrapper. The candy was warm to her tongue from the sun. So good it brought happy tears. She stood still as long as she dared while the sweetness flooded her dry mouth, coated her throat. Feeling anything was a novelty.

She cried easily over small pleasures: a liquid orange sunset, the wild horses she'd seen roaming a field, freed to their original destiny. She wondered if he had left her the Twizzlers in a survivors' courtship rite, until she found a half-eaten rope of the red candy discarded a few steps away. A Red Vines man, then. She could live with that. They would work it out.

By noon on Twizzlers Day, she saw him again, a long shadow stretching only half a mile ahead of her. Time was, she could have jogged to catch up to him easily, but the idea of hurry made her want to vomit. Her stomach wasn't as happy with the candy feast as the rest of her.

So she walked.

He passed a large wooden sign—not quite a billboard, but big—and when she followed behind him, she read the happy script:

COUNTY LINE ROAD FAIR!!!!
June 1-30 2 MI

Beneath that, cartoon renderings of pigs with blue ribbons, a hot dog grinning in his bun, and a Ferris wheel. A dull fucking name for a fair, she thought. Or a road, for that matter. She vowed that when the renaming of things began, she and the man on the road would do better. The Fair of Ultimate Rainbows, on Ultimate Rainbow Road. A name worthy of the sign's colors.

She was nearly close enough to touch the sign before she made out the papers tacked on the right side, three age-faded, identical handbills in a vertical line:

RESCUE CENTER

Stamped with a Red Cross insignia.

Red Crap. Red Death. Red Loss.

Nayima fought dueling urges to laugh and scream. Her legs nearly buckled in rebellion. The sun felt ten degrees hotter, sizzling her neck.

"You have got to be goddamn kidding," she said.

The man on the road could not hear her.

She cupped her hands to her mouth. "Do you still believe there's a Wizard too?"

Moron.

But she kept the last word silent. She shouldn't be rude. They needed to get along.

He didn't stop walking, but he gave her a grumpy old man wave over his shoulder. Finally—communication. Candor was the greatest courtesy in the land of the 72-Hour Flu, so she told him the truth. "They're just big petri dishes, you know! Best way to get sick is in evac camps! *Was*, I mean. Sorry to bear bad news, but there's no rescue center here!"

Nine months ago, she would have believed in that sign. She'd believed in her share. Back when the best minds preached hope for a vaccine that would help communities avoid getting sick with precautions, she'd heard the term on the CDC and WHO press conferences: herd immunity. As it turned out, the vaccine was a fable and herd immunity was an oxymoron.

Only NIs were left now: naturally immune. The only people she'd seen since June were other NIs floating through the rubble, shy about contact for fear of the attacks of rage and mass insanity. Nayima had escaped Bakersfield, where anyone walking with pep was a traitor to the human experience. Nayima had seen radiant satisfaction on the face of an axe-wielding old woman who, with her last gasps of breath, had split open the skull of the NI nurse offering her a sip of water. No good deed, as they say. This man was the first NI she'd met on the road in the three months since.

The formerly populated areas would be quieter now. That was the thing about the 72-Hour Flu: it settled disputes quickly. The buzzards were building new kingdoms in the cities, their day come at last.

"The dead can't rescue the living!" Nayima shouted up the godless road.

Her new friend kept walking. No matter. He would be stopping in two miles anyway.

She could smell the fair already.

SHE THOUGHT maybe, just maybe—not enough to speed her heart, but enough to make her eyes go sharp—when the rows of neatly parked cars appeared on the west side of the road. A makeshift parking lot, with rows designated in letter-number pairs on new cedar poles, A-1 through M-20. Because of the daylight's furious glare across the chrome and glass, the cars seemed to glitter like fairy-tale carriages. It was the most order Nayima had seen in months.

Then she saw the dust across their windows.

Everywhere she went, too late for the party. Even at the fair.

Buzzards and crows sat atop the COUNTY LINE ROAD FAIR—FREE PARKING banner, bright white and red, that hung across the gravel driveway from SR-46. The Ferris wheel stood frozen beyond, marking where the fair began, but it was so small it seemed sickly. The cartoon had been so much grander. Everything about the sign had been a lie.

The sound of mournful guitar came—picking, not strumming. She had never heard the melody before, but she knew the song well. "The 72-Hour Blues."

In the parking lot, she glanced through enough rear windows to start smiling. The Corolla had a backpack in plain sight. A few had keys in their ignitions. One was bound to have gas. This was a car lot Christmas sale. The cars on the road were from the people who'd given up on driving and left nothing behind. These cars were satisfied at their destination, although their drivers had left unfinished business inside. A few cars with windows cracked open stank of dead pets; she saw a large dog's white fur carpeting the back seat floor of a Ford Explorer. A child's baseball cap near the fur made her think of a pudgy-cheeked boy giving his dog a last hug before his parents hurried him away.

The cars screamed stories.

She saw her own face in the window. Hooded. Brown face sun-darkened by two shades. Jaw thin, showing too much bone. *You gotta eat, girl*, Gram would say. Nayima blinked and looked away from the stranger in the glass.

Tears. Damn, damn, damn.

Nayima dug her fingernails into her palm, hard. She drew blood. The cars went silent.

The guitar player could claim he'd found the treasure first, but there was enough to share. She had a .38 if he needed convincing, but she hoped it wouldn't come to that. Even the idea of her .38 made her feel sullied. She didn't want to hurt him. She didn't want him to try to hurt her. She wanted the opposite; someone to keep watch while she slept, to help her find food, to keep her warm. She couldn't remember the last time she'd wanted anything so badly.

The music soothed the graveyard in the parking lot. The guitarist might be the best musician she would ever know; just enough sour, not too much sweet. He was playing a song her grandmother might have hummed, but had forgotten to teach her.

Dear Old Testament God of Noah, please don't let him be another asshole.

He was out of sight again, so she followed the music through the remains of the fair.

The Ferris wheel wasn't the only no-frills part of the County Line Road Fair, which had been named right after all. She counted fewer than a dozen rides—the anemic Ferris wheel was the belle of the ball. The rest was two kiddie fake pony rides she might have found at a good-sized shopping mall, a merry-go-round with mermaids among the horses (that one actually wasn't too bad), a spinner ride in cars for four she'd always hated because she got crushed from centrifugal force, and a Haunted Castle with empty cars waiting to slip into the mouth of hellfire. A giant with a molten face guarded the castle's door, draped in black rags. Even now the Haunted Castle scared her. As she passed it, she spat into one of the waiting cars.

Crows scattered as she walked.

This fair was organized like all small fairs—a row of games on one side, food vendors on the other. Birds and scavengers had picked over the empty paper popcorn cups and foil hot dog wrappers, but only a few of the vendors had locked their booths tight with aluminum panels. A large deep fryer stood in plain sight at Joe's Beef Franks as she passed—nothing but an open doorway between them—so she was free to explore. Cabinets. Trash. Counters. So many possibilities. Now her heartbeat did speed up.

With a car and enough essential items, she could think about a future somewhere. The guitar seemed to agree, picking up tempo and passion. The music reminded her that she didn't have to be alone in her getaway car.

Words were nearly useless now, so she didn't speak right away when she found his camp alongside the elephant ear vendor's booth. He had laid out a sleeping bag in the shade of the awning promising "Taysteee Treets," his back supported against the booth. She stood across the fairway by the ringtoss and took him in.

First surprise: he was wearing a dust mask. A summer look for the fall. Ridiculous.

The mask was particularly disappointing because it was already hard to make out his face beneath his hair and the dirt. He had light brown skin, she guessed, a dark tangle of thinly textured hair, a half-fed build to match hers. He looked nearly a foot taller, so he would have an advantage if they had to fight. Nayima slipped her hand to the compartment in her backpack she kept in easy reach. She took hold of the gun slowly, but she didn't pull it out.

"Guitar's mine to keep, and nothin' else is worth taking," he said. His voice was gravel. "Grab your pick of whatever you find here and move on."

"You think I followed you three days to rob you?"

"I don't try to guess why."

Nayima shook off her light jacket's hood. She'd shaved her head in Bakersfield so she wouldn't be such an obvious rape target. Most of her hair was close to her scalp—but she had a woman's face. She imagined his eyes flickering, just a flash.

"I'm Nayima," she said.

He concentrated on his guitar strings. "Keep your distance."

"You're immune." Dummy. She didn't call him names, but it dripped in her voice.

He stopped playing. "Who says?"

"You do," she said. "Because you're still breathing."

He went back to playing, uninterested.

"Let me guess," she said. "Everyone in your family got sick and died—including people you saw every day—but you never got even a tummy-ache."

"I was careful."

"You think you're still alive because you're smarter than the rest?"

"I didn't say that." He sounded angry. "But I was very careful."

"No touching? No breathing?"

"Yes. Even learned how to play with these on." He held up his right hand. She hadn't seen his thin, dirty gloves at first glance.

"Your fingertips never brushed a countertop or a window pane or a slip of paper?"

"Doing my best."

"You never once got unlucky."

"Until now, I guess," he said.

"Bullshit," she said. Now she felt angry. More hurt, but angry too. She hadn't realized any stranger still held the power to hurt her feelings, or that any feelings were still so raw. "You're living scared. You're like one of those Japanese soldiers in World War II who didn't know the war was over."

"You think it's all over. In less than a year."

"Might as well be. Look how fast the UK went down."

His eyes dropped away. Plenty had happened since, but London had been the first proof that China's 72-Hour Virus was waging a world war instead of only a genocide. Cases hadn't appeared in the U.S. until a full two days after London burned—those last two days of worry over the problems that seemed far away, people that were none of their business. The televisions had still been working, so they had all heard the news unfolding. An entire tribe at the fire, just before the rains.

"What have you seen?" Finally, he wasn't trying to push her away.

"I can only report on Southern and Central California. Almost everybody's gone. The rest of us, we're spread out. You're the only breather I've seen in two months. That's why it's time for us to stop hiding and start finding each other."

"'Us?'" he repeated, hitched brow incredulous.

"NIs," she said. "Naturally Immunes. One in ten thousand, but that's a guess."

"Jesus." A worthy response, but Nayima didn't like the hard turn of his voice.

"Yes." She realized she didn't sound sad enough. He might not understand how sadness made her legs collapse, made it hard to breathe. She tried harder. "It's terrible."

"Not that—you." He sang the rest. "*Welcome, one and all, to the new super race . . .*"

Song as mockery, especially in his soulful, road-toughened tenor, hurt more than a physical blow. Nayima's anger roiled from the memory of rivulets of poisoned saliva running down her cheeks from hateful strangers making a last wish. "They spit in my face, whenever they could. They tried to take me with them—yet here I stand. You can stop being a slave to that filthy paper you're wearing, giving yourself rashes. We're immune. Congratulations."

"Swell," he said. "I don't suppose you can back any of that up with lab tests? Studies?"

"We will one day," she said. "But so far it's you, and me, and some cop I saw high-tailing out of Bakersfield who should not have still been breathing. Believe me when I tell you: This bad-boy virus takes everybody, eventually. Except NIs."

"What if I just left a bunker? A treehouse? A cave?"

"Wouldn't matter. You've been out now. Something you touched. It lives on glass for thirty days, maybe forty-five. That was what the lab people in China said, when they finally started talking. Immunity—that's not a theory. There were always people who didn't get it when they should've dropped. Doctors. Old People."

"People who were careful," he said.

"This isn't survival of the smartest," she said. "It's dumb luck. In our genes."

"So, basically, Madame Curie," he said, drawing out his words, "you don't know shit."

Arrogant. Rude. Condescending. He was a disappointment after three days' walk, no question about it. But that was to be expected, Nayima reminded herself. She went on patiently. "The next one we find, we'll ask what they know. That's how we'll learn. Get a handle on the numbers. Start with villages again. I like the Central Valley. Good farmland. We just have to be sure of a steady water supply." It was a relief to let her thoughts out for air.

He laughed. "Whoa, sister. Don't start picking out real estate. You and me ain't a village. I'll shoot you if you come within twenty yards."

So—he was armed. Of course. His gun didn't show, but she couldn't see his left hand, suddenly hidden beneath a fold in his sleeping bag. He had been waiting for her.

"Oh," she said. "This again."

"Yeah—this," he said. "This is called common sense. Go on about your business. You can spend the night here, but I want you gone by morning. This is mine."

"Rescue's coming?"

He coughed a shallow, thirsty cough—not the rattling cough of the plague. "I'm not here for rescue. Didn't know a thing about that."

"I have water," she said. "I bet there's more in the vendor booths." Let him remember what it felt like to be fussed over. Let him see caring in her eyes.

His chuckle turned into another cough. "Yeah, no thanks. Got my own."

"If you didn't come here to get rescued, then why? Jonesing for hot dog buns?"

He moved his left hand away from his gun and back to his guitar strings. He plinked.

"My family used to come," he said. "Compete in Four-H. Eat fried dough 'til we puked. Ride those cheap-ass rides. This area's real close-knit, so you'd see everybody like a backyard party. That's all I wanted—to be somewhere I knew. Somewhere I would remember."

The wind shifted. Could be worse, but the dead were in the breeze.

"Smells like their plan didn't work out," Nayima said.

"Unless it did." He shrugged. "You need to leave me alone now."

Coming as it did at the end of the living portrait he'd just painted, the theft of his company burned a hole in her. She needed him already. Father, son, brother, lover, she didn't care which. She didn't want to be without him. Couldn't be without him, maybe.

His silence turned the fairgrounds gloomy again. This smell was the reason she preferred the open road, for now.

"At least tell me your name," she said. Her voice quavered.

But he only played his fantasy of bright, spinning lights.

WITH ONLY two hours left before dark, Nayima remembered her situation. She was down to her last two bottles of water—so there was that. She noted every hose and spigot, mapping the grounds in her mind. Even with the water turned off, sometimes the reserves weren't dry.

Nayima went to search for a car first, since that would decide what else she needed. She didn't break into cars with locked doors during her first sweep. She decided she would only break a window if she saw a key. Glass was unpredictable, and her life was too fragile for everyday infections. The first vehicles she found with keys—the first engines she heard turn—had less than an eighth of a tank. Not enough.

Then she saw the PT Cruiser parked at B-7. Berry purple. The cream-colored one she'd driven in college at Spelman had been reincarnated in her favorite color, calling to her. Unlocked door. No stench inside. Half a bottle of water waiting in the beverage cup, nearly hot as steam from the sun. No keys in the ignition, but they were tucked in the passenger visor, ready to be found. The engine choked complaints about long neglect, but finally hummed to life. And the gas tank, except by a hair, was full. Nayima felt so dizzy with relief that she sank into the car's bucket seat and closed her eyes. She thanked the man on the road and his music in the sky.

She could pack a working car with enough supplies for a month or more. With so much gas, she would easily make it to the closest town. She would stake out the periphery, find an old farmhouse in the new quiet. Clean up its mess. Rest with a proper roof.

Nayima's breath caught in her throat like a stone. Her first miracle in the New World.

The rest of her searching took on a leisurely pace, one step ahead of the setting sun. Nayima avoided the guitar player while she scouted, honoring his perimeter. She drove from the parking lot to the fairway, her slow-moving wheels chewing the gravel. Her driver's seat was a starship captain's throne.

Weather and dust were no match for the colors at the County Line Road Fair. Painted clowns and polar bears and ringmasters in top hats shouted red, blue, and yellow from wildly named booths promising sweet, salty, and cold. In the colors and the guitar music, ghostly faces emerged, captured at play. The fairground teemed with children. Nayima heard their carefree abandon.

For an instant, she let in the children's voices—until her throat burned. The sky seemed ready to fall. She held her breath until her lungs forced her to suck in the air. To breathe in that smell she hated. The false memory was gone.

As she'd expected, airtight packages of hot dog buns looked fresh enough to last for millennia. She found boxes of protein bars in a vendor's cabinet and a sack of unshelled peanuts so large she had to carry it over her back like a child. She stuffed the PT Cruiser with a growing bounty of clean blankets, an unopened twenty-four pack of water bottles and her food stash—even a large purple stuffed elephant, just because she could. The PT Cruiser, her womb on wheels, cast a fresh light on the world.

But there was the question of the passenger seat, still empty. The may, maybe, might part was making her too anxious to enjoy her fair prizes.

Then Nayima saw the stenciled sign:

RESCUE CENTER ⇨

The arrow pointed away from the vendors' booths, toward the Farm World side of the fair, with its phantom Petting Zoo and Pony Rides in dull earth tones; really more an alleyway than a world. On the other end, a long wood-plank horse stall like one she had seen at the Kentucky Derby stood behind an empty corral, doors firmly shut.

Nayima climbed out of her PT Cruiser, pocketing her precious keys. She followed the dried tracks of man and beast side by side, walking on crushed hay. On the Farm World side, she could barely make out the sounds of the guitar. She felt like she had as a kid swimming in the ocean, testing a greater distance from shore. He might stop playing and disappear. It seemed more and more likely that she had only dreamed him.

But she had to see the rescue center. Like the driver from the PT Cruiser who had left her water bottle half full, she followed the sign. In her imagination, Nayima melted into scuffling feet, complaining children, muffled sobs.

The signs were posted on neatly spaced posts. Each sign, helpful and profound.

FAMILIES SHOULD REMAIN TOGETHER

YOUR CALM HELPS OTHERS STAY CALM

SMILE—REMOVE YOUR MASK

The smell worsened with each step toward the looming structure. In front of the closed double doors stood two eight-foot folding tables—somewhat rusted now. Sun-faded pages flapped from a clipboard. Nayima glanced at a page of dull bureaucracy: handwritten names and addresses: *Gerald Hillbrandt, Party of 4.* As she'd guessed, a few hundred people had come.

SHOES ⇨

Nayima's eyes followed the next sign to the southwest corner of the stall, where she found rows of shoes neatly paired against the wall. Mama Bear, Papa Bear, Baby Bear, all side by side. Cheerfully surrendered. Nayima, who wore through shoes quickly, felt a strange combination of exhilaration and sorrow at the sight of the shoes on merry display.

ENTRANCE ⇨

The next sign pointed around the corner, away from the registration table and cache of shoes. The entrance to the intake center had been in the rear, not the front. The rear double barn doors were closed, but they also had tables on either side, each with a large opaque beverage dispenser half-filled with a dark liquid that could be iced tea.

A refreshments table, she thought—until she saw the signs.

MAKE SURE EVERYONE IN YOUR PARTY TAKES A FULL CUP

PARENTS, WATCH YOUR CHILDREN DRINK
BEFORE DRINKING YOURSELF

MAKE SURE CUPS ARE EMPTIED BEFORE ENTERING

TRASH HERE, PLEASE

Beneath the last sign, a large garbage can halfway filled with crumpled plastic cups. Nayima stared. Some cups were marked with lipstick. Several, actually. Had they come to the Rescue Center wearing their Sunday best? Had they dressed up to meet their maker?

The smell, strongest here, was not fresh; it was the smell of older, dry death. The door waited—locked, perhaps—but Nayima did not want to go inside. Nayima laid her palm across the building's warm wooden wall, a communion with whoever had left her the PT Cruiser. And the shoes she would choose. What visionary had brought them here in this humane way? Had they known what was waiting? Her questions filled her with acid grief. She was startled by her longing to be with them, calm and resting.

Just in time, she heard the music.

• • •

"LOOK WHAT I found," she said, and held up the sign for him to see.

"Can't read that from here."

"I can come closer."

"Wouldn't do that."

So, nothing had changed. She sighed. "It says—'Smile, Remove Your Mask.'"

He laughed. She already loved the sound. And then, the second miracle—he tugged his mask down to his chin. "Hell, since it's on the sign." He pointed a finger of judgment at her. "You stay way over there, I'll keep it off."

His voice was clearer. It was almost too dark to see him now, but she guessed he couldn't be older than fifty, perhaps as young as forty. He was young. Young enough. She wasn't close enough to see his eyes, but she imagined they were kind.

"I'm Kyle," he said.

She grinned so widely that she might have blinded him.

"Easy there, sister," he said. "That's all you get—my name. And a little guitar, if you can be a quiet audience. Like I said, you're moving on."

"Some of the other cars have gas. But this one has a full tank."

"Good for you," he said, not unkindly.

"You'll die here if you're afraid to touch anything."

"My cross to bear."

"How will you ever know you're immune?" she said.

He only shrugged. "I expect it'll become clear."

"But I won't be here. I don't know where I'll be. We have to . . . " She almost said *We have to fight back and make babies and see if they can survive.* " . . . stay together. Help protect each other. We're herd animals, not solitary. We always have been. We need each other."

Too much to comprehend lay in his silence.

"All you need is a full tank of gas," he said at last. "All I need is my guitar. Nothing personal—but ever hear of Typhoid Mary?"

Yes, of course she had heard of Typhoid Mary, had lived under the terror of her legacy. In high school, she'd learned that the poor woman died in isolation after thirty years, with no one allowed close to her. Nayima had decided long ago not to live in fear.

"We have immunity," she said. "I won't get you sick."

"That's a beautiful idea." His voice softened practically to a song. "You'll be the one who got away, Nayima."

She couldn't remember the last time anyone had called her by name. And he'd pronounced it as if he'd known her all her life. Not to mention how the word beautiful cascaded up and down her spine. While her hormones raged, she loved him more with each breath. Nayima was tempted to jump into her PT Cruiser and drive away then, the way she had learned to flee all hopeless scenarios.

Instead, she pulled her car within fifteen yards of him and reclined in the driver's seat with her door open, watching him play until he stopped. The car's clock said it was midnight when he finally slept. Hours had melted in his music. She couldn't sleep, feverish with the thought of losing him.

At first, she only climbed out of the car to stretch her limbs. She took a tentative step toward him. Then, another. Soon, she was standing over him while he slept.

She took in his bright guitar strap, woven from a pattern that looked Native American. The wiry hairs on his dark beard where they grew thick to protect his pink lips. The moonlight didn't show a single gray hair. He could be strong, with better feeding. Beneath his dusty camo jacket, he wore a Pink Floyd concert shirt. He could play her all of the old songs, and she could teach him music he didn't know. The moonlight cradled his curls across his forehead, gleamed on his exposed nose. He was altogether magnificent.

Nayima was sure he would wake when she knelt beside him, but he was a strong sleeper. His chest rose and fell, rose and fell, even as she leaned over him.

Was the stone rolling across her chest only her heartbeat? Her palms itched, hot. She was seventeen again, unexpectedly alone in a corner with Darryn Stephens at her best friend's house party, so aware of every prickling pore where they touched. And when he'd bent close, she'd thought he was going to whisper something in her ear over the noise of the world's last dance. His breath blew across her lips, sweet with beer. Then his lips grazed hers, lightning strikes down her spine, and the softness . . . the softness . . .

Kyle slept on as Nayima pressed her lips to his. Was he awake? Had his lips yielded to her? It seemed so much like Kyle was kissing her too, but his eyes were still closed, his breathing uninterrupted even as she pulled away.

She crept back to her PT Cruiser, giddy as a twelve-year-old. Oh, but he would be furious! The idea of his anger made her giggle. She dozed to sleep thinking of the gift of liberation she had given Kyle. Freedom from masks. Freedom from fear. Freedom to live his life with her, to build their village.

BY DAWN, Nayima woke to the sound of his retching.

She thought she'd dreamed the sound at first—tried to will herself to stay in her happy dream of singing "Kumbaya" with well-groomed strangers in the horse stalls, hand in hand—but she opened her eyes and saw the guitar player hunched away from her. He had pushed his guitar aside. She heard the splatter of his vomit.

Nausea came first. Nausea came fast.

Shit, she thought. Her mind was a vast white prairie, emptied, save that one word. She remembered his laughter, realized she would never hear him laugh again now.

"I'm sorry," she said. "I thought for sure you were like me. An NI."

She wished her voice had sounded sadder, but she didn't know how. She wanted to explain that he might have contracted the virus somewhere else in the past twenty-four hours, not necessarily from her. But despite the odds and statistics on her side, even she didn't believe that.

It's only a mistake if you don't learn from it, Gram would say. Nayima clamped her fingernails into both palms. Her wrist tendons popped out from the effort. Hot pain. The numbness that had thawed with his music and 4-H stories crept over her again, calcified.

The man didn't turn to look at her as she stood over him and picked through his things. His luggage carrier held six water bottles and a mountain of candy bars. The necessities. She left him his candy and water. His 9mm had no ammo, but she took it. She left his guitar—although she took the strap to remember him by. She might take up guitar herself one day.

The man gagged and vomited again. Most people choked to death by the third day.

"I'm leaving now," she said, and knelt behind him. She searched for something to say that might matter to him. "Kyle, I found that Rescue Center over in Farm Land—Farm *World*—and it looks nice. Somebody really thought the whole thing through. You were right to come here. Where I grew up, they just burned everything."

Even now, she craved his voice. Wanted so badly for him to hear her. To affirm her. To learn her grandmother's name and say, "Yes, she was. Yes, you were. Yes, you are."

The man did not answer or turn her way. Like the others before him, he was consumed with his illness. Just as well, Nayima thought as she climbed back into her car. Just as well. She glanced at her visor mirror and saw her face: dirt-streaked, unrepentant. She blinked and looked away.

Nayima never had been able to stomach the eyes of the dead.

Asked to write a story about the end of the world for The End Is Now, *edited by John Joseph Adams and Hugh Howey, I decided to imagine what the end of the world would feel like to one character. My answer: isolation.*

Carriers

Republic of Sacramento
Carrier Territories
2055

NAYIMA'S SLEEP had turned restless as she aged, so the rattling from the chicken coop outside woke her before her hens raised the alarm. The intruder was likely either feline or human, and she hoped it was the former. A cat, no matter how big, wasn't as dangerous as a person.

Nayima ignored the sharp throb in her knee when she jumped from her bed and ran outside with her sawed-off in time to see a hound-sized tabby scurrying away with a young hen pinned in its teeth, a snow globe of downy white feathers trailing behind. The army of night cats scattered in swishing bushes and brittle leaves. The giant thief paused to look back at her, his eyes glowing gold with threat. The cats were getting bigger.

Nayima had been saving that hen for Sunday dinner, but she was too winded to chase the thief. Now both knees throbbed. And her lower back, right on schedule. She fired once into the dark and hoped she'd hit him.

Fucking cats.

The dark was thick to the forsaken east, but to the west she saw the gentle orange glow from the colony in Sacramento, the fortress she would never enter. The town folk had electricity to spare, since their lights never went fully dark anymore. They were building a real-life Emerald City from the ruins, with bright lights and fresh water flowing in the streets—literally, after the levees flooded back in the '20s.

By contrast, her tract, Nayimaland, was two-hundred acres of dead farmland she shared with feral cats made bold because food was scarce—taken by drought, not the Plague. The late State of California had yet more dying to do.

287

Nayima felt thirsty, but she didn't stop at her sealed barrel to take a scoop. She couldn't guess how long her standing water would have to last. Sacramento owed her water credits, but she would be a fool to trust their promises.

At the rear of the chicken coop, Nayima found the hole the cat had torn in the mesh and lashed loose wires to close it. The hens were unsettled, so she could expect broken eggs. And she couldn't afford to cook one of her reliable laying hens, so she'd have to wait for meat at least another week, until trading day.

By the time Nayima came back to her porch, her two house cats, Tango and Buster, had gathered enough courage to poke their heads up in the window. For an instant, her pets looked like the thief cat, no better.

"It's okay, babies," she said. "One of 'em got a chicken."

Buster, still aloof, raised his tail good night and went to his sofa. But Tango followed her to her bedroom and jumped beside her to sleep. Nayima preferred a bare mattress to the full bed that had been in this room—fewer places for intruders to hide and surprise her. She slept beneath the window, where she could always open her eyes and see the sky. Tango rested his weight against her; precious warmth and a thrumming heartbeat to calm her nerves.

"I can't feed you all," she told Tango. "I'm crazy for taking in just you two."

Tango slowly blinked his endless green eyes at her, his cat language for love. Nayima returned Tango's long, slow blink.

NAYIMA THOUGHT the jangling bells outside soon after dawn meant that a cat had been caught in a cage, but when she went to investigate, she found Raul's mud-painted red pickup slewed across the dirt path to her ranch house. He was cursing in Spanish. His front tire had caught a camouflaged cage, and he was stooping to check the damage. At least a dozen sets of cats' eyes floated like marbles in the dry shrubbery.

"Don't shoot!" Raul called to her. He knew she had her little sawed-off without looking back. "You'll blow off your own culo with that rusty thing one day. ¿Es todo, Nayima?"

Despite the disturbance and his complaining, Nayima was glad to see Raul. He looked grand in morning sunshine. Raul's eyes drooped slightly, giving the impression of drowsiness, but he was handsome, with a fine jaw and silvering hair he wore in two long braids like his Apache forebears. Since reconciliation and the allotment of the Carrier Territories eight years ago, Raul looked younger every time she saw him.

Nayima had turned sixty-one or sixty-two in December—she barely tracked her age anymore—and she and Raul were among the youngest left, so most carriers had died before the territories were allotted. In their human cages.

Captivity had been their repayment for the treatment and vaccine from the antibodies in their blood. They were outcasts, despite zero human transmissions of the virus after Year One. The single new case twenty-five years ago had been a lab accident, and the serum had knocked it out quick.

The Ward B carriers Nayima had barely known still lived communally, or close enough to walk to each other's ranches. But Nayima had chosen seclusion on an airy expanse of unruly farmland that stretched as far as she could see. In containment, she'd never had the luxury of community, except Raul. She had enough human contact on her market trips, where she made transactions through a wall. Or her hour-long ride on her ATV to see Raul, if she wanted conversation. Other people wearied her.

"Sorry—cat problem," she told Raul. "Did it rip?" She had a few worn tires in her shed from the previous owner, but they were at least forty years old.

Raul exhaled, relieved. "No, creo que está bien."

She squatted beside him, close enough to smell the sun on his clothes. She had not seen Raul in at least thirty days. He had begged her to share his house, but she had refused. She needed to talk to him from time to time, but she remembered why she did not want to live with him, and why she had slept with him only once: Raul's persistent recollections about his old neighborhood in Rancho Cucamonga and his grandparents' house in Nogales were unbearable. He always wanted to talk about the days before the Plague.

But after forty years, he was family. He'd been a gangly fifteen-year-old when the lab-coats captured him. Shivering and crying, he had webbed his fingers to reach toward her hand against the sheet of glass.

Nayima missed skin. She felt sorry for the new children, being raised not to touch. She absently ran her fingertips along the dirt-packed ridges in the tire's warm rubber.

"Do you have meat?" she said.

"Five pounds of dried beef," he said. Nayima didn't care much for beef, but meat was meat. "In the back of the truck. And a couple of water barrels."

Water barrels? A gift that large probably wasn't from Raul alone, and she didn't like owing anyone.

"From Sacramento?"

"You're doing a school talk today, I heard. Liaison's office asked me to come out."

Nayima's temper flared. She could swear she'd felt a *ping* at her right temple an hour before, waking her from fractured sleep. The lab-coats denied that they abused her tracking chip, but was it a coincidence she had a school obligation that day? And how dare they send so little water!

Nayima was so angry that her first words came in Spanish, because she wanted Raul's full attention. He had taught her Spanish, just as she had taught him so much else, patient lessons through locked doors. "Que me deben créditos, Raul. They owe a lot more than two barrels."

"You'll get your créditos. This is just . . . " He waved his hand, summoning the right word. Then he gave up. "Por favor, Nayima. Take them. You earned them." He tested the air pressure in his tire with a pound of his fist. "Gracias a Díos this is okay."

Nayima's shaky faith had been shattered during the Plague, but Raul still held fast to his God. *He told us the Apocalypse was coming in Revelation*, he always said, as if that excused it all. Nayima still believed Sunday dinner should be special, but only to honor the memory of her grandmother's weekly feasts.

Two new orange water barrels stood in the bed of Raul's truck. Large ones. She needed more credits to get her faucets running, but the barrels would last a while. Nayima climbed up, grabbing the bed's door to swing her leg over. She winced at the pain in her knees as she landed. She treasured the freedom to move her body, but movement came with a cost.

"¿Estás bien, querida?" Raul said.

"Just my knees. Stop fussing."

Nayima fumbled with an unmarked plastic crate tied beside the closest barrel.

"Don't open that yet," Raul said.

But she already had. Inside, she found the beef, wrapped in paper and twine. Still not quite dry, judging by the grease spots.

But she forgot the jerky when she saw two dolls, both long-haired girls, one with brown skin, one white. The dolls' hands were painted with blue plastic gloves, but nothing else. They had lost their clothes, lying atop a folded, obscenely pink blanket.

"What the hell's this?" Nayima said.

Raul walked closer as if he carried a heavy sack of across his shoulders. "I wanted to talk to you," he said, voice low. He reached toward her. "Come down. Walk with me."

"Bullshit," she said. "Why is Sacramento sending me dolls?"

"Bejar de la truck," Raul insisted. "Por favor. Let's walk. I have to tell you something."

Nayima was certain Raul had sold her out in some way, she just couldn't guess how. Raul had always been more willing to play political games; he'd been so much younger when he'd been found, raised without knowing any better. So Raul's house had expensive solar panels that kept his water piping hot and other niceties she did not bother to covet. His old pickup truck, which ran on precious ethanol and gasoline, was another of his luxuries for the extra time and blood he was always willing to give the lab-coats.

Nayima climbed out of the truck more carefully than she'd climbed in, refusing Raul's aid. Living in small spaces for most of her life had left her joints irritable and stiff, even with daily exercises to loosen them. If she'd had the energy or balance, she would have shoved Raul down on his ass.

"Start talking," she said. "What have you done?"

"Put the gun down first."

Nayima hadn't realized she was pointing the shotgun at him. She lowered it. "Tell me ahora, Raul. No hay más secretos." Raul's secrets stung more than anyone else's.

"I won a ruling," Raul said.

"About what? Free toys?"

Raul stared out toward the thirsty grasslands. "I have a library portal at my house . . . " he began.

Of course he did. Toys and gadgets. That was Raul.

Raul went on. "I did some research on . . . the embryos."

Nayima's cheek flared as if he'd struck her. During Reconciliation, she and Raul had learned that dozens of embryos had been created from her eggs and his sperm, more than they'd known. They had been the cocktail du jour: something about their blood types. Her heart gave a sudden sick tumbling in her chest, as if to drown him out.

"There's a bebé, Nayima," he said, whispering like wind. "One survived."

The world went white. Her eyesight, her thoughts, lost.

"What? When?"

"She just turned four," he said. "She's still in the research compound."

There was a *she* somewhere?

"How long have you known?"

"Six months," he said. "When I got the portal. I saw rumors of the surviving infant, did the research. She's one of ours. They never told us."

Now Nayima's sacrifices seemed fresh: the involuntary harvesting of her eggs, three first-trimester miscarriages after forced insemination, a succession of unviable embryos created in labs, and two premature live births of infants from artificial wombs who had never survived beyond a day. Pieces of her chopped away.

"We can't reproduce," she said.

"But one lived," Raul said. "They don't know why."

"You've known all this time? And you never told me?"

He sighed. "Lo siento, Nayima. I hated hiding it. But I knew it would upset you. Or you might work against me. I didn't want to say anything until I got a ruling. As the biological father, I have rights."

"Carriers don't have rights."

"Parental rights," Raul said. "For the first time—yes, we do."

Nayima despised herself for her volcanic emotions. How could Raul be naïve enough to believe Sacramento's lies? If there was a surviving child—

which she did not believe—they would not release their precious property to carriers.

"It's a trick," she said. "To get us to go back there."

Raul shook his head slowly. Impossibly, he smiled. "No, Nayima," he said. "They're sending her to us. To you. She's free under Reconciliation to be with her parents. All you have to do is sign the consent when they come."

Nayima needed to sit, so she ignored her sore joints and sat where she'd been standing, on the caked dirt of her road. The air felt thick and heavy in her lungs.

"No," Nayima said. Saying the word gave her strength. "No no no. We can't. It's a trap. Even if there's a girl . . . " It was so improbable, Nayima could barely say the words. "And there isn't . . . But even if there is, why would they offer her except as a weapon against us? To threaten us? To control us? Why do they keep trying so hard to make children from us? She's not from my womb, so she doesn't have the antibodies. Think about it! We're just . . . reserves for them. A blood supply, if they ever need it. That's the only reason we're still alive."

Raul's eyes dropped. He couldn't deny it.

"She's our child," Raul said. "Ella es nuestra bebé. We can't leave her there."

"You can't—but I can," she said. "Watch me."

Raul's voice cracked. "The ruling says both living parents must consent. I need you with me on this, Nayima."

"I'm an old woman now!" Nayima said. Her throat burned hot.

"And I'm fifty-six," Raul said. "But we had una hija together. The marshals are bringing her here tomorrow."

"You're sending marshals to me?" The last time marshals came to see her in the territories after only nine months, a pack of them had removed her from the house she had chosen and stolen half of her chickens, shooting a dozen dead just for fun. Her earliest taste of freedom had been a false start, victim to a government property dispute.

"Marshals aren't like they were," Raul said. "Things are changing, Nayima." Like he was scolding her.

Raul lowered the truck's bed door and pulled out the plastic crate. He carried it to her porch. Next, he took down the barrels and rolled them to the house one by one. The heavy barrels thundered across the soil.

When he returned, breathing hard, Nayima was on her feet again, with her gun. She jacked a shell into the chamber.

"You could've shot me before I did all that work," Raul said.

"I'm not shooting you yet," she said. "But any marshals that show up here tomorrow are declaring war. They might bring her, but they could take her at any time. We're all property! I won't give them that power over me. She's better off dead. I'm not afraid to die too."

Raul gave her a forlorn look before he walked past her and slammed the bed of his truck shut. "I was hoping for some eggs, pero maybe mañana."

"I swear to your God, Raul, I will kill anyone who comes to this house."

Raul opened his driver's side door and began to climb back inside, but he stopped to look at her over his shoulder. He had left his truck idling. He had never planned to stay long.

"She doesn't have a name," he said.

"What?"

"Nobody bothered to name her. In the records, she's called Specimen 120. Punto. Some of the researchers call her Chubby for a nickname. Like a pet, Nayima. Our hija."

The weight of the shotgun made Nayima's arms tremble.

"Don't bring anyone here," she said. "Please."

Raul got in the truck and slammed the door. He lurched into reverse, turned the truck away, and drove. Nayima fired once into the air, a roar of rage that echoed across the flatlands. The shotgun kicked in her arms like an angry baby.

After the engine's hum was lost in the open air, the only sound was Nayima's wretched sobs.

IN HER front room, Nayima's comm screen flared white, turning itself on. A minder waited in five-by-five on her wall, as though she'd been invited to breakfast. The light haloing her was bright enough to show old acne stars. Makeup had yet to make a comeback, except the enhanced red lips favored by both men and women. Full of life.

"Hello, Nayima," the minder said. Then she corrected herself: "Ms. Dixon."

Nayima nodded cordially. Nayima's grandmother, born in Alabama, had never stood for being called by her first name, and neither did Nayima—an admittedly old-fashioned trait at a time when numbers mattered more than names.

The minder seemed to notice Nayima's puffed eyes, and her polite veneer dulled. "You remember the guidelines?"

Guideline One and Only: She was not to criticize the lab-coats or make it sound as if she had been treated badly. Blah blah blah and so forth. Questions about the embryo—the *girl*—broiled in Nayima's mind, but she didn't dare bring her up. Maybe the marshals wouldn't come. Maybe she could still get her water credits.

"Yes," Nayima said, testing her thin voice.

"We added younger students this year," the minder said. "Stand by."

Three smaller squares appeared inset beneath the girl's image—classrooms, the children progressively older in each. The far left square held the image of twelve wriggling, worming children ages about three to six sprawled across a floor with a red mat. A few in the front sat transfixed by her image on what seemed to be a looming screen, high above them. Every child wore tiny, powder blue plastic gloves.

Nayima had to look away from the smallest children. She had not seen children so young in forty years, and the sight of them was acid to her eyes.

Hadn't Raul said the girl was four?

Nayima blinked rapidly, her eyes itching with tears.

Crying, she was certain, was against the guidelines.

Nayima willed herself to look at the young, moony faces, braving memories of tiny bodies rotting on sidewalks, in cars, on the roadways, mummified in closets. These were new children—untouched by Plague. Their parents had been the wealthy, the isolated, the truly Chosen—the infinitesimal number of survivors who were not carriers, who did not have the antibodies, but had simply, somehow, survived.

Nayima leaned closer to her screen. "Boo!" she said.

Young eyes widened with terror. Children scooted away.

But when Nayima smiled, the entire mass of them quivered with laughter, a sea of perfect teeth.

Nayima's teeth were not perfect. She had never replaced the lower front tooth she'd lost to a lab-coat she'd smacked across his nose, drawing blood. He'd strapped her to a table, raped her, and extracted her tooth on the spot, without anesthesia.

Nayima had been offered a dental implant during Reconciliation, but a new tooth felt like a lie, so she had refused. In previous classroom visits, she had answered the question *What happened to your tooth?* without bitterness—why should she feel contempt for brutes any more than she would a tree dropping leaves?—until a minder pointed out that the anecdote about her extracted tooth violated the guidelines.

The guidelines left Nayima with very little to say. She chose each word with painful care.

These schoolchildren asked the usual questions: why she had survived (genetic predisposition), how many people she had infected (only one personally, as far as she knew), how many carriers were left (fifteen, since most known carriers were "gone now"). By the fourth question, Nayima had lost her will to look at the children's faces. It was harder all the time.

The girl who spoke up next was not yet eight. Her face held a whisper of brown; a girl who might have been hers. And Raul's.

"Do you have any children?" the girl said.

All of Nayima's work, gone. No composure. No smile. A sharp pain in her belly.

"No, I've never had children," she said. "None that survived."

Nayima shot a pointed gaze at the minder, who did not contradict her. Maybe the minder didn't know about Specimen 120. Maybe a bureaucrat had made up the story to tease Raul.

"Okay," the girl said, shrugging, not yet schooled in the art of condolences. "What do you miss the most about the time before the Plague?"

An easy answer came right away, and it almost wasn't a lie. "Halloween."

When she explained what Halloween had been, the children sat literally open-mouthed. She wondered which part of her story most stupefied them. The ready access to sweets? The trust of strangers? The costumes?

The host looked relieved with the children's enchantment and announced that the visit was over. A flurry of waving blue gloves. Nayima waved back. She even smiled again.

"Don't forget my water credits," Nayima said from behind her happy teeth.

But the minder's image had already flashed away.

NAYIMA LINED UP her contraband on the front table—the sawed-off, a box of shells, an old Colt she'd found in the attic with its full magazine, the baseball bat she kept at her bedside. She'd even found a gas mask she'd bartered for at market. When the marshals came, she would be prepared. In her younger years, she would have boarded up at least her front windows, but her weapons would have to do.

"Raul is the real child," she told Tango and Buster while they watched her work. Buster swatted at a loose shell at the edge of the table, but Nayima caught it before it hit the floor. "He believes every word they say. 'Things are changing,' he says. Believing in miracles. Sending marshals here—to me!"

Tango mewed softly. A question.

"Of course they're not bringing a child here," she said. "A judge's ruling? In favor of carriers? You know the lab-coats would fight to keep her." She shook her head, angry with herself for her weakness. "Besides, there is no child. Babies with carrier genes don't live."

The crate was light enough to lift to the table with only slight pressure in her lower back, gone when she stretched. But she could only roll a barrel slowly, oh-so-slowly, across her threshold. How had Raul managed so easily? She left the second barrel outside. By the time she closed her door again, her lower back pulsed with pain and she felt aged by a decade.

"Lies," Nayima said.

Tango and Buster agreed with frenzied mews.

She would have no Sunday dinner if she died tomorrow, Nayima reminded herself. So she got her cleaver from the kitchen, unwrapped the beef, and began chopping the meat on the table, not caring about dents in the wood. She chopped until she was perspiring and sweat stung her eyes.

Nayima held a chunk with both hands and sank in her teeth. She mostly did not bother with salt in her own cooking, so the taste was overwhelming at first. The cats gnawed at the meat beside her on the table with loud purrs.

"Could there be a child?"

Suppose they'd had a breakthrough, found a way to rewire the genes? But why go through that trouble and expense when other children were being born? The girl must be a failed experiment. A laboratory fluke. Did they need caretakers for a child born with half a brain—was that it? Nayima swore she'd be damned if she'd spend the years she had left tending the lab-coats' mistakes.

"But there is no child," she reminded Tango and Buster. "It's all a lie."

After dark, with her flashlight to guide her, Nayima set her traps for the thief cat with slices of meat and visited the wooden chicken coop Raul had helped her build, as big as her grandmother's backyard shed. She checked the loose wires in the rear, but the hole was still secure. She hadn't collected eggs earlier, so chickens had defecated on some. A few eggs lay entirely crushed, yolks seeping across the straw.

Nayima was exhausted by the time she'd cleaned the nest boxes, scrubbed the surviving eggs, and set them on a bowl on her kitchen for Raul to find later—but she couldn't afford to sleep tonight. The marshals might come at any time.

Nayima fixed herself a cup of black tea from her new water—so fresh!— and sat vigil by her front window with her shotgun, watching the empty pathway. Sometimes her eyes played tricks, animating the darkness. A far-off cat's cry sounded like a baby's, waking Nayima when she dozed.

Just before dawn, bells jingled near the chicken coop. Heart clambering, Nayima ran outside. The food was gone from the first trap she reached, but the door had not properly sprung. Shit.

More frantic jingling came from the trap twenty yards farther. Nayima raced toward it, her light in one hand and her gun in the other.

A pair of eyes glared out at her from beyond the bars.

The cat scrambled to every corner of the cage, desperate to escape while bells mocked him. This was the one. Nayima recognized the monster tabby's unusual size.

"Buddy, you stole the wrong chicken."

Nayima could not remember the last time she had felt so giddy. She carefully lowered her flashlight to the ground, keeping it trained on the trap. Then she raised her shotgun, aiming. She'd blow a hole in her trap this way, but she had caught the one she was looking for.

The cat mewed—not angry, beseeching. With a clear understanding of his situation.

"You started it, not me," Nayima said. "Don't sit there begging now."

The cat's trapped eyes glowed in her bright beam. Another plaintive mew.

"Shut up, you hear me? This is your fault." But her resolve was flagging.

The cat raised his paw, shaking the cage door. How many times had she done the very same thing? How many locks had she tested, searching for freedom?

Could there really be a child?

Nayima sobbed. Her throat was already raw from crying. Never again, she had said. No more tears. No more.

Nayima went to the trap's door and flipped up the latch. The cat hissed at her and raced away like a jaguar, melting into the dark. She hoped he would run for miles, never looking back.

Is my little girl with those zookeepers without even a name?

"But it's all lies," she whispered at the window, as she stroked Tango in her lap. "Isn't it?"

Dawn came and went with the roosters' crowing. Nayima did not move to collect the morning eggs, or to eat any of the beef she and the cats had left, or to empty her bulging bladder. She watched the sky light up her empty pathway, her open gate.

Why hadn't she closed the gate?

Based on the sun high above, it was nearly noon when Nayima finally stood up.

The metallic glint far down the roadway looked imaginary at first. To be sure, Nayima wiped away dust on her windowpane with her shirt, although the spots outside still clouded it. The gleam seemed to vanish, but then it was back, this time with bright cobalt blue lights that looked out of place against the browns and grays of the road. Two sets of blue lights danced in regimented patterns, back and forth.

Nayima's breath fogged her window as she leaned closer, so she wiped it again.

Hoverbikes!

Two large hoverbikes were speeding toward her house, one on each side of the road at a matching pace, blue lights snaking across their underbellies. At least it wasn't an army, unless more were coming. Marshals' hoverbikes were only big enough for two, at most.

"You damn fool, Raul," she whispered again, but she already had forgiven him too.

Nayima was too exhausted to pick up her shotgun. She had failed the test with her cat thief, so what made her think she could fight marshals? Let them take what they wanted. As long as she had Tango and Buster, she could start again. She always did.

As the hoverbikes flew past her gate, Nayima counted one front rider on each bike in the marshals' uniform: black jackets with orange armbands. The second rider on the lead bike was only Raul—his face was hidden behind the black helmet, but she knew his red hickory shirt. His father had worn one just like it, Raul had told her until she wanted to scream.

"Nayima!" Raul called. He flung his helmet to the ground.

The hoverbike Raul was riding hadn't quite slowed to a stop, floating six inches above the ground, so Raul stumbled when he leaped off in a hurry. The marshal grabbed his arm to help hold him steady while the bike bobbing obediently in place.

"Querida, it's me," Raul said. "Don't worry about the marshals. Please open the door."

Nayima stared as both marshals took off their helmets, almost in unison, and rested them in the crooks of their arms. One was a young man, one a woman, neither older than twenty-five. The man was fair-haired and ruddy. The woman's skin was nearly as dark as her own, her hair also trimmed to fuzz. Had she seen this man during an earlier classroom visit? He looked familiar, and he was smiling. They both were. She had never seen a marshal smile.

The marshals wore no protective suits. No masks. They did not hide their faces or draw weapons. Even ten yards away, through a dirty window, Nayima saw their eyes.

Nayima jumped when Raul banged on her door. "Nayima, ella está aqui!"

"I don't see her." Nayima tried to shout, but her throat nearly strangled her breath.

Raul motioned to the woman marshal, and she dismounted her hoverbike. For the first time, Nayima saw her bike's passenger—not standing, but in a backward facing seat. A child stirred as the woman unstrapped her.

It couldn't be. *Couldn't* be.

Nayima closed her eyes. Had they drugged her meat? Was it a hallucination?

"Do you see, Nayima?" Raul said. "Ven afuera conmigo. Please come."

Raul left her porch to run back to the hoverbike. Freed from her straps, a child reached out for a hand for Raul's help from the seat. Raul made a game of it, lifting the child up high. Curly spirals of dark hair nestled her shoulders. For an instant, the child was silhouetted in the sunlight, larger than life in Raul's sturdy upward grasp.

The girl giggled loudly enough for Nayima to hear her through the windowpane. Raul was a good father. Nayima could see it already.

"Now you're going to meet your mamí," Raul said.

Nayima hid behind her faded draperies as Raul took the girl's hand and walked to the porch with her. When she heard the twin footsteps on her wooden planks, Nayima's world swayed. She ventured a peek and saw the girl's inquisitive face turned toward the window—dear Jesus, this angel had Gram's nose and plump, cheerful cheeks. Raul's lips. Buried treasure was etched in her delicate features.

Jesus. Jesus. *Thank you, Dear Lord.*

Nayima opened her door.

⌒⌒

This is Nayima's final story in the post-apocalyptic trilogy edited by John Joseph Adams and Hugh Howey. Each story, in its own way, is about seeking or trying to hold on to family. Nayima had resigned herself to be without human contact—or a human experience as a mother. After all she had been through, I wanted her to experience the kind of Change we see unfolding daily even in the face of fear and pain that has lasted for generations.

VANISHINGS

She could never catch hold of a moment.

Señora Suerte

I HATE this place.

Someone got the idea—brilliant or inane, depending on how the meds are tickling my brain that day—to dress up this place with games. Someone thought the general air of Death might smell better with a whiff of Fortune. General collection of losers that we are, it would be nice if someone could win something once in a while. That's the idea.

Brilliant or inane, it truly does not matter. You'd have to live here to see the boldness of the notion. You'd have to be breathing in the urine-soaked air. Picture Fidel's worst prisons with festive shooting galleries—not with real bullets, mind you, but pellets knocking over rows of smiling duckies—and maybe you would get the picture.

Have I mentioned yet that I don't like it here?

I hate this place.

A few years ago, I could have sat you down over a few rounds of mojitos and sifted through other facts that could have been called pertinent, at least at the time: Born in La Habana province outside of Mariel, Cuba. Second of five children. Bank manager in Hialeah, Florida, for thirty years. Married twice, once happily. Widower twice, once unhappily.

Brace yourself: Only child, a son, died in a car crash at seventeen. That was once the defining fact of my existence. A whisper of my son's death, and I got hisses, moans, blinking eyes, tears. I got laid, even. It was a powerful fact. That's Gilberto. His son died. His only son. His namesake. (Gilberto. Not Gil. Not Bert, for God's sake. Gilberto.) Gilberto lost two wives and a son, they clucked. What an unlucky man. Come to me, pobrecito.

But before I came here, I was a virgin. I thought bad luck was a myth, and had vastly underestimated the phrase's meaning in either Spanish (mala suerte) or the English I worked so hard to learn as a young man in my twenties, when I had to begin my life anew. Mala suerte. Now, I live

305

in bad luck's bosom. It suckles me to sleep—that, and the meds. Thank goodness for sleep. My only goal in life is more sleep. I'm so far behind. Raul, in the bed next to mine, sleeps all day, the lucky bastardo. All day, and no one bothers him.

No sleeping for me. When I first arrived, I got trotted around like a poster boy for recovery. Look at Gilberto, Mrs. Sanchez. He had a stroke only three months ago, and he can stand on his own two feet. Look at Gilberto, Mr. Ortiz. He's already feeding himself with both hands. Look at Gilberto, Mr. Benton. Look at Gilberto.

The day of the stroke, I had a beautiful dream. No pain, just visions. One minute I'm munching on pastelitos at my favorite Cuban bakery on Flagler, and the next minute I'm at the emergency room. In my dream, I see my first wife, Maritza. The woman had a beautiful face, but I called her El Diablo. She was a horror. When I saw her again, I thought I must be on my way to Hell. So I asked her: "Why were you so unkind?" And she shrugged her shoulders in her awkward, unrefined manner. "I didn't know how to be another way," she said softly. Of course, no? It made sense at the time, so I forgave her. Deep in my heart, I forgave her. I told her I was sorry for the way I danced when her headache turned out to be a brain aneurysm, my problems gone like that. And she smiled. Such a weight was lifted from me!

Then, her face became Camila's. Mi reina. Mi vida. Not as beautiful as Maritza—in her younger years, judged by her face, Camila had been lonely—but I saw her clean, pure spirit. All kindness. And I understood: As in life, I had to pass my first test, Maritza, to see Camila again. Perhaps it was Heaven calling for me. She touched my face, and an indescribable feeling bathed me. Better than sex, better than rum, better than music. A feeling we don't find in this world.

The next thing I knew, no Camila. I was in a hospital room. I could not speak, I could not move the right side of my body. After an eternity, in answer to my prayers for a cessation of misery, I was brought here. So, either God has a grudge against me or has no better way to amuse himself. Either way, we don't speak anymore.

Was it not enough I was an exile? Exiled first from my homeland, and next from my loved ones? Did I ever complain? When others would have cursed God, I never did. But for this place, God has some answering to do.

There is no excuse.

I hate this place.

Here, we are not exiles, engineers, postal workers, grocers, bankers, grandparents, or deserted lovers. No—here, we are beds. Sixty beds. This is a place where people come to die when there is no one to take them in, like unwanted mongrels. Most of us are helpless to carry out even the most basic dignities of life, worse than babies. And someone of authority—the new administrator, or someone trying to impress him—looked out at this collection of sad human debris and said, "Ah! Let the games begin." So now, there is bingo. B-I-N-G-O, like the gringo children's song.

I can hear you laughing, so you must get the joke. Bingo in Hell's parlor.

"You have a very bad attitude, Gilberto," a young nurse, Antoinette, chides me. No one has taught her not to call her elders by their Christian names, but I tolerate this because she understands the words from my ruined mouth. My translator.

"¿Que? Did I say anything?"

"You don't have to say it. I see it in your face. They like the bingo. Why come watch others play every day just to make fun? You should play, too."

But she is wrong. I don't come to watch the others play. Only a sadist would be entertained watching scarecrows listing in their wheelchairs, raising trembling fingers when they win, hardly realizing when they are wetting themselves. Does this sound like a sane person's amusement? Yet, it is true. I come every Friday. I wheel myself to the lounge by 2:00 p.m. without fail. I am the first one inside, the last one to leave.

But I never win. Remember? Mala suerte. Playing to win would be a waste of my time.

I come for Her. My angel.

Unlike me, she doesn't come every week. Angels cannot be summoned like pizza delivery, and I accept this. But the entire room changes when she walks inside. The light shifts to a bright golden hue, the exact color of twilight. The walls, which are usually growling at us with the promise of suffering, begin to sing.

The first day I saw her, I admit it, I believed it was only the meds at work. At first glance, she seemed to be a typical nurse, invisible in a powder-blue uniform that would make any woman seem boyish, white shoes squeaking across the floor, and a name tag that read ROSARIA. Her skin was browned with the echoes of an abuela negra whose African genes kinked her hair into tight brown ringlets she wore like a crown atop her head.

Then I noticed her eyes.

Dios mío, such eyes! Beneath her luxuriant lashes, her eyes are black coffee beans, shining like the night itself. I saw her eyes from across the room, and they stole my concentration from the droning call of the bingo numbers, my hand frozen above my cards. Her eyes held none of the dull dispassion or thinly masked contempt of the other nurses who occasionally gazed upon our pathetic game. Her eyes darted and dashed the way my little Gilberto chased our housecat to and fro when he was small, soaking up every detail about us. Instead of seeing only our tubes and wheelchairs, she lingered on our faces, memorizing our existence, blessing us with personhood.

You can believe me or not, but I swear to what happened next on my dear Camila's soul: As soon as I noticed her eyes, I gained new eyes myself. Her image changed. I was no longer staring at a nurse in a uniform, but a visage who glided across the floor in a sheen of pale light. Floating, you see. Her hair was suddenly an impossibly long mane behind her, following her on the floor like a wedding train spun of dark lamb's wool.

She met my eyes and smiled at me. I have seen dying men resuscitated with electric shock, and that sensation can be no more jarring than her eyes. Her gaze shocked me back to life.

No one else at the bingo game seemed to notice her. Not Pedro, who breathed through oxygen tubes and coughed blood into his handkerchief, making such a racket that it was hard to hear the numbers—not Dixon Washington (or Washington Dixon, I forget which), who always sat with his hand shielding his bingo cards as if his neighbors could somehow cheat if they saw what Fate had dealt him—not Mrs. Martinez, who dressed up for bingo games in her fading white lace dress and spring hat as if bingo days were Easter Sunday—not Stella Rothman, a World War II widow who

308

always cupped her ear to try to hear the numbers, complaining that her hearing aid was made in Japan and therefore wasn't worth a damn—and not Crazy Joe, who called *Bingo!* every other number even though he was the only one with worse luck than mine.

No one else glanced in the direction of this magnificent creature. Only me. To them, she was a nurse named Rosaria making an obligatory tour to see to it that no one dropped dead at a table. Such a death, after all, might ruin the game.

But she is much more than a nurse. I know that now. Perhaps she is Oyá herself. I have reasons for speaking so. I alone see her. I alone know what she does.

Our game is the perfect place for her to visit undetected. Bingo, you see, is not a game of skill, nor of will. There are no true choices—only luck. Each player is issued six cards, so in our game, anyone can expect to win at least once, even in a fellowship as cursed as ours. During the three hours we play, there are three or four winners. Sometimes more. Not me, of course—winning is not in my makeup—but usually. From time to time, even Crazy Joe is right when he claims he has his bingo numbers lined up. A broken clock tells the time twice a day, after all.

So, I do not blame the others for not seeing it as I do. They would have to see her.

The first day Rosaria arrived in the bingo room—the first time her eyes gave me access to the truer vision of her—I watched her glide from table to table, pausing like a honeybee collecting nectar. She lingered over one wheelchair for a time, then moved to the next. And the next. With each person she passed, she seemed to be listening for something only her ears could discern. I watched her so closely that I lost my concentration, forgetting the administrator's bored drone as he called the bingo numbers. How I longed for her!

Not as a woman, mind you. I will confess she is beautiful—with a face that is fine-featured and yet ever-changing, with cheeks as hollow as an Indian princess in one moment and then as full as my Camila's in the next—but it was not her beauty that commanded my eyes. I have not known hunger in my loins since Camila left this Earth, and my body no longer craves a woman's touch. But as I watched her, even the first time, all of my heart cried out: Choose me.

Bless me. Save me. Choose me.

But she did not.

Several minutes passed before she made her decision. My eyes had never left her, so I saw the exact moment: She took her hand and rested it across Pedro's shoulder, her lithe fingers weightless. He was so intent on smothering his constant cough in his handkerchief that he never noticed the rare gesture of kindness. But I did. All at once, Pedro's cough went silent.

The visage was gone. And the nurse Rosaria, unnoticed, slipped away to her duties.

But the change that came over Pedro! Without his cough to bedevil him, Pedro sat straighter in his chair, with a young man's posture. He marked his cards with fervor, his ears virtually twitching every time a number was called. His pencil flew. I heard him laugh to himself, a sound of boyish joy. On that day, as I witnessed the transformation, I believed the bingo games were a brilliant stroke, and felt my faith in our caretakers renewed. I shared Pedro's sudden belief that he could win, and that winning a simple game could matter to creatures such as we.

As I had anticipated, it was only moments before Pedro's voice rose, silencing the room: "Bingo!" he called through phlegm. Like a conqueror. He waved his card above his head.

The prizes in our bingo game are nothing to speak of. What is money to us? The staff gives the winners little tokens—brightly wrapped sugarless candies, postcards of beaches and mountain ranges, photo frames in which to display the evidences of younger days on our nightstands—but winning the game meant everything to Pedro that day. His skin flushed pink. His eyes danced. I never heard him cough again the entire game. When he won the second time, he nearly leaped from his wheelchair.

Pedro was not the only winner that day. But he was the only one chosen.

That very night, you see, Pedro died in his sleep. His monitors made no sound to alert the nurses, and later it was discovered that his oxygen machine had been unplugged. His roommate, Ben Wallenbech, said he slept so soundly that he never heard his neighbor's machine stop.

There was no outraged family to answer to, so the "investigation" amounted mostly to shrugged shoulders and shaking heads. Many speculated that Pedro himself had unplugged his oxygen. Those who had seen him at bingo recalled his last moment of triumph, saying he chose death on that night because he wanted to leave this world on a winning streak.

After that, I kept a special eye for the nurse, Rosaria. She frequently visited the bingo games, but I never saw the amazing metamorphosis I saw the day she chose Pedro. I came to believe I had hallucinated, or perhaps that I'd simply had a flash of premonition like my Tía Maria, the way I knew in my bones that my little Gilberto would not come home from football practice the night he died.

A week after Pedro's death, I suffered another stroke, one so minor that I did not notice it while it happened. But one morning I realized I could no longer stand and walk even the few steps I had mastered a short time before, the model of recovery. To this day, whenever I try to stand, my legs tremble as if I have no bones.

I can still mark the bingo cards. But most days for a time after that, I only watched. Even the sight of Rosaria could not cheer me, because she never again appeared as she had that day, and I stopped believing in magic.

I lost my spirit of play.

Until a month passed. And everything changed.

The bingo game was flourishing. A male nurse named Jackson volunteered to be the new caller, and he was so animated that he might have been a preacher at a Baptist church. Jackson made all the difference. The sound of laughter regularly filled our tiny bingo hall now, ringing through the hallways to the ears of those who were not well enough to participate. But I could not share their laughter.

"Gilberto, your face is gonna be in a permanent frown if you don't practice smiling again," Antoinette told me as she wheeled me into the hall, as she always does. "Don't worry, papi. Your legs will grow stronger." Such a sweet, young face to already be such a liar! The truth is plain to me now. I believed their lies, even when I fought not to. No one here grows stronger. No one here gets better.

And on that day, when I felt most mired in my helplessness, I saw her again.

This time, I did not even see her as plain-dressed Rosaria, the nurse who came and went without notice. I saw a shadow emerge in the doorway, impossibly long for the lighting from the hall, and at its tip was a large, winding spiral shape I could hardly make sense of.

She followed her shadow into the doorway. This time, she wore her dark hair in thick, ropy shapes splaying from all sides of her head. The largest was an oversized, upright whorl the size of a python that looked as if it weighed several pounds. Her face was obscured behind the light that floated around her like a swampland mist, but how could I mistake her?

This time, I knew. My veins raced with adrenaline.

"We got luck-y number O-72, ya'll. That's the year the Dolphins went undefeated, so you know that's lucky. You got O-72, you're a winner." Jackson called on, unaware.

She floated serenely down the rows of tables, toward mine. Something blocked my ears suddenly; perhaps my heart itself, silencing everything except its own excited thrashing. If my legs had obeyed me, I would have stood up and fallen to my knees in her path. When she passed only a foot from me, I nearly pissed myself. I smelled Camila's favorite perfume in her wake, and tears came to my eyes. I opened my mouth to speak, but I had forgotten all language.

"What's that? N-32?" Stella Rothman said, cupping her ear.

"O-72," someone yelled. "Jesus, will you get that thing fixed?"

Stella tugged at her hearing aid. "It's my fault it's made in Japan? Not worth a damn."

The entity did not dally this time, as she had the first time I saw her. She went straight to Stella. She glided behind her, and laid her hand gently on Stella's shoulder, her fingers like twigs.

"Seventy-two?" Stella said. "Wait a second. Just a second." As she stared at her cards, light brightened her face, erasing her furrowed brow. She had told me once that her life ended the day the telegram from the War Department came; I couldn't remember the last time I had seen her smile. "Seventy-two? I can't believe . . . I got it! Bingo!"

Need I tell you? It was only Rosaria who stood behind Stella then, stripped of her magnificent visage. Amidst the groans of disappointment from players who had not been as lucky as Stella, no one saw Rosaria lower her face, hiding her inscrutable eyes. I was the only one who watched the nurse leave, back to her mundane duties.

I was in a state that night, as you can guess. I had less appetite than even this food deserves. I could not sleep. Had I more control of my limbs, I might have taken myself to Stella's room to watch her doorway. To see the outcome for myself.

But in the end, of course, I already knew.

Stella died in her sleep. There were no machines unplugged this time, and fewer questions. She was eighty-six, after all. When an eighty-six-year-old dies, it isn't a mystery.

I wrestled with myself in the days to come, as anyone would. Should I report the girl, Rosaria? And tell the administrators what, exactly? That she touched the dying? That she gave them one last smile? That I suspected she was sneaking into their rooms at night? Or that she was Oyá herself coming to call, shepherding her chosen from one realm to the next?

No one listens to our kind, those who are cloistered away from the raging world outside. That is why living here is worse than death, you see. Bingo for the damned? The idea seems brilliant or inane to me, depending on how the meds are tickling my brain that day.

I hate this place.

"I'll never understand you, Gilberto," my young Antoinette says. "You complain about the bingo game, but you're always first at the door."

Of course I am, and now you see why. I no longer simply watch—I play. I listen closely, and I mark my cards when my numbers are called. I feel my heart leap as the rows fill.

Because she is here today. Rosaria is here. She has not yet shed her human form, but I see the light glowing in embers from her skin. Her dainty nest of hair will grow. Her white nurse's shoes are mewling against the floor now, but soon her feet will glide on the air itself.

She passes from one table to the next, closer to me. Studying me.

And I am a believer again. Perhaps my mala suerte is banished at last. Will my number come up this time? Just this once, Rosaria—this one time—will you give me luck? Will I win?

Bless me. Save me. Choose me.

⌒

I wrote this at the invitation of Gordon Van Gelder of The Magazine of Fantasy and Science Fiction, *who was editing a tribute edition for Harlan Ellison with a prompt Harlan wrote: "What if the unluckiest man alive met Lady Luck?" This was my interpretation.*

I met Harlan Ellison at the Bram Stoker Awards in 1995, the year I published my first novel, The Between, *and gave him a signed copy (which he still has on his bookshelf). Not only did Harlan read it, but he tracked me down by phone to point out grammatical errors.*

Vintage Harlan. He loves writers and the written word.

Vanishings

va-nish (v) 1: to pass quickly from sight: disappear
2: to pass completely from existence

THERE'S NO *easy way to say this, ma'am,* the memory of the highway patrolman's voice repeated in her head, a loop. *Your husband's vanished.*

Vanished.

Nidra shuddered. A year had passed, and no time at all. Frost clung to the windshield, so the wipers dragged and whined. She was almost driving blind. Visiting the place where Karl's truck had wrecked was dangerous in dawn's tricky light.

Nidra's skin vibrated when she approached the ramp to Interstate 285, where the curve grew sharp and a driver might spin and slide backward down a steep embankment, crashing into a stand of hardy Georgia pines. Like Karl. Nidra stopped a few yards before the exit, since it wasn't safe to linger near the curve. She parked on the shoulder with her flashers on. Her tiny Corolla shuddered when the semis thundered past with their urgent loads, spraying gravel from monstrous tires. The spot reeked of tragic endings.

Karl had been on his way back home. At least she knew that much.

Dead leaves made the grass so slick that Nidra nearly slipped as she made her way down the sharp grade. She wasn't sure she could find the exact place a year later, but a crumpled diet soda can winked from the bed of leaves, marking the spot. A long scrape remained across the thick-trunked tree where the Ford's rear fender had rested. The ugly white smear of exposed bark reminded Nidra of an open scab; no longer bleeding, not yet healed.

Nidra expected to find the truck waiting, an apparition. To find him. His voice. His face. Every shadow was Karl hiding in the shrubs; every

315

rustle was Karl swinging from the tree branches. The Queen of Denial, her daughter Sharlene had called her last night.

That night, police had called Karl by all three of his names and asked if he was her husband. She said she'd rather they didn't come in, thank you, and waited to find out what the bail was. She knew the situation was bound to be bad, since they had come to the house instead of calling and used his full name like he was a serial killer. *We found this wallet in your pickup rolled over off 285 near the Atlanta Road exit. There's no easy way to say this, but your husband's vanished.*

Then the officers had waited as if they expected her to cry or have a fit like on TV.

But they didn't know Karl. They didn't know about The Talk they'd had from Dr. Ross, Asia's pediatric oncologist, about their youngest daughter's white cell count. Karl might wish he'd vanished, all right.

"He didn't vanish," she told the police. "He ran—I guarantee it."

Karl would come back. And when he did, he would wish he had never left. One year ago, this was where he had changed his mind and decided he wouldn't come home. Decided to flee to a secret life. To leave her and Sharlene to manage Asia's fevers and whimpers when it was time to go back to the doctors.

Nidra wiped away angry tears.

"Cowardly sonofabitch," she said to the tree.

ASIA'S SCHOOL was a twenty-minute drive each way. In a rare moment of solidarity, Nidra and Karl had petitioned the county to pull Asia out of Glory Elementary around the corner because she'd come home crying every day from the teasing. The kids had called her *Ghost* because she was so ill. They bumped into her in the hallways purposely, pretending they could not see her as she passed them. Nidra had never seen Karl so mad. To keep him from doing something drastic and going to jail, they decided to find Asia a new school.

Spring Valley had better manners, smaller class sizes, and fresher paint. The only drawback was the long drive. When Karl's office shut down, he had been Asia's "designated driver," as he liked to say, hardy har. In the months before Karl left, Asia often needed to come home from school early because she felt weak or sick. They had spent entire days shuttling back and forth between Asia's school, her doctor, and the hospital. Or just the hospital.

But not today.

Asia sat safely strapped on the passenger side, her bright red ski cap bent forward as she scribbled in her composition book. Asia had taken up drawing during her last long stay at Piedmont Children's. Asia was drawing Karl's profile again; his bushy mop of hair, the rounded tip of his nose, pronounced shading of his skin.

"Looks just like him," Nidra said. Down to the knot in her stomach.

Asia didn't answer, absorbed by her pencil's even strokes.

The school driveway was lit up in brake lights from waiting cars. Asia might still be marked tardy. Nidra wished she hadn't slipped out earlier to go to the interstate. The day had just started, and she was already behind.

A family of stick figures was pasted to the rear window of the SUV directly in front of Nidra's car, even a dog at the end. But a space stood empty between the tallest and third tallest. Nidra wondered who had vanished, and how. A parent? Had some poor soul been left alone with four children to raise? She only had two, but some mornings she dreaded getting out of bed. She wished she had a time machine to go back and stop Karl from getting in his truck. Or else jump in with him.

"Did you know black walnut trees have a poison so nothing else will grow near them?" Asia said. She learned a new thing about trees each week in third-grade science.

"Nope, didn't know that."

"Does every plant and animal do something special no one else does?"

"Maybe," Nidra said. "Probably, yes."

"What about me?" Asia said.

"Everything about you is special."

"No, really, Mom."

Asia's first teacher had advised Nidra to smile more, advice that was harder to remember each day. But she tried. "There."

"What? You're smiling?"

317

Nidra nodded and kissed the top of her cap. "Yep. You're the only one who can make me do that, pumpkin."

"Good one. Love you, Mom."

Asia sprang out of her door before Nidra could say *I love you, too*.

Asia watched the easy bounce in her daughter's gait. Asia wasn't dragging like she used to before Karl left. She walked just like the other kids, her backpack swinging between her shoulders like the pendulum on a grandfather clock.

Still, Spring Valley's students and parents stared, heads slowly turning to watch her daughter as she walked up the stairs and into the school's freshly painted doors.

"Didn't anyone teach you manners?" she called out, too loudly. She sounded like Karl, but she couldn't help it. Even Asia turned her head with the rest to see what the fuss was about.

Nidra waved at her daughter and drove away.

THE SEDAN parked outside her house looked like an undercover police car: a dark blue Crown Victoria. Nidra's heart beat so quickly that the rush of blood dizzied her. Karl had been in jail, that was all. Or on the run. Of course! He'd been a petty thief and a dealer in high school and promised he'd never stray again, so he'd been too ashamed to tell her and the girls. Nidra heard herself make a sound that was half laugh, half sob, an ecstatic rage.

But it was only Lenore Augustine waiting in the driver's seat, studying *Vogue* like it was contagious. Nidra was so disappointed to find Lenore that she nearly cried.

"Nidra!" Lenore said. "There you are. Have you seen that mess across the way? Hard to believe my brothers used to hunt squirrels and rabbits out here."

The nearby construction site hadn't seemed so bad when the foliage in Nidra's yard kept the new development hidden. Their house was built high atop a slope, so it had seemed like a tree house in the forest even though they lived only ten minutes from I-285 and five minutes from Publix. The builders' noise hadn't bothered Nidra as long as she could feel enfolded in the woods. But winter was coming, leaves were thinning, and the ugliness was in plain view.

"Answer's still no," Nidra said.

"Hear me out this time. It's almost a year. Next week is the anniversary."

"You don't have to tell me it's been a year," Nidra said.

Lenore came by every three months. She and Karl had both worked at the same Realty office before Clarkson/Myers shut down and everyone scattered for new jobs. Lenore had ended up in insurance, and Karl had ended up nowhere. Lenore and Karl had been so close, hitting Happy Hour at Parkfield Lanes two or three times a month, that Nidra would have suspected them of an affair if Lenore hadn't been a year older than his mother. Right before Asia's diagnosis, Lenore had told Nidra they had married too young. *Nobody warns young people not to get married unless you can march into Hell side by side.*

When Lenore gave her car door a push, Nidra had no choice but to step back and let her out. Microscopic wrinkles painted a patchwork across Lenore's face, barely hidden by her caked makeup's false glow of youth. Had Karl showered with Lenore at cheap motels, run his fingers through her lifeless hair? Nidra couldn't quite see it, but she couldn't quite unsee it either.

"Do you know how hard it is to get a vanishing cert from the Georgia Highway Patrol?" Lenore said. "My client list would kill for your incident report—not to mention, my boss would kill me if he knew I was out here. In seven days, the insurance will be a much bigger fight. But you paid extra for the comp package, and Karl made me promise I'd look out for you."

"So he planned it," Nidra said. "With you. That's what you're saying." Karl was a con artist through and through. He'd put on a hell of a show with his tears and carrying on before he'd driven off in the Ford.

"You know you don't mean that, Nidra. I'm saying to fill out the paperwork. The money is yours, and you should have it. You need it for Asia. For the medical bills."

Lenore's eyes reminded Nidra of the smug pity in Dr. Ross's face when he saw Asia waiting in his examination room, her cap bobbing as she swung her legs to and fro on the table's perch. *Can't you see how pale Asia is?* Sharlene had screamed during their fight last night. *You just don't want to look, Mom!*

But no. That couldn't be. Asia had three more weeks before her next doctor's appointment. Asia was symptom-free, without the high temperatures, loss of appetite, or vomiting that had sent her and Karl to the emergency room with her bundled like a foundling night after night. Three weeks before Dr. Ross would test Asia's levels and start the next horror show ride.

"Asia is fine."

"Of course she's fine," Lenore said. "But you have bills—"

"Cut the bullshit," Nidra said. "Just tell me where he is."

Lenore pursed her lips, a portrait of heartbreak.

"He's gone, sugar," Lenore said. "That's what I keep trying to tell you. There are support groups, if that's what you need. Books I can give you. I went through it with my mom, so I know. I expect her to tap me on the shoulder every day. It's been hell. But read what the police said—no one could have walked away from that crash alive. I wish it wasn't true—I loved him like a baby brother—but Karl has vanished. He's gone."

SHARLENE HAD seen Nidra with Devon last night. That was what started their fight.

Devon was Shar's high school geometry teacher. He'd asked Nidra out for coffee after a parent conference three months before, as if to soften his report. That first night, they had only talked about Shar; how bright she was, how frustrating. They shared a common passion. Nidra sometimes went out to Devon's townhouse for a couple of hours three times a week now, usually after seven, when Asia was ready for bed and Shar was home for the night.

Nidra's agreement with Devon was firm: he could pick her up if he waited at the curb, but he had to take her straight to his place. The sex was great, like breathing again, but that was all it ever would be. She was a married woman, and she had to sort out her family when Karl came back. Besides, dating had never led her anywhere except where she was.

Gawd, Mom, what do you SEE in him? Sharlene had wailed last night, and Nidra understood her point. Devon had braces at forty-five. He said he would wear the braces for "only" nine months, as if people in their forties had months to spare. Nidra was ten years younger than Devon, but his braces made her feel like his mother. He also had a weak chin and small frame. And Nidra loathed math, which she had yet to confess. But none of that mattered.

Devon was parked in his usual place, across the street in front of their neighbor's house. When she climbed in, she wondered if Karl had felt as free as she did.

"Shar saw you drop me off last night," Nidra said.

Devon's hand lingered on the gearshift. "Meaning?"

"I need to start meeting you at your place."

The car almost trembled with his relief. They both knew she was looking for an excuse to remind him she was married. Even if she signed the paperwork and took the payout, certification from the Georgia Highway Patrol couldn't change what would happen when Karl came home. How happy their daughters would be to see him. The light it would bring to Asia.

"I think this part makes it harder for her," Devon said. "The hiding."

"She's making a C in your class," Nidra said. "You're not her favorite person."

"You want me to raise her grade?" He sounded scandalized. "Because then I would have to sleep with every other kid's mother, and I don't think I have the stamina." He winked at her.

Nidra barked a laugh so loud that she covered her mouth. She felt a foreign, giddy impulse to lean over and kiss him. No kissing was another one of her rules.

Devon grew serious. "If the grade bothers her, she should stop gliding and engage. It's locus theorems, parallel lines, transformations. The rules don't change. She knows all of this."

Sharlene had screamed hateful things at Nidra last night—terrible words with claws, leaving them both gasping and sobbing. Thank goodness Asia had slept through it all.

"We fight about it," Nidra said, "so after tonight, I'll drive myself."

The silence was an escape for the first who grabbed the chance. Neither of them did.

"We need to stop at the corner market," Devon said. "I have a mango emergency."

Nidra had never known anyone else with mango emergencies. Devon had lived in the U.S. since he was fifteen, but Trinidad survived in his habits and his carefully modulated lilt.

"All right," Nidra said. "But just a hot minute."

Nidra didn't want to be seen in public with Devon, but she was a stranger at World Foods. The market was closer than Publix or Kroger, but the lighting was dim, the aisles were poorly marked, and she had trouble finding even simple foods. The store bustled with sure-footed Koreans, Jamaicans, Taiwanese, Mexicans, Cubans, and others like Devon looking for flavors of home. Nidra didn't recognize most of the fruit in the produce section. The rows were stuffed with odd shapes and colors, misshapen. Who ate this angry red fruit shaped like a banana? Whose worlds bore these fruits?

Devon took forever choosing his mangoes, clucking over them like baby chicks. He bagged his ripened fruit one by one, careful not to bruise them. That done, he moved to dried dates. They were nearly as large as figs, mutants.

When Devon spoke to her, his voice was so low that she might have imagined it.

"Sharlene is worried about her sister."

Nidra's stomach dropped. The floor dropped. The lighting seemed to brighten, then dim.

"She told you that?"

"Not me," Devon said. "But she talks to her friends, and they say she's deathly worried. Her sister is very ill, they say, and she isn't getting proper care. That's what she's telling them."

His voice was mere breath. So, so gentle a voice for such impaling words. Devon patted her hand and moved away to knot his produce bags. They did not talk about Asia's illness: that was the first rule, the reason for the other rules. They did not talk about Asia, and they did not talk about Karl.

"I'll wait in the car," Nidra said.

Alone, she spent two minutes crying, two minutes drying her face and eyes. Devon opened his car door just as she snapped her purse shut.

"Do you still want to come with me?" Devon said.

Nidra shook her head. "Take me back, please."

Devon's anxiousness to find the right words filled the car with pained silence. "Nidra . . . "

"I left mac and cheese for Shar and Asia in my fridge," she said. "We can whip something together at my place."

Devon considered and nodded. Without a word, he drove her home.

"Eww," Shar said when she saw Devon in the living room. She froze mid-step on the staircase, her face puckered. With her hair cut short, she looked like a willowy version of Karl; Nidra saw the resemblance most when Shar frowned. "What's Mr. Roy doing here?"

"Good to see you too, Sharlene."

"It's Shar," she said. "In my house, you call me Shar. And you can go now."

"Shar, don't," Nidra said. Her spontaneous plan had felt foolish as soon as she opened her door—indecent, really—but Shar had started downstairs before she could tell Devon she'd changed her mind. Shar stood halfway down the stairs, knuckles tight on the railing, undecided.

When Nidra saw the living room through Devon's eyes, everything was crooked: the books, the rug, the sofa cushions, the photo frames. Everything.

"Did Asia finish her homework?" Nidra said.

Shar stared at Nidra with what looked like real loathing. "Yes, Mother. Anything else?"

"Are you done with yours?" Devon muttered, and Shar's eyes shot lasers at him.

"Yes, there's something else," Nidra said. "Devon's having dinner with us tonight. That all right with you?" She tried to sound casual. Like she wasn't begging.

Shar's lips shrank, tightening. "Is it all right if my arch-nemesis Mr. Roy, my geometry teacher drone, has dinner with us here in our house? At our table?"

"Yes, Shar. Is it all right?"

Shar still hadn't moved from the stairs. Nidra braced for the storm, in front of company this time. None came. "Your life," Shar said. "But he's a royal pain."

"Only during daylight hours," Devon said. "After dark, my true personality emerges."

He picked up the Christmas portrait Nidra and the girls had taken at Sears last year at her parents' insistence, their smiles so forced they looked manic.

"I'm sorry, Shar," Nidra said. "Hiding doesn't feel right. You said to stop pretending."

"It's nothing at all to you," Devon told Shar. "You're any other student, and your mother and I are friends."

Shar shrugged and went to the kitchen to get the dinner plates. Shar used to hide in her room to avoid her chores, but she never needed reminding since Karl left.

"Asia?" Nidra called upstairs.

"Right here, Mom."

The voice came from the stairs, but hung weightless in the corner shadows. Then, just that fast, Asia was midway down the stairs in a long black T-shirt. Asia's skin was the color of the stained teak-colored paneling on the wall behind her. Light from the foyer lamp shimmered, making her face seem to phase in and out against the wood's grains, like an optical illusion.

When Devon drew a hitched breath, Nidra realized she'd been holding her own since she heard *Right here, Mom* from thin air.

"Well," Devon said, sunshine in his voice. "It's good to meet you, Asia. Your mother has told me a great deal about you."

A lie, but a forgivable one for the way it made Asia's teeth gleam with a smile.

"This is my friend, Mr. Roy. He's—"

"I know," Asia said. "I heard."

Nidra served the macaroni and cheese as they sat at the table. Devon silently said grace before he ate, a habit she had never noticed. Could it be they had never eaten together? She remembered the sound of his lungs hissing when he'd seen Asia.

Why had everyone seen how sick Asia was but her?

"My daddy's vanished," Asia said to Devon.

Quickly, Nidra patted Asia's hand. "That's just what the police told us. We don't know."

Shar's stare was so pointed that Nidra had to fight to hold her daughter's eyes.

"He's not coming back," Shar told Asia, an assurance, as if Nidra were a stranger who had just said something profane. Her stare held, daring Nidra to dispute her.

"No," Nidra said. "Probably not."

Packed molecules in the air seemed to drift clear of each other, making it easier to breathe. Karl would want them to have the insurance money. Both of the girls needed new jackets instead of the old ones she'd had to dig out of the coat closet. It was only late November, but it was cold.

Maybe Karl's truck had skidded in icy rain. Maybe that was how it had happened. He'd been on his way home. Maybe his last thoughts on this Earth had been of them.

"How do you like school?" Devon asked Asia.

Asia shook her head. "I hate it. Everybody looks at me because I'm sick."

Nidra tried to keep the panic she felt from her face.

"Yes, that's very rude," she heard Devon say somewhere far beneath her. "It was that way for me, too, when my parents first moved us from my country. I was in a private school where no one had brown skin but me. They all stared. I ignored it."

"Yeah, screw them," Shar said.

"Who wants dessert?" Devon said, pulling out a produce bag.

Shar peered into the bag and blanched. "Do you know what those look like?"

"They're dates," he said.

Karl didn't like dates, so Nidra had gotten out of the habit of buying them by the time the Shar was old enough to eat them. She could hardly remember who she had been when she was twenty, dropping out of Georgia State and marrying Karl because he had plans and made her laugh. Two months later, she was pregnant with Sharlene. Eight years after Sharlene, Asia. A life lived in a blur.

"I don't think they've ever tasted dates," Nidra said.

Devon cast Nidra a playful look. "Why are you depriving these girls?"

While Devon helped Asia choose the plumpest date, Shar peered over to study them.

"I'll try one," Shar said.

Asia squealed when she took her first bite. "It's so sweet! Like cake." She ate three more. She had a good appetite. Watching the fruit find Asia's mouth, Nidra remembered the bubbles in Asia's baby bottle when she drank, the way their dance had quieted Nidra's worries when Asia was small.

"Well?" Nidra said, watching Sharlene wrap her date pit in her napkin.

"It's okay." Shar scooted out her chair. "It's time for Asia's bath."

"I'll take her up in a minute."

Shar stood and reached for Asia's hand the way she would at a busy intersection. "It's a school night, so the sooner the better. Come on, Asia."

After the polite good-nights, Devon watched as they walked away.

"You're so lucky," Devon said once he was alone at the table with Nidra.

"Which part?"

Devon slipped his hand over hers on the tabletop.

"Sharlene is such a big help to you," he said. "You have a lovely family."

THE BATHTUB was full, the water crowned with bright white suds.

When Asia was two and Karl got a bonus at work, they'd used most of the check to refurbish the main bathroom upstairs. The floor, wall tiles, and bathtub were slick aquamarine, the color of the bathroom in her grandmother's house. The picture window overlooking the backyard was the biggest luxury of her lifetime.

Neighbors' lights twinkled in the dark like constellations. When the treetops were a full canopy, they never saw lights at night. Now, even in the darkness, her backyard trees' steady shedding unmasked the lighted construction site down the hill: bare concrete walls half finished, machinery painted brightly in unnatural colors. She'd stopped noticing the view when it was pretty, and now it was gone. She could never catch hold of a moment.

Karl's good razor hung suspended in the toothbrush rack, coated with dust and powdery shaving cream residue. Nidra took the razor and almost put it in the drawer, but she buried it in her front pocket instead. It would still smell like his face.

"Asia?" Nidra called into the hall.

"I'm right here."

A splash echoed behind Nidra, from the bathtub. Suds parted at the foot of the tub as Asia sat up, a watery shadow against bathwater the color of the ocean. The bubbles clinging to Asia's hair and face framed her features. Nidra couldn't believe how pale Asia was since her last bath. Her bare skin was nearly invisible.

She would call Dr. Ross as soon as Asia was in bed. Nidra knew his cell phone number by heart. She wondered at her calm, but knew she was not calm anywhere except on the outside.

"You were hiding," Nidra said.

Asia giggled. "If I was a snake, I woulda bit you," she said, imitating Grandma.

Nidra sat on the rim of the tub and dunked Asia's washcloth into the warm water. "Here comes the snake," she said, slithering the cloth beneath the suds toward Asia's back. Asia pretended to scream, splashing to the other side of the tub. Nidra wanted to ask why Asia never told her she wasn't feeling well again, but she didn't have to. She probably had tried to say it, or expected Nidra to notice. She was Asia's mother, after all. A mother should see it first, not last.

Water splashed again, and a stream trickled from Asia's fingers. Asia played with the water for a long time. Nidra ran Dr. Ross's telephone number through her head, sixes and threes.

"After your bath, you pick a story and I'll read it to you," Nidra said.

"Anansi, then."

However small, it was a plan. No mysteries or new tragedies waited in the next thirty minutes. A maw gnawing inside Nidra's stomach felt like a scream from her heart and womb, but Nidra enjoyed the sound of Asia splashing in the water, playing unafraid.

"Look, Mom," Asia said in a hush, entranced. "I'm vanishing."

Crystalline threads twined Asia's fingers, blending her skin to the color of blue bathwater where her fading flesh rose and fell, rose and fell, across the liquid plane.

⌒⌒

Throughout my writing career, I have sought ways to convey the feelings and images of death and dying as my own coping mechanism. This story, first written in the wake of my mother's death in 2012, has never before been published.

I am still trying to understand how our loved ones can simply disappear.

Afterword: On Tananarive Due

Steven Barnes

In 1997, I met Tananarive Due at the African-American Fantastic Imagination conference hosted by Clark Atlanta University. She was cute and smart and terribly young, and when I heard her explain how she combined social networking, musical skill, and raw chutzpah to get a cover blurb from Stephen King, it was pretty much love at first sight. Literally, within three days we were all but engaged, sitting in the airport holding hands, our heads resting together, speaking of building empire . . . and a life . . . together.

And in 1998 we were married in her parents' house, by her father, and she moved to Washington State, where I was raising my daughter, Nicki, in a little lumber town called Longview. When Nicki graduated high school, the idea was that we would move down to California and my home town of Los Angeles, and take on Hollywood.

In the mean time, we wrote. T (as I call her, figuring that there was no reason to invest the extra syllables, or even fearing that by the time I got out "Tananarive" I could have said "T . . . the bus!" and saved her life) was a writer of such clarity, imagination and emotion that Hollywood immediately saw the value of her work, and fought to back dump trucks filled with money up to our door. We believed that if we could learn to work together, we could graft the best of her approach and mine together, and create something extraordinary, and effective.

Well . . . anyone who has tried to collaborate with anyone at all has experienced the difficulty of weaving two creative instincts into a single braid. Now add being married. The natural jostling and arguing that is a natural part of the collaborative process now has to also carry the weight of the natural stresses of living and loving. One answer was to take the relationship itself "off the table." In other words, no matter how passionate the fight, it was never personal. It was just about the work.

To a degree it worked, although our initial attempts to work with movie studios were pretty much stillborn. We just couldn't figure out how to leverage our different approaches.

Then in 2005 we were asked to submit a story to a horror anthology, and wrote the tale "Danger Word," which is also included in this collection. This was our first fictive collaboration, and we bounced ideas back and forth until we came up with the idea of a grandfather trying to protect his immature and traumatized grandson post zombie apocalypse. (By the way, this simple short story led, in time to our Devil's Wake young adult zombie series, and the short film we co-produced and wrote, *Danger Word*, in which the young boy protagonist of the original story morphed into a slightly older girl. But that's another story.)

What happened during the writing of the short story was fascinating and educational. The process moved from plot to character to rough draft to polished draft. But it was in the polishing that something remarkable happened. The first time I read Tananarive's work, a passage of her first novel, *The Between*, I recognized that this young woman had phenomenal storytelling skills, but I didn't fully understand what it was I was seeing.

When we worked on "Danger Word" on the other hand, we talked about every sequence, every scene, every paragraph, every sentence, every word. And as we "passionately discussed" all these things, what became clear is that she did not use the same dyadic relationship that had been so valuable in my own career. Yes, she understood plot beautifully. And her characterization was superb—she had a feeling for humanity that simply shone from the page. But there was something else: poetics.

The language itself. And more than that, please remember the saying that "poetry is what happens between the lines" in the same way that "jazz is what happens between the notes."

Tananarive was looking at the invisible world of the almost psychic connection between the writer and the reader, the creative dream-space that the storyteller creates where emotions trump logic, and we are willing to accept the fantastic as real.

Plot, yes. Characters, yes. But the POETRY of the language, the imagery, the rhythms, the secret meldings of their proportions, the thing that can't quite be quantified but is the instinctive gift of the natural storyteller, that thing that teachers seek to educe from their students, often with despair. It is indeed a gift that keeps on giving, and Tananarive Due, my darling wife, has it in spades.

I fought her for a couple of years, but finally surrendered, and added that third element to my basic structure, which then became: Plot, Character, Language (what I call "poetics"). Each has a relationship with the other two. Each can be viewed individually, or in dyadic relationship with one of the others.

View this as life itself. We have human beings. And we have the world that they inhabit. And the lives they create in reaction with that world.
And then there is the poetry, the world of meaning they seek to create . . . we seek to create . . . out of our day-to-day lives. Seeking every day to not merely survive another sunset, but to find pleasure, and beauty, and even that elusive quality called "art," spinning gold from the straw of our existence.

Tananarive's fiction seeks to add or extract meaning from the chaos of life, to give us the perspective that helps us see that the crying child, the departing lover, the discontented customer, the senile grandparent who used to be so alive and wise, are somehow all part of a world of meaning. We see the people. We experience the events. But it is the poetry we yearn for.

We work, we play, we give, we share . . . seeking that poetry. Seeking love, and connection with our own hearts. And fiction reduces the infinite universe into a knowable few words and scenes that represent a greater whole, and to the degree that the writer is honest about their own experiences, needs, strengths and weaknesses their characters live more vibrantly than the actual "real" human beings in our lives. There is something magical about a writer who can do this, give us these insights, extract and convey that meaning.

And Tananarive is a magician. She loves her characters, because she loves people deeply. Her connection to her family, her friends, her readers, her students, and even teachers is profound. And as the man fortunate

331

enough to share her life, I have been able to observe her in all moods and times, through triumph and tragedy, and seen the depths of her strength and the very real and tender weaknesses, all of them connected to how very much she loves life, and fears what that life can do to those she loves.

The poetry of life is the invisible connection between people, things, and events. Love is the binding emotion between those exact same things. By seeking to orchestrate the emotions and images experienced by the audience when they read her stories, she is saying: I love these things. These people. This world. I want you to experience that love. To open your heart, despite the fact that there is much to fear. Do not let fear stop you from loving, ever, because it is, in the final analysis, the only thing that blunts the terror of existence.

Tananarive Due's stories are filled with terrors, extraordinary and mundane. And with beauty. And love. And poetry.

The human heart is just that large, that immense, with that many chambers. If all there was in the world was people and problems . . . character and plot . . . it would be a sterile world indeed.

But there is more. There is poetry.

There is love.

She is mine.

Steven Barnes
June 10, 2015

Acknowledgments

"The Lake" © 2011 Tananarive Due. First published: *The Lake* (St. Martin's Press).

"Summer" © 2007 Tananarive Due. First published: *Whispers in the Night,* ed. Brandon Massey (Dafina Books/Kensington Corp.).

"Ghost Summer" © 2008 Tananarive Due. First published: *The Ancestors,* ed. Brandon Massey (Dafina Books/Kensington Corp.).

"Free Jim's Mine" © 2014 Tananarive Due. First published: *Long Hidden: Speculative Fiction from the Margins of History,* eds. Daniel José Older & Rose Fox (Crossed Genres Publications).

"The Knowing" © 2002 Tananarive Due. First published: *Gumbo: A Celebration of African-American Writing,* eds. Marita Golden & E. Lynn Harris (Harlem Moon).

"Like Daughter" © 2000 *Dark Matter: A Century of Speculative Fiction from the African Diaspora,* ed. Sheree R. Thomas (Aspect/Warner Books).

"Aftermoon" © 2004 Tananarive Due. First published: *Dark Matter: Reading the Bones,* ed. Sheree R. Thomas (Aspect/Warner Books).

"Trial Day" © 2003 Tananarive Due. First published: *Mojo: Conjure Stories,* ed. Nalo Hopkinson (Aspect/Warner Books).

"Patient Zero" © 2000 Tananarive Due. First published: *The Magazine of Fantasy and Science Fiction,* August 2000.

"Danger Word" © 2004 Steven Barnes and Tananarive Due. First published: *Dark Dreams: A Collection of Horror and Suspense by Black Writers,* ed. Brandon Massey (Dafina Books/Kensington Corp.).

About Tananarive Due

Tananarive Due is a former Cosby Chair in the Humanities at Spelman College (2012-2014), where she taught screenwriting, creative writing. and journalism. She also teaches in the creative writing MFA program at Antioch University Los Angeles. The American Book Award winner and NAACP Image Award recipient is the author of twelve novels and a civil rights memoir. In 2010, she was inducted into the Medill School of Journalism's Hall of Achievement at Northwestern University.

Due's novella "Ghost Summer" received the 2008 Kindred Award from the Carl Brandon Society, and her short fiction has appeared in best-of-the-year anthologies of science fiction and fantasy. Due is a leading voice in black speculative fiction; a paper on Due's work recently was presented at the College Language Association Conference.

Due collaborates on the Tennyson Hardwick mystery series with her husband, author Steven Barnes, in partnership with actor Blair Underwood. Due also wrote *The Black Rose*—a historical novel about the life of Madam C. J. Walker, based on the research of Alex Haley—and *Freedom in the Family: A Mother-Daughter Memoir of the Fight for Civil Rights*, which she co-authored with her mother, the late civil rights activist Patricia Stephens Due. *Freedom in the Family* was named 2003's Best Civil Rights Memoir by *Black Issues Book Review*.

In 2004, alongside such luminaries as Nobel Prize-winner Toni Morrison, Due received the New Voice in Literature Award at the Yari Yari Pamberi conference co-sponsored by New York University's Institute of African-American Affairs and African Studies Program and the Organization of Women Writers of Africa.

Due has a BS in journalism from Northwestern University and an MA in English literature from the University of Leeds, where she specialized in Nigerian literature as a Rotary Foundation Scholar. Due lives in Southern California with Barnes and their son, Jason. Her writing blog is tananarivedue. wordpress.com. Her website is tananarivedue.com.

Ghost Summer is her first short story collection.